A TREASURY
OF
DAMON RUNYON

A
TREASURY
OF
DAMON
RUNYON

Selected, with an Introduction,
by CLARK KINNAIRD

THE MODERN LIBRARY · NEW YORK

Random House IS THE PUBLISHER OF *The Modern Library*

Manufactured in the United States of America by H. Wolff

Contents

Foreword

by CLARK KINNAIRD

"Ça, dit Butch, c'est du boulot de l'ancien temps."

Big Butch and those three parties from Brooklyn, Harry the Horse, Little Isadore, and Spanish John, now speak French, Spanish, German and assorted languages besides Brooklynese. The characters with whom Damon Runyon peopled his stories have become world citizens, in company with Leatherstocking, C. Auguste Dupin, Huckleberry Finn, Nick Adams, Eugene Gant.

"Damon Runyon est probablement un cas unique dans l'histoire des lettres," R. N. Raimbault begins his introduction to a collection* composed of *Johnny-n'-a-Qu'un-Ceil, Une Côte Advantageuse, Rose de la Rue des Rêves* and five other Runyon tales in vernacular French, which has been a popular seller in France.

In England, where one or more of his books has been in print for twenty-five years, there is a Damon Runyon Society according him honor such as the Baker Street Irregulars in this country bestow on Conan-Doyle or the devotees of *Alice in Wonderland* on its author. The London *Evening Standard*'s literary critic called Runyon a genius as authentic as Laurence Sterne or James M. Barrie, saying Runyon had "invented a humanity as new and startling as Lewis Carroll did."

The *Evening Standard*'s appraisal was made of Runyon's Broadway stories, the first of which was *Romance in the Roaring Forties,* published in 1929.

A careless commentator on Runyon fostered a legend about Damon's start as a fiction writer. He said Runyon was on the skids, a neglected sports columnist, when *Cosmopolitan* magazine published *Romance in the Roaring Forties* and "made" Runyon as a fiction writer practically overnight. The facts are that at the time Runyon

* *Broadway Mon Village:* Librairie Gaillimard, Paris.

was under long-term newspaper contract at about $500 a week, the equivalent of several thousand dollars a week now. Furthermore, Runyon had scores of short stories and fiction sketches behind him when he wrote *Romance in the Roaring Forties. As Between Friends, The Old Men of the Mountain, At Dead Mule Crossing* and *The Wooing of Nosey Gillespie* in this volume are examples of them.

Runyon's name first became known outside of his native Southwest through the stories and verses he contributed to *Harper's Weekly, Lippincott*'s, *Metropolitan, Hampton*'s, and *Century*. In the verses he evidenced vision and the gift for metaphor which Aristotle defined as the supreme power of the poet. Some were extraordinarily prophetic. In his *The Sky Marines,* written in 1908, when the military airplane was still untried, the Runyon protagonist declared,

> With a dynamite bomb in me hand,
> A-sailin' the deep-blue sky,
> You'll reckon with me on land or on sea
> Sometime in the sweet bye an' bye.

Runyon's *The Song of the Submarine* was perhaps the first poetic recognition given to the men of the "silent service." Its grimly ominous lines were written in 1910, before the U-boats had made the potentialities of submarines fully understood.

The Funeral of Madame Chase, a Runyon story-poem of those early days in this volume, has the quality which critics hailed a few years later in Edgar Lee Masters' *Spoon River Anthology*.

The first two books bearing Runyon's name were collections of his verses published in 1911 and 1912, right after he moved from Denver to New York for good.

While writing fiction under his own name, Runyon contributed ideas, and perhaps more, to H. H. Van Loan, a sports writer who had broken into the slick magazines with short stories having sports backgrounds.

After Van Loan moved his operating base to New York, he was asked to write sports for Hearst's New York *American*. But Van Loan was determined to sell his talents to the slick magazines, where the pay was better. He recommended the *American*'s hiring of Runyon instead, and had his uncredited collaborator close at hand.

Runyon also generated fiction ideas for pay for Irvin S. Cobb, who had to turn out short stories fast to keep up with the demand from George Horace Lorimer of the *Saturday Evening Post* and other editors.

There was a letup in his own fiction writing in 1914, when he was catapulted from sports into the position of star reporter for the Hearst newspapers, covering Mexican border incidents, the war in France, first Atlantic flights, murder trials, and what not.

Runyon's name began to appear in fiction again regularly in 1922, when he began a series of *My Old Home Town* sketches in the Hearst Sunday papers. The evolution of such phraseology as "more than somewhat" and of humorous slants characteristic of the Broadway guys and dolls stories is evident in these tales. The narrator of *The Wooing of Nosey Gillespie* and the narrator of *The Idyll of Miss Sarah Brown* are the same in spirit.

A highlight of the stage play and movie *Guys and Dolls* is a scene at "the oldest established floating crap game" in New York. Both the play and the movie derive from two Runyon stories, *The Idyll of Miss Sarah Brown* and *Pick the Winner,* in this book. The latter is the chronicle of Nathan Detroit (called Hot Horse Herbie in the original) and his ever-loving fiancée, Miss Cutie Singleton. The former is the account of the subjugation by a doll of Sky Masterson, "the highest player this country ever sees."

Sky was "originally out of a little town in southern Colorado where he learns to shoot craps, and play cards and one thing and another, and where his old man is a very well-known citizen, and something of a sport himself." Runyon could have been describing himself in that sentence. The advice Sky Masterson's father gives him

in the story is a paraphrase of advice Runyon attributed
to My Old Man earlier. In *The Idyll of Miss Sarah
Brown*, old man Masterson says, "Some day, somewhere,
a guy is going to show you a nice brand-new deck of
cards on which the seal is never broken, and this guy
is going to offer to bet you that the jack of spades will
jump out of this deck and squirt cider in your ear. But,
son, do not bet him, for as sure as you do you are going to get an ear full of cider in your ear." In a poem,
Runyon had written:

> There are the words my daddy said,
> (Poor old daddy, long since dead):
> "Son," he said, "you're goin' away,
> Into the world so cold and gray,
> And son," he said, "all I've got to say
> Is don't play 'em unless you've got 'em.

> "Your maw'll give you advice," he said,
> "On goin' to church, and goin' to bed.
> What's good fer your health, and good to read,
> But son," he said, "the thing that you need
> To keep in your mind, and always heed,
> Is don't play 'em unless you've got 'em.

> "Many a time," my daddy said,
> "You'll git some idea into your head;
> Many a time you'll risk your stack
> And back a king to hell and back—
> But, son, thar's aces in every pack,
> And don't play 'em unless you've got 'em."

Runyon wrote several ballads about dice addicts that
anticipated the famous crapshooting scene in *Guys and
Dolls*. It seemed altogether appropriate to include *Vers
Libre* and *Them Dice'll Make You Talk* in this collection.

Guys and Dolls was not the first Runyon creation to
become a part of Broadway theatrical history. Damon

had a direct hand in two earlier attractions in which characters of his came to life. He collaborated with Irving Caesar on *Saratoga Chips,* a comedy about racing with a locale, as the title suggests, in the New York State resort. Subsequently, Runyon wrote *A Slight Case of Murder* with Howard Lindsay, who, it must be said, had greater success as a collaborator with Russel Crouse, with whom he wrote *Life with Father.*

Nice and Quiet, She Was, one of the "Joe and Ethel Turp" stories in this book, is reminiscent of Runyon's *A Slight Case of Murder.*

After beginning the Broadway Guys and Dolls series with *Romance in the Roaring Forties* in 1929, Runyon wrote four other fictional series: "A Detective's Confession," which satirized the Hammett-Chandler private-eye school of whodunit writing; "In Our Town," in which his sketches of his figurative Old Home Town became more acid, a new group of "My Old Man" tales, and the "Joe and Ethel Turp" bagatelles.

Runyon tired of his Broadway stories before his readers did and offered the "In Our Town" pieces to *Collier's* magazine as a substitute for more contrivances about Harry the Horse, Nicely-Nicely, et al. After *Collier's* had published a few of them with misgivings, the editors were prodded by letter-writers into extracting more of the stuff of Broadway legend from Runyon. While responding to this popular demand, Runyon practically gave away a batch of "In Our Town" sketches to a magazine which promised to print them.

It is said that Runyon "glorified" the murderers, dope-dealers, rum-runners, thieves, kidnapers, bookmakers, horse-players and parasitical hangers-on who comprised most of the principal protagonists in the Broadway stories. But I believe the impression may be due to too hasty or unperceptive reading, or lack of understanding of the background of the stories.

When Runyon began his satiric Broadway saga, a new phenomenon was making itself felt in the American press. This was the Broadway columnist who sought all his news or what passed for it in speakeasies and wrote of gunmen, hijackers, union racketeers, dope-smugglers and white-slavers in somewhat more glamorous terms than honest citizens were described. Runyon began by poking fun at the Broadway columnists; the Waldo Winchester of *Romance in the Roaring Forties* is a "hundred per cent sucker," a two-timer, a craven. Deliberately, Runyon made his outlaws Robin Hoods or Galahads in modern bullet-proof vests. This was not a new device in fiction, for Western outlaws had been treated in similar fashion by Alfred Henry Lewis and other humorists, but Runyon used it skillfully and distinctively. With the result that he captivated readers of *Cosmopolitan, Saturday Evening Post,* and *Collier's* with his humor, his realistic reporting of human nature, and his inventive argot.

Runyon had no illusions concerning the stuff of which his Broadway characters were made. In one of his newspaper columns of the time he remarked, "There are only three men in the night life of Broadway whose word is worth a nickel." Similar realistic views of the habitues of Broadway and the sporting fraternity run through the verse he produced in the Thirties. *The Three Cheers Boys, Ghosts of the Great White Way, The Manly Art, The Old Horse Player,* are Runyon poems that leave us without doubts about his feelings.

Evidence that Joe and Ethel Turp were perhaps Runyon's favorite characters, next to My Old Man, is that he made the Turps the principals in a long series of his daily columns and in his weekly contributions to *Pictorial Review,* in which he had complete freedom of choice of subjects.

The Turps were introduced to the reading public in *Nothing Happens in Brooklyn,* in 1937. After a second long story about the young couple, *A Visit to the President,* in 1938, Runyon realized that the stories would be more effective and easier for him to write if Joe's letters were shorter. He therefore reduced the wordage to about a thousand a tale, and wrote enough about the Turps to fill a couple of books. Several dozen of the Turp tales postdate *Blonde Mink* and *Big Boy Blues,** which were the end of his *Broadway Guys and Dolls* saga. *Home-Cooking,* an inclusion in this book, was one of the last Turp stories.

The Turps delineated by Runyon are basic Americans having all of the homely and broad virtues, and without much in common with people of the narrow world of Broadway. When the Turps visit that small world, Runyon makes them feel out of place and glad to get away from it. He endows them with the traits of which he wrote with sentiment in his earliest fiction. They obviously are folks whom he cherished, as he did My Old Man. To more than one reader, they form as distinct a series of Runyonese commentaries on life and manners in and about New York City as his guys and dolls on Broadway.

My Old Man is the most frequently recurring character in Damon Runyon's literary work. One of Damon's earliest stories in a national magazine was a semi-fictional portrait of his Old Man, Alfred Runyan. The latter spelled the family name with an "a," as did many of the family back in New Jersey. Originally it was Ruiniong, or something like that, Damon once said; the earliest of his paternal ancestors in this country were from France.

Damon's paternal grandfather, William Runyan, left New Jersey in the California gold rush. However, like many others, he and his companions found the hardships and deprivations of the rush too much and fell by the wayside. In his case the wayside was Kansas. After

---

* These stories were written when he was a dying man—and knew it. He had written his will and directed that his ashes be "scattered over the place that I have truly loved and that was so good to me"—Broadway. Looking along Broadway one night, Runyon remarked proudly, "I took one little section and made a half million dollars writing about it." Actually, the sum returned him in tribute from readers and viewers of the tales of West Side Willie, Rosie Flynn and their likes, was larger.

trying farming, William Runyan reverted to his old trade; he opened a printing business in Manhattan, Kansas, in 1855. Damon's father, Alfred, who was born there and educated in his father's shop, became a roving printer. He had some connection with dozens of newspapers both before and after he married. Damon's mother, Elizabeth Damon, who came of a Kansas family transplanted from New England, died when Damon was young, and Damon literally grew up in newspaper plants in Kansas and Colorado where his father was employed. He knew the West as it really was.

Two stories in back pages of this book, *At Dead Mule Crossing* and *The Old Men of the Mountain,* are Runyonesque commentaries on the dime-novel and movie-scenario fiction which created a fabulous Wild West.

The Turp story, *One of Those Things,* was the last piece Runyon wrote about his favorite spectator sport, boxing. As a reporter, he covered every kind of athletic spectacle from yacht-racing to pole-vaulting, and wrote memorable news stories about most of them. Still, nothing ever won his interest and devotion as thoroughly as prize-fighting. He was fascinated with its ins and outs and was happiest when he had a hand in arranging a championship bout. It appears he yearned to be the "owner," i.e., manager of a champion, more than anything else. Much "Runyonese" was inspired by his knowledge of the way boxing industry figures talked.

Ironically, the piece of Runyon sports writing best remembered is, as he foresaw, a poem about a jockey. He told a later-day Broadway acquaintance, Leonard Lyons: "If I'm remembered, it will not be for the millions of words I've written for the papers but for some 3500 words in a short story or the 200 words about Sande."

"Sande" is a reference, of course, to *A Handy Guy Like Sande.* Runyon wrote five versions of this often misquoted poem between 1922 and 1930 (see pages 421 to 426 of this book.)

Although Runyon did not lack appreciation of his

craftsmanship, he lacked confidence in his ability to produce longer works. He thought he could not write a novel and rejected proposals that he work on one. Yet he maintained interest in the Turps, My Old Man, and another, unnamed, character of his through hundreds of thousands of words—more than the average novel contains. The unnamed character is the narrator of the Broadway Guys and Dolls stories who tells us, "names make no difference to me, especially on Broadway, because no matter what name a man has, it is not his square moniker," and offers us no square moniker, or any shape moniker at all, for himself—one of the most artfully delineated characters in modern literature.

Runyon also refused to write an autobiography, proposed by the J. B. Lippincott Co. He commented in his daily column:

"If I told the truth, a lot of persons, including myself, might go to jail. If I held out the truth or just told it half way, a lot of my pals who now have confidence in me would be saying:

"'That Runyon is a scaredy-cat and a phony bum. As long as he was going to write his life at all, why didn't he write it on the emmus.' *

"Of course, an even more potent reason why I am never going to write my own tale is that there is no sure money in that tripe. It is purely speculative. It might sell but the odds are against it. . . .

"I do not think my material would ever pass on the basis of importance. My life has been made up of trivialities. I have accomplished no great deeds. I have met no considerable number of the high muck-a-mucks of the world, and when I did I was always too self-conscious to hear what they said."

At another time, commenting on a published collection of his columns, Runyon had this to say about himself:

"Damon Runyon is not a humorist per se. He is more

* On the level.

of a dramatic writer, but in a simulation of humor he often manages to say things which if said in a serious tone might be erased because he is not supposed to say things like that. By saying something with a half-boob air, by conveying an air of jocularity, he gets ideas out of his system on the wrongs of this world which indicate that he must have been a great rebel at heart but lacking moral courage. . . .

"He is a disguised defeatist in that he is always saying with a sort of smirk as if he is half kidding that the world will not change as long as we have human greed and man's inhumanity to man, that dames will continue to doublecross their husbands and sweethearts and vice versa, that politicians will continue to rob the public and that the public will remain as dumb as ever, but these are generalities to which no one is apt to object and the saying of which is not calculated to disturb the author's status quo, if you get what I mean.

"He has one not easily acquired trick which is conveying a thought for indirection. He makes it appear that he is not personally responsible for the thought, but there it is. This has something of the form and something of the effect of dropping rumors on someone where it will do the most harm. I tell you Runyon has subtlety but it is the considered opinion of this reviewer that it is a great pity the guy did not remain a rebel out-and-out, even at the cost of a good position at the feed trough."

Did any author ever appraise himself more frankly?

A TREASURY
OF
DAMON RUNYON

The Idyll of Miss Sarah Brown

Of all the high players this country ever sees, there is no doubt but that the guy they call The Sky is the highest. In fact, the reason he is called The Sky is because he goes so high when it comes to betting on any proposition whatever. He will bet all he has, and nobody can bet any more than this.

His right name is Obadiah Masterson, and he is originally out of a little town in southern Colorado, where he learns to shoot craps, and play cards, and one thing and another, and where his old man is a very well-known citizen, and something of a sport himself. In fact, The Sky tells me that when he finally cleans up all the loose scratch around his home town and decides he needs more room, his old man has a little private talk with him and says to him like this:

"Son," the old guy says, "you are now going out into the wide, wide world to make your own way, and it is a very good thing to do, as there are no more opportunities for you in this burg. I am only sorry," he says, "that I am not able to bank-roll you to a very large start, but," he says, "not having any potatoes to give you, I am now going to stake you to some very valuable advice, which I personally collect in my years of experience around and about, and I hope and trust you will always bear this advice in mind.

"Son," the old guy says, "no matter how far you travel, or how smart you get, always remember this: Some day, somewhere," he says, "a guy is going to come to you and show you a nice brand-new deck of cards on which the seal is never broken, and this guy is going

3

to offer to bet you that the jack of spades will jump out of this deck and squirt cider in your ear. But, son," the old guy says, "do not bet him, for as sure as you do you are going to get an ear full of cider."

Well, The Sky remembers what his old man says, and he is always very cautious about betting on such propositions as the jack of spades jumping out of a sealed deck of cards and squirting cider in his ear, and so he makes few mistakes as he goes along. In fact, the only real mistake The Sky makes is when he hits St. Louis after leaving his old home town, and loses all his potatoes betting a guy St. Louis is the biggest town in the world.

Now of course this is before The Sky ever sees any bigger towns, and he is never much of a hand for reading up on matters such as this. In fact, the only reading The Sky ever does as he goes along through life is in these Gideon Bibles such as he finds in the hotel rooms where he lives, for The Sky never lives anywhere else but in hotel rooms for years.

He tells me that he reads many items of great interest in these Gideon Bibles, and furthermore The Sky says that several times these Gideon Bibles keep him from getting out of line, such as the time he finds himself pretty much frozen-in over in Cincinnati, what with owing everybody in town except maybe the mayor from playing games of chance of one kind and another.

Well, The Sky says he sees no way of meeting these obligations and he is figuring the only thing he can do is to take a run-out powder, when he happens to read in one of these Gideon Bibles where it says like this:

"Better is it," the Gideon Bible says, "that thou shouldest not vow, than that thou shouldest vow and not pay."

Well, The Sky says he can see that there is no doubt whatever but that this means a guy shall not welsh, so he remains in Cincinnati until he manages to wiggle himself out of the situation, and from that day to this, The Sky never thinks of welshing.

He is maybe thirty years old, and is a tall guy with a round kisser, and big blue eyes, and he always looks as innocent as a little baby. But The Sky is by no means as innocent as he looks. In fact, The Sky is smarter than three Philadelphia lawyers, which makes him very smart, indeed, and he is well established as a high player in New Orleans, and Chicago, and Los Angeles, and wherever else there is any action in the way of card-playing, or crap-shooting, or horse-racing, or betting on the baseball games, for The Sky is always moving around the country following the action.

But while The Sky will bet on anything whatever, he is more of a short-card player and a crap shooter than anything else, and furthermore he is a great hand for propositions, such as are always coming up among citizens who follow games of chance for a living. Many citizens prefer betting on propositions to anything you can think of, because they figure a proposition gives them a chance to outsmart somebody, and in fact I know citizens who will sit up all night making up propositions to offer other citizens the next day.

A proposition may be only a problem in cards, such as what is the price against a guy getting aces back-to-back, or how often a pair of deuces will win a hand in stud, and then again it may be some very daffy proposition, indeed, although the daffier any proposition seems to be, the more some citizens like it. And no one ever sees The Sky when he does not have some proposition of his own.

The first time he ever shows up around this town, he goes to a baseball game at the Polo Grounds with several prominent citizens, and while he is at the ball game, he buys himself a sack of Harry Stevens' peanuts, which he dumps in a side pocket of his coat. He is eating these peanuts all through the game, and after the game is over and he is walking across the field with the citizens, he says to them like this:

"What price," The Sky says, "I cannot throw a peanut from second base to the home plate?"

Well, everybody knows that a peanut is too light for anybody to throw it this far, so Big Nig, the crap shooter, who always likes to have a little the best of it running for him, speaks as follows:

"You can have three to one from me, stranger," Big Nig says.

"Two C's against six," The Sky says, and then he stands on second base, and takes a peanut out of his pocket, and not only whips it to the home plate, but on into the lap of a fat guy who is still sitting in the grandstand putting the zing on Bill Terry for not taking Walker out of the box when Walker is getting a pasting from the other club.

Well, naturally, this is a most astonishing throw, indeed, but afterwards it comes out that The Sky throws a peanut loaded with lead, and of course it is not one of Harry Stevens' peanuts, either, as Harry is not selling peanuts full of lead at a dime a bag, with the price of lead what it is.

It is only a few nights after this that The Sky states another most unusual proposition to a group of citizens sitting in Mindy's restaurant when he offers to bet a C note that he can go down into Mindy's cellar and catch a live rat with his bare hands, and everybody is greatly astonished when Mindy himself steps up and takes the bet, for ordinarily Mindy will not bet you a nickel he is alive.

But it seems that Mindy knows that The Sky plants a tame rat in the cellar, and this rat knows The Sky and loves him dearly, and will let him catch it any time he wishes, and it also seems that Mindy knows that one of his dishwashers happens upon this rat, and not knowing it is tame, knocks it flatter than a pancake. So when The Sky goes down into the cellar and starts trying to catch a rat with his bare hands, he is greatly surprised how inhospitable the rat turns out to be, because it is one of Mindy's personal rats, and Mindy is around afterwards saying he will lay plenty of seven to five against even

Strangler Lewis being able to catch one of his rats with his bare hands, or with boxing gloves on.

I am only telling you all this to show you what a smart guy The Sky is, and I am only sorry I do not have time to tell you about many other very remarkable propositions that he thinks up outside of his regular business.

It is well known to one and all that he is very honest in every respect, and that he hates and despises cheaters at cards, or dice, and furthermore The Sky never wishes to play with any the best of it himself, or anyway not much. He will never take the inside of any situation, as many gamblers love to do, such as owning a gambling house, and having the percentage run for him instead of against him, for always The Sky is strictly a player, because he says he will never care to settle down in one spot long enough to become the owner of anything.

In fact, in all the years The Sky is drifting around the country, nobody ever knows him to own anything except maybe a bank roll, and when he comes to Broadway the last time, which is the time I am now speaking of, he has a hundred G's in cash money, and an extra suit of clothes, and this is all he has in the world. He never owns such a thing as a house, or an automobile, or a piece of jewelry. He never owns a watch, because The Sky says time means nothing to him.

Of course some guys will figure a hundred G's comes under the head of owning something, but as far as The Sky is concerned, money is nothing but just something for him to play with and the dollars may as well be doughnuts as far as value goes with him. The only time The Sky ever thinks of money as money is when he is broke, and the only way he can tell he is broke is when he reaches into his pocket and finds nothing there but his fingers.

Then it is necessary for The Sky to go out and dig up some fresh scratch somewhere, and when it comes to digging up scratch, The Sky is practically supernatural. He can get more potatoes on the strength of a telegram to some place or other than John D. Rockefeller can get on collateral, for everybody knows The Sky's word is as good as wheat in the bin.

Now one Sunday evening The Sky is walking along Broadway, and at the corner of Forty-ninth Street he comes upon a little bunch of mission workers who are holding a religious meeting, such as mission workers love to do of a Sunday evening, the idea being that they may round up a few sinners here and there, although personally I always claim the mission workers come out too early to catch any sinners on this part of Broadway. At such an hour the sinners are still in bed resting up from their sinning of the night before, so they will be in good shape for more sinning a little later on.

There are only four of these mission workers, and two of them are old guys, and one is an old doll, while the other is a young doll who is tootling on a cornet. And after a couple of ganders at this young doll, The Sky is a goner, for this is one of the most beautiful young dolls anybody ever sees on Broadway, and especially as a mission worker. Her name is Miss Sarah Brown.

She is tall, and thin, and has a first-class shape, and her hair is a light brown, going on blond, and her eyes are like I do not know what, except that they are one-hundred-per-cent eyes in every respect. Furthermore, she is not a bad cornet player, if you like cornet players, although at this spot on Broadway she has to play against a scat band in a chop-suey joint near by, and this is tough competition, although at that many citizens believe Miss Sarah Brown will win by a large score if she only gets a little more support from one of the old guys with her who has a big bass drum, but does not pound it hearty enough.

Well, The Sky stands there listening to Miss Sarah Brown tootling on the cornet for quite a spell, and then he hears her make a speech in which she puts the blast on sin very good, and boosts religion quite some, and says if there are any souls around that need saving, the owners of same may step forward at once. But no one steps forward, so The Sky comes over to Mindy's restaurant where many citizens are congregated, and starts telling us about Miss Sarah Brown. But of course we already know about Miss Sarah Brown, because she is so beautiful, and so good.

Furthermore, everybody feels somewhat sorry for Miss Sarah Brown, for while she is always tootling the cornet, and making speeches, and looking to save any souls that need saving, she never seems to find any souls to save, or at least her bunch of mission workers never gets any bigger. In fact, it gets smaller, as she starts out with a guy who plays a very fair sort of trombone, but this guy takes it on the lam one night with the trombone, which one and all consider a dirty trick.

Now from this time on, The Sky does not take any interest in anything but Miss Sarah Brown, and any night she is out on the corner with the other mission workers, you will see The Sky standing around looking at her, and naturally after a few weeks of this, Miss Sarah Brown must know The Sky is looking at her, or she is dumber than seems possible. And nobody ever figures Miss Sarah Brown dumb, as she is always on her toes, and seems plenty able to take care of herself, even on Broadway.

Sometimes after the street meeting is over, The Sky follows the mission workers to their headquarters in an old storeroom around in Forty-eighth Street where they generally hold an indoor session, and I hear The Sky drops many a large coarse note in the collection box while looking at Miss Sarah Brown, and there is no doubt these notes come in handy around the mission, as I hear business is by no means so good there.

It is called the Save-a-Soul Mission, and it is run mainly by Miss Sarah Brown's grandfather, an old guy with whiskers, by the name of Arvide Abernathy, but Miss Sarah Brown seems to do most of the work, including tootling the cornet, and visiting the poor people around and about, and all this and that, and many citizens claim it is a great shame that such a beautiful doll is wasting her time being good.

How The Sky ever becomes acquainted with Miss Sarah Brown is a very great mystery, but the next thing anybody knows, he is saying hello to her, and she is smiling at him out of her one-hundred-per-cent eyes, and one evening when I happen to be with The Sky we run into her walking along Forty-ninth Street, and The Sky hauls off and stops her, and says it is a nice evening, which it is, at that. Then The Sky says to Miss Sarah Brown like this:

"Well," The Sky says, "how is the mission dodge going these days? Are you saving any souls?" he says.

Well, it seems from what Miss Sarah Brown says, the soul-saving is very slow, indeed, these days.

"In fact," Miss Sarah Brown says, "I worry greatly about how few souls we seem to save. Sometimes I wonder if we are lacking in grace."

She goes on up the street, and The Sky stands looking after her, and he says to me like this:

"I wish I can think of some way to help this little doll," he says, "especially," he says, "in saving a few souls to build up her mob at the mission. I must speak to her again, and see if I can figure something out."

But The Sky does not get to speak to Miss Sarah Brown again, because somebody weighs in the sacks on him by telling her he is nothing but a professional gambler, and that he is a very undesirable character, and that his only interest in hanging around the mission is because she is a good-looking doll. So all of a sudden Miss Sarah Brown plays plenty of chill for The Sky. Furthermore, she sends him word that she does not care to accept any more of his potatoes in the collection box, because his potatoes are nothing but ill-gotten gains.

Well, naturally, this hurts The Sky's feelings no little, so he quits standing around looking at Miss Sarah Brown, and going to the mission, and takes to mingling again with the citizens in Mindy's, and showing some interest in the affairs of the community, especially the crap games.

Of course the crap games that are going on at this time are nothing much, because practically everybody in the world is broke, but there is a head-and-head game run by Nathan Detroit over a garage in Fifty-second Street where there is occasionally some action, and who shows up at this crap game early one evening but The Sky, although it seems he shows up there more to find company than anything else.

In fact, he only stands around watching the play, and talking with other guys who are also standing around and watching, and many of these guys are very high shots during the gold rush, although most of them are now as clean as a jaybird, and maybe cleaner. One of these guys is a guy by the name of Brandy Bottle Bates, who is known from coast to coast as a high player when he has anything to play with, and who is called Brandy Bottle Bates because it seems that years ago he is a great hand for belting a brandy bottle around.

This Brandy Bottle Bates is a big, black-looking guy, with a large beezer, and a head shaped like a pear, and he is considered a very immoral and wicked character, but he is a pretty slick gambler, and a fast man with a dollar when he is in the money.

Well, finally The Sky asks Brandy Bottle why he is not playing and Brandy laughs, and states as follows:

"Why," he says, "in the first place I have no potatoes, and in the second place I doubt if it will do me much good if I do have any potatoes the way I am going the past year. Why," Brandy Bottle says, "I cannot win a bet to save my soul."

Now this crack seems to give The Sky an idea, as he stands looking at Brandy Bottle very strangely, and while he is looking, Big Nig, the crap shooter, picks up the dice and hits three times hand-running, bing, bing, bing. Then Big Nig comes out on a six and Brandy Bottle Bates speaks as follows:

"You see how my luck is," he says. "Here is Big Nig hotter than a stove, and here I am without a bob to follow him with, especially," Brandy says, "when he is looking for nothing but a six. Why," he says, "Nig can make sixes all night when he is hot. If he does not make this six, the way he is, I will be willing to turn square and quit gambling forever."

"Well, Brandy," The Sky says, "I will make you a proposition. I will lay you a G note Big Nig does not get his six. I will lay you a G note against nothing but your soul," he says. "I mean if Big Nig does not get his six, you are to turn square and join Miss Sarah Brown's mission for six months."

"Bet!" Brandy Bottle Bates says right away, meaning the proposition is on, although the chances are he does not quite understand the proposition. All Brandy understands is The Sky wishes to wager that Big Nig does not make his six, and Brandy Bottle Bates will be willing to bet his soul a couple of times over on Big Nig making his six, and figure he is getting the best of it, at that, as Brandy has great confidence in Nig.

Well, sure enough, Big Nig makes the six, so The Sky weeds Brandy Bottle Bates a G note, although everybody around is saying The Sky makes a terrible overlay of the natural price in giving Brandy Bottle a G against his soul. Furthermore, everybody around figures the chances are The Sky only wishes to give Brandy an opportunity to get in action, and nobody figures The Sky is on the level about trying to win Brandy Bottle Bates' soul, especially as The Sky does not seem to wish to go any further after paying the bet.

He only stands there looking on and seeming somewhat depressed as Brandy Bottle goes into action on his own account with the G note, fading other guys around the table with cash money. But Brandy Bottle Bates seems to figure what is in The Sky's mind pretty well, because Brandy Bottle is a crafty old guy.

It finally comes his turn to handle the dice, and he hits a couple of times, and then he comes out on a four, and anybody will tell you that a four is a very tough point to make, even with a lead pencil. Then Brandy Bottle turns to The Sky and speaks to him as follows:

"Well, Sky," he says, "I will take the odds off you on this one. I know you do not want my dough," he says. "I know you only want my soul for Miss Sarah Brown, and," he says, "without wishing to be fresh about it, I know why you want it for her. I am young once myself," Brandy Bottle says. "And you know if I lose to you, I will be over there in Forty-eighth Street in an hour pounding on the door, for Brandy always settles.

"But, Sky," he says, "now I am in the money, and my price goes up. Will you lay me ten G's against my soul I do not make this four?"

"Bet!" The Sky says, and right away Brandy Bottle hits with a four.

Well, when word goes around that The Sky is up at Nathan Detroit's crap game trying to win Brandy Bottle Bates' soul for Miss Sarah Brown, the excitement is practically intense. Somebody telephones Mindy's, where a large number of citizens are sitting around arguing about this and that, and telling one another how much they will bet in support of their arguments, if only they have something to bet, and Mindy himself is almost killed in the rush for the door.

One of the first guys out of Mindy's and up to the crap game is Regret, the horse player, and as he comes in, Brandy Bottle is looking for a nine, and The Sky is laying him twelve G's against his soul that he does not make this nine, for it seems Brandy Bottle's soul keeps getting more and more expensive.

Well, Regret wishes to bet his soul against a G that Brandy Bottle gets his nine, and is greatly insulted when The Sky cannot figure his price any better than a double saw, but finally Regret accepts this price, and Brandy Bottle hits again.

Now many other citizens request a little action from The Sky, and if there is one thing The Sky cannot deny a citizen it is action, so he says he will lay them according to how he figures their word to join Miss Sarah Brown's mission if Brandy Bottle misses out, but about this time The Sky finds he has no more potatoes on him, being now around thirty-five G's loser, and he wishes to give markers.

But Brandy Bottle says that while ordinarily he will be pleased to extend The Sky this accommodation, he does not care to accept markers against his soul, so then The Sky has to leave the joint and go over to his hotel two or three blocks away, and get the night clerk to open his damper so The Sky can get the rest of his bank roll. In the meantime the crap game continues at Nathan Detroit's among the small operators, while the other citizens stand around and say that while they hear of many a daffy proposition in their time, this is the daffiest that ever comes to their attention, although Big Nig claims he hears of a daffier one, but cannot think what it is.

Big Nig claims that all gamblers are daffy anyway, and in fact he says if they are not daffy they will not be gamblers, and while he is arguing this matter, back comes The Sky with fresh scratch, and Brandy Bottle Bates takes up where he leaves off, although Brandy says he is accepting the worst of it, as the dice have a chance to cool off.

Now the upshot of the whole business is that Brandy Bottle hits thirteen licks in a row, and the last lick he makes is on a ten, and it is for twenty G's against his soul, with about a dozen other citizens getting anywhere from one to five C's against their souls, and complaining bitterly of the price.

And as Brandy Bottle makes his ten, I happen to look at The Sky and I see him watching Brandy with a very peculiar expression on his face, and furthermore I see The Sky's right hand creeping inside his coat where I know he always packs a Betsy in a shoulder holster, so I can see something is wrong somewhere.

But before I can figure out what it is, there is quite a fuss at the door, and loud talking, and a doll's voice, and all of a sudden in bobs nobody else but Miss Sarah Brown. It is plain to be seen that she is all steamed up about something.

She marches right up to the crap table where Brandy Bottle Bates and The Sky and the other citizens are standing, and one and all are feeling sorry for Dobber, the doorman, thinking of what Nathan Detroit is bound to say to him for letting her in. The dice are still lying on the table showing Brandy Bottle Bates' last throw, which cleans The Sky and gives many citizens the first means they enjoy in several months.

Well, Miss Sarah Brown looks at The Sky, and The Sky looks at Miss Sarah Brown, and Miss Sarah Brown looks at the citizens around and about, and one and all are somewhat dumfounded, and nobody seems to be able to think of much to say, although The Sky finally speaks up as follows:

"Good evening," The Sky says. "It is a nice evening," he says. "I am trying to win a few souls for you around here, but," he says, "I seem to be about half out of luck."

"Well," Miss Miss Sarah Brown says, looking at The Sky most severely out of her hundred-per-cent eyes, "you are taking too much upon yourself. I can win any souls I need myself. You better be thinking of your own soul. By the way," she says, "are you risking your own soul, or just your money?"

Well, of course up to this time The Sky is not risking anything but his potatoes, so he only shakes his head to Miss Sarah Brown's question, and looks somewhat disorganized.

"I know something about gambling," Miss Sarah Brown says, "especially about crap games. I ought to," she says. "It ruins my poor papa and my brother Joe. If you wish to gamble for souls, Mister Sky, gamble for your own soul."

Now Miss Sarah Brown opens a small black leather pocketbook she is carrying in one hand, and pulls out a

two-dollar bill, and it is such a two-dollar bill as seems
to have seen much service in its time, and holding up
this deuce, Miss Sarah Brown speaks as follows:

"I will gamble with you, Mister Sky," she says. "I will
gamble with you," she says, "on the same terms you
gamble with these parties here. This two dollars against
your soul, Mister Sky. It is all I have, but," she says,
"it is more than your soul is worth."

Well, of course anybody can see that Miss Sarah
Brown is doing this because she is very angry, and wishes
to make The Sky look small, but right away The Sky's
duke comes from inside his coat, and he picks up the
dice and hands them to her and speaks as follows:

"Roll them," The Sky says, and Miss Sarah Brown
snatches the dice out of his hand and gives them a quick
sling on the table in such a way that anybody can see
she is not a professional crap shooter, and not even an
amateur crap shooter, for all amateur crap shooters first
breathe on the dice, and rattle them good, and make
remarks to them, such as "Come on, baby!"

In fact, there is some criticism of Miss Sarah Brown
afterwards on account of her haste, as many citizens are
eager to string with her to hit, while others are just as
anxious to bet she misses, and she does not give them a
chance to get down.

Well, Scranton Slim is the stick guy, and he takes a
gander at the dice as they hit up against the side of the
table and bounce back, and then Slim hollers, "Winner,
winner, winner," as stick guys love to do, and what is
showing on the dice as big as life, but a six and a five,
which makes eleven, no matter how you figure, so The
Sky's soul belongs to Miss Sarah Brown.

She turns at once and pushes through the citizens
around the table without even waiting to pick up the
deuce she lays down when she grabs the dice. Afterwards a most obnoxious character by the name of Red
Nose Regan tries to claim the deuce as a sleeper and
gets the heave-o from Nathan Detroit, who becomes very

indignant about this, stating that Red Nose is trying to give his joint a wrong rap.

Naturally, The Sky follows Miss Brown, and Dobber, the doorman, tells me that as they are waiting for him to unlock the door and let them out, Miss Sarah Brown turns on The Sky and speaks to him as follows:

"You are a fool," Miss Sarah Brown says.

Well, at this Dobber figures The Sky is bound to let one go, as this seems to be most insulting language, but instead of letting one go, The Sky only smiles at Miss Sarah Brown and says to her like this:

"Why," The Sky says, "Paul says, 'If any man among you seemeth to be wise in this world, let him become a fool, that he may be wise.' I love you, Miss Sarah Brown," The Sky says.

Well, now, Dobber has a pretty fair sort of memory, and he says that Miss Sarah Brown tells The Sky that since he seems to know so much about the Bible, maybe he remembers the second verse of the Song of Solomon, but the chances are Dobber muffs the number of the verse, because I look the matter up in one of these Gideon Bibles, and the verse seems a little too much for Miss Sarah Brown, although of course you never can tell.

Anyway, this is about all there is to the story, except that Brandy Bottle Bates slides out during the confusion so quietly even Dobber scarcely remembers letting him out, and he takes most of The Sky's potatoes with him, but he soon gets batted in against the faro bank out in Chicago, and the last anybody hears of him he gets religion all over again, and is preaching out in San José, so The Sky always claims he beats Brandy for his soul, at that.

I see The Sky the other night at Forty-ninth Street and Broadway, and he is with quite a raft of mission workers, including Mrs. Sky, for it seems that the soul-saving business picks up wonderfully, and The Sky is giving a big bass drum such a first-class whacking that the scat band in the chop-suey joint can scarcely be heard. Furthermore, The Sky is hollering between whacks, and I never see a guy look happier, especially when Mrs. Sky smiles at him out of her hundred-percent eyes. But I do not linger long, because The Sky gets a gander at me, and right away he begins hollering:

"I see before me a sinner of deepest dye," he hollers. "Oh, sinner, repent before it is too late. Join with us, sinner," he hollers, "and let us save your soul."

Naturally, this crack about me being a sinner embarrasses me no little, as it is by no means true, and it is a good thing for The Sky there is no copper in me, or I will go to Mrs. Sky, who is always bragging about how she wins The Sky's soul by outplaying him at his own game, and tell her the truth.

And the truth is that the dice with which she wins The Sky's soul, and which are the same dice with which Brandy Bottle Bates wins all his potatoes, are strictly phony, and that she gets into Nathan Detroit's just in time to keep The Sky from killing old Brandy Bottle.

Pick the Winner

What I am doing in Miami associating with such a character as Hot Horse Herbie is really quite a long story, and it goes back to one cold night when I am sitting in Mindy's restaurant on Broadway thinking what a cruel world it is, to be sure, when in comes Hot Horse Herbie and his ever-loving fiancée, Miss Cutie Singleton.

This Hot Horse Herbie is a tall, skinny guy with a most depressing kisser, and he is called Hot Horse Herbie because he can always tell you about a horse that is so hot it is practically on fire, a hot horse being a horse that is all readied up to win a race, although sometimes Herbie's hot horses turn out to be so cold they freeze everybody within fifty miles of them.

He is following the races almost since infancy, to hear him tell it. In fact, old Captain Duhaine, who has charge of the Pinkertons around the race tracks, says he remembers Hot Horse Herbie as a little child, and that even then Herbie is a hustler, but of course Captain Duhaine does not care for Hot Horse Herbie, because he claims Herbie is nothing but a tout, and a tout is something that is most repulsive to Captain Duhaine and all other Pinkertons.

A tout is a guy who goes around a race track giving out tips on the races, if he can find anybody who will listen to his tips, especially suckers, and a tout is nearly always broke. If he is not broke, he is by no means a tout, but a handicapper, and is respected by one and all, including the Pinkertons, for knowing so much about the races.

Well, personally, I have nothing much against Hot Horse Herbie, no matter what Captain Duhaine says he is, and I certainly have nothing against Herbie's everloving fiancée, Miss Cutie Singleton. In fact, I am rather in favor of Miss Cutie Singleton, because in all the years I know her, I wish to say I never catch Miss Cutie Singleton out of line, which is more than I can say of many other dolls I know.

She is a little, good-natured blond doll, and by no means a crow, if you care for blondes, and some people say that Miss Cutie Singleton is pretty smart, although I never can see how this can be, as I figure a smart doll will never have any truck with a guy like Hot Horse Herbie, for Herbie is by no means a provider.

But for going on ten years, Miss Cutie Singleton and Hot Horse Herbie are engaged, and it is well known to one and all that they are to be married as soon as Herbie makes a scratch. In fact, they are almost married in New Orleans in 1928, when Hot Horse Herbie beats a good thing for eleven C's, but the tough part of it is the good thing is in the first race, and naturally Herbie bets the eleven C's right back on another good thing in the next race, and this good thing blows, so Herbie winds up with nothing but the morning line and is unable to marry Miss Cutie Singleton at this time.

Then again in 1929 at Churchill Downs, Hot Horse Herbie has a nice bet on Naishapur to win the Kentucky Derby, and he is so sure Naishapur cannot miss, that the morning of the race he sends Miss Cutie Singleton out to pick a wedding ring. But Naishapur finishes second, so naturally Hot Horse Herbie is unable to buy the ring, and of course Miss Cutie Singleton does not wish to be married without a wedding ring.

They have another close call in 1931 at Baltimore when Hot Horse Herbie figures Twenty Grand a standout in the Preakness, and in fact is so sure of his figures that he has Miss Cutie Singleton go down to the city hall to find out what a marriage license costs. But of course Twenty Grand does not win the Preakness, so the information Miss Cutie Singleton obtains is of no use to them, and anyway Hot Horse Herbie says he can beat the price on marriage licenses in New York.

However, there is no doubt but what Hot Horse Herbie and Miss Cutie Singleton are greatly in love, although I hear rumors that for a couple of years past, Miss Cutie Singleton is getting somewhat impatient about Hot Horse Herbie not making a scratch as soon as he claims he is going to when he first meets up with her in Hot Springs in 1923.

In fact, Miss Cutie Singleton says if she knows Hot Horse Herbie is going to be so long delayed in making his scratch she will never consider becoming engaged to him, but will keep her job as a manicurist at the Arlington Hotel, where she is not doing bad, at that.

It seems that the past couple of years Miss Cutie Singleton is taking to looking longingly at the little houses in the towns they pass through going from one race track to another, and especially at little white houses with green shutters and yards and vines all around and about, and saying it must be nice to be able to live in such places instead of in a suitcase.

But of course Hot Horse Herbie does not put in with her on these ideas, because Herbie knows very well if he is placed in a little white house for more than fifteen minutes the chances are he will lose his mind, even if the house has green shutters.

Personally, I consider Miss Cutie Singleton somewhat ungrateful for thinking of such matters after all the scenery Hot Horse Herbie lets her see in the past ten years. In fact, Herbie lets her see practically all the scenery there is in this country, and some in Canada, and all she has to do in return for all this courtesy is to occasionally get out a little crystal ball and deck of cards and let on she is a fortuneteller when things are going especially tough for Herbie.

Of course Miss Cutie cannot really tell fortunes, or she will be telling Hot Horse Herbie's fortune, and maybe her own, too, but I hear she is better than a raw hand at making people believe she is telling their fortunes, especially old maids who think they are in love, or widows who are looking to snare another husband, and other such characters.

Well, anyway, when Hot Horse Herbie and his everloving fiancée come into Mindy's, he gives me a large hello, and so does Miss Cutie Singleton, so I hello them right back, and Hot Horse Herbie speaks to me as follows:

"Well," Herbie says, "we have some wonderful news for you. We are going to Miami," he says, "and soon we will be among the waving palms, and reveling in the warm waters of the Gulf Stream."

Now of course this is a lie, because while Hot Horse Herbie is in Miami many times, he never revels in the warm waters of the Gulf Stream, because he never has time for such a thing, what with hustling around the race tracks in the daytime, and around the dog tracks and the gambling joints at night, and in fact I will lay plenty of six to five Hot Horse Herbie cannot even point in the direction of the Gulf Stream when he is in Miami, and I will give him three points, at that.

But naturally, what he says gets me to thinking how pleasant it is in Miami in the winter, especially when it is snowing up north, and a guy does not have a flogger to keep himself warm, and I am commencing to feel very envious of Hot Horse Herbie and his ever-loving fiancée when he says like this:

"But," Herbie says, "our wonderful news for you is not about us going. It is about you going," he says. "We already have our railroad tickets," he says, "as Miss Cutie Singleton, my ever-loving fiancée here, saves up three C's for her hope chest the past summer, but when it comes to deciding between a hope chest and Miami, naturally she chooses Miami, because," Herbie says, "she claims she does not have enough hope left to fill a chest. Miss Cutie Singleton is always kidding," he says.

"Well, now," Herbie goes on, "I just run into Mr. Edward Donlin, the undertaker, and it seems that he is sending a citizen of Miami back home tomorrow night, and of course you know," he says, "that Mr. Donlin must purchase two railroad tickets for this journey, and as the citizen has no one else to accompany him, I got to thinking of you. He is a very old and respected citizen of Miami," Herbie says, "although of course," he says, "he is no longer with us, except maybe in spirit."

Of course such an idea is most obnoxious to me, and I am very indignant that Hot Horse Herbie can even think I will travel in this manner, but he gets to telling me that the old and respected citizen of Miami that Mr. Donlin is sending back home is a great old guy in his day, and that for all anybody knows he will appreciate having company on the trip, and about this time Big Nig, the crap shooter, comes into Mindy's leaving the door open behind him so that a blast of cold air hits me, and makes me think more than somewhat of the waving palms and the warm waters of the Gulf Stream.

So the next thing I know, there I am in Miami with

Hot Horse Herbie, and it is the winter of 1931, and everybody now knows that this is the winter when the suffering among the horse players in Miami is practically horrible. In fact, the suffering is so intense that many citizens are wondering if it will do any good to appeal to Congress for relief for the horse players, but The Dancer says he hears Congress needs a little relief itself.

Hot Horse Herbie and his ever-loving fiancée, Miss Cutie Singleton, and me have rooms in a little hotel on Flagler Street, and while it is nothing but a fleabag, and we are doing the landlord a favor by living there, it is surprising how much fuss he makes any time anybody happens to be a little short of the rent. In fact, the landlord hollers and yells so much any time anybody is a little short of the rent that he becomes a very great nuisance to me, and I have half a notion to move, only I cannot think of any place to move to. Furthermore, the landlord will not let me move unless I pay him all I owe him, and I am not in a position to take care of this matter at the moment.

Of course I am not very dirty when I first come in as far as having any potatoes is concerned, and I start off at once having a little bad luck. It goes this way awhile, and then it gets worse, and sometimes I wonder if I will not be better off if I buy myself a rope and end it all on a palm tree in the park on Biscayne Boulevard. But the only trouble with the idea is I do not have the price of a rope, and anyway I hear most of the palm trees in the park are already spoken for by guys who have the same notion.

And bad off as I am, I am not half as bad off as Hot Horse Herbie, because he has his ever-loving fiancée, Miss Cutie Singleton, to think of, especially as Miss Cutie Singleton is putting up quite a beef about not having any recreation, and saying if she only has the brains God gives geese she will break off their engagement at once and find some guy who can show her a little speed, and she seems to have no sympathy whatever for Hot Horse Herbie when he tells her how many tough snoots he gets beat at the track.

But Herbie is very patient with her, and tells her it will not be long now, because the law of average is such that his luck is bound to change, and he suggests to Miss Cutie Singleton that she get the addresses of a few preachers in case they wish to locate one in a hurry. Furthermore, Hot Horse Herbie suggests to Miss Cutie Singleton that she get out the old crystal ball and her deck of cards, and hang out her sign as a fortuneteller while they are waiting for the law of averages to start working for him, although personally I doubt if she will be able to get any business telling fortunes in Miami at this time because everybody in Miami seems to know what their fortune is already.

Now I wish to say that after we arrive in Miami I have very little truck with Hot Horse Herbie, because I do not approve of some of his business methods, and furthermore I do not wish Captain Duhaine and his Pinkertons at my hip all the time, as I never permit myself to get out of line in any respect, or anyway not much. But of course I see Hot Horse Herbie at the track every day, and one day I see him talking to the most innocent-looking guy I ever see in all my life.

He is a tall, spindling guy with a soft brown Vandyke beard, and soft brown hair, and no hat, and he is maybe forty-odd, and wears rumpled white flannel pants, and a rumpled sports coat, and big horn cheaters, and he is smoking a pipe that you can smell a block away. He is such a guy as looks as if he does not know what time it is, and furthermore he does not look as if he has a quarter, but I can see by the way Hot Horse Herbie is warming his ear that Herbie figures him to have a few potatoes.

Furthermore, I never know Hot Horse Herbie to make many bad guesses in this respect, so I am not surprised when I see the guy pull out a long flat leather from the inside pocket of his coat and weed Herbie a bank note. Then I see Herbie start for the mutuels windows, but I am quite astonished when I see that he makes for a two-dollar window. So I follow Hot Horse Herbie to see what this is all about, because it is certainly not like Herbie to dig up a guy with a bank roll and then only promote him for a deuce.

When I get hold of Herbie and ask him what this means, he laughs, and says to me like this:

"Well," he says, "I am just taking a chance with the guy. He may be a prospect, at that," Herbie says. "You never can tell about people. This is the first bet he ever makes in his life, and furthermore," Herbie says, "he does not wish to bet. He says he knows one horse can beat another, and what of it? But," Herbie says, "I give him a good story, so he finally goes for the deuce. I think he is a college professor somewhere," Herbie says, "and he is only wandering around the track out of curiosity. He does not know a soul here. Well," Herbie says, "I put him on a real hot horse, and if he wins, maybe he can be developed into something. You know," Herbie says, "they can never rule you off for trying."

Well, it seems that the horse Herbie gives the guy wins all right and at a fair price, and Herbie lets it go at that for the time being, because he gets hold of a real good guy, and cannot be bothering with guys who only bet deuces. But every day the professor is at the track and I often see him wandering through the crowds, puffing at his old stinkaroo and looking somewhat bewildered.

I get somewhat interested in the guy myself, because he seems so much out of place, but I wish to say I never think of promoting him in any respect, because this is by no means my dodge, and finally one day I get to talking to him and he seems just as innocent as he looks. He is a professor at Princeton, which is a college in New Jersey, and his name is Woodhead, and he has been very sick, and is in Florida to get well, and he thinks the track mob is the greatest show he ever sees, and is sorry he does not study this business a little earlier in life.

Well, personally, I think he is a very nice guy, and he seems to have quite some knowledge of this and that and one thing and another, although he is so ignorant about racing that it is hard to believe he is a college guy.

Even if I am a hustler, I will just as soon try to hustle Santa Claus as Professor Woodhead, but by and by Hot Horse Herbie finds things getting very desperate indeed, so he picks up the professor again and starts working on him, and one day he gets him to go for another deuce, and then for a fin, and both times the horses Herbie gives him are winners, which Herbie says just goes to show you the luck he is playing in, because when he has a guy who is willing to make a bet for him, he cannot pick one to finish fifth.

You see, the idea is, when Hot Horse Herbie gives a guy a horse, he expects the guy to bet for him, too, or maybe give him a piece of what he wins, but of course Herbie does not mention this to Professor Woodhead as yet, because the professor does not bet enough to bother with, and anyway Herbie is building him up by degrees, although if you ask me, it is going to be slow work, and finally Herbie himself admits as much, and says to me like this:

"It looks as if I will have to blast," Herbie says. "The professor is a nice guy, but," he says, "he does not loosen so easy. Furthermore," Herbie says, "he is very dumb about horses. In fact," he says, "I never see a guy so hard to educate, and if I do not like him personally, I will have no part of him whatever. And besides liking him personally," Herbie says, "I get a gander into that leather he carries the other day, and what do I see," he says, "but some large, coarse notes in there back to back."

Well, of course this is very interesting news, even to me, because large, coarse notes are so scarce in Miami at this time that if a guy runs into one he takes it to bank to see if it is counterfeit before he changes it, and even then he will scarcely believe it.

I get to thinking that if a guy such as Professor Woodhead can be going around with large, coarse notes in his possession, I make a serious mistake in not becoming a college professor myself, and naturally after this I treat Professor Woodhead with great respect.

Now what happens one evening, but Hot Horse Herbie and his ever-loving fiancée, Miss Cutie Singleton, and me are in a little grease joint on Second Street putting on the old hot tripe à la Creole, which is a very pleasant dish, and by no means expensive, when who wanders in but Professor Woodhead.

Naturally Herbie calls him over to our table and introduces Professor Woodhead to Miss Cutie Singleton, and Professor Woodhead sits there with us looking at Miss Cutie Singleton with great interest, although Miss Cutie Singleton is at this time feeling somewhat peevish because it is the fourth evening hand running she has to eat tripe à la Creole, and Miss Cutie Singleton does not care for tripe under any circumstances.

She does not pay any attention whatever to Professor Woodhead, but finally Hot Horse Herbie happens to mention that the professor is from Princeton, and then Miss Cutie Singleton looks at the professor, and says to him like this:

"Where is this Princeton?" she says. "Is it a little town?"

"Well," Professor Woodhead says, "Princeton is in New Jersey, and it is by no means a large town, but," he says, "it is thriving."

"Are there any little white houses in this town?" Miss Cutie Singleton asks. "Are there any little white houses with green shutters and vines all around and about?"

"Why," Professor Woodhead says, looking at her with more interest than somewhat, "you are speaking of my own house," he says. "I live in a little white house with green shutters and vines all around and about, and," he says, "it is a nice place to live in, at that, although it is sometimes a little lonesome, as I live there all by myself, unless," he says, "you wish to count old Mrs. Bixby, who keeps house for me. I am a bachelor," he says.

Well, Miss Cutie Singleton does not have much to say after this, although it is only fair to Miss Cutie Singleton to state that for a doll, and especially a blond doll, she is never so very gabby, at that, but she watches Professor Woodhead rather closely, as Miss Cutie Singleton never before comes in contact with anybody who lives in a little white house with green shutters.

Finally we get through with the hot tripe à la Creole and walk around to the fleabag where Hot Horse Herbie and Miss Cutie Singleton and me are residing, and Professor Woodhead walks around with us. In fact, Professor Woodhead walks with Miss Cutie Singleton, while Hot Horse Herbie walks with me, and Hot Horse Herbie is telling me that he has the very best thing of his entire life in the final race at Hialeah the next day, and he is expressing great regret that he does not have any potatoes to bet on this thing, and does not know where he can get any potatoes.

It seems that he is speaking of a horse by the name of Breezing Along, which is owned by a guy by the name of Moose Tassell, who is a citizen of Chicago, and who tells Hot Horse Herbie that the only way Breezing Along can lose the race is to have somebody shoot him at the quarter pole, and of course nobody is shooting horses at the quarter pole at Hialeah, though many citizens often feel like shooting horses at the half.

Well, by this time we get to our fleabag, and we all stand there talking when Professor Woodhead speaks as follows:

"Miss Cutie Singleton informs me," he says, "that she dabbles somewhat in fortunetelling. Well," Professor Woodhead says, "this is most interesting to me, because I am by no means skeptical of fortunetelling. In fact," he says, "I make something of a study of the matter. and there is no doubt in my mind that certain human beings

do have the faculty of foretelling future events with remarkable accuracy."

Now I wish to say one thing for Hot Horse Herbie,
and this is that he is a quick-thinking guy when you put
him up against a situation that calls for quick thinking,
for right away he speaks up and says like this:

"Why, Professor," he says, "I am certainly glad to
hear you make this statement, because," he says, "I am
a believer in fortunetelling myself. As a matter of fact,
I am just figuring on having Miss Cutie Singleton look
into her crystal ball and see if she can make out anything on a race that is coming up tomorrow, and which
has me greatly puzzled, what with being undecided
between a couple of horses."

Well, of course up to this time Miss Cutie Singleton
does not have any idea she is to look into any crystal
ball for a horse, and furthermore, it is the first time in
his life Hot Horse Herbie ever asks her to look into the
crystal ball for anything whatever, except to make a
few bobs for them to eat on, because Herbie by no
means believes in matters of this nature.

But naturally Miss Cutie Singleton is not going to display any astonishment, and when she says she will be
very glad to oblige, Professor Woodhead speaks up and
says he will be glad to see this crystal gazing come off,
which makes it perfect for Hot Horse Herbie.

So we all go upstairs to Miss Cutie Singleton's room,
and the next thing anybody knows there she is with her
crystal ball, gazing into it with both eyes.

Now Professor Woodhead is taking a deep interest
in the proceedings, but of course Professor Woodhead
does not hear what Hot Horse Herbie tells Miss Cutie
Singleton in private, and as far as this is concerned
neither do I, but Herbie tells me afterwards that he tells
her to be sure and see a breeze blowing in the crystal
ball. So by and by, after gazing into the ball a long time,
Miss Cutie Singleton speaks in a low voice as follows:

"I seem to see trees bending to the ground under the
force of a great wind," Miss Cutie Singleton says. "I see

houses blown about by the wind," she says. "Yes," Miss Cutie Singleton says, "I see pedestrians struggling along and shivering in the face of this wind, and I see waves driven high on a beach and boats tossed about like paper cups. In fact," Miss Singleton says, "I seem to see quite a blow."

Well, then, it seems that Miss Cutie Singleton can see no more, but Hot Horse Herbie is greatly excited by what she sees already, and he says like this:

"It means this horse Breezing Along," he says. "There can be no doubt about it. Professor," he says, "here is the chance of your lifetime. The horse will be not less than six to one," he says. "This is the spot to bet a gob, and," he says, "the place to bet it is downtown with a bookmaker at the opening price, because there will be a ton of money for the horse in the machines. Give me five C's," Hot Horse Herbie says, "and I will bet four for you, and one for me."

Well, Professor Woodhead seems greatly impressed by what Miss Cutie Singleton sees in the crystal ball, but of course taking a guy from a finnif to five C's is carrying him along too fast, especially when Herbie explains that five C's is five hundred dollars, and naturally the professor does not care to bet any such money as this. In fact, the professor does not seem anxious to bet more than a sawbuck, tops, but Herbie finally moves him up to bet a yard, and of this yard twenty-five bobs is running for Hot Horse Herbie, as Herbie explains to the professor that a remittance he is expecting from his New York bankers fails him.

The next day Herbie takes the hundred bucks and bets it with Gloomy Gus downtown, for Herbie really has great confidence in the horse.

We are out to the track early in the afternoon and the first guy we run into is Professor Woodhead, who is very much excited. We speak to him, and then we do not see him again all day.

Well, I am not going to bother telling you the details of the race, but this horse Breezing Along is nowhere.

In fact, he is so far back that I do not recollect seeing him finish, because by the time the third horse in the field crosses the line, Hot Horse Herbie and me are on our way back to town, as Herbie does not feel that he can face Professor Woodhead at such a time as this. In fact, Herbie does not feel that he can face anybody, so we go to a certain spot over on Miami Beach and remain there drinking beer until a late hour, when Herbie happens to think of his ever-loving fiancée, Miss Cutie Singleton, and how she must be suffering from lack of food, so we return to our fleabag so Herbie can take Miss Cutie Singleton to dinner.

But he does not find Miss Cutie Singleton. All he finds from her is a note, and in this note Miss Cutie Singleton says like this: "Dear Herbie," she says, "I do not believe in long engagements any more, so Professor Woodhead and I are going to Palm Beach to be married tonight, and are leaving for Princeton, New Jersey, at once, where I am going to live in a little white house with green shutters and vines all around and about. Good-by, Herbie," the note says. "Do not eat any bad fish. Respectfully, Mrs. Professor Woodhead."

Well, naturally this is most surprising to Hot Horse Herbie, but I never hear him mention Miss Cutie Singleton or Professor Woodhead again until a couple of weeks later when he shows me a letter from the professor.

It is quite a long letter, and it seems that Professor Woodhead wishes to apologize, and naturally Herbie has a right to think that the professor is going to apologize for marrying his ever-loving fiancée, Miss Cutie Singleton, as Herbie feels he has an apology coming on this account.

But what the professor seems to be apologizing about is not being able to find Hot Horse Herbie just before the Breezing Along race to explain a certain matter that is on his mind.

"It does not seem to me," the professor says, as near as I can remember the letter, "that the name of your se-

lection is wholly adequate as a description of the present
Mrs. Professor Woodhead's wonderful vision in the crystal ball, so," he says, "I examine the program further,
and finally discover what I believe to be the name of the
horse meant by the vision, and I wager two hundred dollars on this horse, which turns out to be the winner at
ten to one, as you may recall. It is in my mind," the
professor says, "to send you some share of the proceeds,
inasmuch as we are partners in the original arrangement,
but the present Mrs. Woodhead disagrees with my view,
so all I can send you is an apology, and best wishes."

Well, Hot Horse Herbie cannot possibly remember
the name of the winner of any race as far back as this,
and neither can I, but we go over to the *Herald* office
and look at the files, and what is the name of the winner
of the Breezing Along race but Mistral, and when I look
in the dictionary to see what this word means, what does
it mean but a violent, cold and dry northerly wind.

And of course I never mention to Hot Horse Herbie
or anybody else that I am betting on another horse in
this race myself, and the name of the horse I am betting
on is Leg Show, for how do I know for certain that Miss
Cutie Singleton is not really seeing in the crystal ball
just such a blow as she describes?

Vers Libre

(By a gentleman who feels himself "right")

Two bits I shoot; two bits!
Aw' righ'? Come on, now! Look out there! Gimme room!
HAH!
What do they say? 'Leven!
I shoot four bits!

HAH!
Read 'em; read 'em to me! Seven! Ol' sev'!
I shoot the buck!
HAH!
Gimme the news! Don't hold nothin' back!
Four!
I kin do it. Haffah dollar I four or ten!
Anybody want it! Haffah dollar I four or ten!
HAH!
What is it? Nine! Nine the line! Ol' nine!
Come on, now, four! Come on, Joe! We kin do it!
HAH!
Lookit refuse me! Lookit! Oh, Joe! Oh, Joe-dey!
HAH!
Why, there you are, you lil' fat Joe. There you are!
I knowed we could do it!
I shoot four bucks!
HAH!
What? Three!
Well, she mus' happen sometimes!
Bound to happen now 'n then!
I shoot two bits!
Nev' mind! Thass aw righ'!
I know when I'm hot 'n when I ain't in this game!
Two bits, I shoot! Two bits! I'm comin' out!
HAH!
'Lev'! Oh, you natch!
I shoot four bits!
HAH!
Sev'! Oh, you sweet lil' sev'!
I'm gittin' hot, boys; I'm gittin' hot!
I shoot the buck; one man I shoot!
HAH!
Five, hey? Git yer foot away there!
Five—we kin do it!
Feevy, dice! Oh, feeve! Fever in the south!
HAH!
Pair o' mules!
HAH!

Eight—eight the fav'rit!

Haffah buck I five or nine—hello, feeve! Feeveedy-
feeve!

HAH!

Whuddid I tell you? I shoot the two! Who fades me?

HAH!

Cocked-dice! Yes, it is! Lookit!

HAH!

Read 'em to me! I can't see good!

Ten! Oh, you Dick!

Oh, you big fellow! Come on, Dick!

Oh, Dick! Where are you, Dick?

Six 'n four, or five 'n five!

HAH!

Twelve in the high field! We're gittin' close!

Where's Dick? Hey, Dick! Oh, Dick! Say, Dick!

HAH!

There he is! There's Dick! I shoot four bucks!

Come on, boys; I'm comin' out! I'm comin' out!

Rattle 'n' roll, I'm comin' out!

Four I shoot! How much am I in 'at bill?

Wait'll I breathe on 'em! Wait!

Aw righ'! They're warm! Here we go!

HAH!

What is it? I can't bear to look!

'Lev'! Whoa! Whoa!

Let 'er ride! I shoot the chunk; I shoot 'er all!

Come on, boys, sixteen seeds I shoot!

Oh, I bin waitin' for this day!

Are you all down?

Gimme room! Gimme a lottah room!

Man, oh, man! Sixteen bucks! Look out! Look out!

HAH!

Sixteen buckos—whoa-up! Six!

Nev' missed it in my life!

Wait, now, wait!

Wait'll I whisper to 'em!

Don't touch 'at dough! Let 'er lay!

Don't gather it together! Don't touch it!

Dice! Listen, dice!
I've always bin yer frien'!
Gimme a six, lil' dice! Pretty lil' dice!
Thutty-two bucks there, dice, for you 'n me!
Please, dice!
You know, dice—four 'n two!
Three 'n three, dice!
Six, dice! Just a six!
Only six!
Thass all! Just six!
Sixty days!
Thutty-two bucks! You hear me, dice!
One roll for thutty-two! I'm a bum or a millionaire,
    dice!
Oh, six! Nice six! Sweet six!
Just this one time, dice!
Won't ask you no more!
I'll go righ' home, dice!
Gimme room, boys! Don't get excited!
Thutty-two bucks!
Thutty-two bucks for a six!
I bin waitin' for this! I just bin waitin'!
Here we go. Remember, dice! Remember!
HAH!
What?
Sev'?
'At rotten sev'!
Well, I nev' did have no luck in my whole life!
I fade two bits o' 'at piece!

Them Dice'll Make You Talk

Yes, sir!
One o' the high shots, mister, a cold, cold clammy guy,

He'd roll those bones to a blister with never a word or
   sigh.
Never a word he'd utter, if the luck was good or bad,
Never a cuss he'd mutter, or a sign that he was glad.
And far and near, for many a year, a brother-in-law to
   the clam,
He was the quietest man you'd hope to see, and we
   called him Silent Sam.
Yes, sir!
Silent Sam was his handle, a wonder at keeping still,
And never a breath of scandal touched his amazing skill.
You could talk to him by the hour, and he'd only wag-
   gle his head,
And some of us thought he was sour, while others
   thought he was dead—
But he'd bet 'em long, either right or wrong, and never a
   single jam,
The quietest man in seventeen states, and we called him
   Silent Sam.
Yes, sir!
A dummy has plenty of prattle, the Sphinx is a noisy
   slob,
Compared to Sam as he'd rattle, them dice and bet you
   a gob.
One of the highest players, he often hooked with The
   Greek,
And one of the longest stayers, but gosh how you'd wish
   he'd speak!
But never a squawk, or any talk, as he'd send it in, ker-
   zam!
The quietest man you ever saw, and we called him
   Silent Sam.

Yes, sir!
Finally his luck deserted, his Fortune went on the lam—
'Twas Tuesday I hear he blurted a word that sounded
   like "Damn!"
And then from his lips in a torrent, as water might gush
   from a rock,

Came language, the like, I warrant, would give you a
    terrible shock.
And for years and years into any ears his conversation
    he'd cram—
This fellow who was once so quiet that we called him
    Silent Sam.

Yes, sir!
Since then he buzzes and gabbles, since then he chatters
    and drones;
In every subject he dabbles, the weather, as well as the
    bones.
He can't make six with a pencil, but he can talk 'til the
    cows come home;
He can't make a point with a stencil, but he can churn
    the air to a foam—
With boast and brag he can chew the rag, and his tongue
    goes biffity-bam,
This beezark who was once so quiet that we called him
    Silent Sam.

Yes, sir!
I have a moral, for what would a story be if it didn't
    have a moral
As a warning to you and me?
And this is the moral I'm pointing; you can write it in
    ink or chalk—
You can be born dumb, you can be born numb—
Them Dice'll Make You Talk!

Blonde Mink

Now of course there are many different ways of cooking
tripe but personally I prefer it stewed with tomatoes

and mushrooms and a bit of garlic and in fact I am partaking of a portion in this form in Mindy's restaurant on
Broadway one evening in January when a personality
by the name of Julie the Starker sits down at my table
and leans over and sniffs my dish and says to me like
this:

"Tripe," he says. "With garlic," he says. "Why, this
is according to the recipe of the late Slats Slavin, who
obtains it from his old Aunt Margaret in Troy. Waiter,"
he says, "bring me an order of this delicious concoction
only with more garlic. It is getting colder outside and a
guy needs garlic in his system to thicken his blood.
Well," he says, "this is indeed a coincidence because I
just come from visiting the late Slats and having a small
chat with him."

Naturally I am somewhat surprised by this statement,
as I know the late Slats is resting in Woodlawn Cemetery
and to tell the truth I remember I am present as a pall-
bearer when he is placed there to rest, but I am also
pleased to hear these tidings as Slats is always a good
friend of mine and no nicer guy ever steps in shoe
leather.

"Well," I say to Julie, "and how is Slats these days?"

"He is cold," Julie says. "He states that it is very
crimpy around the edges up there in Woodlawn especially at night. You know the late Slats always hates cold
weather. He is usually in Florida by this time of year to
duck the chill.

"Furthermore," Julie says, "he is greatly embarrassed
up there without a stone over him such as Beatrice promises to get him. He says it makes him feel like a bum
with nothing to show who he is when all around him
are many fine markers including one of black marble
to the memory of the late Cockeyed Corrigan who as
you know is of no consequence compared to the late
Slats who is really somebody."

Well, of course this is very true because the late Slats
is formerly known and esteemed by one and all on

Broadway as one of the smartest operators in horse-racing that ever draws breath. He is a handicapper by trade and his figures on the horses that are apt to win are so highly prized that one night he is stuck up by a couple of guys when he has six thou in cash money on him, but all they want is his figures on the next day's races.

He is a player and a layer. He will bet on the horses himself when he sees spots he fancies or he will let you bet him on them, and he has clients all over the United States who call him up at his office on Broadway and transact business with him one way or the other. He is a tall guy in his late forties who is not much thicker than a lath, which is why he is called Slats though his first name is really Terence.

He is by no means Mr. America for looks but he dresses well and he is very rapid with a dollar. He is the softest touch in town for busted guys and he will get up in the middle of the night to do somebody a favor, consequently no one gets more or larger hellos along the main drag than the late Slats.

He comes from a little burg upstate by the name of Cohoes and I hear that he and Julie the Starker are friends from their short-pants days there, although Julie is about the last one in the world you will expect to see a guy of class like Slats associating with, as Julie is strictly in the muggola department.

He is about Slats' age and is short and thick and has a kisser that is surely a pain to even his own mamma. He is called Julie the Starker because starker means a strong rough guy and there is no doubt that Julie answers this description in every manner, shape and form.

He is at one time in his life a prize fighter but strictly a catcher, which is a way of saying he catches everything the other guy throws at him and at other times he is a bouncer; I do not know what all else except that he has some Sing Sing background.

At all times he is a most undesirable personality but

he is very fond of the late Slats Slavin and vice versa, and they get along together in a way that is most astonishing to behold.

He is not only a handy guy for Slats but he is also a social companion, and for some years wherever you see Slats you are apt to see Julie the Starker except when Slats is with his fiancée, Miss Beatrice Gee, and even then you may see Julie though as a rule Miss Beatrice Gee does not approve of him any more than she does of leprosy. In fact, she makes no bones about considering the very sight of Julie revolting to her.

In addition to being the late Slats' fiancée, Miss Beatrice Gee is at this time a prominent show girl in one of Mike Todd's musical shows and she is conceded by one and all to be the most beautiful object on Manhattan Island or anyway no worse than a photo finish for the most beautiful.

She is an original brunette and is quite tall and carries herself in a way that the late Slats says is dignity, though it really comes of Mike Todd's director putting a big copy of the Bible on her head and saying she will either learn to walk balancing it or else, though he never does tell her or else what.

Other dolls call Miss Beatrice Gee a clothes horse because it seems she wears clothes with great skill, and furthermore she is crazy about them although her best hold is not wearing them, which she also does with great skill but of course only on the stage. When she is not on the stage she is always groomed like a stake horse going to the post for a big race, and no one takes greater pride in her appearance than the late Slats Slavin, except Miss Beatrice Gee herself.

While I do not believe the story that once when she has a headache and Doc Kelton puts his thermometer in her mouth, to see if she is running a temperature, the mercury freezes tight, there is no doubt that Beatrice is not the emotional type, and to be very frank about the matter many think she is downright frosty. But of course no one ever mentions this to the late Slats because he is greatly in love and the chances are he maybe thinks Beatrice is hotter than a stove and personally I am in no position to deny it.

Well, in much less time than it takes me to tell you all this, Julie the Starker has his tripe and is eating it with more sound than is altogether necessary for tripe no matter how it is cooked, and to tell the truth I have to wait until he pauses before I can make him hear my voice above his eating. Then I say to him like this:

"Why, Julie," I say, "I cannot understand why Slats is in the plight you describe with reference to the stone. I am under the impression that he leaves Beatrice well loaded as far as the do-re-mi is concerned and I take it for granted that she handles the stone situation. By the way, Julie," I say, "does Slats say anything to you about any horses anywhere for tomorrow?"

"No," Julie says. "But if you have a minute to spare I will tell you the story of Beatrice and her failure to take care of the matter of the stone for the late Slats. It is really a great scandal."

Then without waiting to hear if I have a minute to spare or not, he starts telling me, and it seems it all goes back to a night in late September when Beatrice informs Slats that she just comes upon a great bargain in a blonde mink coat for twenty-three thousand dollars and that she desires same at once to keep herself warm during the impending winter although she already had enough fur coats in her closet to keep not only herself warm but half of Syracuse, too.

"Pardon me, Julie," I say at this point, "but what is a blonde mink?"

"Why," Julie says, "that is the very question Slats asks and he learns from Beatrice that it is a new light-colored mink fur that is sometimes called blue mink and sometimes platinum mink and sometimes blonde mink and he also learns that no matter what it is called, it is very, very expensive, and after Slats gets all this info he speaks to Beatrice as follows:

" 'Baby,' he says, 'you cut right to the crimp when you

mention twenty-three thou because that is exactly the size of the bank roll at the moment. But I just come off a tough season and I will need all my ready for navigating purposes the next few months and besides it looks like a mild winter and you can wear your old last season's leopard or caracul or ermine or Persian lamb or beaver until I get going again.' "

Now at this (Julie the Starker says) Beatrice flies into a terrible rage and tells Slats that he is a tightwad and a skinflint and a miser, and that he has no heart and no pride or he will not suggest that she go around in such shabby old floogers and that she will never humiliate herself in this manner. She says if she waits even a few minutes, someone else is sure to snap up the blonde mink and that she may never again meet with a similar opportunity.

"Well, they have a large quarrel," Julie says, "and when Slats and I get back to his hotel apartment that night he complains of not feeling any too well and in fact he finally keels over on the bed with his tongue hanging out and I send for Doc Kelton, who says it is a heart attack and very bad.

"He says to tell the truth it is a hundred to one Slats will not beat it, and then Doc takes his departure stating that he has so many shorter-priced patients he cannot afford to waste time on long shots and he leaves it to me to notify Slats that his number is up.

"On receiving this information, Slats requests me to find Miss Beatrice Gee and bring her to his bedside, which I do, although at first she is much opposed to leaving her table in the Stork Club where she is the center of a gay throng, until I whisper to her that I will be compelled to flatten her and carry her unless she does.

"But on arriving at Slats' apartment and realizing that he is indeed an invalid, Beatrice seems to be quite downcast and starts to shed tears all over the joint, and I have no doubt that some of them are on the level because surely she must remember how kind Slats is to her.

"Then Slats say he wishes to talk to Beatrice alone and requests me to go into the next room, but of course I have a crack in the door so I can hear what goes on between them, and what I hear is Slats saying to Beatrice like this:

" 'Baby,' he says, 'reach in under my pillow and get the package of currency there. It is the twenty-three I tell you about and it is all the dough I have in the world. It is all yours except twenty-six hundred which you are to pay Clancy Brothers the tombstone makers in Yonkers for a stone I pick out for myself some time ago and forget to pay for although my plot in Woodlawn is free and clear.

" 'It is a long stone of white Carrara marble in excellent taste,' Slats says. 'It is to lie flat over my last resting place, not to stand upright, and it is cut to exactly cover same from end to end and side to side. I order it in this form,' Slats says, 'because I am always a restless soul and long have a fear I may not lie quietly in my last resting place but may wish to roam around unless there is a sort of lid over me such as this stone. And besides,' he says, 'it will keep the snow off me. I loathe and despise the snow. I will leave the engraving to you, Baby, but promise you will take care of the stone at once.'

"Well, I hear Beatrice promise between sobs, and also no doubt as she is reaching under the pillow for Slats' plant, and when I step back into the room a little later, Slats is a goner and Beatrice is now really letting the salt water flow freely, although her best effort is in Woodlawn two days later when it looks as if we will have to send for a siphon to unflood the premises.

"But to show you what a smart strudel Beatrice is, she is around the day after we place the late Slats to rest, saying that he does not leave her a thin dime. You see, she is figuring against the chance that relatives of Slats may show up and claim his estate and she even lets Slats' lodge pay the funeral expenses although of course this is no more than is coming to any departed brother.

"I do not dispute her statement because I think she is entitled to the dough as long as Slats gives it to her, and of course I take it for granted that she will split herself out from enough of the swag to buy the stone according to her promise, and in fact I am so sure of this that one afternoon last week I go out to Woodlawn not only to pay my respects to the memory of the late Slats but to see how his last resting place looks with the stone over it.

"Well, what do I see but Slats himself walking around and around a mound of dried earth with some withered flowers scattered over it and among these flowers I recognize my own wreath which says 'So long, pal' on it and which costs me a double-saw, but there is no stone whatsoever over the mound, not even as much as a weentsy little pebble."

"Just a minute, Julie," I say. "You state that you see the late Slats walking around and about. Do you see him all pale and vapory?"

"Well," Julie says, "now you mention it, I do seem to recall that Slats is a little on the pale side of what he used to be. But he is otherwise unchanged except that he is not wearing his derby hat as usual. We do not give him his derby hat when we place him to rest, as the undertaker guy says it is not necessary. Anyway, when he spies me, Slats stops walking and sits down on the edge of the late Cockeyed Corrigan's black marble marker, which is practically next door to him and says to me like this:

" 'Hello, Julie,' he says. 'I am commencing to wonder what becomes of you. I am walking around here for weeks trying to keep warm and I am all tuckered out. What do you suppose is the idea of not providing people with overcoats when they are placed to rest? Only I do not rest, Julie. Do you see Beatrice lately and what does she say about my stone?'

" 'Slats,' I say, 'I must confess I do not see Beatrice lately, but I never dream she does not provide the stone long before this as per her promise which I can tell you

now I overhear her make to you. A solemn deathbed
promise.'

" 'Never mind what kind of bed it is,' Slats says. 'It is
a morbid topic. And I think you have plenty of gall to
be on the Erie when I am saying my last good-by to
my baby. You owe us both an apology. Look her up
right away and give her a good one and ask her what
about my stone. The chances are there is a hitch somewhere. Maybe the engraving is causing the delay. I am
sure Beatrice will wish something sentimental on it like
"Sleep well, my beloved," and engraving takes time.'

"Well, I am about to mention that she already takes
time enough to have George Washington's farewell address engraved on it, but all of a sudden the late Slats
disappears from sight and I take this as a hint for me to
blow, too, and that very night I hunt up Beatrice to
give her Slats' message.

"I find her standing at the bar of a gaff called the
Palmetto with a couple of guys and I notice she is wearing a fur coat the color of mist that I do not remember
ever seeing on her before and I turn to a dame who is
sitting at a table and say to her like this:

" 'Pardon me, little miss,' I say, 'but just to satisfy my
curiosity, can you tell me the name of the fur that party
over yonder is wearing?'

" 'Blonde mink,' she says. 'It is perfectly beautiful too.'

" 'And what does such a garment cost?' I ask.

" 'Why,' she says, 'that one seems to be first-class
merchandise. It costs twenty-five thousand dollars.
Maybe more, but not much less. It is the very newest
fur out!'

"Then I walk over to Beatrice and tap her on the
shoulder, and when she turns I motion her out of hearing distance of the guys she is with and speak to her as
follows:

" 'Well, Bea,' I say, 'your new coat must hang a little
heavy on you considering that it represents the weight
of a nice tombstone. I never mention it to you before

but I hear your last chat with the late Slats Slavin including your promise but until I find you in this lovely benny no one will ever make me believe you mean to welsh on your word.'

" 'All right, all right,' she says. 'So I do not buy the stone. But it costs twenty-six hundred and all I have is twenty-three thousand and an odd tenner and this coat is a steal at twenty-three. If I wait another minute longer someone else is sure to snap it up and the dealer wants his all cash. Besides, Slats will never know he does not get the stone.'

" 'Bea,' I say, 'I have a talk with Slats today at Woodlawn. He knows he has no stone and he is upset about it. But he is making excuses for you, Bea. He figures you are unexpectedly delayed a bit in getting it there. You have the guy fooled even yet.'

"At this Beatrice gazes at me for some time without saying a word and I notice that looking into her eyes is just the same as looking into a couple of ice cubes. Then she gives her coat a hitch and brings it closer around her and finally she says:

" 'Julie,' she says, 'I want to tell you something. If ever again you speak to me or about me I will start remembering out loud that Slats has a large bundle of cash on him that last night and I will also start wondering out loud what becomes of it, and a guy with your biography cannot stand much wonderment such as that. And if you see Slats again tell him how I look in my new coat.'

" 'Bea,' I say, 'you will never have any luck with your new coat because it means leaving poor Slats up there in Woodlawn restless and cold.'

" 'No luck?' she says. 'Listen,' she says, 'do you see the dopey-looking little punk in the uniform leaning against the bar? His name is Freddy Voogan and his papa is a squillionaire out in Denver and I am going to marry the kid any minute, and what do you think gets him for me? My blonde mink. He notices how nice I look in it and insists on meeting me. No luck?' Beatrice says. 'Is kicking up a gold mine no luck?'

" 'Bea,' I say, 'it is bad enough to rob the grave as you already do but it is even worse to rob the cradle.'

" 'Good-by, Julie,' Bea says. 'Do not forget to tell Slats how I looked in my new coat.'

"Well, I will say she looks wonderful in it even though I am greatly disappointed in her because it is plain to be seen that Beatrice has no sentiment about the past. So now I am compelled to report back to the late Slats Slavin that he is on a bust as far as the stone is concerned and I hope and trust that my revelation will not cause him too much anguish."

And with this, Julie the Starker dunks up the last of the tripe gravy on his plate with a piece of rye bread and gets up to take his departure and I say to him like this:

"Julie," I say, "if you happen to think of it, kindly ask the late Slats to look over the entries at Hialeah for the next few days and if he can send me a winner now and then I can get parties to bet a little for me."

"Well," Julie says, "Slats has other things on his mind besides horses right now, but," he says, "I will try to remember your request although of course you will carry me for a small piece of your end."

Then he leaves me and I am still sitting there when a plain-clothes copper by the name of Johnny Brannigan comes in and sits down in the chair Julie just vacates and orders some Danish pastry and a cup of Java, and then almost as if he hears the conversation between Julie and me he says:

"Oh, hello," he says. "How well do you know Miss Beatrice Gee who is formerly the fiancée of the late Slats Slavin? I mean how well do you know her history and most especially do you know any knocks against her?"

"Why?" I say.

"Well," Johnny says, "it is strictly an unofficial question. There is hell up Ninth Street over her. A family out in Denver that must have more weight than Pike's Peak gets the Denver police department to ask our department very quietly about her, and our department requests me to make a few inquiries. Of course it is not an official police matter. It is an exchange of courtesies. It seems," Johnny says, "that Miss Beatrice Gee is going to marry a member of this family who is under twenty-one years of age and his papa and mamma are doing handstands about it, though personally," Johnny says, "I believe in letting love take its course. But," he says, "my theory has nothing to do with the fact that I promise to make a return of some kind on this blintz."

"Well, Johnny," I say, "I do not know anything whatever about her but you just miss a guy who can probably give you a complete run-down on her. You just miss Julie the Starker. However," I say, "I am pretty sure to run into him tomorrow and will tell him to contact you."

But I do not see Julie the next day or for several days after that and I am greatly disappointed as I not only wish to tell him to get in touch with Johnny but I am anxious to learn if Slats sends me any info on the horses. For that matter I do not see Johnny Brannigan either until late one afternoon I run into him on Broadway and he says to me like this:

"Say," he says, "you are just the guy I am looking for. Do you see the late editions of the blats?"

"No," I say, "why?"

"Well," Johnny says, "they are carrying big stories about the finding of Miss Beatrice Gee in her apartment in East Fifty-seventh Street as dead as a doornail. It looks as if the young guy from Denver she is going to marry bounces a big bronze lamp off her coco, in what the scribes will undoubtedly call a fit of jealous rage, because he has a big row with her early in the evening in the Canary Club when he finds a Marine captain from the Pacific teaching her how the island natives in those parts rub noses when they greet each other, although the young guy claims he walks away from her then and does not see her again because he is too busy loading himself up with champagne.

"But," Johnny says, "he is found unconscious from

the champagne in his hotel room today and admits he does not remember when or where or what or why. My goodness," Johnny says, "the champagne they sell nowadays is worse than an anesthetic."

Naturally this news about Miss Beatrice Gee is quite distressing to me if only because of her former association with the late Slats Slavin and I am sorry to hear of the young guy's plight, too, even though I do not know him. I am always sorry to hear of young guys in trouble and especially rich young guys but of course if they wish to mix bronze lamps with champagne they must take the consequences and I so state to Johnny Brannigan.

"Well," Johnny says, "he does not seem to be the bronze-lamp type, and yet who else has a motive to commit this deed? You must always consider the question of motive in crimes of this nature."

"What about robbery?" I say.

"No," Johnny says. "All her jewelry and other belongings are found in the apartment. The only thing missing as far as her maid and acquaintances can tell seems to be a new fur coat which she probably leaves some place in her wanderings during the evening. But now I remember why I am looking for you. I am still collecting data on Miss Beatrice Gee's background though this time officially and I recall you tell me that maybe Julie the Starker can give me some information and I wish to know where I am apt to find Julie."

"A new fur coat, Johnny?" I say. "Well," I say, "as a rule I am not in favor of aiding and abetting coppers but this matter seems different and if you will take a ride with me I think I may be able to lead you to Julie."

So I call a taxicab, and as we get in I tell the jockey to drive us to Woodlawn Cemetery, and if Johnny Brannigan is surprised by our destination he does not crack but whiles away the time on the journey by relating many of his experiences as a copper, some of which are very interesting.

It is coming on dusk when we reach Woodlawn and while I have an idea of the general direction of the late

Slats Slavin's last resting place, I have to keep the taxi
guy driving around inside the gates for some time before
I spot the exact location through recognizing the late
Cockeyed Corrigan's black marble marker.

It is a short distance off the auto roadway so I have
the hackie stop and Johnny Brannigan and I get out of
the cab to walk a few yards to the mound and as we approach same who steps out from the shadow of the late
Cockeyed Corrigan's marker but Julie the Starker, who
speaks to me as follows:

"Hello, hello," he says. "I am glad to see you and I
know you will be pleased to learn that the late Slats
gives me a tip for you on a horse that goes at Hialeah
tomorrow but the name escapes me at the moment. He
says his figures make it an absolute kick in the pants.
Well," Julie says, "stick around a while and maybe I will
remember it."

Then he seems to notice the presence of Johnny Brannigan for the first time and to recognize him, too, because all of a sudden he outs with Captain Barker and
says:

"Oh, a copper, eh?" he says. "Well, copper, here is a
little kiss for you."

And with this he lets go a slug that misses Johnny
Brannigan and knocks an arm off a pink stone cherub in
the background and he is about to encore when Johnny
blasts ahead of him, and Julie the Starker drops his
pizzolover and his legs begin bending under him like
Leon Errol's when Leon is playing a drunk.

He finally staggers up to the last resting place of the
late Slats Slavin and falls there with the blood bumping
from the hole that Johnny Brannigan drills in his chest
and as I notice his lips moving I hasten to his side figuring that he may be about to utter the name of the horse
Slats gives him for me.

Then I observe that there is something soft and fuzzy
spread out on the mound under him that Julie the
Starker pats weakly with one hand as he whispers to me
like this:

"Well," he says, "the late Slats is not only resting in peace now with the same as his stone over him but he is as warm as toast and in fact warmer."

"The horse, Julie," I say. "What is the name of the horse?"

But Julie only closes his eyes and as it is plain to be seen that he now joins out permanently with the population of Woodlawn. Johnny Brannigan steps forward and rolls him off the mound with his foot and picks up the object that is under Julie and examines it in the dim light.

"I always think Julie is a little stir-crazy," Johnny says, "but I wonder why he takes a pop at me when all I want of him is to ask him some questions and I wonder, too, where this nice red fox fur coat comes from?"

Well, of course I know that Johnny will soon realize that Julie probably thinks Johnny wishes to chat with him about the job he does on Miss Beatrice Gee, but at the moment I am too provoked about Julie holding out the tip the late Slats Slavin gives him for me to discuss the matter or even to explain that the red is only Julie's blood and that the coat is really blonde mink.

Lillian

What I always say is that Wilbur Willard is nothing but a very lucky guy, because what is it but luck that has him teetering along Forty-ninth Street one cold snowy morning when Lillian is mer-owing around the sidewalk looking for her mamma?

And what is it but luck that has Wilbur Willard all mulled up to a million, what with him having been sitting out a few seidels of Scotch with a friend by the name of Haggerty in an apartment over in Fifty-ninth

Street? Because if Wilbur Willard is not mulled up he
will see Lillian as nothing but a little black cat, and give
her plenty of room, for everybody knows that black cats
are terribly bad luck, even when they are only kittens.

But being mulled up like I tell you, things look very
different to Wilbur Willard, and he does not see Lillian
as a little black kitten scrabbling around in the snow.
He sees a beautiful leopard, because a copper by the
name of O'Hara, who is walking past about then, and
who knows Wilbur Willard, hears him say: "Oh, you
beautiful leopard!"

The copper takes a quick peek himself, because he
does not wish any leopards running around his beat, it
being against the law, but all he sees, as he tells me afterwards, is this rumpot ham, Wilbur Willard, picking up
a scrawny little black kitten and shoving it in his overcoat pocket, and he also hears Wilbur say: "Your name
is Lillian."

Then Wilbur teeters on up to his room on the top
floor of an old fleabag in Eighth Avenue that is called
the Hotel de Brussels, where he lives quite a while, be
cause the management does not mind actors, the man
agement of the Hotel de Brussels being very broad
minded, indeed.

There is some complaint this same morning from one
of Wilbur's neighbors, an old burlesque doll by the name
of Minnie Madigan, who is not working since Abraham
Lincoln is assassinated, because she hears Wilbur going
on in his room about a beautiful leopard, and calls up
the clerk to say that a hotel which allows wild animals
is not respectable. But the clerk looks in on Wilbur and
finds him playing with nothing but a harmless-looking
little black kitten, and nothing comes of the old doll's
beef, especially as nobody ever claims the Hotel de
Brussels is respectable anyway, or at least not much.

Of course when Wilbur comes out from under the
ether next afternoon he can see Lillian is not a leopard,
and in fact Wilbur is quite astonished to find himself in
bed with a little black kitten, because it seems Lillian is

sleeping on Wilbur's chest to keep warm. At first Wilbur does not believe what he sees, and puts it down to Haggerty's Scotch, but finally he is convinced, and so he puts Lillian in his pocket, and takes her over to the Hot Box night club and gives her some milk, of which it seems Lillian is very fond.

Now where Lillian comes from in the first place of course nobody knows. The chances are somebody chucks her out of a window into the snow, because people are always chucking kittens, and one thing and another, out of windows in New York. In fact, if there is one thing this town has plenty of, it is kittens, which finally grow up to be cats, and go snooping around ash cans, and merowing on roofs, and keeping people from sleeping good.

Personally, I have no use for cats, including kittens, because I never see one that has any too much sense, although I know a guy by the name of Pussy McGuire who makes a first-rate living doing nothing but stealing cats, and sometimes dogs, and selling them to old dolls who like such things for company. But Pussy only steals Persian and Angora cats, which are very fine cats, and of course Lillian is no such cat as this. Lillian is nothing but a black cat, and nobody will give you a dime a dozen for black cats in this town, as they are generally regarded as very bad jinxes.

Furthermore, it comes out in a few weeks that Wilbur Willard can just as well name her Herman, or Sidney, as not, but Wilbur sticks to Lillian, because this is the name of his partner when he is in vaudeville years ago. He often tells me about Lillian Withington when he is mulled up, which is more often than somewhat, for Wilbur is a great hand for drinking Scotch, or rye, or bourbon, or gin, or whatever else there is around for drinking, except water. In fact, Wilbur Willard is a high-class drinking man, and it does no good to tell him it is against the law to drink in this country, because it only makes him mad, and he says to the dickens with the law, only Wilbur Willard uses a much rougher word than dickens.

"She is like a beautiful leopard," Wilbur says to me

about Lillian Withington. "Black-haired, and black-eyed, and all ripply, like a leopard I see in an animal act on the same bill at the Palace with us once. We are headliners then," he says, "Willard and Withington, the best singing and dancing act in the country.

"I pick her up in San Antonio, which is a spot in Texas," Wilbur says. "She is not long out of a convent, and I just lose my old partner, Mary McGee, who ups and dies on me of pneumonia down there. Lillian wishes to go on the stage, and joins out with me. A natural-born actress with a great voice. But like a leopard," Wilbur says. "Like a leopard. There is cat in her, no doubt of this, and cats and women are both ungrateful. I love Lillian Withington. I wish to marry her. But she is cold to me. She says she is not going to follow the stage all her life. She says she wishes money, and luxury, and a fine home, and of course a guy like me cannot give a doll such things.

"I wait on her hand and foot," Wilbur says. "I am her slave. There is nothing I will not do for her. Then one day she walks in on me in Boston very cool and says she is quitting me. She says she is marrying a rich guy there. Well, naturally it busts up the act and I never have the heart to look for another partner, and then I get to belting that old black bottle around, and now what am I but a cabaret performer?"

Then sometimes he will bust out crying, and sometimes I will cry with him, although the way I look at it, Wilbur gets a pretty fair break, at that, in getting rid of a doll who wishes things he cannot give her. Many a guy in this town is tangled up with a doll who wishes things he cannot give her, but who keeps him tangled up just the same and busting himself trying to keep her quiet.

Wilbur makes pretty fair money as an entertainer in the Hot Box, though he spends most of it for Scotch, and he is not a bad entertainer, either. I often go to the Hot Box when I am feeling blue to hear him sing "Melancholy Baby," and "Moonshine Valley," and other sad songs which break my heart. Personally, I do not see

why any doll cannot love Wilbur, especially if they listen to him sing such songs as "Melancholy Baby" when
he is mulled up good, because he is a tall, nice-looking
guy, with long eyelashes and sleepy brown eyes, and his
voice has a low moaning sound that usually goes very
big with the dolls. In fact, many a doll does do some
pitching to Wilbur when he is singing in the Hot Box,
but somehow Wilbur never gives them a tumble, which
I suppose is because he is thinking only of Lillian Withington.

Well, after he gets Lillian, the black kitten, Wilbur
seems to find a new interest in life, and Lillian turns out
to be right cute, and not bad-looking after Wilbur gets
her fed up good. She is blacker than a yard up a chimney,
with not a white spot on her, and she grows so fast that
by and by Wilbur cannot carry her in his pocket any
more, so he puts a collar on her and leads her around.
So Lillian becomes very well known on Broadway, what
with Wilbur taking her many places, and finally she does
not even have to be led around by Willard, but follows
him like a pooch. And in all the Roaring Forties there
is no pooch that cares to have any truck with Lillian, for
she will leap aboard them quicker than you can say scat,
and scratch and bite them until they are very glad indeed
to get away from her.

But of course the pooches in the Forties are mainly
nothing but Chows, and Pekes, and Poms, or little woolly
white poodles, which are led around by blond dolls, and
are not fit to take their own part against a smart cat. In
fact, Wilbur Willard is finally not on speaking terms with
any doll that owns a pooch between Times Square and
Columbus Circle, and they are all hoping that both
Wilbur and Lillian will go lay down and die somewhere.
Furthermore, Wilbur has a couple of battles with guys
who also belong to the dolls, but Wilbur is no sucker in a
battle if he is not mulled up too much and leg-weary.

After he is through entertaining people in the Hot
Box, Wilbur generally goes around to any speakeasies
which may still be open, and does a little offhand drink-

ing on top of what he already drinks down in the Hot Box, which is plenty, and although it is considered very risky in this town to mix Hot Box liquor with any other, it never seems to bother Wilbur. Along toward daylight he takes a couple of bottles of Scotch over to his room in the Hotel de Brussels and uses them for a nightcap, so by the time Wilbur Willard is ready to slide off to sleep he has plenty of liquor of one kind and another inside him, and he sleeps pretty good.

Of course nobody on Broadway blames Wilbur so very much for being such a rumpot, because they know about him loving Lillian Withington, and losing her, and it is considered a reasonable excuse in this town for a guy to do some drinking when he loses a doll, which is why there is so much drinking here, but it is a mystery to one and all how Wilbur stands off all this liquor without croaking. The cemeteries are full of guys who do a lot less drinking than Wilbur, but he never even seems to feel extra tough, or if he does he keeps it to himself and does not go around saying it is the kind of liquor you get nowadays.

He costs some of the boys around Mindy's plenty of dough one winter, because he starts in doing most of his drinking after hours in Good Time Charley's speakeasy, and the boys lay a price of four to one against him lasting until spring, never figuring a guy can drink very much of Good Time Charley's liquor and keep on living. But Wilbur Willard does it just the same, so everybody says the guy is just naturally superhuman, and lets it go a that.

Sometimes Wilbur drops into Mindy's with Lillian following him on the lookout for pooches, or riding on his shoulder if the weather is bad, and the two of them will sit with us for hours chewing the rag about one thing and another. At such times Wilbur generally has a bottle on his hip and takes a shot now and then, but of course this does not come under the head of serious drinking with him. When Lillian is with Wilbur she always lays as close

to him as she can get and anybody can see that she seems
to be very fond of Wilbur, and that he is very fond of
her, although he sometimes forgets himself and speaks
of her as a beautiful leopard. But of course this is only a
slip of the tongue, and anyway if Wilbur gets any pleasure
out of thinking Lillian is a leopard, it is nobody's business but his own.

"I suppose she will run away from me some day,"
Wilbur says, running his hand over Lillian's back until
her fur crackles. "Yes, although I give her plenty of
liver and catnip, and one thing and another, and all my
affection, she will probably give me the shake. Cats are
like women, and women are like cats. They are both very
ungrateful."

"They are both generally bad luck," Big Nig, the crap
shooter, says. "Especially cats, and most especially black
cats."

Many other guys tell Wilbur about black cats being
bad luck, and advise him to slip Lillian into the North
River some night with a sinker on her, but Wilbur claims
he already has all the bad luck in the world when he
loses Lillian Withington, and that Lillian, the cat, cannot
make it any worse, so he goes on taking extra good care
of her, and Lillian goes on getting bigger and bigger until
I commence thinking maybe there is some St. Bernard
in her.

Finally I commence to notice something funny about
Lillian. Sometimes she will be acting very loving toward
Wilbur, and then again she will be very unfriendly to
him, and will spit at him, and snatch at him with her
claws, very hostile. It seems to me that she is all right
when Willard is mulled up, but is as sad and fretful as
he is himself when he is only a little bit mulled. And
when Lillian is sad and fretful she makes it very tough
indeed on the pooches in the neighborhood of the Brussels.

In fact, Lillian takes to pooch-hunting, sneaking off
when Wilbur is getting his rest, and running pooches

bowlegged, especially when she finds one that is not on a leash. A loose pooch is just naturally cherry pie for Lillian.

Well, of course this causes great indignation among the dolls who own the pooches, particularly when Lillian comes home one day carrying a Peke as big as she is herself by the scruff of the neck, and with a very excited blond doll following her and yelling bloody murder outside Wilbur Willard's door when Lillian pops into Wilbur's room through a hole he cuts in the door for her, still lugging the Peke. But it seems that instead of being mad at Lillian and giving her a pasting for such goings-on, Wilbur is somewhat pleased, because he happens to be still in a fog when Lillian arrives with the Peke, and is thinking of Lillian as a beautiful leopard.

"Why," Wilbur says, "this is devotion, indeed. My beautiful leopard goes off into the jungle and fetches me an antelope for dinner."

Now of course there is no sense whatever to this, because a Peke is certainly not anything like an antelope, but the blond doll outside Wilbur's door hears Wilbur mumble, and gets the idea that he is going to eat her Peke for dinner and the squawk she puts up is very terrible. There is plenty of trouble around the Brussels in chilling the blond doll's beef over Lillian snagging her Peke, and what is more the blond doll's ever-loving guy, who turns out to be a tough Ginney bootlegger by the name of Gregorio, shows up at the Hot Box the next night and wishes to put the slug on Wilbur Willard.

But Wilbur rounds him up with a few drinks and by singing "Melancholy Baby" to him, and before he leaves, the Ginney gets very sentimental toward Wilbur, and Lillian, too, and wishes to give Wilbur five bucks to let Lillian grab the Peke again, if Lillian will promise not to bring it back. It seems Gregorio does not really care for the Peke, and is only acting quarrelsome to please the blond doll and make her think he loves her dearly.

But I can see Lillian is having different moods, and finally I ask Wilbur if he notices it.

"Yes," he says, very sad, "I do not seem to be holding her love. She is getting very fickle. A guy moves onto my floor at the Brussels the other day with a little boy, and Lillian becomes very fond of this kid at once. In fact, they are great friends. Ah, well," Wilbur says, "cats are like women. Their affection does not last."

I happen to go over to the Brussels a few days later to explain to a guy by the name of Crutchy, who lives on the same floor as Wilbur Willard, that some of our citizens do not like his face and that it may be a good idea for him to leave town, especially if he insists on bringing ale into their territory, and I see Lillian out in the hall with a youngster which I judge is the kid Wilbur is talking about. This kid is maybe three years old, and very cute, what with black hair, and black eyes, and he is wooling Lillian around the hall in a way that is most surprising, for Lillian is not such a cat as will stand for much wooling around, not even from Wilbur Willard.

I am wondering how anybody comes to take such a kid to a joint like the Brussels, but I figure it is some actor's kid, and that maybe there is no mamma for it. Later I am talking to Wilbur about this, and he says: "Well, if the kid's old man is an actor, he is not working at it. He sticks close to his room all the time, and he does not allow the kid to go anywhere but in the hall, and I feel sorry for the little guy, which is why I allow Lillian to play with him."

Now it comes on a very cold spell, and a bunch of us are sitting in Mindy's along toward five o'clock in the morning when we hear fire engines going past. By and by in comes a guy by the name of Kansas, who is named Kansas because he comes from Kansas, and who is a crap shooter by trade.

"The old Brussels is on fire," this guy Kansas says.

"She is always on fire," Big Nig says, meaning there is always plenty of hot stuff going on around the Brussels.

About this time who walks in but Wilbur Willard, and anybody can see he is just naturally floating. The chances are he comes from Good Time Charley's, and he is cer-

tainly carrying plenty of pressure. I never see Wilbur
Willard mulled up more. He does not have Lillian with
him, but then he never takes Lillian to Good Time
Charley's, because Charley hates cats.

"Hey, Wilbur," Big Nig says, "your joint, the Brussels,
is on fire."

"Well," Wilbur says, "I am a little firefly, and I need
a light. Let us go where there is fire."

The Brussels is only a few blocks from Mindy's, and
there is nothing else to do just then, so some of us walk
over to Eighth Avenue, with Wilbur teetering along
ahead of us. The old shack is certainly roaring good
when we get in sight of it, and the firemen are tossing
water into it, and the coppers have the fire lines out to
keep the crowd back, although there is not much of a
crowd at such an hour in the morning.

"Is it not beautiful?" Wilbur Willard says, looking up
at the flames. "Is it not like a fairy palace all lighted up
this way?"

You see, Wilbur does not realize the joint is on fire,
although guys and dolls are running out of it every which
way, most of them half dressed, or not dressed at all,
and the firemen are getting out the life nets in case anybody wishes to hop out of the windows.

"It is certainly beautiful," Wilbur says. "I must get
Lillian so she can see this."

And before anybody has time to think, there is Wilbur
Willard walking into the front door of the Brussels as if
nothing happens. The firemen and the coppers are so
astonished all they can do is holler at Wilbur, but he pays
no attention whatever. Well, naturally everybody figures
Wilbur is a gone gosling, but in about ten minutes he
comes walking out of this same door through the fire
and smoke as cool as you please, and he has Lillian in his
arms.

"You know," Wilbur says, coming over to where we
are standing with our eyes popping out, "I have to walk
all the way up to my floor because the elevators seem to

be out of commission. The service is getting terrible in this hotel. I will certainly make a strong beef to the management about it as soon as I pay something on my account."

Then what happens but Lillian lets out a big mer-ow, and hops out of Wilbur's arms and skips past the coppers and the firemen with her back all humped up, and the next thing anybody knows she is tearing through the front door of the old hotel and making plenty of speed.

"Well, well," Wilbur says, looking much surprised, "there goes Lillian."

And what does this daffy Wilbur Willard do but turn and go marching back into the Brussels again, and by this time the smoke is pouring out of the front doors so thick he is out of sight in a second. Naturally he takes the coppers and firemen by surprise, because they are not used to guys walking in and out of fires on them.

This time anybody standing around will lay you plenty of odds—two and a half and maybe three to one that Wilbur never shows up again, because the old Brussels is now just popping with fire and smoke from the lower windows, although there does not seem to be quite so much fire in the upper story. Everybody seems to be out of the joint, and even the firemen are fighting the blaze from the outside because the Brussels is so old and ramshackly there is no sense in them risking the floors.

I mean everybody is out of the joint except Wilbur Willard and Lillian, and we figure they are getting a good frying somewhere inside, although Feet Samuels is around offering to take thirteen to five for a few small bets that Lillian comes out okay, because Feet claims that a cat has nine lives and that is a fair bet at the price.

Well, up comes a swell-looking doll all heated up about something and pushing and clawing her way through the crowd up to the ropes and screaming until you can hardly hear yourself think, and about this same minute everybody hears a voice going ai-lee-hi-hee-hoo, like a Swiss yodeler, which comes from the roof of the

Brussels, and looking up what do we see but Wilbur Willard standing up there on the edge of the roof, high above the fire and smoke, and yodeling very loud.

Under one arm he has a big bundle of some kind, and under the other he has the little kid I see playing in the hall with Lillian. As he stands up there going ai-lee-hi-hee-hoo, the swell-dressed doll near us begins yipping louder than Wilbur is yodeling, and the firemen rush over under him with a life net.

Wilbur lets go another ai-lee-hi-hee-hoo, and down he comes all spraddled out, with the bundle and the kid, but he hits the net sitting down and bounces up and back again for a couple of minutes before he finally settles. In fact, Wilbur is enjoying the bouncing, and the chances are he will be bouncing yet if the firemen do not drop their hold on the net and let him fall to the ground.

Then Wilbur steps out of the net, and I can see the bundle is a rolled-up blanket with Lillian's eyes peeking out of one end. He still has the kid under the other arm with his head stuck out in front, and his legs stuck out behind, and it does not seem to me that Wilbur is handling the kid as careful as he is handling Lillian. He stands there looking at the firemen with a very sneering look, and finally he says: "Do not think you can catch me in your net unless I wish to be caught. I am a butterfly, and very hard to overtake."

Then all of a sudden the swell-dressed doll who is doing so much hollering, piles on top of Wilbur and grabs the kid from him and begins hugging and kissing it.

"Wilbur," she says, "God bless you, Wilbur, for saving my baby! Oh, thank you, Wilbur, thank you! My wretched husband kidnaps and runs away with him, and it is only a few hours ago that my detectives find out where he is."

Wilbur gives the doll a funny look for about half a minute and starts to walk away, but Lillian comes wiggling out of the blanket, looking and smelling pretty much singed up, and the kid sees Lillian and begins hollering for her, so Wilbur finally hands Lillian over to the kid. And not wishing to leave Lillian, Wilbur stands around somewhat confused, and the doll gets talking to him, and finally they go away together, and as they go Wilbur is carrying the kid, and the kid is carrying Lillian, and Lillian is not feeling so good from her burns.

Furthermore, Wilbur is probably more sober than he ever is before in years at this hour in the morning, but before they go I get a chance to talk some to Wilbur when he is still rambling somewhat, and I make out from what he says that the first time he goes to get Lillian he finds her in his room and does not see hide or hair of the little kid and does not even think of him, because he does not know what room the kid is in, anyway, having never noticed such a thing.

But the second time he goes up, Lillian is sniffing at the crack under the door of a room down the hall from Wilbur's and Wilbur says he seems to remember seeing a trickle of something like water coming out of the crack.

"And," Wilbur says, "as I am looking for a blanket for Lillian, and it will be a bother to go back to my room, I figure I will get one out of this room. I try the knob but the door is locked, so I kick it in, and walk in to find the room is full of smoke, and fire is shooting through the windows very lovely, and when I grab a blanket off the bed for Lillian, what is under the blanket but the kid?

"Well," Wilbur says, "the kid is squawking, and Lillian is mer-owing, and there is so much confusion generally that it makes me nervous, so I figure we better go up on the roof and let the stink blow off us, and look at the fire from there. It seems there is a guy stretched out on the floor of the room alongside an upset table between the door and the bed. He has a bottle in one hand, and he is dead. Well, naturally there is no percentage in lugging a dead guy along, so I take Lillian and the kid and go up on the roof, and we just naturally fly off like humming birds. Now I must get a drink," Wilbur says. "I wonder if anybody has anything on their hip?"

Well, the papers are certainly full of Wilbur and Lillian the next day, especially Lillian, and they are both great heroes.

But Wilbur cannot stand the publicity very long, because he never has no time to himself for his drinking, what with the scribes and the photographers hopping on him every few minutes wishing to hear his story, and to take more pictures of him and Lillian, so one night he disappears, and Lillian disappears with him.

About a year later it comes out that he marries his old doll, Lillian Withington-Harmon, and falls into a lot of dough, and what is more he cuts out the liquor and becomes quite a useful citizen one way and another. So everybody has to admit that black cats are not always bad luck, although I say Wilbur's case is a little exceptional because he does not start out knowing Lillian is a black cat, but thinking she is a leopard.

I happen to run into Wilbur one day all dressed up in good clothes and jewelry and chucking quite a swell.

"Wilbur," I say to him, "I often think how remarkable it is the way Lillian suddenly gets such an attachment for the little kid and remembers about him being in the hotel and leads you back there a second time to the right room. If I do not see this come off with my own eyes, I will never believe a cat has brains enough to do such a thing, because I consider cats extra dumb."

"Brains nothing," Wilbur says. "Lillian does not have brains enough to grease a gimlet. And what is more she has no more attachment for the kid than a jack rabbit. The time has come," Wilbur says, "to expose Lillian. She gets a lot of credit which is never coming to her. I will now tell you about Lillian, and nobody knows this but me.

"You see," Wilbur says, "when Lillian is a little kitten I always put a little Scotch in her milk, partly to help make her good and strong, and partly because I am never no hand to drink alone, unless there is nobody with me. Well, at first Lillian does not care so much for this Scotch in her milk, but finally she takes a liking to it, and I keep making her toddy stronger until in the end she will lap up a good big snort without any milk for a chaser, and yell for more. In fact, I suddenly realize that Lillian becomes a rumpot, just like I am in those days, and simply must have her grog, and it is when she is good and rummed up that Lillian goes off snatching Pekes, and acting tough generally.

"Now," Wilbur says, "the time of the fire is about the time I get home every morning and give Lillian her schnapps. But when I go into the hotel and get her the first time, I forget to Scotch her up, and the reason she runs back into the hotel is because she is looking for her shot. And the reason she is sniffing at the kid's door is not because the kid is in there but because the trickle that is coming through the crack under the door is nothing but Scotch that is running out of the bottle in the dead guy's hand. I never mention this before because I figure it may be a knock to a dead guy's memory," Wilbur says. "Drinking is certainly a disgusting thing, especially secret drinking."

"But how is Lillian getting along these days?" I ask Wilbur Willard.

"I am greatly disappointed in Lillian," he says. "She refuses to reform when I do and the last I hear of her she takes up with Gregorio, the Ginney bootlegger, who keeps her well Scotched up all the time so she will lead his blond doll's Peke a dog's life."

Johnny One-Eye

This cat I am going to tell you about is a very small cat, and in fact it is only a few weeks old, consequently it is really nothing but an infant cat. To tell the truth, it is just a kitten.

It is gray and white and very dirty and its fur is all

frowzled up, so it is a very miserable-looking little kitten to be sure the day it crawls through a broken basement window into an old house in East Fifty-third Street over near Third Avenue in the city of New York and goes from room to room saying mer-ow, mer-ow in a low, weak voice until it comes to a room at the head of the stairs on the second story where a guy by the name of Rudolph is sitting on the floor thinking of not much.

One reason Rudolph is sitting on the floor is because there is nothing else to sit on as this is an empty house that is all boarded up for years and there is no furniture whatever in it, and another reason is that Rudolph has a .38 slug in his side and really does not feel like doing much of anything but sitting. He is wearing a derby hat and his overcoat as it is in the wintertime and very cold and he has an automatic Betsy on the floor beside him and naturally he is surprised quite some when the little kitten comes mer-owing into the room and he picks up the Betsy and points it at the door in case anyone he does not wish to see is with the kitten. But when he observes that it is all alone, Rudolph puts the Betsy down again and speaks to the kitten as follows:

"Hello, cat," he says.

Of course the kitten does not say anything in reply except mer-ow but it walks right up to Rudolph and climbs on his lap, although the chances are if it knows who Rudolph is, it will hightail it out of there quicker than anybody can say scat. There is enough daylight coming through the chinks in the boards over the windows for Rudolph to see that the kitten's right eye is in bad shape, and in fact it is bulged half out of its head in a most distressing manner and it is plain to be seen that the sight is gone from this eye. It is also plain to be seen that the injury happens recently and Rudolph gazes at the kitten a while and starts to laugh and says like this:

"Well, cat," he says, "you seem to be scuffed up almost as much as I am. We make a fine pair of invalids here together. What is your name, cat?"

Naturally the kitten does not state its name but only

goes mer-ow and Rudolph says, "All right, I will call you Johnny. Yes," he says, "your tag is now Johnny One-Eye."

Then he puts the kitten in under his overcoat and pretty soon it gets warm and starts to purr and Rudolph says:

"Johnny," he says, "I will say one thing for you and that is you are plenty game to be able to sing when you are hurt as bad as you are. It is more than I can do."

But Johnny only goes mer-ow again and keeps on purring and by and by it falls sound asleep under Rudolph's coat, and Rudolph is wishing the pain in his side will let up long enough for him to do the same.

Well, I suppose you are saying to yourself, what is this Rudolph doing in an old empty house with a slug in his side, so I will explain that the district attorney is responsible for this situation. It seems that the D.A. appears before the grand jury and tells it that Rudolph is an extortion guy and a killer and I do not know what all else, though some of these statements are without doubt a great injustice to Rudolph as, up to the time the D.A. makes them, Rudolph does not kill anybody of any consequence in years.

It is true that at one period of his life he is considered a little wild but this is in the 1920's when everybody else is, too, and for seven or eight years he is all settled down and is engaged in business organization work, which is very respectable work, indeed. He organizes quite a number of businesses on a large scale and is doing very good for himself. He is living quietly in a big hotel all alone, as Rudolph is by no means a family guy, and he is highly spoken of by one and all when the D.A. starts poking his nose into his affairs, claiming that Rudolph has no right to be making money out of the businesses, even though Rudolph gives these businesses plenty of first-class protection.

In fact, the D.A. claims that Rudolph is nothing but a racket guy and a great knock to the community, and all this upsets Rudolph no little when it comes to his ears in a roundabout way. So he calls up his lawbooks and requests legal advice on the subject, and lawbooks says the best thing he can think of for Rudolph to do is to become as inconspicuous as possible right away but to please not mention to anyone that he gives this advice.

Lawbooks says he understands the D.A. is requesting indictments and is likely to get them and furthermore that he is rounding up certain parties that Rudolph is once associated with and trying to get them to remember incidents in Rudolph's early career that may not be entirely to his credit. Lawbooks says he hears that one of these parties is a guy by the name of Cute Freddy and that Freddy makes a deal with the D.A. to lay off of him if he tells everything he knows about Rudolph, so under the circumstances a long journey by Rudolph will be in the interest of everybody concerned.

So Rudolph decides to go on a journey but then he gets to thinking that maybe Freddy will remember a little matter that Rudolph long since dismisses from his mind and does not wish to have recalled again, which is the time he and Freddy do a job on a guy by the name of The Icelander in Troy years ago and he drops around to Freddy's house to remind him to be sure not to remember this.

But it seems that Freddy, who is an important guy in business organization work himself, though in a different part of the city than Rudolph, mistakes the purpose of Rudolph's visit and starts to out with his rooty-toot-toot, and in order to protect himself it is necessary for Rudolph to take his Betsy and give Freddy a little tattooing. In fact, Rudolph practically crochets his monogram on Freddy's chest and leaves him exceptionally deceased.

But as Rudolph is departing from the neighborhood, who bobs up but a young guy by the name of Buttsy Fagan, who works for Freddy as a chauffeur and one thing and another, and who is also said to be able to put a slug through a keyhole at forty paces without touching the sides, though I suppose it will have to be a pretty good-sized keyhole. Anyway, he takes a long-distance crack at Rudolph as Rudolph is rounding a corner but all Buttsy can see of Rudolph at the moment is a little piece of his left side and this is what Buttsy hits, although no one knows it at the time, except of course Rudolph, who just keeps on departing.

Now this incident causes quite a stir in police circles, and the D.A. is very indignant over losing a valuable witness, and when they are unable to locate Rudolph at once, a reward of five thousand dollars is offered for information leading to his capture alive or dead and some think they really mean dead. Indeed, it is publicly stated that it is not a good idea for anyone to take any chances with Rudolph as he is known to be armed and is such a character as will be sure to resent being captured, but they do not explain that this is only because Rudolph knows the D.A. wishes to place him in the old rocking chair at Sing Sing and that Rudolph is quite allergic to the idea.

Anyway, the cops go looking for Rudolph in Hot Springs and Miami and every other place except where he is, which is right in New York wandering around town with the slug in his side, knocking at the doors of old friends requesting assistance. But all the old friends do for him is to slam the doors in his face and forget they ever see him, as the D.A. is very tough on parties who assist guys he is looking for, claiming that this is something most illegal called harboring fugitives. Besides Rudolph is never any too popular at best with his old friends as he always plays pretty much of a lone duke and takes the big end of everything for his.

He cannot even consult a doctor about the slug in his side as he knows that nowadays the first thing a doctor will do about a guy with a gunshot wound is to report him to the cops, although Rudolph can remember when there is always a sure-footed doctor around who will consider it a privilege and a pleasure to treat him and keep his trap closed about it. But of course this is in the good old days and Rudolph can see they are gone forever. So he just does the best he can about the slug and

goes on wandering here and there and around and about
and the blats keep printing his picture and saying, Where
is Rudolph?

Where he is some of the time is in Central Park trying to get some sleep, but of course even the blats will
consider it foolish to go looking for Rudolph there in
such cold weather, as he is known as a guy who enjoys
his comfort at all times. In fact, it is comfort that Rudolph misses more than anything as the slug is commencing to cause him great pain and naturally the pain turns
Rudolph's thoughts to the author of same and he remembers that he once hears somebody say that Buttsy
lives over in East Fifty-third Street.

So one night Rudolph decides to look Buttsy up and
cause him a little pain in return, and he is moseying
through Fifty-third when he gets so weak he falls down
on the sidewalk in front of the old house and rolls down
a short flight of steps that lead from the street level to a
little railed-in areaway and ground floor or basement
door, and before he stops rolling he brings up against the
door itself and it creaks open inward as he bumps it.
After he lays there a while Rudolph can see that the
house is empty and he crawls on inside.

Then, when he feels stronger, Rudolph makes his
way upstairs because the basement is damp and mice
keep trotting back and forth over him and eventually
he winds up in the room where Johnny One-Eye finds
him the following afternoon, and the reason Rudolph
settles down in this room is because it commands the
stairs. Naturally, this is important to a guy in Rudolph's
situation, though after he is sitting there for about fourteen hours before Johnny comes along he can see that
he is not going to be much disturbed by traffic. But he
considers it a very fine place, indeed, to remain planted
until he is able to resume his search for Buttsy.

Well, after a while Johnny One-Eye wakes up and
comes from under the coat and looks at Rudolph out of
his good eye and Rudolph waggles his fingers and
Johnny plays with them, catching one finger in his front

paws and biting it gently and this pleases Rudolph no little as he never before has any personal experience with a kitten. However, he remembers observing one when he is a boy down in Houston Street, so he takes a piece of paper out of his pocket and makes a little ball of it and rolls it along the floor and Johnny bounces after it very lively indeed. But Rudolph can see that the bad eye is getting worse and finally he says to Johnny like this:

"Johnny," he says, "I guess you must be suffering more than I am. I remember there are some pet shops over on Lexington Avenue not far from here and when it gets good and dark I am going to take you out and see if we can find a cat croaker to do something about your eye. Yes, Johnny," Rudolph says, "I will also get you something to eat. You must be starved."

Johnny One-Eye says mer-ow to this and keeps on playing with the paper ball but soon it comes on dark outside and inside, too, and, in fact, it is so dark inside that Rudolph cannot see his hand before him. Then he puts his Betsy in a side pocket of his overcoat and picks up Johnny and goes downstairs, feeling his way in the dark and easing along a step at a time until he gets to the basement door. Naturally, Rudolph does not wish to strike any matches because he is afraid someone outside may see the light and get nosey.

By moving very slowly, Rudolph finally gets to Lexington Avenue and while he is going along he remembers the time he walks from 125th Street in Harlem down to 110th with six slugs in him and never feels as bad as he does now. He gets to thinking that maybe he is not the guy he used to be, which of course is very true, as Rudolph is now forty-odd years of age and is fat around the middle and getting bald, and he also does some thinking about what a pleasure it will be to him to find this Buttsy and cause him the pain he is personally suffering.

There are not many people in the streets and those that are go hurrying along because it is so cold and none of them pay any attention to Rudolph or Johnny One-Eye either, even though Rudolph staggers a little now and then like a guy who is rummed up, although of course it is only weakness. The chances are he is also getting a little feverish and light-headed because finally he stops a cop who is going along swinging his arms to keep warm and asks him if he knows where there is a pet shop, and it is really most indiscreet of such a guy as Rudolph to be interviewing cops. But the cop just points up the street and goes on without looking twice at Rudolph and Rudolph laughs and pokes Johnny with a finger and says:

"No, Johnny One-Eye," he says, "the cop is not a dope for not recognizing Rudolph. Who can figure the hottest guy in forty-eight states to be going along a street with a little cat in his arms? Can you, Johnny?"

Johnny says mer-ow and pretty soon Rudolph comes to the pet shop the cop points out. Rudolph goes inside and says to the guy like this:

"Are you a cat croaker?" Rudolph says. "Do you know what to do about a little cat that has a hurt eye?"

"I am a kind of a vet," the guy says.

"Then take a glaum at Johnny One-Eye here and see what you can do for him," Rudolph says.

Then he hands Johnny over to the guy and the guy looks at Johnny a while and says:

"Mister," he says, "the best thing I can do for this cat is to put it out of its misery. You better let me give it something right now. It will just go to sleep and never know what happens."

Well, at this, Rudolph grabs Johnny One-Eye out of the guy's hands and puts him under his coat and drops a duke on the Betsy in his pocket as if he is afraid the guy will take Johnny away from him again and he says to the guy like this:

"No, no, no," Rudolph says. "I cannot bear to think of such a thing. What about some kind of an operation? I remember they take a bum lamp out of Joe the Goat at Bellevue one time and he is okay now."

"Nothing will do your cat any good," the guy says. "It is a goner. It will start having fits pretty soon and die sure. What is the idea of trying to save such a cat as this? It is no kind of a cat to begin with. It is just a cat. You can get a million like it for a nickel."

"No," Rudolph says, "this is not just a cat. This is Johnny One-Eye. He is my only friend in the world. He is the only living thing that ever comes pushing up against me warm and friendly and trusts me in my whole life. I feel sorry for him."

"I feel sorry for him, too," the guy says. "I always feel sorry for animals that get hurt and for people."

"I do not feel sorry for people," Rudolph says. "I only feel sorry for Johnny One-Eye. Give me some kind of stuff that Johnny will eat."

"Your cat wants milk," the guy says. "You can get some at the delicatessen store down at the corner. Mister," he says, "you look sick yourself. Can I do anything for you?"

But Rudolph only shakes his head and goes on out and down to the delicatessen joint where he buys a bottle of milk and this transaction reminds him that he is very short in the moo department. In fact, he can find only a five-dollar note in his pockets and he remembers that he has no way of getting any more when this runs out, which is a very sad predicament indeed for a guy who is accustomed to plenty of moo at all times.

Then Rudolph returns to the old house and sits down on the floor again and gives Johnny One-Eye some of the milk in his derby hat as he neglects buying something for Johnny to drink out of. But Johnny offers no complaint. He laps up the milk and curls himself into a wad in Rudolph's lap and purrs.

Rudolph takes a swig of the milk himself but it makes him sick, for by this time Rudolph is really far from being in the pink of condition. He not only has the pain in his side but he has a heavy cold which he probably catches from lying on the basement floor or maybe sleeping in the park and he is wheezing no little. He com-

mences to worry that he may get too ill to continue looking for Buttsy, as he can see that if it is not for Buttsy
he will not be in this situation, suffering the way he is,
but on a long journey to some place.

He takes to going off into long stretches of a kind of
stupor and every time he comes out of one of these stu-
pors the first thing he does is to look around for Johnny
One-Eye and Johnny is always right there either playing with the paper ball or purring in Rudolph's lap. He
is a great comfort to Rudolph but after a while Rudolph
notices that Johnny seems to be running out of zip and
he also notices that he is running out of zip himself especially when he discovers that he is no longer able to
get to his feet.

It is along in the late afternoon of the day following
the night Rudolph goes out of the house that he hears
someone coming up the stairs and naturally he picks up
his Betsy and gets ready for action when he also hears
a very small voice calling kitty, kitty, kitty, and he realizes that the party that is coming can be nobody but a
child. In fact, a minute later a little pretty of maybe six
years of age comes into the room all out of breath and
says to Rudolph like this:

"How do you do?" she says. "Have you seen my
kitty?"

Then she spots Johnny One-Eye in Rudolph's lap
and runs over and sits down beside Rudolph and takes
Johnny in her arms, and at first Rudolph is inclined to
resent this and has a notion to give her a good boffing
but he is too weak to exert himself in such a manner.

"Who are you?" Rudolph says to the little pretty,
"and," he says, "where do you live and how do you get
in this house?"

"Why," she says, "I am Elsie, and I live down the
street and I am looking everywhere for my kitty for
three days and the door is open downstairs and I know
kitty likes to go in doors that are open so I came to find
her and here she is."

"I guess I forgot to close it last night," Rudolph says. "I seem to be very forgetful lately."

"What is your name?" Elsie asks, "and why are you sitting on the floor in the cold and where are all your chairs? Do you have any little girls like me and do you love them dearly?"

"No," Rudolph says. "By no means and not at all."

"Well," Elsie says, "I think you are a nice man for taking care of my kitty. Do you love kitty?"

"Look," Rudolph says, "his name is not kitty. His name is Johnny One-Eye, because he has only one eye."

"I call her kitty," Elsie says. "But," she says, "Johnny One-Eye is a nice name too and if you like it best I will call her Johnny and I will leave her here with you to take care of always and I will come to see her every day. You see," she says, "if I take Johnny home Buttsy will only kick her again."

"Buttsy?" Rudolph says. "Do I hear you say Buttsy? Is his other name Fagan?"

"Why, yes," Elsie says. "Do you know him?"

"No," Rudolph says, "but I hear of him. What is he to you?"

"He is my new daddy," Elsie says. "My other one and my best one is dead and so my mamma makes Buttsy my new one. My mamma says Buttsy is her mistake. He is very mean. He kicks Johnny and hurts her eye and makes her run away. He kicks my mamma too. Buttsy kicks everybody and everything when he is mad and he is always mad."

"He is a louse to kick a little cat," Rudolph says.

"Yes," Elsie says, "that is what Mr. O'Toole says he is for kicking my mamma but my mamma says it is not a nice word and I am never to say it out loud."

"Who is Mr. O'Toole?" Rudolph says.

"He is the policeman," Elsie says. "He lives across the street from us and he is very nice to me. He says Buttsy is the word you say just now, not only for kicking my mamma but for taking her money when she brings

it home from work and spending it so she cannot buy
me nice things to wear. But do you know what?" Elsie
says. "My mamma says some day Buttsy is going far
away and then she will buy me lots of things and send
me to school and make me a lady."

Then Elsie begins skipping around the room with
Johnny One-Eye in her arms and singing I am going to
be a lady, I am going to be a lady, until Rudolph has to
tell her to pipe down because he is afraid somebody
may hear her. And all the time Rudolph is thinking of
Buttsy and regretting that he is unable to get on his pins
and go out of the house.

"Now I must go home," Elsie says, "because this is a
night Buttsy comes in for his supper and I have to be
in bed before he gets there so I will not bother him.
Buttsy does not like little girls. Buttsy does not like little
kittens. Buttsy does not like little anythings. My mamma
is afraid of Buttsy and so am I. But," she says, "I will
leave Johnny here with you and come back tomorrow
to see her."

"Listen, Elsie," Rudolph says, "does Mr. O'Toole
come home tonight to his house for his supper, too?"

"Oh, yes," Elsie says. "He comes home every night.
Sometimes when there is a night Buttsy is not coming
in for his supper my mamma lets me go over to Mr.
O'Toole's and I play with his dog Charley but you must
never tell Buttsy this because he does not like O'Toole
either. But this is a night Buttsy is coming and that is
why my mamma tells me to get in early."

Now Rudolph takes an old letter out of his inside
pocket and a pencil out of another pocket and he scrib-
bles a few lines on the envelope and stretches himself
out on the floor and begins groaning oh, oh, oh, and then
he says to Elsie like this:

"Look, Elsie," he says, "you are a smart little kid and
you pay strict attention to what I am going to say to you.
Do not go to bed tonight until Buttsy gets in. Then,"
Rudolph says, "you tell him you come in this old house
looking for your cat and that you hear somebody groan-

ing like I do just now in the room at the head of the stairs and that you find a guy who says his name is Rudolph lying on the floor so sick he cannot move. Tell him the front door of the basement is open. But," Rudolph says, "you must not tell him that Rudolph tells you to say these things. Do you understand?"

"Oh," Elsie says, "do you want him to come here? He will kick Johnny again if he does."

"He will come here, but he will not kick Johnny," Rudolph says. "He will come here, or I am the worst guesser in the world. Tell him what I look like, Elsie. Maybe he will ask you if you see a gun. Tell him you do not see one. You do not see a gun, do you, Elsie?"

"No," Elsie says, "only the one in your hand when I come in but you put it under your coat. Buttsy has a gun and Mr. O'Toole has a gun but Buttsy says I am never, never to tell anybody about this or he will kick me the way he does my mamma."

"Well," Rudolph says, "you must not remember seeing mine, either. It is a secret between you and me and Johnny One-Eye. Now," he says, "if Buttsy leaves the house to come and see me, as I am pretty sure he will, you run over to Mr. O'Toole's house and give him this note, but do not tell Buttsy or your mamma either about the note. If Buttsy does not leave, it is my hard luck but you give the note to Mr. O'Toole anyway. Now tell me what you are to do, Elsie," Rudolph says, "so I can see if you have got everything correct."

"I am to go on home and wait for Buttsy," she says, "and I am to tell him Rudolph is lying on the floor of this dirty old house with a fat stomach and a big nose making noises and that he is very sick and the basement door is open and there is no gun if he asks me, and when Buttsy comes to see you I am to take this note to Mr. O'Toole but Buttsy and my mamma are not to know I have the note and if Buttsy does not leave I am to give it to Mr. O'Toole anyway and you are to stay here and take care of Johnny my kitten."

"That is swell," Rudolph says. "Now you run along."

So Elsie leaves and Rudolph sits up again against the wall because his side feels easier this way and Johnny One-Eye is in his lap purring very low and the dark comes on until it is blacker inside the room than in the middle of a tunnel and Rudolph feels that he is going into another stupor and he has a tough time fighting it off.

Afterward some of the neighbors claim they remember hearing a shot inside the house and then two more in quick succession and then all is quiet until a little later when Officer O'Toole and half a dozen other cops and an ambulance with a doctor come busting into the street and swarm into the joint with their guns out and their flashlights going. The first thing they find is Buttsy at the foot of the stairs with two bullet wounds close together in his throat, and naturally he is real dead.

Rudolph is still sitting against the wall with what seems to be a small bundle of bloody fur in his lap but which turns out to be what is left of this little cat I am telling you about, although nobody pays any attention to it at first. They are more interested in getting the come-alongs on Rudolph's wrists, but before they move him he pulls his clothes aside and shows the doctor where the slug is in his side and the doctor takes one glaum and shakes his head and says:

"Gangrene," he says. "I think you have pneumonia, too, from the way you are blowing."

"I know," Rudolph says. "I know this morning. Not much chance, hey, croaker?"

"Not much," the doctor says.

"Well, cops," Rudolph says, "load me in. I do not suppose you want Johnny, seeing that he is dead."

"Johnny who?" one of the cops says.

"Johnny One-Eye," Rudolph says. "This little cat here in my lap. Buttsy shoots Johnny's only good eye out and takes most of his noodle with it. I never see a more wonderful shot. Well, Johnny is better off but I feel sorry about him as he is my best friend down to the last."

Then he begins to laugh and the cop asks him what tickles him so much and Rudolph says:

"Oh," he says, "I am thinking of the joke on Buttsy. I am positive he will come looking for me, all right, not only because of the little altercation between Cute Freddy and me but because the chances are Buttsy is greatly embarrassed by not tilting me over the first time, as of course he never knows he wings me. Furthermore," Rudolph says, "and this is the best reason of all, Buttsy will realize that if I am in his neighborhood it is by no means a good sign for him, even if he hears I am sick.

"Well," Rudolph says, "I figure that with any kind of a square rattle I will have a better chance of nailing him than he has of nailing me, but that even if he happens to nail me, O'Toole will get my note in time to arrive here and nab Buttsy on the spot with his gun on him. And," Rudolph says, "I know it will be a great pleasure to the D.A. to settle Buttsy for having a gun on him.

"But," Rudolph says, "as soon as I hear Buttsy coming on the sneaksby up the stairs, I can see I am taking all the worst of it because I am now wheezing like a busted valve and you can hear me a block away except when I hold my breath, which is very difficult indeed, considering the way I am already greatly tuckered out. No," Rudolph says, "it does not look any too good for me as Buttsy keeps coming up the stairs, as I can tell he is doing by a little faint creak in the boards now and then. I am in no shape to maneuver around the room and pretty soon he will be on the landing and then all he will have to do is to wait there until he hears me which he is bound to do unless I stop breathing altogether. Naturally," Rudolph says, "I do not care to risk a blast in the dark without knowing where he is, as something tells me Buttsy is not a guy you can miss in safety.

"Well," Rudolph says, "I notice several times before this that in the dark Johnny One-Eye's good glim shines like a big spark, so when I feel Buttsy is about to hit the landing, although of course I cannot see him, I flip Johnny's ball of paper across the room to the wall just opposite the door, and tough as he must be feeling Johnny chases after it when he hears it light. I figure Buttsy will hear Johnny playing with the paper and see his eye shining and think it is me and take a pop at it and that his gun flash will give me a crack at him.

"It all works out just like I dope it," Rudolph says, "but," he says, "I never give Buttsy credit for being such a marksman as to be able to hit a cat's eye in the dark. If I know this, maybe I will never stick Johnny out in front the way I do. It is a good thing I never give Buttsy a second shot. He is a lily. Yes," Rudolph says, "I can remember when I can use a guy like him."

"Buttsy is no account," the cop says. "He is a good riddance. He is the makings of a worse guy than you."

"Well," Rudolph says, "it is a good lesson to him for kicking a little cat."

Then they take Rudolph to a hospital and this is where I see him and piece out this story of Johnny One-Eye, and Officer O'Toole is at Rudolph's bedside keeping guard over him, and I remember that not long before Rudolph chalks out he looks at O'Toole and says to him like this:

"Copper," he says, "there is no chance of them out-juggling the kid on the reward moo, is there?"

"No," O'Toole says, "no chance. I keep the note you send me by Elsie saying she will tell me where you are. It is information leading to your capture just as the reward offer states. Rudolph," he says, "it is a nice thing you do for Elsie and her mother, although," he says, "it is not nearly as nice as icing Buttsy for them."

"By the way, copper," Rudolph says, "there is the remainders of a pound note in my pants pocket when I am brought here. I want you to do me a favor. Get it from the desk and buy Elsie another cat and name it Johnny, will you?"

"Sure," O'Toole says. "Anything else?"

"Yes," Rudolph says, "be sure it has two good eyes."

Butch Minds the Baby

One evening along about seven o'clock I am sitting in Mindy's restaurant putting on the gefillte fish, which is a dish I am very fond of, when in comes three parties from Brooklyn wearing caps as follows: Harry the Horse, Little Isadore and Spanish John.

Now these parties are not such parties as I will care to have much truck with, because I often hear rumors about them that are very discreditable, even if the rumors are not true. In fact, I hear that many citizens of Brooklyn will be very glad indeed to see Harry the Horse, Little Isadore and Spanish John move away from there, as they are always doing something that is considered a knock to the community, such as robbing people, or maybe shooting or stabbing them, and throwing pineapples, and carrying on generally.

I am really much surprised to see these parties on Broadway, as it is well known that the Broadway coppers just naturally love to shove such parties around, but here they are in Mindy's, and there I am, so of course I give them a very large hello, as I never wish to seem inhospitable, even to Brooklyn parties. Right away they come over to my table and sit down, and Little Isadore reaches out and spears himself a big hunk of my gefillte fish with his fingers, but I overlook this, as I am using the only knife on the table.

Then they all sit there looking at me without saying anything, and the way they look at me makes me very nervous indeed. Finally I figure that maybe they are a little embarrassed being in a high-class spot such as Mindy's, with legitimate people around and about, so I say to them, very polite: "It is a nice night."

"What is nice about it?" asks Harry the Horse, who is a thin man with a sharp face and sharp eyes.

Well, now that it is put up to me in this way, I can see there is nothing so nice about the night, at that, so I try to think of something else jolly to say, while Little Isadore keeps spearing at my gefillte fish with his fingers, and Spanish John nabs one of my potatoes.

"Where does Big Butch live?" Harry the Horse asks.

"Big Butch?" I say, as if I never hear the name before in my life, because in this man's town it is never a good idea to answer any question without thinking it over, as some time you may give the right answer to the wrong guy, or the wrong answer to the right guy. "Where does Big Butch live?" I ask them again.

"Yes, where does he live?" Harry the Horse says, very impatient. "We wish you to take us to him."

"Now wait a minute, Harry," I say, and I am now more nervous than somewhat. "I am not sure I remember the exact house Big Butch lives in, and furthermore I am not sure Big Butch will care to have me bringing people to see him, especially three at a time, and especially from Brooklyn. You know Big Butch has a very bad disposition, and there is no telling what he may say to me if he does not like the idea of me taking you to him."

"Everything is very kosher," Harry the Horse says. "You need not be afraid of anything whatever. We have a business proposition for Big Butch. It means a nice score for him, so you take us to him at once, or the chances are I will have to put the arm on somebody around here."

Well, as the only one around there for him to put the arm on at this time seems to be me, I can see where it will be good policy for me to take these parties to Big Butch, especially as the last of my gefillte fish is just going down Little Isadore's gullet, and Spanish John is finishing up my potatoes, and is dunking a piece of rye bread in my coffee, so there is nothing more for me to eat.

So I lead them over into West Forty-ninth Street, near Tenth Avenue, where Big Butch lives on the ground floor of an old brownstone-front house, and who is sitting out on the stoop but Big Butch himself. In fact, everybody in the neighborhood is sitting out on the front stoops over there, including women and children, because sitting out on the front stoops is quite a custom in this section.

Big Butch is peeled down to his undershirt and pants, and he has no shoes on his feet, as Big Butch is a guy who likes his comfort. Furthermore, he is smoking a cigar, and laid out on the stoop beside him on a blanket is a little baby with not much clothes on. This baby seems to be asleep, and every now and then Big Butch fans it with a folded newspaper to shoo away the mosquitoes that wish to nibble on the baby. These mosquitoes come across the river from the Jersey side on hot nights and they seem to be very fond of babies.

"Hello, Butch," I say, as we stop in front of the stoop.

"Sh-h-h-h!" Butch says, pointing at the baby, and making more noise with his shush than an engine blowing off steam. Then he gets up and tiptoes down to the sidewalk where we are standing, and I am hoping that Butch feels all right, because when Butch does not feel so good he is apt to be very short with one and all. He is a guy of maybe six foot two and a couple of feet wide, and he has big hairy hands and a mean look.

In fact, Big Butch is known all over this man's town as a guy you must not monkey with in any respect, so it takes plenty of weight off of me when I see that he seems to know the parties from Brooklyn, and nods at them very friendly, especially at Harry the Horse. And right away Harry states a most surprising proposition to Big Butch.

It seems that there is a big coal company which has an office in an old building down in West Eighteenth Street, and in this office is a safe, and in this safe is the company pay roll of twenty thousand dollars cash money. Harry the Horse knows the money is there because a personal friend of his who is the paymaster for the company puts it there late this very afternoon.

It seems that the paymaster enters into a dicker with Harry the Horse and Little Isadore and Spanish John for them to slug him while he is carrying the pay roll from the bank to the office in the afternoon, but something happens that they miss connections on the exact spot, so the paymaster has to carry the sugar on to the office without being slugged, and there it is now in two fat bundles.

Personally it seems to me as I listen to Harry's story that the paymaster must be a very dishonest character to be making deals to hold still while he is being slugged and the company's sugar taken away from him, but of course it is none of my business, so I take no part in the conversation.

Well, it seems that Harry the Horse and Little Isadore and Spanish John wish to get the money out of the safe, but none of them knows anything about opening safes, and while they are standing around over in Brooklyn talking over what is to be done in this emergency Harry suddenly remembers that Big Butch is once in the business of opening safes for a living.

In fact, I hear afterwards that Big Butch is considered the best safe opener east of the Mississippi River in his day, but the law finally takes to sending him to Sing Sing for opening these safes, and after he is in and out of Sing Sing three different times for opening safes Butch gets sick and tired of the place, especially as they pass what is called the Baumes Law in New York, which is a law that says if a guy is sent to Sing Sing four times hand running, he must stay there the rest of his life, without any argument about it.

So Big Butch gives up opening safes for a living, and goes into business in a small way, such as running beer, and handling a little Scotch now and then, and becomes an honest citizen. Furthermore, he marries one of the neighbor's children over on the West Side by the name of Mary Murphy, and I judge the baby on this stoop comes of this marriage between Big Butch and Mary because I can see that it is a very homely baby, indeed. Still, I never see many babies that I consider rose geraniums for looks, anyway.

Well, it finally comes out that the idea of Harry the Horse and Little Isadore and Spanish John is to get Big Butch to open the coal company's safe and take the payroll money out, and they are willing to give him fifty per cent of the money for his bother, taking fifty per cent for themselves for finding the plant, and paying all the overhead, such as the paymaster, out of their bit, which strikes me as a pretty fair sort of deal for Big Butch. But Butch only shakes his head.

"It is old-fashioned stuff," Butch says. "Nobody opens pete boxes for a living any more. They make the boxes too good, and they are all wired up with alarms and are a lot of trouble generally. I am in a legitimate business now and going along. You boys know I cannot stand another fall, what with being away three times already, and in addition to this I must mind the baby. My old lady goes to Mrs. Clancy's wake tonight up in the Bronx, and the chances are she will be there all night, as she is very fond of wakes, so I must mind little John Ignatius Junior."

"Listen, Butch," Harry the Horse says, "this is a very soft pete. It is old-fashioned, and you can open it with a toothpick. There are no wires on it, because they never put more than a dime in it before in years. It just happens they have to put the twenty G's in it tonight because my pal the paymaster makes it a point not to get back from the jug with the scratch in time to pay off today, especially after he sees we miss out on him. It is the softest touch you will ever know, and where can a guy pick up ten G's like this?"

I can see that Big Butch is thinking the ten G's over very seriously, at that, because in these times nobody can afford to pass up ten G's, especially a guy in the beer business, which is very, very tough just now. But finally he shakes his head again and says like this:

"No," he says, "I must let it go, because I must mind the baby. My old lady is very, very particular about this, and I dast not leave little John Ignatius Junior for a minute. If Mary comes home and finds I am not minding the baby she will put the blast on me plenty. I like to turn a few honest bobs now and then as well as anybody, but," Butch says, "John Ignatius Junior comes first with me."

Then he turns away and goes back to the stoop as much as to say he is through arguing, and sits down beside John Ignatius Junior again just in time to keep a mosquito from carrying off one of John's legs. Anybody can see that Big Butch is very fond of this baby, though personally I will not give you a dime a dozen for babies, male and female.

Well, Harry the Horse and Little Isadore and Spanish John are very much disappointed, and stand around talking among themselves, and paying no attention to me, when all of a sudden Spanish John, who never has much to say up to this time, seems to have a bright idea. He talks to Harry and Isadore, and they get all pleasured up over what he has to say, and finally Harry goes to Big Butch.

"Sh-h-h-h!" Big Butch says, pointing to the baby as Harry opens his mouth.

"Listen, Butch," Harry says in a whisper, "we can take the baby with us, and you can mind it and work, too."

"Why," Big Butch whispers back, "this is quite an idea indeed. Let us go into the house and talk things over."

So he picks up the baby and leads us into his joint, and gets out some pretty fair beer, though it is needled a little, at that, and we sit around the kitchen chewing the fat in whispers. There is a crib in the kitchen, and Butch puts the baby in his crib, and it keeps on snoozing away first rate while we are talking. In fact, it is sleeping so sound that I am commencing to figure that

Butch must give it some of the needled beer he is feeding us, because I am feeling a little dopey myself.

Finally Butch says that as long as he can take John
Ignatius Junior with him he sees no reason why he shall
not go and open the safe for them, only he says he must
have five per cent more to put in the baby's bank when
he gets back, so as to round himself up with his ever-
loving wife in case of a beef from her over keeping the
baby out in the night air. Harry the Horse says he considers this extra five per cent a little strong, but Spanish
John, who seems to be a very square guy, says that
after all it is only fair to cut the baby in if it is to be
with them when they are making the score, and Little
Isadore seems to think this is all right, too. So Harry
the Horse gives in, and says five per cent it is.

Well, as they do not wish to start out until after midnight, and as there is plenty of time, Big Butch gets out
some more needled beer, and then he goes looking for
the tools with which he opens safes, and which he says
he does not see since the day John Ignatius Junior is
born, and he gets them out to build the crib.

Now this is a good time for me to bid one and all
farewell, and what keeps me there is something I cannot tell you to this day, because personally I never
before have any idea of taking part in a safe opening,
especially with a baby, as I consider such actions very
dishonorable. When I come to think things over afterwards, the only thing I can figure is the needled beer,
but I wish to say I am really very much surprised at myself when I find myself in a taxicab along about one
o'clock in the morning with these Brooklyn parties and
Big Butch and the baby.

Butch has John Ignatius Junior rolled up in a blanket,
and John is still pounding his ear. Butch has a satchel
of tools, and what looks to me like a big flat book, and
just before we leave the house Butch hands me a package and tells me to be very careful with it. He gives
Little Isadore a smaller package, which Isadore shoves

into his pistol pocket, and when Isadore sits down in the taxi something goes wa-wa, like a sheep, and Big Butch becomes very indignant because it seems Isador is sitting on John Ignatius Junior's doll, which says "Mamma" when you squeeze it.

It seems Big Butch figures that John Ignatius Junior may wish something to play with in case he wakes up, and it is a good thing for Little Isadore that the mamma doll is not squashed so it cannot say "Mamma" any more, or the chances are Little Isadore will get a good bust in the snoot.

We let the taxicab go a block away from the spot we are headed for in West Eighteenth Street, between Seventh and Eighth Avenues, and walk the rest of the way two by two. I walk with Big Butch, carrying my package, and Butch is lugging the baby and his satchel and the flat thing that looks like a book. It is so quiet down in West Eighteenth Street at such an hour that you can hear yourself think, and in fact I hear myself thinking very plain that I am a big sap to be on a job like this, especially with a baby, but I keep going just the same, which shows you what a very big sap I am, indeed.

There are very few people in West Eighteenth Street when we get there, and one of them is a fat guy who is leaning against a building almost in the center of the block, and who takes a walk for himself as soon as he sees us. It seems that this fat guy is the watchman at the coal company's office and is also a personal friend of Harry the Horse, which is why he takes the walk when he sees us coming.

It is agreed before we leave Big Butch's house that Harry the Horse and Spanish John are to stay outside the place as lookouts, while Big Butch is inside opening the safe, and that Little Isadore is to go with Butch. Nothing whatever is said by anybody about where I am to be at any time, and I can see that, no matter where I am, I will still be an outsider, but, as Butch gives me the package to carry, I figure he wishes me to remain with him.

It is no bother at all getting into the office of the coal company, which is on the ground floor, because it seems the watchman leaves the front door open, this watchman being a most obliging guy, indeed. In fact he is so obliging that by and by he comes back and lets Harry the Horse and Spanish John tie him up good and tight, and stick a handkerchief in his mouth and chuck him in an areaway next to the office, so nobody will think he has anything to do with opening the safe in case anybody comes around asking.

The office looks out on the street, and the safe that Harry the Horse and Little Isadore and Spanish John wish Big Butch to open is standing up against the rear wall of the office facing the street windows. There is one little electric light burning very dim over the safe so that when anybody walks past the place outside, such as a watchman, they can look in through the window and see the safe at all times, unless they are blind. It is not a tall safe, and it is not a big safe, and I can see Big Butch grin when he sees it, so I figure this safe is not much of a safe, just as Harry the Horse claims.

Well, as soon as Big Butch and the baby and Little Isadore and me get into the office, Big Butch steps over to the safe and unfolds what I think is the big flat book, and what is it but a sort of screen painted on one side to look exactly like the front of a safe. Big Butch stands this screen up on the floor in front of the real safe, leaving plenty of space in between, the idea being that the screen will keep anyone passing in the street outside from seeing Butch while he is opening the safe, because when a man is opening a safe he needs all the privacy he can get.

Big Butch lays John Ignatius Junior down on the floor on the blanket behind the phony safe front and takes his tools out of the satchel and starts to work opening the safe, while Little Isadore and me get back in a corner where it is dark, because there is not room for all of us back of the screen. However, we can see what Big Butch is doing, and I wish to say while I never before see a professional safe opener at work, and never wish to see another, this Butch handles himself like a real artist.

He starts drilling into the safe around the combination lock, working very fast and very quiet, when all of a sudden what happens but John Ignatius Junior sits up on the blanket and lets out a squall. Naturally this is most disquieting to me, and personally I am in favor of beaning John Ignatius Junior with something to make him keep still, because I am nervous enough as it is. But the squalling does not seem to bother Big Butch. He lays down his tools and picks up John Ignatius Junior and starts whispering, "There, there, there, my itty oddleums. Da-dad is here."

Well, this sounds very nonsensical to me in such a situation, and it makes no impression whatever on John Ignatius Junior. He keeps on squalling, and I judge he is squalling pretty loud because I see Harry the Horse and Spanish John both walk past the window and look in very anxious. Big Butch jiggles John Ignatius Junior up and down and keeps whispering baby talk to him, which sounds very undignified coming from a high-class safe opener, and finally Butch whispers to me to hand him the package I am carrying.

He opens the package, and what is in it but a baby's nursing bottle full of milk. Moreover, there is a little tin stew pan, and Butch hands the pan to me and whispers to me to find a water tap somewhere in the joint and fill the pan with water. So I go stumbling around in the dark in a room behind the office and bark my shins several times before I find a tap and fill the pan. I take it back to Big Butch, and he squats there with the baby on one arm, and gets a tin of what is called canned heat out of the package, and lights this canned heat with his cigar lighter, and starts heating the pan of water with the nursing bottle in it.

Big Butch keeps sticking his finger in the pan of water while it is heating, and by and by he puts the rubber nipple of the nursing bottle in his mouth and takes a pull at it to see if the milk is warm enough, just like I see dolls who have babies do. Apparently the milk is okay, as Butch hands the bottle to John Ignatius Junior, who grabs hold of it with both hands and starts sucking on the business end. Naturally he has to stop squalling, and Big Butch goes to work on the safe again, with John Ignatius Junior sitting on the blanket, pulling on the bottle and looking wiser than a treeful of owls.

It seems the safe is either a tougher job than anybody figures, or Big Butch's tools are not so good, what with being old and rusty and used for building baby cribs, because he breaks a couple of drills and works himself up into quite a sweat without getting anywhere. Butch afterwards explains to me that he is one of the first guys in this country to open safes without explosives, but he says to do this work properly you have to know the safes so as to drill to the tumblers of the lock just right, and it seems that this particular safe is a new type to him, even if it is old, and he is out of practice.

Well, in the meantime John Ignatius Junior finishes his bottle and starts mumbling again, and Big Butch gives him a tool to play with, and finally Butch needs this tool and tries to take it away from John Ignatius Junior, and the baby lets out such a squawk that Butch has to let him keep it until he can sneak it away from him, and this causes more delay.

Finally Big Butch gives up trying to drill the safe open, and he whispers to us that he will have to put a little shot in it to loosen up the lock, which is all right with us, because we are getting tired of hanging around and listening to John Ignatius Junior's glug-glugging. As far as I am personally concerned, I am wishing I am home in bed.

Well, Butch starts pawing through his satchel looking for something and it seems that what he is looking for is a little bottle of some kind of explosive with which to shake the lock on the safe up some, and at first he cannot find this bottle, but finally he discovers that John Ignatius Junior has it and is gnawing at the cork, and

Butch has quite a battle making John Ignatius Junior give it up.

Anyway, he fixes the explosive in one of the holes he drills near the combination lock on the safe, and then he puts in a fuse, and just before he touches off the fuse Butch picks up John Ignatius Junior and hands him to Little Isadore, and tells us to go into the room behind the office. John Ignatius Junior does not seem to care for Little Isadore, and I do not blame him, at that, because he starts to squirm around quite some in Isadore's arms and lets out a squall, but all of a sudden he becomes very quiet indeed, and, while I am not able to prove it, something tells me that Little Isadore has his hand over John Ignatius Junior's mouth.

Well, Big Butch joins us right away in the back room, and sound comes out of John Ignatius Junior again as Butch takes him from Little Isadore, and I am thinking that it is a good thing for Isadore that the baby cannot tell Big Butch what Isadore does to him.

"I put in just a little bit of a shot," Big Butch says, "and it will not make any more noise than snapping your fingers."

But a second later there is a big whoom from the office, and the whole joint shakes, and John Ignatius Junior laughs right out loud. The chances are he thinks it is the Fourth of July.

"I guess maybe I put in too big a charge," Big Butch says, and then he rushes into the office with Little Isadore and me after him, and John Ignatius Junior still laughing very heartily for a small baby. The door of the safe is swinging loose, and the whole joint looks somewhat wrecked, but Big Butch loses no time in getting his dukes into the safe and grabbing out two big bundles of cash money, which he sticks inside his shirt.

As we go into the street Harry the Horse and Spanish John come running up much excited, and Harry says to Big Butch like this:

"What are you trying to do," he says, "wake up the whole town?"

"Well," Butch says, "I guess maybe the charge is too strong, at that, but nobody seems to be coming, so you and Spanish John walk over to Eighth Avenue, and the rest of us will walk to Seventh, and if you go along quiet, like people minding their own business, it will be all right."

But I judge Little Isadore is tired of John Ignatius Junior's company by this time, because he says he will go with Harry the Horse and Spanish John, and this leaves Big Butch and John Ignatius Junior and me to go the other way. So we start moving, and all of a sudden two cops come tearing around the corner toward which Harry and Isadore and Spanish John are going. The chances are the cops hear the earthquake Big Butch lets off and are coming to investigate.

But the chances are, too, that if Harry the Horse and the other two keep on walking along very quietly like Butch tells them to, the coppers will pass them up entirely, because it is not likely that coppers will figure anybody to be opening safes with explosives in this neighborhood. But the minute Harry the Horse sees the coppers he loses his nut, and he outs with the old equalizer and starts blasting away, and what does Spanish John do but get his out, too, and open up.

The next thing anybody knows, the two coppers are down on the ground with slugs in them, but other coppers are coming from every which direction, blowing whistles and doing a little blasting themselves, and there is plenty of excitement, especially when the coppers who are not chasing Harry the Horse and Little Isadore and Spanish John start poking around the neighborhood and find Harry's pal, the watchman, all tied up nice and tight where Harry leaves him, and the watchman explains that some scoundrels blow open the safe he is watching.

All this time Big Butch and me are walking in the other direction toward Seventh Avenue, and Big Butch has John Ignatius in his arms, and John Ignatius is now squalling very loud, indeed. The chances are he is still thinking of the big whoom back there which tickles him so and is wishing to hear some more whooms. Anyway, he is beating his own best record for squalling, and as we go walking along Big Butch says to me like this:

"I dast not run," he says, "because if any coppers see me running they will start popping at me and maybe hit John Ignatius Junior, and besides running will joggle the milk up in him and make him sick. My old lady always warns me never to joggle John Ignatius Junior when he is full of milk."

"Well, Butch," I say, "there is no milk in me, and I do not care if I am joggled up, so if you do not mind, I will start doing a piece of running at the next corner."

But just then around the corner of Seventh Avenue toward which we are headed comes two or three coppers with a big fat sergeant with them, and one of the coppers, who is half out of breath as if he has been doing plenty of sprinting, is explaining to the sergeant that somebody blows a safe down the street and shoots a couple of coppers in the getaway.

And there is Big Butch, with John Ignatius Junior in his arms and twenty G's in his shirt front and a tough record behind him, walking right up to them.

I am feeling very sorry, indeed, for Big Butch, and very sorry for myself, too, and I am saying to myself that if I get out of this I will never associate with anyone but ministers of the gospel as long as I live. I can remember thinking that I am getting a better break than Butch, at that, because I will not have to go to Sing Sing for the rest of my life, like him, and I also remember wondering what they will give John Ignatius Junior, who is still tearing off these squalls, with Big Butch saying: "There, there, there, Daddy's itty woogleums." Then I hear one of the coppers say to the fat sergeant: "We better nail these guys. They may be in on this."

Well, I can see it is good-by to Butch and John Ignatius Junior and me, as the fat sergeant steps up to Big Butch, but instead of putting the arm on Butch, the fat sergeant only points at John Ignatius Junior and asks very sympathetic: "Teeth?"

"No," Big Butch says. "Not teeth. Colic. I just get the doctor here out of bed to do something for him, and we are going to a drug store to get some medicine."

Well, naturally I am very much surprised at this statement, because of course I am not a doctor, and if John Ignatius Junior has colic it serves him right, but I am only hoping they do not ask for my degree, when the fat sergeant says: "Too bad. I know what it is. I got three of them at home. But," he says, "it acts more like it is teeth than colic."

Then as Big Butch and John Ignatius Junior and me go on about our business I hear the fat sergeant say to the copper, very sarcastic: "Yea, of course a guy is out blowing safes with a baby in his arms! You will make a great detective, you will!"

I do not see Big Butch for several days after I learn that Harry the Horse and Little Isadore and Spanish John get back to Brooklyn all right, except they are a little nicked up here and there from the slugs the coppers toss at them, while the coppers they clip are not damaged so very much. Furthermore, the chances are I will not see Big Butch for several years, if it is left to me, but he comes looking for me one night, and he seems to be all pleasured up about something.

"Say," Big Butch says to me, "you know I never give a copper credit for knowing any too much about anything, but I wish to say that this fat sergeant we run into the other night is a very, very smart duck. He is right about it being teeth that is ailing John Ignatius Junior, for what happens yesterday but John cuts in his first tooth."

The Snatching of Bookie Bob

Now it comes on the spring of 1931, after a long hard winter, and times are very tough indeed, what with the stock market going all to pieces, and banks busting right and left, and the law getting very nasty about this and that, and one thing and another, and many citizens of this town are compelled to do the best they can.

There is very little scratch anywhere and along Broadway many citizens are wearing their last year's clothes and have practically nothing to bet on the races or anything else, and it is a condition that will touch anybody's heart.

So I am not surprised to hear rumors that the snatching of certain parties is going on in spots, because while snatching is by no means a high-class business, and is even considered somewhat illegal, it is something to tide over the hard times.

Furthermore, I am not surprised to hear that this snatching is being done by a character by the name of Harry the Horse, who comes from Brooklyn, and who is a character who does not care much what sort of business he is in, and who is mobbed up with other characters from Brooklyn such as Spanish John and Little Isadore, who do not care what sort of business they are in, either.

In fact, Harry the Horse and Spanish John and Little Isadore are very hard characters in every respect, and there is considerable indignation expressed around and about when they move over from Brooklyn into Manhattan and start snatching, because the citizens of Manhattan feel that if there is any snatching done in their territory, they are entitled to do it themselves.

But Harry the Horse and Spanish John and Little Isadore pay no attention whatever to local sentiment and
go on the snatch on a pretty fair scale, and by and by
I am hearing rumors of some very nice scores. These
scores are not extra large scores, to be sure, but they
are enough to keep the wolf from the door, and in fact
from three different doors, and before long Harry the
Horse and Spanish John and Little Isadore are around
the race tracks betting on the horses, because if there is
one thing they are all very fond of, it is betting on the
horses.

Now many citizens have the wrong idea entirely of
the snatching business. Many citizens think that all there
is to snatching is to round up the party who is to be
snatched and then just snatch him, putting him away
somewhere until his family or friends dig up enough
scratch to pay whatever price the snatchers are asking.
Very few citizens understand that the snatching business
must be well organized and very systematic.

In the first place, if you are going to do any snatching,
you cannot snatch just anybody. You must know who
you are snatching, because naturally it is no good snatching somebody who does not have any scratch to settle
with. And you cannot tell by the way a party looks or
how he lives in town if he has any scratch, because
many a party who is around in automobiles, and wearing
good clothes, and chucking quite a swell is nothing but
the phonus bolonus and does not have any real scratch
whatever.

So of course such a party is no good for snatching, and
of course guys who are on the snatch cannot go around
inquiring into bank accounts, or asking how much this
and that party has in a safe-deposit vault, because such
questions are apt to make citizens wonder why, and it
is very dangerous to get citizens to wondering why about
anything. So the only way guys who are on the snatch
can find out about parties worth snatching is to make a
connection with some guy who can put the finger on the
right party.

The finger guy must know the party he fingers has plenty of ready scratch to begin with, and he must also know that this party is such a party as is not apt to make too much disturbance about being snatched, such as telling the gendarmes. The party may be a legitimate party, such as a business guy, but he will have reasons why he does not wish it to get out that he is snatched, and the finger must know these reasons. Maybe the party is not leading the right sort of life, such as running around with blondes when he has an ever-loving wife and seven children in Mamaroneck, but does not care to have his habits known, as is apt to happen if he is snatched, especially if he is snatched when he is with a blonde.

And sometimes the party is such a party as does not care to have matches run up and down the bottom of his feet, which often happens to parties who are snatched and who do not seem to wish to settle their bill promptly, because many parties are very ticklish on the bottom of the feet, especially if the matches are lit. On the other hand, maybe the party is not a legitimate guy, such as a party who is running a crap game or a swell speakeasy, or who has some other dodge he does not care to have come out, and who also does not care about having his feet tickled.

Such a party is very good indeed for the snatching business, because he is pretty apt to settle without any argument. And after a party settles one snatching, it will be considered very unethical for anybody else to snatch him again very soon, so he is not likely to make any fuss about the matter. The finger guy gets a commission of twenty-five per cent of the settlement, and one and all are satisfied and much fresh scratch comes into circulation, which is very good for the merchants. And while the party who is snatched may know who snatches him, one thing he never knows is who puts the finger on him, this being considered a trade secret.

I am talking to Waldo Winchester, the newspaper scribe, one night and something about the snatching

business comes up, and Waldo Winchester is trying to
tell me that it is one of the oldest dodges in the world,
only Waldo calls it kidnaping, which is a title that will
be very repulsive to guys who are on the snatch nowadays. Waldo Winchester claims that hundreds of years
ago guys are around snatching parties, male and female,
and holding them for ransom, and furthermore Waldo
Winchester says they even snatch very little children
and Waldo states that it is all a very, very wicked proposition.

Well, I can see where Waldo is right about it being
wicked to snatch dolls and little children, but of course
no guys who are on the snatch nowadays will ever think
of such a thing, because who is going to settle for a doll
in these times when you can scarcely even give them
away? As for little children, they are apt to be a great
nuisance, because their mammas are sure to go running
around hollering bloody murder about them, and furthermore little children are very dangerous, indeed,
what with being apt to break out with measles and
mumps and one thing and another any minute and give
it to everybody in the neighborhood.

Well, anyway, knowing that Harry the Horse and
Spanish John and Little Isadore are now on the snatch,
I am by no means pleased to see them come along one
Tuesday evening when I am standing at the corner of
Fiftieth and Broadway, although of course I give them
a very jolly hello, and say I hope and trust they are feel-
ing nicely.

They stand there talking to me a few minutes, and *I*
am very glad indeed that Johnny Brannigan, the strong-
arm cop, does not happen along and see us, because it
will give Johnny a very bad impression of me to see me
in such company, even though I am not responsible for
the company. But naturally I cannot haul off and walk
away from this company at once, because Harry the
Horse and Spanish John and Little Isadore may get the
idea that I am playing the chill for them, and will feel
hurt.

"Well," I say to Harry the Horse, "how are things going, Harry?"

"They are going no good," Harry says. "We do not beat a race in four days. In fact," he says, "we go overboard today. We are washed out. We owe every bookmaker at the track that will trust us, and now we are out trying to raise some scratch to pay off. A guy must pay his bookmaker no matter what."

Well, of course this is very true, indeed, because if a guy does not pay his bookmaker it will lower his business standing quite some, as the bookmaker is sure to go around putting the blast on him, so I am pleased to hear Harry the Horse mention such honorable principles.

"By the way," Harry says, "do you know a guy by the name of Bookie Bob?"

Now I do not know Bookie Bob personally, but of course I know who Bookie Bob is, and so does everybody else in this town that ever goes to a race track, because Bookie Bob is the biggest bookmaker around and about, and has plenty of scratch. Furthermore, it is the opinion of one and all that Bookie Bob will die with this scratch, because he is considered a very close guy with his scratch. In fact, Bookie Bob is considered closer than a dead heat.

He is a short fat guy with a bald head, and his head is always shaking a little from side to side, which some say is a touch of palsy, but which most citizens believe comes of Bookie Bob shaking his head "No" to guys asking for credit in betting on the races. He has an ever-loving wife, who is a very quiet little old doll with gray hair and a very sad look in her eyes, but nobody can blame her for this when they figure that she lives with Bookie Bob for many years.

I often see Bookie Bob and his ever-loving wife eating in different joints along in the Forties, because they seem to have no home except a hotel, and many a time I hear Bookie Bob giving her a going-over about something or other, and generally it is about the price of something she orders to eat, so I judge Bookie Bob is

as tough with his ever-loving wife about scratch as he
is with everybody else. In fact, I hear him bawling her
out one night because she has on a new hat which she
says costs her six bucks, and Bookie Bob wishes to know
if she is trying to ruin him with her extravagances.

But of course I am not criticizing Bookie Bob for
squawking about the hat, because for all I know six
bucks may be too much for a doll to pay for a hat, at that.
And furthermore, maybe Bookie Bob has the right idea
about keeping down his ever-loving wife's appetite, because I know many a guy in this town who is practically
ruined by dolls eating too much on him.

"Well," I say to Harry the Horse, "if Bookie Bob is
one of the bookmakers you owe, I am greatly surprised
to see that you seem to have both eyes in your head,
because I never before hear of Bookie Bob letting anybody owe him without giving him at least one of their
eyes for security. In fact," I say, "Bookie Bob is such a
guy as will not give you the right time if he has two
watches."

"No," Harry the Horse says, "we do not owe Bookie
Bob. But," he says, "he will be owing us before long.
We are going to put the snatch on Bookie Bob."

Well, this is most disquieting news to me, not because
I care if they snatch Bookie Bob or not, but because
somebody may see me talking to them who will remember about it when Bookie Bob is snatched. But of course
it will not be good policy for me to show Harry the
Horse and Spanish John and Little Isadore that I am
nervous, so I only speak as follows:

"Harry," I say, "every man knows his own business
best, and I judge you know what you are doing. But," I
say, "you are snatching a hard guy when you snatch
Bookie Bob. A very hard guy, indeed. In fact," I say,
"I hear the softest thing about him is his front teeth,
so it may be very difficult for you to get him to settle
after you snatch him."

"No," Harry the Horse says, "we will have no trouble
about it. Our finger gives us Bookie Bob's hole card,

and it is a most surprising thing, indeed. But," Harry the Horse says, "you come upon many surprising things in human nature when you are on the snatch. Bookie Bob's hole card is his ever-loving wife's opinion of him.

"You see," Harry the Horse says, "Bookie Bob has been putting himself away with his ever-loving wife for years as a very important guy in this town, with much power and influence, although of course Bookie Bob knows very well he stands about as good as a broken leg. In fact," Harry the Horse says, "Bookie Bob figures that his ever-loving wife is the only one in the world who looks on him as a big guy, and he will sacrifice even his scratch, or anyway some of it, rather than let her know that guys have such little respect for him as to put the snatch on him. It is what you call psychology," Harry the Horse says.

Well, this does not make good sense to me, and I am thinking to myself that the psychology that Harry the Horse really figures to work out nice on Bookie Bob is tickling his feet with matches, but I am not anxious to stand there arguing about it, and pretty soon I bid them all good evening, very polite, and take the wind, and I do not see Harry the Horse or Spanish John or Little Isadore again for a month.

In the meantime, I hear gossip here and there that Bookie Bob is missing for several days, and when he finally shows up again he gives it out that he is very sick during his absence, but I can put two and two together as well as anybody in this town and I figure that Bookie Bob is snatched by Harry the Horse and Spanish John and Little Isadore, and the chances are it costs him plenty.

So I am looking for Harry the Horse and Spanish John and Little Isadore to be around the race track with plenty of scratch and betting them higher than a cat's back, but they never show up, and what is more I hear they leave Manhattan and are back in Brooklyn working every day handling beer. Naturally this is very surprising to me, because the way things are running, beer is a tough dodge just now, and there is very little profit in same, and I figure that with the scratch they must make off Bookie Bob, Harry the Horse and Spanish John and Little Isadore have a right to be taking things easy.

Now one night I am in Good Time Charley Bernstein's little speak in Forty-eighth Street, talking of this and that with Charley, when in comes Harry the Horse looking very weary and by no means prosperous. Naturally I gave him a large hello, and by and by we get to gabbing together and I ask him whatever becomes of the Bookie Bob matter, and Harry the Horse tells me as follows:

Yes [Harry the Horse says], we snatch Bookie Bob all right. In fact, we snatch him the very next night after we are talking to you, or on a Wednesday night. Our finger tells us Bookie Bob is going to a wake over in his old neighborhood on Tenth Avenue, near Thirty-eighth Street, and this is where we pick him up.

He is leaving the place in his car along about midnight, and of course Bookie Bob is alone as he seldom lets anybody ride with him because of the wear and tear on his car cushions, and Little Isadore swings our flivver in front of him and makes him stop. Naturally Bookie Bob is greatly surprised when I poke my head into his car and tell him I wish the pleasure of his company for a short time, and at first he is inclined to argue the matter, saying I must make a mistake, but I put the old convincer on him by letting him peek down the snozzle of my John Roscoe.

We lock his car and throw the keys away, and then we take Bookie Bob in our car and go to a certain spot on Eighth Avenue where we have a nice little apartment all ready. When we get there I tell Bookie Bob that he can call up anybody he wishes and state that the snatch is on him and that it will require twenty-five G's, cash money, to take it off, but of course I also tell Bookie Bob that he is not to mention where he is or something may happen to him.

Well, I will say one thing for Bookie Bob, although

everybody is always weighing in the sacks on him and saying he is no good—he takes it like a gentleman, and very calm and businesslike.

Furthermore, he does not seem alarmed, as many citizens are when they find themselves in such a situation. He recognizes the justice of our claim at once, saying as follows:

"I will telephone my partner, Sam Salt," he says. "He is the only one I can think of who is apt to have such a sum as twenty-five G's cash money. But," he says, "if you gentlemen will pardon the question, because this is a new experience to me, how do I know everything will be okay for me after you get the scratch?"

"Why," I say to Bookie Bob, somewhat indignant, "it is well known to one and all in this town that my word is my bond. There are two things I am bound to do," I say, "and one is to keep my word in such a situation as this, and the other is to pay anything I owe a bookmaker, no matter what, for these are obligations of honor with me."

"Well," Bookie Bob says, "of course I do not know you gentlemen, and, in fact, I do not remember ever seeing any of you, although your face is somewhat familiar, but if you pay your bookmaker you are an honest guy, and one in a million. In fact," Bookie Bob says, "if I have all the scratch that is owing to me around this town, I will not be telephoning anybody for such a sum as twenty-five G's. I will have such a sum in my pants pocket for change."

Now Bookie Bob calls a certain number and talks to somebody there but he does not get Sam Salt, and he seems much disappointed when he hangs up the receiver again.

"This is a very tough break for me," he says. "Sam Salt goes to Atlantic City an hour ago on very important business and will not be back until tomorrow evening, and they do not know where he is to stay in Atlantic City. And," Bookie Bob says, "I cannot think of anybody else to call to get this scratch, especially anybody I will care to have know I am in this situation."

"Why not call your ever-loving wife?" I say. "Maybe she can dig up this kind of scratch."

"Say," Bookie Bob says, "you do not suppose I am chump enough to give my ever-loving wife twenty-five G's, belonging to me, do you? I give my ever-loving wife ten bucks per week for spending money," Bookie Bob says, "and this is enough scratch for any doll, especially when you figure I pay for her meals."

Well, there seems to be nothing we can do except wait until Sam Salt gets back, but we let Bookie Bob call his ever-loving wife, as Bookie Bob says he does not wish to have her worrying about his absence, and tells her a big lie about having to go to Jersey City to sit up with a sick Brother Elk.

Well, it is now nearly four o'clock in the morning, so we put Bookie Bob in a room with Little Isadore to sleep, although, personally, I consider making a guy sleep with Little Isadore very cruel treatment, and Spanish John and I take turns keeping awake and watching out that Bookie Bob does not take the air on us before paying us off. To tell the truth, Little Isadore and Spanish John are somewhat disappointed that Bookie Bob agrees to settle so promptly, because they are looking forward to tickling his feet with great relish.

Now Bookie Bob turns out to be very good company when he wakes up the next morning, because he knows a lot of race-track stories and plenty of scandal, and he keeps us much interested at breakfast. He talks along with us as if he knows us all his life, and he seems very nonchalant indeed, but the chances are he will not be so nonchalant if I tell him about Spanish John's thought.

Well, about noon Spanish John goes out of the apartment and comes back with a racing sheet, because he knows Little Isadore and I will be wishing to know what is running in different spots although we do not have anything to bet on these races, or any way of betting on them, because we are overboard with every bookmaker we know.

Now Bookie Bob is also much interested in the matter of what is running, especially at Belmont, and he is bending over the table with me and Spanish John and Little Isadore, looking at the sheet, when Spanish John speaks as follows:

"My goodness," Spanish John says, "a spot such as this fifth race with Questionnaire at four to five is like finding money in the street. I only wish I have a few bobs to bet on him at such a price," Spanish John says.

"Why," Bookie Bob says, very polite, "if you gentlemen wish to bet on these races I will gladly book to you. It is a good way to pass away the time while we are waiting for Sam Salt, unless you will rather play pinochle?"

"But," I say, "we have no scratch to play the races, at least not much."

"Well," Bookie Bob says, "I will take your markers, because I hear what you say about always paying your bookmaker, and you put yourself away with me as an honest guy, and these other gentlemen also impress me as honest guys."

Now what happens but we begin betting Bookie Bob on the different races, not only at Belmont, but at all the other tracks in the country, for Little Isadore and Spanish John and I are guys who like plenty of action when we start betting on the horses. We write out markers for whatever we wish to bet and hand them to Bookie Bob, and Bookie Bob sticks these markers in an inside pocket, and along in the late afternoon it looks as if he has a tumor on his chest.

We get the race results by phone off a poolroom downtown as fast as they come off, and also the prices, and it is a lot of fun, and Little Isadore and Spanish John and Bookie Bob and I are all little pals together until all the races are over and Bookie Bob takes out the markers and starts counting himself up.

It comes out then that I owe Bookie Bob ten G's,

and Spanish John owes him six G's, and Little Isadore owes him four G's, as Little Isadore beats him a couple of races out west.

Well, about this time, Bookie Bob manages to get Sam Salt on the phone, and explains to Sam that he is to go to a certain safe-deposit box and get out twenty-five G's and then wait until midnight and hire himself a taxicab and start riding around the block between Fifty-first and Fifty-second, from Eighth to Ninth Avenues, and to keep riding until somebody flags the cab and takes the scratch off him.

Naturally Sam Salt understands right away that the snatch is on Bookie Bob, and he agrees to do as he is told, but he says he cannot do it until the following night because he knows there is not twenty-five G's in the box and he will have to get the difference at the track the next day. So there we are with another day in the apartment and Spanish John and Little Isadore and I are just as well pleased because Bookie Bob has us hooked and we naturally wish to wiggle off.

But the next day is worse than ever. In all the years I am playing the horses I never have such a tough day, and Spanish John and Little Isadore are just as bad. In fact, we are all going so bad that Bookie Bob seems to feel sorry for us and often lays us a couple of points above the track prices, but it does no good. At the end of the day, I am in a total of twenty G's, while Spanish John owes fifteen, and Little Isadore fifteen, a total of fifty G's among the three of us. But we are never any hands to hold postmortems on bad days, so Little Isadore goes out to a delicatessen store and lugs in a lot of nice things to eat, and we have a fine dinner, and then we sit around with Bookie Bob telling stories, and even singing songs together until time to meet Sam Salt.

When it comes on midnight Spanish John goes off and lays for Sam, and gets a little valise off Sam Salt. Then Spanish John comes back to the apartment and we open the valise and the twenty-five G's are there okay, and we cut this scratch three ways.

Then I tell Bookie Bob he is free to go about his business, and good luck to him, at that, but Bookie Bob looks at me as if he is very much surprised, and hurt, and says to me like this:

"Well, gentlemen, thank you for your courtesy, but what about the scratch you owe me? What about these markers? Surely, gentlemen, you will pay your bookmaker?"

Well, of course we owe Bookie these markers, all right, and of course a man must pay his bookmaker, no matter what, so I hand over my bit and Bookie Bob puts down something in a little notebook that he takes out of his kick.

Then Spanish John and Little Isadore hand over their dough, too, and Bookie Bob puts down something more in the little notebook.

"Now," Bookie Bob says, "I credit each of your accounts with these payments, but you gentlemen still owe me a matter of twenty-five G's over and above the twenty-five I credit you with, and I hope and trust you will make arrangements to settle this at once because," he says, "I do not care to extend such accommodations over any considerable period."

"But," I say, "we do not have any more scratch after paying you the twenty-five G's on account."

"Listen," Bookie Bob says, dropping his voice down to a whisper, "what about putting the snatch on my partner, Sam Salt, and I will wait over a couple of days with you and keep booking to you, and maybe you can pull yourselves out. But of course," Bookie Bob whispers, "I will be entitled to twenty-five per cent of the snatch for putting the finger on Sam for you."

But Spanish John and Little Isadore are sick and tired of Bookie Bob and will not listen to staying in the apartment any longer, because they say he is a jinx to them and they cannot beat him in any manner, shape or form. Furthermore, I am personally anxious to get away because something Bookie Bob says reminds me of something.

It reminds me that besides the scratch we owe him, we forget to take out six G's two-fifty for the party who puts the finger on Bookie Bob for us, and this is a very serious matter indeed, because everybody will tell you that failing to pay a finger is considered a very dirty trick. Furthermore, if it gets around that you fail to pay a finger, nobody else will ever finger for you.

So [Harry the Horse says] we quit the snatching business because there is no use continuing while this obligation is outstanding against us, and we go back to Brooklyn to earn enough scratch to pay our just debts.

We are paying off Bookie Bob's IOU a little at a time, because we do not wish to ever have anybody say we welsh on a bookmaker, and furthermore we are paying off the six G's two-fifty commission we owe our finger.

And while it is tough going, I am glad to say our honest effort is doing somebody a little good, because I see Bookie Bob's ever-loving wife the other night all dressed up in new clothes, very happy indeed.

And while a guy is telling me she is looking so happy because she gets a large legacy from an uncle who dies in Switzerland, and is now independent of Bookie Bob, I only hope and trust [Harry the Horse says] that it never gets out that our finger in this case is nobody but Bookie Bob's ever-loving wife.

The Lily of St. Pierre

There are four of us sitting in Good Time Charley Bernstein's little joint in Forty-eighth Street one Tuesday morning about four o'clock, doing a bit of quartet singing, very low, so as not to disturb the copper on the beat outside, a very good guy by the name of Carrigan, who likes to get his rest at such an hour.

Good Time Charley's little joint is called the Crystal Room, although of course there is no crystal whatever in the room, but only twelve tables, and twelve hostesses, because Good Time Charley believes in his customers having plenty of social life.

So he has one hostess to a table, and if there are twelve different customers, which is very seldom, each customer has a hostess to talk with. And if there is only one customer, he has all twelve hostesses to gab with and buy drinks for, and no customer can ever go away claiming he is lonesome in Good Time Charley's.

Personally, I will not give you a nickel to talk with Good Time Charley's hostesses, one at a time or all together, because none of them are anything much to look at, and I figure they must be all pretty dumb or they will not be working as hostesses in Good Time Charley's little joint. I happen to speak of this to Good Time Charley, and he admits that I may be right, but he says it is very difficult to get any Peggy Joyces for twenty-five bobs per week.

Of course I never buy any drinks in Good Time Charley's for hostesses, or anybody else, and especially for myself, because I am a personal friend of Good Time Charley's, and he will not sell me any drinks even if I wish to buy any, which is unlikely, as Good Time Charley figures that anybody who buys drinks in his place is apt to drink these drinks, and Charley does not care to see any of his personal friends drinking drinks in his place. If one of his personal friends wishes to buy a drink, Charley always sends him to Jack Fogarty's little speak down the street, and in fact Charley will generally go with him.

So I only go to Good Time Charley's to talk with him, and to sing in quartet with him. There are very seldom any customers in Good Time Charley's until along about five o'clock in the morning after all the other places are closed, and then it is sometimes a very hot spot indeed, and it is no place to sing in quartet at such hours, because everybody around always wishes to join in, and it

ruins the harmony. But just before five o'clock it is okay,
as only the hostesses are there, and of course none of
them dast to join in our singing, or Good Time Charley
will run them plumb out of the joint.

If there is one thing I love to do more than anything
else, it is to sing in quartet. I sing baritone, and I wish
to say I sing a very fine baritone, at that. And what we
are singing—this morning I am talking about—is a lot of
songs such as "Little White Lies," and "The Old Oaken
Bucket," and "My Dad's Dinner Pail," and "Chloe,"
and "Melancholy Baby," and I do not know what else,
including "Home, Sweet Home," although we do not go
so good on this because nobody remembers all the
words, and half the time we are all just going ho-hum-
hum-ho-hum-hum, like guys nearly always do when they
are singing "Home, Sweet Home."

Also we sing "I Can't Give You Anything but Love,
Baby," which is a very fine song for quartet singing, especially when you have a guy singing a nice bass, such
as Good Time Charley, who can come in on every line
with a big bum-bum, like this:

> *I can't give you anything but luh-huh-vuh,*
> *Bay-hay-bee!*
> *BUM-BUM!*

I am the one who holds these last words, such as love,
and baby, and you can hear my fine baritone very far
indeed, especially when I give a little extra roll like bay-
hay-ay-ay-BEE! Then when Good Time Charley comes
in with his old bum-bum, it is worth going a long way
to hear.

Well, naturally, we finally get around to torch songs,
as guys who are singing in quartet are bound to do, especially at four o'clock in the morning, a torch song being
a song which guys sing when they have the big burned-
up feeling inside themselves over a battle with their
dolls.

When a guy has a battle with his doll, such as his

sweetheart, or even his ever-loving wife, he certainly
feels burned up inside himself, and can scarcely think of
anything much. In fact, I know guys who are carrying
the torch to walk ten miles and never know they go an
inch. It is surprising how much ground a guy can cover
just walking around and about, wondering if his doll is
out with some other guy, and everybody knows that at
four o'clock in the morning the torch is hotter than at
any other time of the day.

Good Time Charley, who is carrying a torch longer
than anybody else on Broadway, which is nearly a year,
or ever since his doll, Big Marge, gives him the wind for
a rich Cuban, starts up a torch song by Tommy Lyman,
which goes as follows, very, very slow, and sad:

> *Gee, but it's tough*
> *When the gang's gone home.*
> *Out on the corner*
> *You stand alone.*

Of course there is no spot in this song for Good Time
Charley's bum-bum, but it gives me a great chance with
my fine baritone, especially when I come to the line that
says Gee, I wish I had my old gal back again.

I do not say I can make people bust out crying and
give me money with this song like I see Tommy Lyman
do in night clubs, but then Tommy is a professional
singer, besides writing this song for himself, so naturally
he figures to do a little better with it than me. But I wish
to say it is nothing for me to make five or six of the hostesses in Good Time Charley's cry all over the joint when
I hit this line about Gee, I wish I had my old gal back
again, and making five or six hostesses out of twelve cry
is a fair average anywhere, and especially Good Time
Charley's hostesses.

Well, all of a sudden who comes popping into Good
Time Charley's by way of the front door, looking here
and there, and around and about, but Jack O'Hearts,
and he no sooner pokes his snozzle into the joint than a

guy by the name of Louie the Lug, who is singing a very fair tenor with us, jumps up and heads for the back door.

But just as he gets to the door, Jack O'Hearts outs with the old equalizer and goes whangity-whang-whang at Louie the Lug. As a general proposition, Jack O'Hearts is a fair kind of a shot, but all he does to Louie the Lug is to knock his right ear off. Then Louie gets the back door open and takes it on the lam through an areaway, but not before Jack O'Hearts gets one more crack at him, and it is this last crack which brings Louie down half an hour later on Broadway, where a copper finds him and sends him to the Polyclinic.

Personally, I do not see Louie's ear knocked off, because by the second shot I am out the front door, and on my way down Forty-eighth Street, but they tell me about it afterwards.

I never know Jack O'Hearts is even mad at Louie, and I am wondering why he takes these shots at him, but I do not ask any questions, because when a guy goes around asking questions in this town people may get the idea he is such a guy as wishes to find things out.

Then the next night I run into Jack O'Hearts in Bobby's chophouse, putting on the hot meat, and he asks me to sit down and eat with him, so I sit down and order a hamburger steak, with plenty of onions, and while I am sitting there waiting for my hamburger, Jack O'Hearts says to me like this:

"I suppose," he says, "I owe you guys an apology for busting up your quartet when I toss those slugs at Louie the Lug?"

"Well," I say, "some considers it a dirty trick at that, Jack, but I figure you have a good reason, although I am wondering what it is."

"Louie the Lug is no good," Jack says.

Well, of course I know this much already, and so does everybody else in town for that matter, but I cannot figure what it has to do with Jack shooting off ears in this town for such a reason, or by and by there will be very few people left with ears.

"Let me tell you about Louie the Lug," Jack O'Hearts says. "You will see at once that my only mistake is I do not get my shots an inch to the left. I do not know what is the matter with me lately."

"Maybe you are letting go too quick," I say, very sympathetic, because I know how it annoys him to blow easy shots.

"Maybe," he says. "Anyway, the light in Charley's dump is no good. It is only an accident I get Louie with the last shot, and it is very sloppy work all around. But now I will tell you about Louie the Lug."

It is back in 1924 [Jack O'Hearts says] that I go to St. Pierre for the first time to look after some business matters for John the Boss, rest his soul, who is at this time one of the largest operators in high-grade merchandise in the United States, especially when it comes to Scotch. Maybe you remember John the Boss, and the heat which develops around and about when he is scragged in Detroit? John the Boss is a very fine character, and it is a terrible blow to many citizens when he is scragged.

Now if you are never in St. Pierre, I wish to say you miss nothing much, because what is it but a little squirt of a burg sort of huddled up alongside some big rocks off Newfoundland, and very hard to get to, any way you go. Mostly you go there from Halifax by boat, though personally I go there in 1924 in John the Boss's schooner by the name of the *Maude,* in which we load a thousand cases of very nice merchandise for the Christmas trade.

The first time I see St. Pierre I will not give you eight cents for the whole layout, although of course it is very useful to parties in our line of business. It does not look like much, and it belongs to France, and nearly all the citizens speak French, because most of them are French, and it seems it is the custom of the French people to speak French no matter where they are, even away off up yonder among the fish.

Well, anyway, it is on this trip to St. Pierre in 1924

that I meet an old guy by the name of Doctor Armand Dorval, for what happens to me but I catch pneumonia, and it looks as if maybe I am a gone gosling, especially as there is no place in St. Pierre where a guy can have pneumonia with any comfort. But this Doctor Armand Dorval is a friend of John the Boss, and he takes me into his house and lets me be as sick there as I please, while he does his best to doctor me up.

Now this Doctor Armand Dorval is an old Frenchman with whiskers, and he has a little granddaughter by the name of Lily, who is maybe twelve years old at the time I am talking about, with her hair hanging down her back in two braids. It seems her papa, who is Doctor Armand's son, goes out one day looking for cod on the Grand Banks when Lily is nothing but a baby, and never comes back, and then her mamma dies, so old Doc raises up Lily and is very fond of her indeed.

They live alone in the house where I am sick with this pneumonia, and it is a nice, quiet little house and very old-fashioned, with a good view of the fishing boats, if you care for fishing boats. In fact, it is the quietest place I am ever in in my life, and the only place I ever know any real peace. A big fat old doll who does not talk English comes in every day to look after things for Doctor Armand and Lily, because it seems Lily is not old enough to keep house as yet, although she makes quite a nurse for me.

Lily talks English very good, and she is always bringing me things, and sitting by my bed and chewing the rag with me about this and that, and sometimes she reads to me out of a book which is called *Alice in Wonderland,* and which is nothing but a pack of lies, but very interesting in spots. Furthermore, Lily has a big, blond, dumb-looking doll by the name of Yvonne, which she makes me hold while she is reading to me, and I am very glad indeed that the *Maude* goes on back to the United States and there is no danger of any of the guys walking in on me while I am holding this doll, or they will think I blow my topper.

Finally, when I am able to sit up around the house of an evening I play checkers with Lily, while old Doctor Armand Dorval sits back in a rocking chair, smoking a pipe and watching us, and sometimes I sing for her. I wish to say I sing a first-class tenor, and when I am in the war business in France with the Seventy-seventh Division I am always in great demand for singing a quartet. So I sing such songs to Lily as "There's a Long, Long Trail," and "Mademoiselle from Armentières," although of course when it comes to certain spots in this song I just go dum-dum-dee-dum and do not say the words right out.

By and by Lily gets to singing with me, and we sound very good together, especially when we sing the "Long, Long Trail," which Lily likes very much, and even old Doctor Armand joins in now and then, although his voice is very terrible. Anyway, Lily and me and Doctor Armand become very good pals indeed, and what is more I meet up with other citizens of St. Pierre and become friends with them, and they are by no means bad people to know, and it is certainly a nice thing to be able to walk up and down without being afraid every other guy you meet is going to chuck a slug at you, or a copper put the old sleeve on you and say that they wish to see you at headquarters.

Finally I get rid of this pneumonia and take the boat to Halifax, and I am greatly surprised to find that Doctor Armand and Lily are very sorry to see me go, because never before in my life do I leave a place where anybody is sorry to see me go.

But Doctor Armand seems very sad and shakes me by the hand over and over again, and what does Lily do but bust out crying, and the first thing I know I am feeling sad myself and wishing that I am not going. So I promise Doctor Armand I will come back some day to see him, and then Lily hauls off and gives me a big kiss right in the smush and this astonishes me so much that it is half an hour afterwards before I think to wipe it off.

Well, for the next few months I find myself pretty

busy back in New York, what with one thing and another, and I do not have time to think much of Doctor
Armand Dorval and Lily, and St. Pierre, but it comes
along the summer of 1925, and I am all tired out from
getting a slug in my chest in the run-in with Jerk Dono-
van's mob in Jersey, for I am now in beer and have no
more truck with the boats.

But I get to thinking of St. Pierre and the quiet little
house of Doctor Armand Dorval again, and how peaceful it is up there, and nothing will do but what I must
pop off to Halifax, and pretty soon I am in St. Pierre
once more. I take a raft of things for Lily with me, such
as dolls, and handkerchiefs, and perfume, and a phono-
graph, and also a set of razors for Doctor Armand, although afterwards I am sorry I take these razors because
I remember the old Doc does not shave and may take
them as a hint I do not care for his whiskers. But as it
turns out the Doc finds them very useful in operations,
so the razors are a nice gift after all.

Well, I spend two peaceful weeks there again, walking up and down in the daytime and playing checkers
and singing with Lily in the evening, and it is tough tearing myself away, especially as Doctor Armand Dorval
looks very sad again and Lily bursts out crying, louder
than before. So nearly every year after this I can hardly
wait until I can get to St. Pierre for a vacation, and Doctor Armand Dorval's house is like my home, only more
peaceful.

Now in the summer of 1928 I am in Halifax on my
way to St. Pierre, when I run across Louie the Lug, and
it seems Louie is a lammister out of Detroit on account
of some job or other, and is broke, and does not know
which way to turn. Personally, I always figure Louie a
petty-larceny kind of guy, with no more moxie than a
canary bird, but he always dresses well, and always has
a fair line of guff, and some guys stand for him. Anyway,
here he is in trouble, so what happens but I take him
with me to St. Pierre, figuring he can lay dead there until
things blow over.

Well, Lily and old Doctor Armand Dorval are certainly glad to see me, and I am just as glad to see them, especially Lily, for she is now maybe sixteen years old and as pretty a doll as ever steps in shoe leather, what with her long black hair, and her big black eyes, and a million dollars' worth of personality. Furthermore, by this time she swings a very mean skillet, indeed, and gets me up some very tasty fodder out of fish and one thing and another.

But somehow things are not like they used to be at St. Pierre with this guy Louie the Lug around, because he does not care for the place whatever, and goes roaming about very restless, and making cracks about the citizens, and especially the dolls, until one night I am compelled to tell him to keep his trap closed, although at that the dolls in St. Pierre, outside of Lily, are no such lookers as will get Ziegfeld heated up.

But even in the time when St. Pierre is headquarters for many citizens of the United States who are in the business of handling merchandise out of there, it is always sort of underhand that such citizens will never have any truck with the dolls at St. Pierre. This is partly because the dolls at St. Pierre never give the citizens of the United States a tumble, but more because we do not wish to get in any trouble around there, and if there is anything apt to cause trouble it is dolls.

Now I suppose if I have any brains I will see that Louie is playing the warm for Lily, but I never think of Lily as anything but a little doll with her hair in braids, and certainly not a doll such as a guy will start pitching to, especially a guy who calls himself one of the mob.

I notice Louie is always talking to Lily when he gets a chance, and sometimes he goes walking up and down with her, but I see nothing in this, because after all any guy is apt to get lonesome at St. Pierre and go walking up and down with anybody, even a little young doll. In fact, I never see Louie do anything that strikes me as out of line, except he tries to cut in on the singing between Lily and me, until I tell him one tenor at a time

is enough in any singing combination. Personally, I consider Louie the Lug's tenor very flat, indeed.

Well, it comes time for me to go away, and I take
Louie with me, because I do not wish him hanging
around St. Pierre alone, especially as old Doctor Armand
Dorval does not seem to care for him whatever, and
while Lily seems as sad as ever to see me go I notice that
for the first time she does not kiss me good-bye. But I
figure this is fair enough, as she is now quite a young
lady, and the chances are a little particular about who
she kisses.

I leave Louie in Halifax and give him enough dough
to go on to Denver, which is where he says he wishes to
go, and I never see him again until the other night in
Good Time Charley's. But almost a year later, when I
happen to be in Montreal, I hear of him. I am standing
in the lobby of the Mount Royal Hotel thinking of not
much, when a guy by the name of Bob the Bookie, who
is a hustler around the race tracks, gets to talking to me
and mentions Louie's name. It brings back to me a memory of my last trip to St. Pierre, and I get to thinking that
this is the longest stretch I ever go in several years without a visit there and of the different things that keep me
from going.

I am not paying much attention to what Bob says because he is putting the blast on Louie for running away
from an ever-loving wife and a couple of kids in Cleveland several years before, which is something I do not
know about Louie, at that. Then I hear Bob saying like
this:

"He is an awful rat any way you take him. Why, when
he hops out of here two weeks ago, he leaves a little doll
he brings with him from St. Pierre dying in a hospital
without a nickel to her name. It is a sin and a shame."

"Wait a minute, Bob," I say, waking up all of a sudden. "Do you say a doll from St. Pierre? What-for looking kind of a doll, Bob?" I say.

"Why," Bob says, "she is black-haired, and very
young, and he calls her Lily, or some such. He is knock-

ing around Canada with her for quite a spell. She strikes me as a t.b., but Louie's dolls always look this way after he has them a while. I judge," Bob says, "that Louie does not feed them any too good."

Well, it is Lily Dorval, all right, but never do I see such a change in anybody as there is in the poor little doll I find lying on a bed in a charity ward in a Montreal hospital. She does not look to weigh more than fifty pounds, and her black eyes are sunk away back in her head, and she is in tough shape generally. But she knows me right off the bat and tries to smile at me.

I am in the money very good at this time, and I have Lily moved into a private room, and get her all the nurses the law allows, and the best croakers in Montreal, and flowers, and one thing and another, but one of the medicos tells me it is even money she will not last three weeks, and seven to five she does not go a month. Finally Lily tells me what happens, which is the same thing that happens to a million dolls before and will happen to a million dolls again. Louie never leaves Halifax, but cons her into coming over there to him, and she goes because she loves him, for this is the way dolls are, and personally I will never have them any other way.

"But," Lily whispers to me, "the bad, bad thing I do is to tell poor old Grandfather I am going to meet you, Jack O'Hearts, and marry you, because I know he does not like Louie and will never allow me to go to him. But he loves you, Jack O'Hearts, and he is so pleased in thinking you are to be his son. It is wrong to tell Grandfather this story, and wrong to use your name, and to keep writing him all this time making him think I am your wife, and with you, but I love Louie, and I wish Grandfather to be happy because he is very, very old. Do you understand, Jack O'Hearts?"

Now of course all this is very surprising news to me, indeed, and in fact I am quite flabbergasted, and as for understanding it, all I understand is she got a rotten deal from Louie the Lug and that old Doctor Armand Dorval is going to be all busted up if he hears what really hap-

pens. And thinking about this nice old man, and thinking of how the only place I ever know peace and quiet
is now ruined, I am very angry with Louie the Lug.

But this is something to be taken up later, so I dismiss
him from my mind, and go out and get me a marriage
license and a priest, and have this priest marry me to
Lily Dorval just two days before she looks up at me for
the last time, and smiles a little smile, and then closes
her eyes for good and all. I wish to say, however, that
up to this time I have no more idea of getting myself a
wife than I have of jumping out the window, which is
practically no idea at all.

I take her body back to St. Pierre myself in person,
and we bury her in a little cemetery there, with a big fog
around and about, and the siren moaning away very sad,
and old Doctor Armand Dorval whispers to me like this:
"You will please to sing the song about the long trail,
Jack O'Hearts."

So I stand there in the fog, the chances are looking
like a big sap, and I sing as follows:

> *There's a long, long, trail a-winding*
> *Into the land of my dreams,*
> *Where the nightingale is singing,*
> *And the white moon beams.*

But I can get no farther than this, for something comes
up in my throat, and I sit down by the grave of Mrs.
Jack O'Hearts, who was Lily Dorval, and for the first
time I remember I bust out crying.

So this is why I say Louie the Lug is no good.

Well, I am sitting there thinking that Jack O'Hearts is
right about Louie, at that, when in comes Jack's chauffeur, a guy by the name of Fingers, and he steps up to
Jack and says, very low: "Louie dies half an hour ago
at the Polyclinic."

"What does he say before he goes?" Jack asks.

"Not a peep," Fingers says.

"Well," Jack O'Hearts says, "it is sloppy work, at that. I ought to get him the first crack. But maybe he has a chance to think a little of Lily Dorval."

Then he turns to me and says like this:

"You guys need not feel bad about losing your tenor, because," he says, "I will be glad to fill in for him at all times."

Personally I do not think Jack's tenor is as good as Louie the Lug's, especially when it comes to hitting the very high notes in such songs as "Sweet Adeline," because he does not hold them long enough to let Good Time Charley in with his bum-bum.

But of course this does not go if Jack O'Hearts hears it, as I am never sure he does not clip Louie the Lug just to get a place in our quartet, at that.

Hold 'Em, Yale!

What I am doing in New Haven on the day of a very large football game between the Harvards and the Yales is something which calls for quite a little explanation, because I am not such a guy as you will expect to find in New Haven at any time, and especially on the day of a large football game.

But there I am, and the reason I am there goes back to a Friday night when I am sitting in Mindy's restaurant on Broadway thinking of very little except how I can get hold of a few potatoes to take care of the old overhead. And while I am sitting there, who comes in but Sam the Gonoph, who is a ticket speculator by trade, and who seems to be looking all around and about.

Well, Sam the Gonoph gets to talking to me, and it turns out that he is looking for a guy by the name of Gigolo Georgie, who is called Gigolo Georgie because he is always hanging around night clubs wearing a little mustache and white spats, and dancing with old dolls. In fact, Gigolo Georgie is nothing but a gentleman bum, and I am surprised that Sam the Gonoph is looking for him.

But it seems that the reason Sam the Gonoph wishes to find Gigolo Georgie is to give him a good punch in the snoot, because it seems that Gigolo Georgie promotes Sam for several duckets to the large football game between the Harvards and the Yales to sell on commission, and never kicks back anything whatever to Sam. Naturally Sam considers Gigolo Georgie nothing but a rascal for doing such a thing to him, and Sam says he will find Gigolo Georgie and give him a going-over if it is the last act of his life.

Well, then, Sam explains to me that he has quite a few nice duckets for the large football game between the Harvards and the Yales and that he is taking a crew of guys with him to New Haven the next day to hustle these duckets, and what about me going along and helping to hustle these duckets and making a few bobs for myself, which is an invitation that sounds very pleasant to me, indeed.

Now of course it is very difficult for anybody to get nice duckets to a large football game between the Harvards and the Yales unless they are personally college guys, and Sam the Gonoph is by no means a college guy. In fact, the nearest Sam ever comes to a college is once when he is passing through the yard belonging to the Princetons, but Sam is on the fly at the time as a gendarme is after him, so he does not really see much of the college.

But every college guy is entitled to duckets to a large football game with which his college is connected, and it is really surprising how many college guys do not care to see large football games even after they get their duckets, especially if a ticket spec such as Sam the Gonoph comes along offering them a few bobs more than the duckets are worth. I suppose this is because a college guy figures he can see a large football game when he is old, while many things are taking place around and about that it is necessary for him to see while he is young enough to really enjoy them, such as the Follies.

Anyway, many college guys are always willing to listen to reason when Sam the Gonoph comes around offering to buy their duckets, and then Sam takes these duckets and sells them to customers for maybe ten times the price the duckets call for, and in this way Sam does very good for himself.

I know Sam the Gonoph for maybe twenty years, and always he is speculating in duckets of one kind and another. Sometimes it is duckets for the world's series, and sometimes for big fights, and sometimes it is duckets for nothing but lawn-tennis games, although why anybody wishes to see such a thing as lawn tennis is always a very great mystery to Sam the Gonoph and everybody else.

But in all those years I see Sam dodging around under the feet of the crowds of these large events, or running through the special trains offering to buy or sell duckets, I never hear of Sam personally attending any of these events except maybe a baseball game, or a fight, for Sam has practically no interest in anything but a little profit on his duckets.

He is a short, chunky, black-looking guy with a big beezer, and he is always sweating even on a cold day, and he comes from down around Essex Street, on the lower East Side. Moreover, Sam the Gonoph's crew generally comes from the lower East Side, too, for as Sam goes along he makes plenty of potatoes for himself and branches out quite some, and has a lot of assistants hustling duckets around these different events.

When Sam is younger the cops consider him hard to get along with, and in fact his monicker, the Gonoph, comes from his young days down on the lower East Side, and I hear it is Yiddish for thief, but of course as Sam gets older and starts gathering plenty of potatoes, he will not think of stealing anything. At least not much, and especially if it is anything that is nailed down.

Well, anyway, I meet Sam the Gonoph and his crew at the information desk in Grand Central the next morning, and this is how I come to be in New Haven on the day of the large football game between the Harvards and the Yales.

For such a game as this, Sam has all his best hustlers, including such as Jew Louie, Nubbsy Taylor, Benny South Street and old Liverlips, and to look at these parties you will never suspect that they are topnotch ducket hustlers. The best you will figure them is a lot of guys who are not to be met up with in a dark alley, but then ducket-hustling is a rough-and-tumble dodge and it will scarcely be good policy to hire female impersonators.

Now while we are hustling these duckets out around the main gates of the Yale Bowl I notice a very beautiful little doll of maybe sixteen or seventeen standing around watching the crowd, and I can see she is waiting for somebody, as many dolls often do at football games. But I can also see that this little doll is very much worried as the crowd keeps going in, and it is getting on toward game time. In fact, by and by I can see this little doll has tears in her eyes and if there is anything I hate to see it is tears in a doll's eyes.

So finally I go over to her, and I say as follows: "What is eating you, little miss?"

"Oh," she says, "I am waiting for Elliot. He is to come up from New York and meet me here to take me to the game, but he is not here yet, and I am afraid something happens to him. Furthermore," she says, the tears in her eyes getting very large, indeed, "I am afraid I will miss the game because he has my ticket."

"Why," I say, "this is a very simple proposition. I will sell you a choice ducket for only a sawbuck, which is ten dollars in your language, and you are getting such a bargain only because the game is about to begin, and the market is going down."

"But," she says, "I do not have ten dollars. In fact, I have only fifty cents left in my purse, and this is worrying me very much, for what will I do if Elliot does not meet me? You see," she says, "I come from Miss Peevy's school at Worcester, and I only have enough money to pay my railroad fare here, and of course I cannot ask Miss Peevy for any money as I do not wish her to know I am going away."

Well, naturally all this is commencing to sound to me like a hard-luck story such as any doll is apt to tell, so I go on about my business because I figure she will next be trying to put the lug on me for a ducket, or maybe for her railroad fare back to Worcester, although generally dolls with hard-luck stories live in San Francisco.

She keeps on standing there, and I notice she is now crying more than somewhat, and I get to thinking to myself that she is about as cute a little doll as ever I see, although too young for anybody to be bothering much about. Furthermore, I get to thinking that maybe she is on the level, at that, with her story.

Well, by this time the crowd is nearly all in the Bowl, and only a few parties such as coppers and hustlers of one kind and another are left standing outside, and there is much cheering going on inside, when Sam the Gonoph comes up looking very much disgusted, and speaks as follows:

"What do you think?" Sam says. "I am left with seven duckets on my hands, and these guys around here will not pay as much as face value for them, and they stand me better than three bucks over that. Well," Sam says, "I am certainly not going to let them go for less than they call for if I have to eat them. What do you guys say we use these duckets ourselves and go in and see the game? Personally," Sam says, "I often wish to see one of these large football games just to find out what makes suckers willing to pay so much for duckets."

Well, this seems to strike one and all, including myself, as a great idea, because none of the rest of us ever see a large football game either, so we start for the gate, and as we pass the little doll who is still crying, I say to Sam the Gonoph like this:

"Listen, Sam," I say, "you have seven duckets, and

we are only six, and here is a little doll who is stood up by her guy, and has no ducket, and no potatoes to buy one with, so what about taking her with us?"

Well, this is all right with Sam the Gonoph, and none of the others object, so I step up to the little doll and invite her to go with us, and right away she stops crying and begins smiling, and saying we are very kind indeed. She gives Sam the Gonoph an extra big smile, and right away Sam is saying she is very cute, indeed, and then she gives old Liverlips an even bigger smile, and what is more she takes old Liverlips by the arm and walks with him, and old Liverlips is not only very much astonished, but very much pleased. In fact, old Liverlips begins stepping out very spry, and Liverlips is not such a guy as cares to have any part of dolls, young or old.

But while walking with old Liverlips, the little doll talks very friendly to Jew Louie and to Nubbsy Taylor and Benny South Street, and even to me, and by and by you will think to see us that we are all her uncles, although of course if this little doll really knows who she is with, the chances are she will start chucking faints one after the other.

Anybody can see that she has very little experience in this wicked old world, and in fact is somewhat rattle-headed, because she gabs away very freely about her personal business. In fact, before we are in the Bowl she lets it out that she runs away from Miss Peevy's school to elope with this Elliot, and she says the idea is they are to be married in Hartford after the game. In fact, she says Elliot wishes to go to Hartford and be married before the game.

"But," she says, "my brother John is playing substitute with the Yales today, and I cannot think of getting married to anybody before I see him play, although I am much in love with Elliot. He is a wonderful dancer," she says, "and very romantic. I meet him in Atlantic City last summer. Now we are eloping," she says, "because my father does not care for Elliot whatever. In fact, my father hates Elliot, although he only sees him once, and it is because he hates Elliot so that my father sends me to Miss Peevy's school in Worcester. She is an old pill. Do you not think my father is unreasonable?" she says.

Well, of course none of us have any ideas on such propositions as this, although old Liverlips tells the little doll he is with her right or wrong, and pretty soon we are inside the Bowl and sitting in seats as good as any in the joint. It seems we are on the Harvards' side of the field, although of course I will never know this if the little doll does not mention it.

She seems to know everything about this football business, and as soon as we sit down she tries to point out her brother playing substitute for the Yales, saying he is the fifth guy from the end among a bunch of guys sitting on a bench on the other side of the field all wrapped in blankets. But we cannot make much of him from where we sit, and anyway it does not look to me as if he has much of a job.

It seems we are right in the middle of all the Harvards and they are making an awful racket, what with yelling, and singing, and one thing and another, because it seems the game is going on when we get in, and that the Harvards are shoving the Yales around more than somewhat. So our little doll lets everybody know she is in favor of the Yales by yelling, "Hold 'em, Yale!"

Personally, I cannot tell which are the Harvards and which are the Yales at first, and Sam the Gonoph and the others are as dumb as I am, but she explains the Harvards are wearing the red shirts and the Yales the blue shirts, and by and by we are yelling for the Yales to hold 'em, too, although of course it is only on account of our little doll wishing the Yales to hold 'em, and not because any of us care one way or the other.

Well, it seems that the idea of a lot of guys and a little doll getting right among them and yelling for the Yales to hold 'em is very repulsive to the Harvards around us, although any of them must admit it is very good advice to the Yales, at that, and some of them start making cracks of one kind and another, especially at our little doll. The chances are they are very jealous because she is outyelling them, because I will say one thing for our little doll, she can yell about as loud as anybody I ever hear, male or female.

A couple of Harvards sitting in front of old Liverlips are imitating our little doll's voice, and making guys around them laugh very heartily, but all of a sudden these parties leave their seats and go away in great haste, their faces very pale, indeed, and I figure maybe they are both taken sick the same moment, but afterwards I learn that Liverlips takes a big shiv out of his pocket and opens it and tells them very confidentially that he is going to carve their ears off.

Naturally, I do not blame the Harvards for going away in great haste, for Liverlips is such a looking guy as you will figure to take great delight in carving off ears. Furthermore, Nubbsy Taylor and Benny South Street and Jew Louie and even Sam the Gonoph commence exchanging such glances with other Harvards around us who are making cracks at our little doll that presently there is almost a dead silence in our neighborhood, except for our little doll yelling, "Hold 'em, Yale!" You see by this time we are all very fond of our little doll because she is so cute-looking and has so much zing in her, and we do not wish anybody making cracks at her or at us either, and especially at us.

In fact, we are so fond of her that when she happens to mention that she is a little chilly, Jew Louie and Nubbsy Taylor slip around among the Harvards and come back with four steamer rugs, six mufflers, two pairs of gloves, and a thermos bottle full of hot coffee for her, and Jew Louie says if she wishes a mink coat to just say the word. But she already has a mink coat. Furthermore, Jew Louie brings her a big bunch of red flowers that he finds on a doll with one of the Harvards, and he is much disappointed when she says it is the wrong color for her.

Well, finally the game is over, and I do not remember

much about it, although afterwards I hear that our little doll's brother John plays substitute for the Yales very good. But it seems that the Harvards win, and our little doll is very sad indeed about this, and is sitting there looking out over the field, which is now covered with guys dancing around as if they all suddenly go daffy, and it seems they are all Harvards, because there is really no reason for the Yales to do any dancing.

All of a sudden our little doll looks toward one end of the field, and says as follows: "Oh, they are going to take our goal posts!"

Sure enough, a lot of the Harvards are gathering around the posts at this end of the field, and are pulling and hauling at the posts, which seem to be very stout posts, indeed. Personally, I will not give you eight cents for these posts, but afterwards one of the Yales tells me that when a football team wins a game it is considered the proper caper for this team's boosters to grab the other guy's goal posts. But he is not able to tell me what good the posts are after they get them, and this is one thing that will always be a mystery to me.

Anyway, while we are watching the goings-on around the goal posts, our little doll says come on and jumps up and runs down an aisle and out on to the field, and into the crowd around the goal posts, so naturally we follow her. Somehow she manages to wiggle through the crowd of Harvards around the posts, and the next thing anybody knows she shins up one of the posts faster than you can say scat, and pretty soon is roosting out on the cross-bar between the posts like a chipmunk.

Afterwards she explains that her idea is the Harvards will not be ungentlemanly enough to pull down the goal posts with a lady roosting on them, but it seems these Harvards are no gentlemen, and keep on pulling, and the posts commence to teeter, and our little doll is teetering with them, although of course she is in no danger if she falls because she is sure to fall on the Harvards' noggins, and the way I look at it, the noggin of anybody who will be found giving any time to pulling down goal posts is apt to be soft enough to break a very long fall.

Now Sam the Gonoph and old Liverlips and Nubbsy Taylor and Benny South Street and Jew Louie and I reach the crowd around the goal posts at about the same time, and our little doll sees us from her roost and yells to us as follows: "Do not let them take our posts!"

Well, about this time one of the Harvards who seems to be about nine feet high reaches over six other guys and hits me on the chin and knocks me so far that when I pick myself up I am pretty well out of the way of everybody and have a chance to see what is going on.

Afterwards somebody tells me that the guy probably thinks I am one of the Yales coming to the rescue of the goal posts, but I wish to say I will always have a very low opinion of college guys, because I remember two other guys punch me as I am going through the air, unable to defend myself.

Now Sam the Gonoph and Nubbsy Taylor and Jew Louie and Benny South Street and old Liverlips somehow manage to ease their way through the crowd until they are under the goal posts, and our little doll is much pleased to see them, because the Harvards are now making the posts teeter more than somewhat with their pulling, and it looks as if the posts will go any minute.

Of course Sam the Gonoph does not wish any trouble with these parties, and he tries to speak nicely to the guys who are pulling at the posts, saying as follows:

"Listen," Sam says, "the little doll up there does not wish you to take these posts."

Well, maybe they do not hear Sam's words in the confusion, or if they do hear them they do not wish to pay any attention to them, for one of the Harvards mashes Sam's derby hat down over his eyes, and another smacks old Liverlips on the left ear, while Jew Louie and Nubbsy Taylor and Benny South Street are shoved around quite some.

"All right," Sam the Gonoph says, as soon as he can pull his hat off his eyes, "all right, gentlemen, if you wish to play this way. Now, boys, let them have it!"

So Sam the Gonoph and Nubbsy Taylor and Jew Louie and Benny South Street and old Liverlips begin letting them have it, and what they let them have it with is not only their dukes, but with the good old difference in their dukes, because these guys are by no means suckers when it comes to a battle, and they all carry something in their pockets to put in their dukes in case of a fight, such as a dollar's worth of nickels rolled up tight.

Furthermore, they are using the old leather, kicking guys in the stomach when they are not able to hit them on the chin, and Liverlips is also using his noodle to good advantage, grabbing guys by their coat lapels and yanking them into him so he can butt them between the eyes with his noggin, and I wish to say that old Liverlips' noggin is a very dangerous weapon at all times.

Well, the ground around them is soon covered with Harvards, and it seems that some Yales are also mixed up with them, being Yales who think Sam the Gonoph and his guys are other Yales defending the goal posts, and wishing to help out. But of course Sam the Gonoph and his guys cannot tell the Yales from the Harvards, and do not have time to ask which is which, so they are just letting everybody have it who comes along. And while all this is going on our little doll is sitting up on the cross-bar and yelling plenty of encouragement to Sam and his guys.

Now it turns out that these Harvards are by no means soft touches in a scrabble such as this, and as fast as they are flattened they get up and keep belting away, and while the old experience is running for Sam the Gonoph and Jew Louie and Nubbsy Taylor and Benny South Street and old Liverlips early in the fight, the Harvards have youth in their favor.

Pretty soon the Harvards are knocking down Sam the Gonoph, then they start knocking down Nubbsy Taylor, and by and by they are knocking down Benny South Street and Jew Louie and Liverlips, and it is so much fun that the Harvards forget all about the goal posts.

Of course as fast as Sam the Gonoph and his guys are knocked down they also get up, but the Harvards are too many for them, and they are getting an awful shellacking when the nine-foot guy who flattens me, and who is knocking down Sam the Gonoph so often he is becoming a great nuisance to Sam, sings out:

"Listen," he says, "these are game guys, even if they do go to Yale. Let us cease knocking them down," he says, "and give them a cheer."

So the Harvards knock down Sam the Gonoph and Nubbsy Taylor and Jew Louie and Benny South Street and old Liverlips just once more and then all the Harvards put their heads together and say rah-rah-rah, very loud, and go away, leaving the goal posts still standing, with our little doll still roosting on the cross-bar, although afterwards I hear some Harvards who are not in the fight get the posts at the other end of the field and sneak away with them. But I always claim these posts do not count.

Well, sitting there on the ground because he is too tired to get up from the last knockdown, and holding one hand to his right eye, which is closed tight, Sam the Gonoph is by no means a well guy, and all around and about him is much suffering among his crew. But our little doll is hopping up and down chattering like a jay-bird and running between old Liverlips, who is stretched out against one goal post, and Nubbsy Taylor, who is leaning up against the other, and she is trying to mop the blood off their kissers with a handkerchief the size of a postage stamp.

Benny South Street is laying across Jew Louie and both are still snoring from the last knockdown, and the Bowl is now pretty much deserted except for the newspaper scribes away up in the press box, who do not seem to realize that the Battle of the Century just comes off in front of them. It is coming on dark, when all of a sudden a guy pops up out of the dusk wearing white spats and an overcoat with a fur collar, and he rushes up to our little doll.

"Clarice," he says, "I am looking for you high and low. My train is stalled for hours behind a wreck the other side of Bridgeport, and I get here just after the game is over. But," he says, "I figure you will be waiting somewhere for me. Let us hurry on to Hartford, darling," he says.

Well, when he hears this voice, Sam the Gonoph opens his good eye wide and takes a peek at the guy. Then all of a sudden Sam jumps up and wobbles over to the guy and hits him a smack between the eyes. Sam is wobbling because his legs are not so good from the shellacking he takes off the Harvards, and furthermore he is away off in his punching as the guy only goes to his knees and comes right up standing again as our little doll lets out a screech and speaks as follows:

"Oo-oo!" she says. "Do not hit Elliot! He is not after our goal posts!"

"Elliot?" Sam the Gonoph says. "This is no Elliot. This is nobody but Gigolo Georgie. I can tell him by his white spats," Sam says, "and I am now going to get even for the pasting I take from the Harvards."

Then he nails the guy again and this time he seems to have a little more on his punch, for the guy goes down and Sam the Gonoph gives him the leather very good, although our little doll is still screeching, and begging Sam not to hurt Elliot. But of course the rest of us know it is not Elliot, no matter what he may tell her, but only Gigolo Georgie.

Well, the rest of us figure we may as well take a little something out of Georgie's hide, too, but as we start for him he gives a quick wiggle and hops to his feet and tears across the field, and the last we see of him is his white spats flying through one of the portals.

Now a couple of other guys come up out of the dusk, and one of them is a tall, fine-looking guy with a white mustache and anybody can see that he is somebody, and what happens but our little doll runs right into his arms and kisses him on the white mustache and calls him daddy and starts to cry more than somewhat, so I can see we lose our little doll then and there. And now the guy with the white mustache walks up to Sam the Gonoph and sticks out his duke and says as follows:

"Sir," he says, "permit me the honor of shaking the hand which does me the very signal service of chastising the scoundrel who just escapes from the field. And," he says, "permit me to introduce myself to you. I am J. Hildreth Van Cleve, president of the Van Cleve Trust. I am notified early today by Miss Peevy of my daughter's sudden departure from school, and we learn she purchases a ticket for New Haven. I at once suspect this fellow has something to do with it. Fortunately," he says, "I have these private detectives here keeping tab on him for some time, knowing my child's schoolgirl infatuation for him, so we easily trail him here. We are on the train with him, and arrive in time for your last little scene with him. Sir," he says, "again I thank you."

"I know who you are, Mr. Van Cleve," Sam the Gonoph says. "You are the Van Cleve who is down to his last forty million. But," he says, "do not thank me for putting the slug on Gigolo Georgie. He is a bum in spades, and I am only sorry he fools your nice little kid even for a minute, although," Sam says, "I figure she must be dumber than she looks to be fooled by such a guy as Gigolo Georgie."

"I hate him," the little doll says. "I hate him because he is a coward. He does not stand up and fight when he is hit like you and Liverlips and the others. I never wish to see him again."

"Do not worry," Sam the Gonoph says. "I will be too close to Gigolo Georgie as soon as I recover from my wounds for him to stay in this part of the country."

Well, I do not see Sam the Gonoph or Nubbsy Taylor or Benny South Street or Jew Louie or Liverlips for nearly a year after this, and then it comes on fall again and one day I get to thinking that here it is Friday and the next day the Harvards are playing the Yales a large football game in Boston.

I figure it is a great chance for me to join up with Sam

the Gonoph again to hustle duckets for him for this game, and I know Sam will be leaving along about midnight with his crew. So I go over to the Grand Central station at such a time, and sure enough he comes along by and by, busting through the crowd in the station with Nubbsy Taylor and Benny South Street and Jew Louie and old Liverlips at his heels, and they seem very much excited.

"Well, Sam," I say, as I hurry along with them, "here I am ready to hustle duckets for you again, and I hope and trust we do a nice business."

"Duckets!" Sam the Gonoph says. "We are not hustling duckets for this game, although you can go with us, and welcome. We are going to Boston," he says, "to root for the Yales to kick hell out of the Harvards and we are going as the personal guests of Miss Clarice Van Cleve and her old man."

"Hold 'em, Yale!" old Liverlips says, as he pushes me to one side and the whole bunch goes trotting through the gate to catch their train, and I then notice they are all wearing blue feathers in their hats with a little white Y on these feathers such as college guys always wear at football games, and that moreover Sam the Gonoph is carrying a Yale pennant.

The Hottest Guy in the World

I wish to say I am very nervous indeed when Big Jule pops into my hotel room one afternoon, because anybody will tell you that Big Jule is the hottest guy in the whole world at the time I am speaking about.

In fact, it is really surprising how hot he is. They wish to see him in Pittsburgh, Pa., about a matter of a mail truck being robbed, and there is gossip about him in Minneapolis, Minn., where somebody takes a fifty G pay roll off a messenger in cash money, and slugs the messenger around somewhat for not holding still.

Furthermore, the Bankers' Association is willing to pay good dough to talk to Big Jule out in Kansas City, Mo., where a jug is knocked off by a stranger, and in the confusion the paying teller, and the cashier, and the second vice president are clouted about, and the day watchman is hurt, and two coppers are badly bruised, and over fifteen G's is removed from the counters, and never returned.

Then there is something about a department store in Canton, O., and a flour mill safe in Toledo, and a grocery in Spokane, Wash., and a branch postoffice in San Francisco, and also something about a shooting match in Chicago, but of course this does not count so much, as only one party is fatally injured. However, you can see that Big Jule is really very hot, what with the coppers all over the country looking for him high and low. In fact, he is practically on fire.

Of course I do not believe Big Jule does all the things the coppers say, because coppers always blame everything no matter where it happens on the most prominent guy they can think of, and Big Jule is quite prominent all over the U.S.A. The chances are he does not do more than half these things, and he probably has a good alibi for the half he does do, at that, but he is certainly hot, and I do not care to have hot guys around me, or even guys who are only just a little bit warm.

But naturally I am not going to say this to Big Jule when he pops in on me, because he may think I am inhospitable, and I do not care to have such a rap going around and about on me, and furthermore Jule may become indignant if he thinks I am inhospitable, and knock me on my potato, because Big Jule is quick to take offense.

So I say hello to Big Jule, very pleasant, and ask him to have a chair by the window where he can see the citizens walking to and fro down in Eighth Avenue and watch the circus wagons moving into Madison Square

Garden by way of the Forty-ninth Street side, for the circus always shows in the Garden in the spring before going out on the road. It is a little warm, and Big Jule takes off his coat, and I can see he has one automatic slung under his arm, and another sticking down in the waistband of his pants, and I hope and trust that no copper steps into the room while Big Jule is there because it is very much against the law for guys to go around rodded up this way in New York City.

"Well, Jule," I say, "this is indeed a very large surprise to me, and I am glad to see you, but I am thinking maybe it is very foolish for you to be popping into New York just now, what with all the heat around here, and the coppers looking to arrest people for very little."

"I know," Jule says. "I know. But they do not have so very much on me around here, no matter what people say, and a guy gets homesick for his old home town, especially a guy who is stuck away where I am for the past few months. I get homesick for the lights and the crowds on Broadway, and for the old neighborhood. Furthermore, I wish to see my maw. I hear she is sick and may not live, and I wish to see her before she goes."

Well, naturally anybody will wish to see their maw under such circumstances, but Big Jule's maw lives over in West Forty-ninth Street near Eleventh Avenue, and who is living in the very same block but Johnny Brannigan, the strong-arm copper, and it is a hundred to one if Big Jule goes nosing around his old neighborhood, Johnny Brannigan will hear of it, and if there is one guy Johnny Brannigan does not care for, it is Big Jule, although they are kids together.

But it seems that even when they are kids they have very little use for each other, and after they grow up and Johnny gets on the strong-arm squad, he never misses a chance to push Big Jule around, and sometimes trying to boff Big Jule with his blackjack, and it is well known to one and all that before Big Jule leaves town the last time, he takes a punch at Johnny Brannigan, and Johnny swears he will never rest until he puts Big Jule where he belongs, although where Big Jule belongs, Johnny does not say.

So I speak of Johnny living in the same block with Big Jule's maw to Big Jule, but it only makes him mad.

"I am not afraid of Johnny Brannigan," he says. "In fact," he says, "I am thinking for some time lately that maybe I will clip Johnny Brannigan good while I am here. I owe Johnny Brannigan a clipping. But I wish to see my maw first, and then I will go around and see Miss Kitty Clancy. I guess maybe she will be much surprised to see me, and no doubt very glad."

Well, I figure it is a sure thing Miss Kitty Clancy will be surprised to see Big Jule, but I am not so sure about her being glad, because very often when a guy is away from a doll for a year or more, no matter how everloving she may be, she may get to thinking of someone else, for this is the way dolls are, whether they live on Eleventh Avenue or over on Park. Still, I remember hearing that this Miss Kitty Clancy once thinks very well of Big Jule, although her old man, Jack Clancy, who runs a speakeasy, always claims it is a big knock to the Clancy family to have such a character as Big Jule hanging around.

"I often think of Miss Kitty Clancy the past year or so," Big Jule says, as he sits there by the window, watching the circus wagons, and the crowds. "I especially think of her the past few months. In fact," he says, "thinking of Miss Kitty Clancy is about all I have to do where I am at, which is in an old warehouse on the Bay of Fundy outside of a town that is called St. Johns, or some such, up in Canada, and thinking of Miss Kitty Clancy all this time, I find out I love her very much indeed.

"I go to this warehouse," Big Jule says, "after somebody takes a jewelry store in the town, and the coppers start in blaming me. This warehouse is not such a place as I will choose myself if I am doing the choosing, because it is an old fur warehouse, and full of strange smells, but in the excitement around the jewelry store, somebody puts a slug in my hip, and Leon Pierre carries me to the old warehouse, and there I am until I get well.

"It is very lonesome," Big Jule says. "In fact, you will be surprised how lonesome it is, and it is very, very cold, and all I have for company is a lot of rats. Personally, I never care for rats under any circumstances because they carry disease germs, and are apt to bite a guy when he is asleep, if they are hungry, which is what these rats try to do to me.

"The warehouse is away off by itself," Jule says, "and nobody ever comes around there except Leon Pierre to bring me grub and dress my hip, and at night it is very still, and all you can hear is the wind howling around outside, and the rats running here and there. Some of them are very, very large rats. In fact, some of them seem about the size of rabbits, and they are pretty fresh, at that. At first I am willing to make friends with these rats, but they seem very hostile, and after they take a few nips at me I can see there is no use trying to be nice to them, so I have Leon Pierre bring me a lot of ammunition for my rods every day and I practice shooting at the rats.

"The warehouse is so far off there is no danger of anybody hearing the shooting," Big Jule says, "and it helps me pass the time away. I get so I can hit a rat sitting, or running, or even flying through the air, because these warehouse rats often leap from place to place like mountain sheep, their idea being generally to take a good nab at me as they fly past.

"Well, sir," Jule says, "I keep score on myself one day, and I hit fifty rats hand running without a miss, which I claim makes me the champion rat shooter of the world with a forty-five automatic, although of course," he says, "if anybody wishes to challenge me to a rat shooting match I am willing to take them on for a side bet. I get so I can call my shots on the rats, and in fact several times I say to myself, I will hit this one in the right eye, and this one in the left eye, and it always turns out just as I say, although sometimes when you hit a rat with a forty-five up close it is not always possible to tell afterwards just where you hit him, because you seem to hit him all over.

"By and by," Jule says, "I seem to discourage the rats somewhat, and they get so they play the chill for me and do not try to nab me even when I am asleep. They find out that no rat dast poke his whiskers out at me or he will get a very close shave. So I have to look around for other amusement, but there is not much doing in such a place, although I finally find a bunch of doctors' books which turn out to be very interesting reading. It seems these books are left there by some croaker who retires there to think things over after experimenting on his ever-loving wife with a knife. In fact, it seems he cuts his ever-loving wife's head off, and she does not continue living, so he takes his books and goes to the warehouse and remains there until the law finds him, and hangs him up very high, indeed.

"Well, the books are a great comfort to me, and I learn many astonishing things about surgery, but after I read all the books there is nothing for me to do but think, and what I think about is Miss Kitty Clancy, and how much pleasure we have together walking around and about and seeing movie shows, and all this and that, until her old man gets so tough with me. Yes, I will be very glad to see Miss Kitty Clancy, and the old neighborhood, and my maw again."

Well, finally nothing will do Big Jule but he must take a stroll over into his old neighborhood, and see if he cannot see Miss Kitty Clancy, and also drop in on his maw, and he asks me to go along with him. I can think of a million things I will rather do than take a stroll with Big Jule, but I do not wish him to think I am snobbish, because as I say, Big Jule is quick to take offense. Furthermore, I figure that at such an hour of the day he is less likely to run into Johnny Brannigan or any other coppers who know him than at any other time, so I say I will go with him, but as we start out, Big Jule puts on his rods.

"Jule," I say, "do not take any rods with you on a stroll, because somebody may happen to see them, such as a copper, and you know they will pick you up for carrying a rod in this town quicker than you can say Jack Robinson, whether they know who you are or not. You know the Sullivan law is very strong against guys carrying rods in this town."

But Big Jule says he is afraid he will catch cold if he goes out without his rods, so we go down into Forty-ninth Street and start west toward Madison Square Garden, and just as we reach Eighth Avenue and are standing there waiting for the traffic to stop, so we can cross the street, I see there is quite some excitement around the Garden on the Forty-ninth Street side, with people running every which way, and yelling no little, and looking up in the air.

So I look up myself, and what do I see sitting up there on the edge of the Garden roof but a big ugly-faced monkey. At first I do not recognize it as a monkey, because it is so big I figure maybe it is just one of the prize fight managers who stand around on this side of the Garden all afternoon waiting to get a match for their fighters, and while I am somewhat astonished to see a prize fight manager in such a position, I figure maybe he is doing it on a bet. But when I take a second look I see that it is indeed a big monk, and an exceptionally homely monk at that, although personally I never see any monks I consider so very handsome, anyway.

Well, this big monk is holding something in its arms, and what it is I am not able to make out at first, but then Big Jule and I cross the street to the side opposite the Garden, and now I can see that the monk has a baby in its arms. Naturally I figure it is some kind of advertising dodge put on by the Garden to ballyhoo the circus, or maybe the fight between Sharkey and Risko which is coming off after the circus, but guys are still yelling and running up and down, and dolls are screaming until finally I realize that a most surprising situation prevails.

It seems that the big monk up on the roof is nobody

but Bongo, who is a gorilla belonging to the circus, and one of the very few gorillas of any account in this country, or anywhere else, as far as this goes, because good gorillas are very scarce, indeed. Well, it seems that while they are shoving Bongo's cage into the Garden, the door becomes unfastened, and the first thing anybody knows, out pops Bongo, and goes bouncing along the street where a lot of the neighbors' children are playing games on the sidewalk, and a lot of mammas are sitting out in the sun alongside baby buggies containing their young. This is a very common sight in side streets such as West Forty-ninth on nice days, and by no means unpleasant, if you like mammas and their young.

Now what does this Bongo do but reach into a baby buggy which a mamma is pushing past on the sidewalk on the Garden side of the street, and snatch out a baby, though what Bongo wants with this baby nobody knows to this day. It is a very young baby, and not such a baby as is fit to give a gorilla the size of Bongo any kind of struggle, so Bongo has no trouble whatever in handling it. Anyway, I always hear a gorilla will make a sucker out of a grown man in a battle, though I wish to say I never see a battle between a gorilla and a grown man. It ought to be a first class drawing card, at that.

Well, naturally the baby's mamma puts up quite a squawk about Bongo grabbing her baby, because no mamma wishes her baby to keep company with a gorilla, and this mamma starts in screaming very loud, and trying to take the baby away from Bongo, so what does Bongo do but run right up on the roof of the Garden by way of a big electric sign which hangs down on the Forty-ninth Street side. And there old Bongo sits on the edge of the roof with the baby in his arms, and the baby is squalling quite some, and Bongo is making funny noises, and showing his teeth as the folks commence gathering in the street below.

There is a big guy in his shirt sleeves running through the crowd waving his hands, and trying to shush everybody, and saying "Quiet, please" over and over, but nobody pays any attention to him. I figure this guy has something to do with the circus, and maybe with Bongo, too. A traffic copper takes a peek at the situation, and calls for the reserves from the Forty-seventh Street station, and somebody else sends for the fire truck down the street, and pretty soon cops are running from every direction, and the fire engines are coming, and the big guy in his shirt sleeves is more excited than ever.

"Quiet, please," he says. "Everybody keep quiet, because if Bongo becomes disturbed by the noise he will throw the baby down in the street. He throws everything he gets his hands on," the guy says. "He acquires this habit from throwing coconuts back in his old home country. Let us get a life net, and if you all keep quiet we may be able to save the baby before Bongo starts heaving it like a coconut."

Well, Bongo is sitting up there on the edge of the roof about seven stories about the ground peeking down with the baby in his arms, and he is holding this baby just like a mamma would, but anybody can see that Bongo does not care for the row below, and once he lifts the baby high above his head as if to bean somebody with it. I see Big Nig, the crap shooter, in the mob, and afterwards I hear he is around offering to lay seven to five against the baby, but everybody is too excited to bet on such a proposition, although it is not a bad price, at that.

I see one doll in the crowd on the sidewalk on the side of the street opposite the Garden who is standing perfectly still staring up at the monk and the baby with a very strange expression on her face, and the way she is looking makes me take a second gander at her, and who is it but Miss Kitty Clancy. Her lips are moving as she stands there staring up, and something tells me Miss Kitty Clancy is saying prayers to herself, because she is such a doll as will know how to say prayers on an occasion like this.

Big Jule sees her about the same time I do, and Big Jule steps up beside Miss Kitty Clancy, and says hello to her, and though it is over a year since Miss Kitty

Clancy sees Big Jule she turns to him and speaks to him as if she is talking to him just a minute before. It is very strange indeed the way Miss Kitty Clancy speaks to Big Jule as if he has never been away at all.

"Do something, Julie," she says. "You are always the one to do something. Oh, please do something, Julie."

Well Big Jule never answers a word, but steps back in the clear of the crowd and reaches for the waistband of his pants, when I grab him by the arm and say to him like this:

"My goodness, Jule," I say, "what are you going to do?"

"Why," Jule says, "I am going to shoot this thieving monk before he takes a notion to heave the baby on somebody down here. For all I know," Jule says, "he may hit me with it, and I do not care to be hit with anybody's baby."

"Jule," I say, very earnestly, "do not pull a rod in front of all these coppers, because if you do they will nail you sure, if only for having the rod, and if you are nailed you are in a very tough spot, indeed, what with being wanted here and there. Jule," I say, "you are hotter than a forty-five all over this country, and I do not wish to see you nailed. Anyway," I say, "you may shoot the baby instead of the monk, because anybody can see it will be very difficult to hit the monk up there without hitting the baby. Furthermore, even if you do hit the monk it will fall into the street, and bring the baby with it."

"You speak great foolishness," Jule says. "I never miss what I shoot at. I will shoot the monk right between the eyes, and this will make him fall backwards, not forwards, and the baby will not be hurt because anybody can see it is no fall at all from the ledge to the roof behind. I make a study of such propositions," Jule says, "and I know if a guy is in such a position as this monk sitting on a ledge looking down from a high spot his defensive reflexes tend backwards, so this is the way he is bound to fall if anything unexpected comes up on him such as a bullet between the eyes. I read all about it in the doctors' books," Jule says.

Then all of a sudden up comes his hand, and in his hand is one of his rods, and I hear a sound like ker-bap. When I come to think about it afterwards, I do not remember Big Jule even taking aim like a guy will generally do if he is shooting at something sitting, but old Bongo seems to lift up a little bit off the ledge at the crack of the gun and then he keels over backwards, the baby still in his arms, and squalling more than somewhat, and Big Jule says to me like this: . .

"Right between the eyes, and I will bet on it," he says, "although it is not much of a target, at that."

Well, nobody can figure what happens for a minute, and there is much silence except from the guy in his shirt sleeves who is expressing much indignation with Big Jule and saying the circus people will sue him for damages sure if he has hurt Bongo because the monk is worth $100,000, or some such. I see Miss Kitty Clancy kneeling on the sidewalk with her hands clasped, and looking upwards, and Big Jule is sticking his rod back in his waistband again.

By this time some guys are out on the roof getting through from the inside of the building with the idea of heading Bongo off from that direction, and they let out a yell, and pretty soon I see one of them holding the baby up so everyone in the street can see it. A couple of other guys get down near the edge of the roof and pick up Bongo and show him to the crowd, as dead as a mackerel, and one of the guys puts a finger between Bongo's eyes to show where the bullet hits the monk, and Miss Kitty Clancy walks over to Big Jule and tries to say something to him, but only busts out crying very loud.

Well, I figure this is a good time for Big Jule and me to take a walk, because everybody is interested in what is going on up on the roof, and I do not wish the circus people to get a chance to serve a summons in a damage

suit on Big Jule for shooting the valuable monk. Furthermore, a couple of coppers in harness are looking Big
Jule over very critically, and I figure they are apt to put
the old sleeve on Jule any second.

All of a sudden a slim young guy steps up to Big Jule
and says to him like this:

"Jule," he says, "I want to see you," and who is it but
Johnny Brannigan. Naturally Big Jule starts reaching for
a rod, but Johnny starts him walking down the street so
fast Big Jule does not have time to get in action just then.

"No use getting it out, Jule," Johnny Brannigan says.
"No use, and no need. Come with me, and hurry."

Well, Big Jule is somewhat puzzled because Johnny
Brannigan is not acting like a copper making a collar, so
he goes along with Johnny, and I follow after them, and
halfway down the block Johnny stops a Yellow short,
and hustles us into it and tells the driver to keep shoving
down Eighth Avenue.

"I am trailing you ever since you get in town, Jule,"
Johnny Brannigan says. "You never have a chance
around here. I was going over to your maw's house to
put the arm on you figuring you are sure to go there,
when the thing over by the Garden comes off. Now I
am getting out of this cab at the next corner, and you
go on and see your maw, and then screw out of town
as quick as you can, because you are red-hot around
here, Jule.

"By the way," Johnny Brannigan says, "do you know
it is my kid you save, Jule? Mine and Kitty Clancy's?
We are married a year ago today."

Well, Big Jule looks very much surprised for a moment, and then he laughs, and says like this: "Well, I
never know it is Kitty Clancy's but I figure it for yours
the minute I see it because it looks like you."

"Yes," Johnny Brannigan says, very proud. "Everybody says he does."

"I can see the resemblance even from a distance," Big
Jule says. "In fact," he says, "it is remarkable how

much you look alike. But," he says, "for a minute,
Johnny, I am afraid I will not be able to pick out the
right face between the two on the roof because it is very
hard to tell the monk and your baby apart."

A Story Goes with It

One night I am in a gambling joint in Miami watching
the crap game and thinking what a nice thing it is, indeed, to be able to shoot craps without having to worry
about losing your potatoes.

Many of the high shots from New York and Detroit
and St. Louis and other cities are around the table, and
there is quite some action in spite of the hard times. In
fact, there is so much action that a guy with only a few
bobs on him, such as me, will be considered very impolite to be pushing into this game, because they are
packed in very tight around the table.

I am maybe three guys back from the table, and I
am watching the game by standing on tiptoe peeking
over their shoulders, and all I can hear is Goldie, the
stick man, hollering money-money-money every time
some guy makes a number, so I can see the dice are
very warm indeed, and that the right betters are doing
first-rate.

By and by a guy by the name of Guinea Joe, out of
Trenton, picks up the dice and starts making numbers
right and left, and I know enough about this Guinea
Joe to know that when he starts making numbers anybody will be very foolish indeed not to follow his hand,
although personally I am generally a wrong better against
the dice, if I bet at all.

Now all I have in my pocket is a sawbuck, and the
hotel stakes are coming up on me the next day, and I

need this saw, but with Guinea Joe hotter than a forty-five it will be overlooking a big opportunity not to go along with him, so when he comes out on an eight, which is a very easy number for Joe to make when he is hot, I dig up my sawbuck, and slide it past the three guys in front of me to the table, and I say to Lefty Park, who is laying against the dice, as follows: "I will take the odds, Lefty."

Well, Lefty looks at my sawbuck and nods his head, for Lefty is not such a guy as will refuse any bet, even though it is as modest as mine, and right away Goldie yells money-money-money, so there I am with twenty-two dollars.

Next Guinea Joe comes out on a nine, and naturally I take thirty to twenty for my sugar, because nine is nothing for Joe to make when he is hot. He makes the nine just as I figure, and I take two to one for my half a yard when he starts looking for a ten, and when he makes the ten I am right up against the table, because I am now a guy with means.

Well, the upshot of the whole business is that I finally find myself with three hundred bucks, and when it looks as if the dice are cooling off, I take out and back off from the table, and while I am backing off I am trying to look like a guy who loses all his potatoes, because there are always many wolves waiting around crap games and one thing and another in Miami this season, and what they are waiting for is to put the bite on anybody who happens to make a little scratch.

In fact, nobody can remember when the bite is as painful as it is in Miami this season, what with the un-employment situation among many citizens who come to Miami expecting to find work in the gambling joints, or around the race track. But almost as soon as these citizens arrive, the gambling joints are all turned off, except in spots, and the bookmakers are chased off the track and the mutuels put in, and the consequences are the suffering is most intense. It is not only intense among the visiting citizens, but it is quite intense among the

Miami landlords, because naturally if a citizen is not working, nobody can expect him to pay any room rent, but the Miami landlords do not seem to understand this situation, and are very unreasonable about their room rent.

Anyway, I back through quite a crowd without anybody biting me, and I am commencing to figure I may escape altogether and get to my hotel and hide my dough before the news gets around that I win about five G's, which is what my winning is sure to amount to by the time the rumor reaches all quarters of the city.

Then, just as I am thinking I am safe, I find I am looking a guy by the name of Hot Horse Herbie in the face, and I can tell from Hot Horse Herbie's expression that he is standing there watching me for some time, so there is no use in telling him I am washed out in the game. In fact, I cannot think of much of anything to tell Hot Horse Herbie that may keep him from putting the bite on me for at least a few bobs, and I am greatly astonished when he does not offer to bite me at all, but says to me like this:

"Well," he says, "I am certainly glad to see you make such a nice score. I will be looking for you tomorrow at the track, and will have some big news for you."

Then he walks away from me and I stand there with my mouth open looking at him, as it is certainly a most unusual way for Herbie to act. It is the first time I ever knew Herbie to walk away from a chance to bite somebody, and I can scarcely understand such actions, for Herbie is such a guy as will not miss a bite, even if he does not need it.

He is a tall, thin guy, with a sad face and a long chin, and he is called Hot Horse Herbie because he nearly always has a very hot horse to tell you about. He nearly always has a horse that is so hot it is fairly smoking, a hot horse being a horse that cannot possibly lose a race unless it falls down dead, and while Herbie's hot horses often lose without falling down dead, this does not keep Herbie from coming up with others just as hot.

In fact, Hot Horse Herbie is what is called a hustler around the race tracks, and his business is to learn about these hot horses, or even just suspect about them, and then get somebody to bet on them, which is a very legitimate business indeed, as Herbie only collects a commission if the hot horses win, and if they do not win Herbie just keeps out of sight awhile from whoever he gets to bet on the hot horses. There are very few guys in this world who can keep out of sight better than Hot Horse Herbie, and especially from old Cap Duhaine, of the Pinkertons, who is always around pouring cold water on hot horses.

In fact, Cap Duhaine, of the Pinkertons, claims that guys such as Hot Horse Herbie are nothing but touts, and sometimes he heaves them off the race track altogether, but of course Cap Duhaine is a very unsentimental old guy and cannot see how such characters as Hot Horse Herbie add to the romance of the turf.

Anyway, I escape from the gambling joint with all my scratch on me, and hurry to my room and lock myself in for the night, and I do not show up in public until along about noon the next day, when it is time to go over to the coffee shop for my java. And of course by this time the news of my score is all over town, and many guys are taking dead aim at me.

But naturally I am now able to explain to them that I have to wire most of the three yards I win to Nebraska to save my father's farm from being seized by the sheriff, and while everybody knows I do not have a father, and that if I do have a father I will not be sending him money for such a thing as saving his farm, with times what they are in Miami, nobody is impolite enough to doubt my word except a guy by the name of Pottsville Legs, who wishes to see my receipts from the telegraph office when I explain to him why I cannot stake him to a double sawbuck.

I do not see Hot Horse Herbie until I get to the track, and he is waiting for me right inside the grandstand

gate, and as soon as I show up he motions me off to one
side and says to me like this:

"Now," Herbie says, "I am very smart indeed about
a certain race today. In fact," he says, "if any guy knowing what I know does not bet all he can rake and scrape
together on a certain horse, such a guy ought to cut his
own throat and get himself out of the way forever. What
I know," Herbie says, "is enough to shake the foundations of this country if it gets out. Do not ask any questions," he says, "but get ready to bet all the sugar you
win last night on this horse I am going to mention to
you, and all I ask you in return is to bet fifty on me.
And," Herbie says, "kindly do not tell me you leave
your money in your other pants, because I know you
do not have any other pants."

"Now, Herbie," I say, "I do not doubt your information, because I know you will not give out information
unless it is well founded. But," I say, "I seldom stand
for a tip, and as for betting fifty for you, you know I
will not bet fifty even for myself if somebody guarantees
me a winner. So I thank you, Herbie, just the same," I
say, "but I must do without your tip," and with this I
start walking away.

"Now," Herbie says, "wait a minute. A story goes
with it," he says.

Well, of course this is a different matter entirely. I am
such a guy as will always listen to a tip on a horse if a
story goes with the tip. In fact, I will not give you a
nickel for a tip without a story, but it must be a first-
class story, and most horse players are the same way.
In fact, there are very few horse players who will not
listen to a tip if a story goes with it, for this is the way
human nature is. So I turn and walk back to Hot Horse
Herbie, and say to him like this:

"Well," I say, "let me hear the story, Herbie."

"Now," Herbie says, dropping his voice away down
low, in case old Cap Duhaine may be around somewhere
listening, "it is the third race, and the horse is a horse
by the name of Never Despair. It is a boat race," Herbie

says. "They are going to shoo in Never Despair. Everything else in the race is a cooler," he says.

"Well," I say, "this is just an idea, Herbie, and not a
story."

"Wait a minute," Herbie says. "The story that goes
with it is a very strange story indeed. In fact," he says,
"it is such a story as I can scarcely believe myself, and
I will generally believe almost any story, including," he
says, "the ones I make up out of my own head. Anyway,
the story is as follows:

"Never Despair is owned by an old guy by the name
of Seed Mercer," Herbie says. "Maybe you remember
seeing him around. He always wears a black slouch hat
and gray whiskers," Herbie says, "and he is maybe a
hundred years old, and his horses are very terrible horses
indeed. In fact," Herbie says, "I do not remember seeing any more terrible horses in all the years I am around
the track, and," Herbie says, "I wish to say I see some
very terrible horses indeed.

"Now," Herbie says, "old Mercer has a granddaughter
who is maybe sixteen years old, come next grass, by the
name of Lame Louise, and she is called Lame Louise
because she is all crippled up from childhood by infan-
tile what-is-this, and can scarcely navigate, and," Herbie
says, "her being crippled up in such a way makes old
Mercer feel very sad, for she is all he has in the world,
except these terrible horses."

"It is a very long story, Herbie," I say, "and I wish to
see Moe Shapoff about a very good thing in the first
race."

"Never mind Moe Shapoff," Herbie says. "He will
only tell you about a bum by the name of Zachary in
the first race, and Zachary has no chance whatever. I
make Your John a standout in the first," he says.

"Well," I say, "let us forget the first and go on with
your story, although it is commencing to sound all mixed
up to me."

"Now," Herbie says, "it not only makes old man
Mercer very sad because Lame Louise is all crippled

up, but," he says, "it makes many of the jockeys and other guys around the race track very sad, because," he says, "they know Lame Louise since she is so high and she always has a smile for them, and especially for Jockey Scroon. In fact," Herbie says, "Jockey Scroon is even more sad about Lame Louise than old man Mercer, because Jockey Scroon loves Lame Louise."

"Why," I say, very indignant, "Jockey Scroon is nothing but a little burglar. Why," I say, "I see Jockey Scroon do things to horses I bet on that he will have to answer for on the Judgment Day, if there is any justice at such a time. Why," I say, "Jockey Scroon is nothing but a Gerald Chapman in his heart, and so are all other jockeys."

"Yes," Hot Horse Herbie says, "what you say is very, very true, and I am personally in favor of the electric chair for all jockeys, but," he says, "Jockey Scroon loves Lame Louise just the same, and is figuring on making her his ever-loving wife when he gets a few bobs together, which," Herbie says, "makes Louise eight to five in my line to be an old maid. Jockey Scroon rooms with me downtown," Herbie says, "and he speaks freely to me about his love for Louise. Furthermore," Herbie says, "Jockey Scroon is personally not a bad little guy, at that, although of course being a jockey he is sometimes greatly misunderstood by the public.

"Anyway," Hot Horse Herbie says, "I happen to go home early last night before I see you at the gambling joint, and I hear voices coming out of my room, and naturally I pause outside the door to listen, because for all I know it may be the landlord speaking about the room rent, although," Herbie says, "I do not figure my landlord to be much worried at this time because I see him sneak into my room a few days before and take a lift at my trunk to make sure I have belongings in the same, and it happens I nail the trunk to the floor beforehand, so not being able to lift it, the landlord is bound to figure me a guy with property.

"These voices," Herbie says, "are mainly soprano

voices, and at first I think Jockey Scroon is in there with
some dolls, which is by no means permissible in my
hotel, but, after listening awhile, I discover they are the
voices of young boys, and I make out that these boys
are nothing but jockeys, and they are the six jockeys
who are riding in the third race, and they are fixing up
this race to be a boat race, and to shoo in Never Despair,
which Jockey Scroon is riding.

"And," Hot Horse Herbie says, "the reason they are
fixing up this boat race is the strangest part of the story.
It seems," he says, "that Jockey Scroon hears old man
Mercer talking about a great surgeon from Europe who
is a shark on patching up cripples such as Lame Louise,
and who just arrives at Palm Beach to spend the winter,
and old man Mercer is saying how he wishes he has
dough enough to take Lame Louise to this guy so he can
operate on her, and maybe make her walk good again.

"But of course," Herbie says, "it is well known to one
and all that old man Mercer does not have a quarter,
and that he has no way of getting a quarter unless one
of his terrible horses accidentally wins a purse. So,"
Herbie says, "it seems these jockeys get to talking it over
among themselves, and they figure it will be a nice thing
to let old man Mercer win a purse such as the thousand
bucks that goes with the third race today, so he can take
Lame Louise to Palm Beach, and now you have a rough
idea of what is coming off.

"Furthermore," Herbie says, "these jockeys wind up
their meeting by taking a big oath among themselves
that they will not tell a living soul what is doing so nobody will bet on Never Despair, because," he says,
"these little guys are smart enough to see if there is any
betting on such a horse there may be a very large
squawk afterwards. And," he says, "I judge they keep
their oath because Never Despair is twenty to one in the
morning line, and I do not hear a whisper about him,
and you have the tip all to yourself."

"Well," I say, "so what?" For this story is now commencing to make me a little tired, especially as I hear

the bell for the first race, and I must see Moe Shapoff.

"Why," Hot Horse Herbie says, "so you bet every nickel you can rake and scrape together on Never Despair, including the twenty you are to bet for me for giving you this tip and the story that goes with it."

"Herbie," I say, "it is a very interesting story indeed, and also very sad, but," I say, "I am sorry it is about a horse Jockey Scroon is to ride, because I do not think I will ever bet on anything Jockey Scroon rides if they pay off in advance. And," I say, "I am certainly not going to bet twenty for you or anybody else."

"Well," Hot Horse Herbie says, "I will compromise with you for a pound note, because I must have something going for me on this boat race."

So I give Herbie a fiver, and the chances are this is about as strong as he figures from the start, and I forget all about his tip and the story that goes with it, because while I enjoy a story with a tip, I feel that Herbie overdoes this one.

Anyway, no handicapper alive can make Never Despair win the third race off the form, because this race is at six furlongs, and there is a barrel of speed in it, and anybody can see that old man Mercer's horse is away over his head. In fact, The Dancer tells me that any one of the other five horses in this race can beat Never Despair doing anything from playing hockey to putting the shot, and everybody else must think the same thing because Never Despair goes to forty to one.

Personally, I like a horse by the name of Loose Living, which is a horse owned by a guy by the name of Bill Howard, and I hear Bill Howard is betting plenty away on his horse, and any time Bill Howard is betting away on his horse a guy will be out of his mind not to bet on this horse, too, as Bill Howard is very smart indeed. Loose Living is two to one in the first line, but by and by I judge the money Bill Howard bets away commences to come back to the track, and Loose Living winds up seven to ten, and while I am generally not a seven-to-ten guy, I can see that here is a proposition I cannot overlook.

So, naturally, I step up to the mutuel window and invest in Loose Living. In fact, I invest everything I have on me in the way of scratch, amounting to a hundred and ten bucks, which is all I have left after taking myself out of the hotel stakes and giving Hot Horse Herbie the finnif, and listening to what Moe Shapoff has to say about the first race, and also getting beat a snoot in the second.

When I first step up to the window, I have no idea of betting all my scratch on Loose Living, but while waiting in line there I get to thinking what a cinch Loose Living is, and how seldom such an opportunity comes into a guy's life, so I just naturally set it all in.

Well, this is a race which will be remembered by one and all to their dying day, as Loose Living beats the barrier a step, and is two lengths in front before you can say Jack Robinson, with a thing by the name of Callipers second by maybe half a length, and with the others bunched except Never Despair, and where is Never Despair but last, where he figures.

Now any time Loose Living busts on top there is no need worrying any more about him, and I am thinking I better get in line at the pay-off window right away, so I will not have to wait long to collect my sugar. But I figure I may as well stay and watch the race, although personally I am never much interested in watching races. I am interested only in how a race comes out.

As the horses hit the turn into the stretch, Loose Living is just breezing, and anybody can see that he is going to laugh his way home from there. Callipers is still second, and a thing called Goose Pimples is third, and I am surprised to see that Never Despair now struggles up to fourth with Jockey Scroon belting away at him with his bat quite earnestly. Furthermore, Never Despair seems to be running very fast, though afterwards I figure this may be because the others are commencing to run very slow.

Anyway, a very strange spectacle now takes place in the stretch, as all of a sudden Loose Living seems to be stopping, as if he is waiting for a street car, and what is all the more remarkable Callipers and Goose Pimples also seem to be hanging back, and the next thing anybody knows, here comes Jockey Scroon on Never Despair sneaking through on the rail, and personally it looks to me as if the jock on Callipers moves over to give Jockey Scroon plenty of elbow room, but of course the jock on Callipers may figure Jockey Scroon has diphtheria, and does not wish to catch it.

Loose Living is out in the middle of the track, anyway, so he does not have to move over. All Loose Living has to do is to keep on running backwards as he seems to be doing from the top of the stretch, to let Jockey Scroon go past on Never Despair to win the heat by a length.

Well, the race is practically supernatural in many respects, and the judges are all upset over it, and they haul all the jocks up in the stand and ask them many questions, and not being altogether satisfied with the answers, they ask these questions over several times. But all the jocks will say is that Never Despair sneaks past them very unexpectedly indeed, while Jockey Scroon, who is a pretty fresh duck at that, wishes to know if he is supposed to blow a horn when he is slipping through a lot of guys sound asleep.

But the judges are still not satisfied, so they go prowling around investigating the betting, because naturally when a boat race comes up there is apt to be some reason for it, such as the betting, but it seems that all the judges find is that one five-dollar win ticket is sold on Never Despair in the mutuels, and they cannot learn of a dime being bet away on the horse. So there is nothing much the judges can do about the proposition, except give the jocks many hard looks, and the jocks are accustomed to hard looks from the judges, anyway.

Personally, I am greatly upset by this business, especially when I see that Never Despair pays $86.34, and

for two cents I will go right up in the stand and start
hollering copper on these little Jesse Jameses for putting on such a boat race and taking all my hard-earned
potatoes away from me, but before I have time to do
this, I run into The Dancer, and he tells me that Dedicate in the next race is the surest thing that ever goes to
the post, and at five to one, at that. So I have to forget
everything while I bustle about to dig up a few bobs
to bet on Dedicate, and when Dedicate is beat a whisker,
I have to do some more bustling to dig up a few bobs
to bet on Vesta in the fifth, and by this time the third
race is such ancient history that nobody cares what
happens in it.

It is nearly a week before I see Hot Horse Herbie
again, and I figure he is hiding out on everybody because he has this dough he wins off the fiver I give him,
and personally I consider him a guy with no manners
not to be kicking back the fin, at least. But before I can
mention the fin, Herbie gives me a big hello, and says to
me like this:

"Well," he says, "I just see Jockey Scroon, and Jockey
Scroon just comes back from Palm Beach, and the operation is a big success, and Lame Louise will walk as
good as anybody again, and old Mercer is tickled silly.
But," Herbie says, "do not say anything out loud, because the judges may still be trying to find out what
comes off in the race."

"Herbie," I say, very serious, "do you mean to say
the story you tell me about Lame Louise, and all this
and that, the other day is on the level?"

"Why," Herbie says, "certainly it is on the level,
and I am sorry to hear you do not take advantage of my
information. But," he says, "I do not blame you for not
believing my story, because it is a very long story for
anybody to believe. It is not such a story," Herbie says,
"as I will tell to any one if I expect them to believe it.
In fact," he says, "it is so long a story that I do not have
the heart to tell it to anybody else but you, or maybe I
will have something running for me on the race.

"But," Herbie says, "never mind all this. I will be plenty smart about a race tomorrow. Yes," Herbie says, "I will be wiser than a treeful of owls, so be sure and see me if you happen to have any coconuts."

"There is no danger of me seeing you," I say, very sad, because I am all sorrowed up to think that the story he tells me is really true. "Things are very terrible with me at this time," I say, "and I am thinking maybe you can hand me back my finnif, because you must do all right for yourself with the fiver you have on Never Despair at such a price."

Now a very strange look comes over Hot Horse Herbie's face, and he raises his right hand, and says to me like this:

"I hope and trust I drop down dead right here in front of you," Herbie says, "if I bet a quarter on the horse. It is true," he says, "I am up at the window to buy a ticket on Never Despair, but the guy who is selling the tickets is a friend of mine by the name of Heeby Rosenbloom, and Heeby whispers to me that Big Joe Gompers, the guy who owns Callipers, just bets half a hundred on his horse, and," Herbie says, "I know Joe Gompers is such a guy as will not bet half a hundred on anything he does not get a Federal Reserve guarantee with it.

"Anyway," Herbie says, "I get to thinking about what a bad jockey this Jockey Scroon is, which is very bad indeed, and," he says, "I figure that even if it is a boat race it is no even-money race they can shoo him in, so I buy a ticket on Callipers."

"Well," I say, "somebody buys one five-dollar ticket on Never Despair, and I figure it can be nobody but you."

"Why," Hot Horse Herbie says, "do you not hear about this? Why," he says, "Cap Duhaine, of the Pinkertons, traces this ticket and finds it is bought by a guy by the name of Steve Harter, and the way this guy Harter comes to buy it is very astonishing. It seems," Herbie says, "that this Harter is a tourist out of Indiana who comes to Miami for the sunshine, and who loses all his dough but six bucks against the faro bank at Hollywood.

"At the same time," Herbie says, "the poor guy gets a telegram from his ever-loving doll back in Indiana saying she no longer wishes any part of him.

"Well," Herbie says, "between losing his dough and his doll, the poor guy is practically out of his mind, and he figures there is nothing left for him to do but knock himself off.

"So," Herbie says, "this Harter spends one of his six bucks to get to the track, figuring to throw himself under the feet of the horses in the first race and let them kick him to a jelly. But he does not get there until just as the third race is coming up and," Herbie says, "he sees this name 'Never Despair,' and he figures it may be a hunch, so he buys himself a ticket with his last fiver. Well, naturally," Herbie says, "when Never Despair pops down, the guy forgets about letting the horses kick him to a jelly, and he keeps sending his dough along until he runs nothing but a nubbin into six G's on the day.

"Then," Herbie says, "Cap Duhaine finds out that the guy, still thinking of Never Despair, calls his ever-loving doll on the phone, and finds she is very sorry she sends him the wire and that she really loves him more than somewhat, especially," Herbie says, "when she finds out about the six G's. And the last anybody hears of the matter, this Harter is on his way home to get married, so Never Despair does quite some good in this wicked old world, after all.

"But," Herbie says, "let us forget all this, because tomorrow is another day. Tomorrow," he says, "I will tell you about a thing that goes in the fourth which is just the same as wheat in the bin. In fact," Hot Horse Herbie says, "if it does not win, you can never speak to me again."

"Well," I say, as I start to walk away, "I am not interested in any tip at this time."

"Now," Herbie says, "wait a minute. A story goes with it."

"Well," I say, coming back to him, "let me hear the story."

That Ever-Loving Wife of Hymie's

If anybody ever tells me I will wake up some morning to find myself sleeping with a horse, I will consider them very daffy indeed, especially if they tell me it will be with such a horse as old Mahogany, for Mahogany is really not much horse. In fact, Mahogany is nothing but an old bum, and you can say it again, and many horse players wish he is dead ten thousand times over.

But I will think anybody is daffier still if they tell me I will wake up some morning to find myself sleeping with Hymie Banjo Eyes, because as between Mahogany and Hymie Banjo Eyes to sleep with, I will take Mahogany every time, even though Mahogany snores more than somewhat when he is sleeping. But Mahogany is by no means as offensive to sleep with as Hymie Banjo Eyes, as Hymie not only snores when he is sleeping, but he hollers and kicks around and takes on generally.

He is a short, pudgy little guy who is called Hymie Banjo Eyes because his eyes bulge out as big and round as banjos, although his right name is Weinstein, or some such, and he is somewhat untidy-looking in spots, for Hymie Banjo Eyes is a guy who does not care if his breakfast gets on his vest, or what. Furthermore, he gabs a lot and thinks he is very smart, and many citizens consider him a pest, in spades. But personally I figure Hymie Banjo Eyes as very harmless, although he is not such a guy as I will ordinarily care to have much truck with.

But there I am one morning waking up to find myself sleeping with both Mahogany and Hymie, and what are we sleeping in but a horse car bound for Miami, and we are passing through North Carolina in a small-time blizzard when I wake up, and Mahogany is snoring and shivering, because it seems Hymie cops the poor horse's blanket to wrap around himself, and I am half frozen and wishing I am back in Mindy's restaurant on Broadway, where all is bright and warm, and that I never see either Mahogany or Hymie in my life.

Of course it is not Mahogany's fault that I am sleeping with him and Hymie, and in fact, for all I know, Mahogany may not consider me any bargain whatever to sleep with. It is Hymie's fault for digging me up in Mindy's one night and explaining to me how wonderful the weather is in Miami in the wintertime, and how we can go there for the races with his stable and make plenty of potatoes for ourselves, although of course I know when Hymie is speaking of his stable he means Mahogany, for Hymie never has more than one horse at any one time in his stable.

Generally it is some broken-down lizard that he buys for about the price of an old wool hat and patches up the best he can, as Hymie Banjo Eyes is a horse trainer by trade, and considering the kind of horses he trains he is not a bad trainer, at that. He is very good indeed at patching up cripples and sometimes winning races with them until somebody claims them on him or they fall down dead, and then he goes and gets himself another cripple and starts all over again.

I hear he buys Mahogany off a guy by the name of O'Shea for a hundred bucks, although the chances are if Hymie waits awhile the guy will pay him at least two hundred to take Mahogany away and hide him, for Mahogany has bad legs and bum feet, and is maybe nine years old, and does not win a race since the summer of 1924, and then it is an accident. But anyway, Mahogany is the stable Hymie Banjo Eyes is speaking of taking to Miami when he digs me up in Mindy's.

"And just think," Hymie says, "all we need to get there is the price of a drawing room on the Florida Special."

Well, I am much surprised by this statement, because it is the first time I ever hear of a horse needing a drawing room, especially such a horse as Mahogany, but it seems the drawing room is not to be for Mahogany, or even for Hymie or me. It seems it is to be for Hymie's ever-loving wife, a blond doll by the name of 'Lasses, which he marries out of some night club where she is what is called an adagio dancer.

It seems that when 'Lasses is very young somebody once says she is just as sweet as Molasses, and this is how she comes to get the name of 'Lasses, although her right name is Maggie Something, and I figure she must change quite a lot since they begin calling her 'Lasses because at the time I meet her she is sweet just the same as green grapefruit.

She has a partner in the adagio business by the name of Donaldo, who picks her up and heaves her around the night club as if she is nothing but a baseball, and it is very thrilling indeed to see Donaldo giving 'Lasses a sling as if he is going to throw her plumb away, which many citizens say may not be a bad idea, at that, and then catching her by the foot in midair and hauling her back to him.

But one night it seems that Donaldo takes a few slugs of gin before going into this adagio business, and he muffs 'Lasses' foot, although nobody can see how this is possible, because 'Lasses' foot is no more invisible than a boxcar, and 'Lasses keeps on sailing through the air. She finally sails into Hymie Banjo Eyes' stomach as he is sitting at a table pretty well back, and this is the way Hymie and 'Lasses meet, and a romance starts, although it is nearly a week before Hymie recovers enough from the body beating he takes off 'Lasses to go around and see her.

The upshot of the romance is 'Lasses and Hymie get married, although up to the time Donaldo slings her into Hymie's stomach, 'Lasses is going around with Brick McCloskey, the bookmaker, and is very loving with him indeed, but they have a row about something and are carrying the old torch for each other when Hymie happens along.

Some citizens say the reason 'Lasses marries Hymie is because she is all sored up on Brick and that she acts without thinking, as dolls often do, especially blond dolls, although personally I figure Hymie takes all the worst of the situation, as 'Lasses is not such a doll as any guy shall marry without talking it over with his lawyer. 'Lasses is one of these little blondes who is full of short answers, and personally I will just as soon marry a porcupine. But Hymie loves her more than somewhat, and there is no doubt Brick McCloskey is all busted up because 'Lasses takes this runout powder on him, so maybe after all 'Lasses has some kind of appeal which I cannot notice offhand.

"But," Hymie explains to me when he is speaking to me about this trip to Miami, " 'Lasses is not well, what with nerves and one thing and another, and she will have to travel to Miami along with her Pekingese dog, Sooey-pow, because," Hymie says, "it will make her more nervous than somewhat if she has to travel with anybody else. And of course," Hymie says, "no one can expect 'Lasses to travel in anything but a drawing room on account of her health."

Well, the last time I see 'Lasses she is making a sucker of a big sirloin in Bobby's restaurant, and she strikes me as a pretty healthy doll, but of course I never examine her close, and anyway, her health is none of my business.

"Now," Hymie says, "I get washed out at Empire, and I am pretty much in hock here and there and have no dough to ship my stable to Miami, but," he says, "a friend of mine is shipping several horses there and he has a whole car, and he will kindly let me have room in one end of the car for my stable, and you and I can ride in there, too.

"That is," Hymie says, "we can ride in there if you

will dig up the price of a drawing room and the two tickets that go with it so 'Lasses' nerves will not be disturbed. You see," Hymie says, "I happen to know you have two hundred and fifty bucks in the jug over here on the corner, because one of the tellers in the jug is a friend of mine, and he tips me off you have this sugar, even though," Hymie says, "you have it in there under another name."

Well, a guy goes up against many daffy propositions as he goes along through life, and the first thing I know I am waking up, like I tell you, to find myself sleeping with Mahogany and Hymie, and as I lay there in the horse car slowly freezing to death, I get to thinking of 'Lasses in a drawing room on the Florida Special, and I hope and trust that she and the Peke are sleeping nice and warm.

The train finally runs out of the blizzard and the weather heats up somewhat, so it is not so bad riding in the horse car, and Hymie and I pass the time away playing two-handed pinochle. Furthermore, I get pretty well acquainted with Mahogany, and I find he is personally not such a bad old pelter as many thousands of citizens think.

Finally we get to Miami, and at first it looks as if Hymie is going to have a tough time finding a place to keep Mahogany, as all the stable room at the Hialeah track is taken by cash customers, and Hymie certainly is not a cash customer and neither is Mahogany. Personally, I am not worried so much about stable room for Mahogany as I am about stable room for myself, because I am now down to a very few bobs and will need same to eat on.

Naturally, I figure Hymie Banjo Eyes will be joining his ever-loving wife 'Lasses, as I always suppose a husband and wife are an entry, but Hymie tells me 'Lasses is parked in the Roney Plaza over on Miami Beach, and that he is going to stay with Mahogany, because it will make her very nervous to have people around her, especially people who are training horses every day, and who may not smell so good.

Well, it looks as if we will wind up camping out with Mahogany under a palm tree, although many of the palm trees are already taken by other guys camping out with horses, but finally Hymie finds a guy who has a garage back of his house right near the race track, and having no use for this garage since his car blows away in the hurricane of 1926, the guy is willing to let Hymie keep Mahogany in the garage. Furthermore, he is willing to let Hymie sleep in the garage with Mahogany, and pay him now and then.

So Hymie borrows a little hay and grain, such as horses love to eat, off a friend who has a big string at the track, and moves into the garage with Mahogany, and about the same time I run into a guy by the name of Pottsville Legs, out of Pottsville, Pa, and he has a room in a joint downtown, and I move in with him, and it is no worse than sleeping with Hymie Banjo Eyes and Mahogany, at that.

I do not see Hymie for some time after this, but I hear of him getting Mahogany ready for a race. He has the old guy out galloping on the track every morning, and who is galloping him but Hymie himself, because he cannot get any stable boys to do the galloping for him, as they do not wish to waste their time. However, Hymie rides himself when he is a young squirt, so galloping Mahogany is not such a tough job for him, except that it gives him a terrible appetite, and it is very hard for him to find anything to satisfy this appetite with, and there are rumors around that Hymie is eating most of Mahogany's hay and grain.

In the meantime, I am going here and there doing the best I can, and this is not so very good, at that, because never is there such a terrible winter in Miami or so much suffering among the horse players. In the afternoon I go out to the race track, and in the evening I go to the dog tracks, and later to the gambling joints try-

168 A TREASURY OF DAMON RUNYON

ing to pick up a few honest bobs, and wherever I go I
seem to see Hymie's ever-loving wife 'Lasses, and she
is always dressed up more than somewhat, and generally
she is with Brick McCloskey, for Brick shows up in
Miami figuring to do a little business in bookmaking at
the track.

When they turn off the books there and put in the
mutuels, Brick still does a little booking to big betters
who do not wish to put their dough in the mutuels for
fear of ruining a price, for Brick is a very large operator
at all times. He is not only a large operator, but he is a
big, good-looking guy, and how 'Lasses can ever give
him the heave-o for such a looking guy as Hymie Banjo
Eyes is always a great mystery to me. But then this is
the way blondes are.

Of course Hymie probably does not know 'Lasses is
running around with Brick McCloskey, because Hymie
is too busy getting Mahogany ready for a race to make
such spots as 'Lasses and Brick are apt to be, and nobody is going to bother to tell him, because so many
ever-loving wives are running around with guys who are
not their ever-loving husbands in Miami this winter that
nobody considers it any news.

Personally, I figure 'Lasses' running around with
Brick is a pretty fair break for Hymie, at that, as it takes
plenty of weight off him in the way of dinners, and
maybe breakfasts, for all I know, although it seems to
me 'Lasses cannot love Hymie as much as Hymie thinks
to be running around with another guy. In fact, I am
commencing to figure 'Lasses does not care for Hymie
Banjo Eyes whatever.

Well, one day I am looking over the entries, and I see
where Hymie has old Mahogany in a claiming race at a
mile and an eighth, and while it is a cheap race, there
are some pretty fair hides in it. In fact, I can figure at
least eight out of the nine that are entered to beat
Mahogany by fourteen lengths.

Well, I go out to Hialeah very early, and I step around
to the garage where Mahogany and Hymie are living,

and Hymie is sitting out in front of the garage on a bucket looking very sad, and Mahogany has his beezer stuck out through the door of the garage, and he is looking even sadder than Hymie.

"Well," I say to Hymie Banjo Eyes, "I see the big horse goes today."

"Yes," Hymie says, "the big horse goes today if I can get ten bucks for the jockey fee, and if I can get a jock after I get the fee. It is a terrible situation," Hymie says. "Here I get Mahogany all readied up for the race of his life in a spot where he can win by as far as from here to Palm Beach and grab a purse worth six hundred fish, and me without as much as a sawbuck to hire one of these hoptoads that are putting themselves away as jocks around here."

"Well," I say, "why do you not speak to 'Lasses, your ever-loving wife, about this situation? I see 'Lasses playing the wheel out at Hollywood last night," I say, "and she has a stack of checks in front of her a greyhound cannot hurdle, and," I say, "it is not like 'Lasses to go away from there without a few bobs off such a start."

"Now there you go again," Hymie says, very impatient, indeed. "You are always making cracks about 'Lasses, and you know very well it will make the poor little doll very nervous if I speak to her about such matters as a sawbuck, because 'Lasses needs all the sawbucks she can get hold of to keep herself and Sooeypow at the Roney Plaza. By the way," Hymie says, "how much scratch do you have on your body at this time?"

Well, I am never any hand for telling lies, especially to an old friend such as Hymie Banjo Eyes, so I admit I have a ten-dollar note, although naturally I do not mention another tenner which I also have in my pocket, as I know Hymie will wish both of them. He will wish one of my tenners to pay the jockey fee, and he will wish the other to bet on Mahogany, and I am certainly not going to let Hymie throw my dough away betting it on such an old crocodile as Mahogany, especially in

a race which a horse by the name of Side Burns is a sure
thing to win.

In fact, I am waiting patiently for several days for a
chance to bet on Side Burns. So I hold out one sawbuck
on Hymie, and then I go over to the track and forget
all about him and Mahogany until the sixth race is coming up, and I see by the jockey board that Hymie has a
jock by the name of Scroon riding Mahogany, and while
Mahogany is carrying only one hundred pounds, which
is the light weight of the race, I will personally just as
soon have Paul Whiteman up as Scroon. Personally I
do not think Scroon can spell "horse," for he is nothing
but a dizzy little guy who gets a mount about once every
Pancake Tuesday. But of course Hymie is not a guy who
can pick and choose his jocks, and the chances are he is
pretty lucky to get anybody to ride Mahogany.

I see by the board where it tells you the approximate
odds that Mahogany is forty to one, and naturally nobody is paying any attention to such a horse, because it
will not be good sense to pay any attention to Mahogany
in this race, what with it being his first start in months,
and Mahogany not figuring with these horses, or with
any horses, as far as this is concerned. In fact, many
citizens think Hymie Banjo Eyes is either crazy, or is
running Mahogany in this race for exercise, although
nobody who knows Hymie will figure him to be spending
dough on a horse just to exercise him.

The favorite in the race is this horse named Side
Burns, and from the way they are playing him right
from taw you will think he is Twenty Grand. He is even
money on the board, and I hope and trust that he will
finally pay as much as this, because at even money I
consider him a very sound investment, indeed. In fact,
I am willing to take four to five for my dough, and will
consider it money well found, because I figure this will
give me about eighteen bobs to bet on Tony Joe in the
last race, and anybody will tell you that you can go to
sleep on Tony Joe winning, unless something happens.

There is a little action on several other horses in the

race, but of course there is none whatever for Mahogany and the last time I look he is up to fifty. So I buy my ticket on Side Burns, and go out to the paddock to take a peek at the horses, and I see Hymie Banjo Eyes in there saddling Mahogany with his jockey, this dizzy Scroon, standing alongside him in Hymie's colors of red, pink and yellow, and making wisecracks to the guys in the next stall about Mahogany.

Hymie Banjo Eyes sees me and motions me to come into the paddock, so I go in and give Mahogany a pat on the snoot, and the old guy seems to remember me right away, because he rubs his beezer up and down my arm and lets out a little snicker. But it seems to me the old plug looks a bit peaked, and I can see his ribs very plain indeed, so I figure maybe there is some truth in the rumor about Hymie sharing Mahogany's hay and grain, after all.

Well, as I am standing there, Hymie gives this dizzy Scroon his riding instructions, and they are very short, for all Hymie says is as follows:

"Listen," Hymie says, "get off with this horse and hurry right home."

And Scroon looks a little dizzier than somewhat and nods his head, and then turns and tips a wink to Kurtsinger, who is riding the horse in the next stall.

Well, finally the post bugle goes, and Hymie walks back with me to the lawn as the horses are coming out on the track, and Hymie is speaking about nothing but Mahogany.

"It is just my luck," Hymie says, "not to have a bob or two to bet on him. He will win this race as far as you can shoot a rifle, and the reason he will win this far," Hymie says, "is because the track is just soft enough to feel nice and soothing to his sore feet. Furthermore," Hymie says, "after lugging my one hundred and forty pounds around every morning for two weeks, Mahogany will think it is Christmas when he finds nothing but this Scroon's one hundred pounds on his back.

"In fact," Hymie says, "if I do not need the purse

money, I will not let him run today, but will hide him for a bet. But," he says, " 'Lasses must have five yards at once, and you know how nervous she will be if she does not get the five yards. So I am letting Mahogany run," Hymie says, "and it is a pity."

"Well," I says, "why do you not promote somebody to bet on him for you?"

"Why," Hymie says, "if I ask one guy I ask fifty. But they all think I am out of my mind to think Mahogany can beat such horses as Side Burns and the rest. Well," he says, "they will be sorry. By the way," he says, "do you have a bet down of any kind?"

Well, now, I do not wish to hurt Hymie's feelings by letting him know I bet on something else in the race, so I tell him I do not play this race at all, and he probably figures it is because I have nothing to bet with after giving him the sawbuck. But he keeps on talking as we walk over in front of the grandstand, and all he is talking about is what a tough break it is for him not to have any dough to bet on Mahogany. By this time the horses are at the post a little way up the track, and as we are standing there watching them, Hymie Banjo Eyes goes on talking, half to me and half to himself, but out loud.

"Yes," he says, "I am the unluckiest guy in all the world. Here I am," he says, "with a race that is a kick in the pants for my horse at fifty to one, and me without a quarter to bet. It is certainly a terrible thing to be poor," Hymie says. "Why," he says, "I will bet my life on my horse in this race, I am so sure of winning. I will bet my clothes. I will bet all I ever hope to have. In fact," he says, "I will even bet my ever-loving wife, this is how sure I am."

Now of course this is only the way horse players rave when they are good and heated up about the chances of a horse, and I hear such conversations as this maybe a million times, and never pay any attention to it whatever, but as Hymie makes this crack about betting his ever-loving wife, a voice behind us says as follows: "Against how much?"

Naturally, Hymie and I look around at once, and who does the voice belong to but Brick McCloskey. Of course I figure Brick is kidding Hymie Banjo Eyes, but Brick's voice is as cold as ice as he says to Hymie like this:

"Against how much will you bet your wife your horse wins this race?" he says. "I hear you saying you are sure this old buzzard meat you are running will win," Brick says, "so let me see how sure you are. Personally," Brick says, "I think they ought to prosecute you for running a broken-down hound like Mahogany on the ground of cruelty to animals, and furthermore," Brick says, "I think they ought to put you in an insane asylum if you really believe your old dog has a chance. But I will give you a bet," he says. "How much do you wish me to lay against your wife?"

Well, this is very harsh language indeed, and I can see that Brick is getting something off his chest he is packing there for some time. The chances are he is putting the blast on poor Hymie Banjo Eyes on account of Hymie grabbing 'Lasses from him, and of course Brick McCloskey never figures for a minute that Hymie will take his question seriously. But Hymie answers like this:

"You are a price maker," he says. "What do you lay?"

Now this is a most astonishing reply, indeed, when you figure that Hymie is asking what Brick will bet against Hymie's ever-loving wife 'Lasses, and I am very sorry to hear Hymie ask, especially as I happen to turn around and find that nobody but 'Lasses herself is listening in on the conversation, and the chances are her face will be very white, if it is not for her make-up, 'Lasses being a doll who goes in for make-up more than somewhat.

"Yes," Brick McCloskey says, "I am a price maker, all right, and I will lay you a price. I will lay you five C's against your wife that your plug does not win," he says.

Brick looks at 'Lasses as he says this, and 'Lasses looks at Brick, and personally I will probably take a pop at a guy who looks at my ever-loving wife in such a way, if I happen to have any ever-loving wife, and maybe I will take a pop at my ever-loving wife, too, if she looks back at a guy in such a way, but of course Hymie is not noticing such things as looks at this time, and in fact he does not see 'Lasses as yet. But he does not hesitate in answering Brick.

"You are a bet," says Hymie. "Five hundred bucks against my ever-loving wife 'Lasses. It is a chiseler's price such as you always lay," he says, "and the chances are I can do better if I have time to go shopping around, but as it is," he says, "it is like finding money and I will not let you get away. But be ready to pay cash right after the race, because I will not accept your paper."

Well, I hear of many a strange bet on horse races, but never before do I hear of a guy betting his ever-loving wife, although to tell you the truth I never before hear of a guy getting the opportunity to bet his wife on a race. For all I know, if bookmakers take wives as a steady thing there will be much action in such matters at every track.

But I can see that both Brick McCloskey and Hymie Banjo Eyes are in dead earnest, and about this time 'Lasses tries to cop a quiet sneak, and Hymie sees her and speaks to her as follows:

"Hello, Baby," Hymie says. "I will have your five yards for you in a few minutes and five more to go with it, as I am just about to clip a sucker. Wait here with me, Baby," Hymie says.

"No," 'Lasses says; "I am too nervous to wait here. I am going down by the fence to root your horse in," she says, but as she goes away I see another look pass between her and Brick McCloskey.

Well, all of a sudden Cassidy gets the horses in a nice line and lets them go, and as they come busting down past the stand the first time who is right there on top but old Mahogany, with this dizzy Scroon kicking at his skinny sides and yelling in his ears. As they make the first turn, Scroon has Mahogany a length in front, and he moves him out another length as they hit the back side.

Now I always like to watch the races from a spot away up the lawn, as I do not care to have anybody much around me when the tough finishes come along in case I wish to bust out crying, so I leave Hymie Banjo Eyes and Brick McCloskey still glaring at each other and go to my usual place, and who is standing there, too, all by herself but 'Lasses. And about this time the horses are making the turn into the stretch and Mahogany is still on top, but something is coming very fast on the outside. It looks as if Mahogany is in a tough spot, because halfway down the stretch the outside horse nails him and looks him right in the eye, and who is it but the favorite, Side Burns.

They come on like a team, and I am personally giving Side Burns a great ride from where I am standing, when I hear a doll yelling out loud, and who is the doll but 'Lasses, and what is she yelling but the following: "Come on with him, jock!"

Furthermore, as she yells, 'Lasses snaps her fingers like a crap shooter and runs a couple of yards one way and then turns and runs a couple of yards back the other way, so I can see that 'Lasses is indeed of a nervous temperament, just as Hymie Banjo Eyes is always telling me, although up to this time I figure her nerves are the old alzo.

"Come on!" 'Lasses yells again. "Let him roll!" she yells. "Ride him, boy!" she yells. "Come on with him, Frankie!"

Well, I wish to say that 'Lasses' voice may be all right if she is selling tomatoes from door to door, but I will not care to have her using it around me every day for any purpose whatever, because she yells so loud I have to move off a piece to keep my eardrums from being busted wide open. She is still yelling when the horses go past the finish line, the snozzles of old Mahogany and Side Burns so close together that nobody can hardly tell which is which.

In fact, there is quite a wait before the numbers go up, and I can see 'Lasses standing there with her program all wadded up in her fist as she watches the board, and I can see she is under a very terrible nervous strain indeed, and I am very sorry I go around thinking her nerves are the old alzo. Pretty soon the guy hangs out No. 9, and No. 9 is nobody but old Mahogany, and at this I hear 'Lasses screech, and all of a sudden she flops over in a faint, and somebody carries her under the grand stand to revive her, and I figure her nerves bog down entirely, and I am sorrier than ever for thinking bad thoughts of her.

I am also very, very sorry I do not bet my sawbuck on Mahogany, especially when the board shows he pays $102, and I can see where Hymie Banjo Eyes is right about the weight and all, but I am glad Hymie wins the purse and also the five C's off of Brick McCloskey and that he saves his ever-loving wife, because I figure Hymie may now pay me back a few bobs.

I do not see Hymie or Brick or 'Lasses again until the races are over, and then I hear of a big row going on under the stand, and go to see what is doing, and who is having the row but Hymie Banjo Eyes and Brick McCloskey. It seems that Hymie hits Brick a clout on the beezer that stretches Brick out, and it seems that Hymie hits Brick this blow because as Brick is paying Hymie the five C's he makes the following crack:

"I do not mind losing the dough to you, Banjo Eyes," Brick says, "but I am sore at myself for overlaying the price. It is the first time in all the years I am booking that I make such an overlay. The right price against your wife," Brick says, "is maybe two dollars and a half."

Well, as Brick goes down with a busted beezer from Hymie's punch, and everybody is much excited, who steps out of the crowd around them and throws her arms around Hymie Banjo Eyes, but his ever-loving wife 'Lasses, and as she kisses Hymie smack dab in the mush, 'Lasses says as follows:

"My darling Hymie," she says, "I hear what this big flannelmouth says about the price on me, and," she says, "I am only sorry you do not cripple him for life. I know now I love you, and only you, Hymie," she says, "and I will never love anybody else. In fact," 'Lasses says, "I just prove my love for you by almost wrecking my nerves in rooting Mahogany home. I am still weak," she says, "but I have strength enough left to go with you to the Sunset Inn for a nice dinner, and you can give me my money then. Furthermore," 'Lasses says, "now that we have a few bobs, I think you better find another place for Mahogany to stay, as it does not look nice for my husband to be living with a horse."

Well, I am going by the jockey house on my way home, thinking how nice it is that Hymie Banjo Eyes will no longer have to live with Mahogany, and what a fine thing it is to have a loyal, ever-loving wife such as 'Lasses, who risks her nerves rooting for her husband's horse, when I run into this dizzy Scroon in his street clothes, and wishing to be friendly, I say to him like this:

"Hello, Frankie," I say. "You put up a nice ride to-day."

"Where do you get this 'Frankie'?" Scroon says. "My name is Gus."

"Why," I say, commencing to think of this and that, "so it is, but is there a jock called Frankie in the sixth race with you this afternoon?"

"Sure," Scroon says. "Frankie Madeley. He rides Side Burns, the favorite; and I make a sucker of him in the stretch run."

But of course I never mention to Hymie Banjo Eyes that I figure his ever-loving wife roots herself into a dead faint for the horse that will give her to Brick McCloskey, because for all I know she may think Scroon's name is Frankie, at that.

The Brakeman's Daughter

It is coming on spring in Newark, N. J., and one nice afternoon I am standing on Broad Street with a guy from Cleveland, O., by the name of The Humming Bird, speaking of this and that, and one thing and another, when along comes a very tasty-looking young doll.

In fact, she is a doll with black hair, and personally I claim there is nothing more restful to the eye than a doll with black hair, because it is even money, or anyway nine to ten, that it is the natural color of the hair, as it seems that dolls will change the color of their hair to any color but black, and why this is nobody knows, except that it is just the way dolls are.

Well, besides black hair, this doll has a complexion like I do not know what, and little feet and ankles, and a way of walking that is very pleasant to behold. Personally, I always take a gander at a doll's feet and ankles before I start handicapping her, because the way I look at it, the feet and ankles are the big tell in the matter of class, although I wish to state that I see some dolls in my time who have large feet and big ankles, but who are by no means bad.

But this doll I am speaking of is one hundred per cent in every respect, and as she passes, The Humming Bird looks at her, and she looks at The Humming Bird, and it is just the same as if they hold a two hours' conversation on the telephone, for they are both young, and it is spring, and the way language can pass between young guys and young dolls in the spring without them saying a word is really most surprising, and in fact it is practically uncanny.

Well, I can see that The Humming Bird is somewhat confused for a minute, while the young doll seems to go right off into a trance, and she starts crossing the street against the lights, which is not only unlawful in Newark, N. J., but most indiscreet, and she is about to be run down and mashed like a turnip by one of Big False Face's beer trucks when The Humming Bird hops out into the street and yanks her out of danger, while the beer truck goes on down the street with the jockey looking back and yelling words you will scarcely believe are known to anybody in Newark, N. J.

Then The Humming Bird and the young doll stand on the sidewalk chewing the fat for a minute or two, and it is plain to be seen that the doll is very much obliged to The Humming Bird, and it is also plain to be seen that The Humming Bird will give anyway four bobs to have the jockey of the beer truck where he can talk to him quietly.

Finally the doll goes on across the street, but this time she keeps her head up and watches where she is going, and The Humming Bird comes back to me, and I ask him if he finds out who she is, and does he date her up, or what? But in answer to my questions, The Humming Bird states to me as follows:

"To tell the truth," The Humming Bird says, "I neglect these details, because," he says, "I am already dated up to go out with Big False Face tonight to call on a doll who is daffy to meet me. Otherwise," he says, "I will undoubtedly make arrangements to see more of this pancake I just save from rack and ruin.

"But," The Humming Bird says, "Big Falsy tells me I am going to meet the most wonderful doll in the world, and one that is very difficult to meet, so I cannot be picking up any excess at this time. In fact," he says, "Big Falsy tells me that every guy in this town will give his right leg for the privilege of meeting the doll in question, but she will have no part of them. But it seems that she sees me talking to Big Falsy on the street yesterday, and now nothing will do but she must meet up with me personally. Is it not remarkable," The Humming Bird says, "the way dolls go for me?"

Well, I says it is, for I can see that The Humming Bird is such a guy as thinks he has something on the dolls, and for all I know maybe he has, at that, for he has plenty of youth, and good looks, and good clothes, and a nice line of gab, and all these matters are given serious consideration by the dolls, especially the youth.

But I cannot figure any doll that Big False Face knows being such a doll as the one The Humming Bird just yanks out the way of the beer truck, and in fact I do not see how any doll whatever can have any truck with a guy as ugly as Big False Face. But then of course Big False Face is now an important guy in the business world, and has plenty of potatoes, and of course potatoes are also something that is taken into consideration by the dolls.

Big False Face is in the brewery business, and he controls a number of breweries in different spots on the Atlantic seaboard, and especially in New Jersey, and the reason The Humming Bird is in Newark, N. J., at this time, is because Big False Face gets a very huge idea in connection with these breweries.

It seems that they are breweries that Big False Face takes over during the past ten years when the country is trying to get along without beer, and the plants are laying idle, and Big False Face opens up these plants, and puts many guys to work, and turns out plenty of beer, and thus becomes quite a philanthropist in his way, especially to citizens who like their beer, although up to the time he gets going good as a brewer, Big False Face is considered a very humble character, indeed.

He comes from the Lower East Side of New York, and he is called Big False Face from the time he is very young, because he has a very large and a very homely kisser, and on this kisser there is always a castor-oil smile that looks as if it is painted on. But this smile is strictly a throw-off, and Big False Face is often smiling when he is by no means amused at anything, though I must say for him that he is generally a very light-hearted guy.

In his early youth, it is Big False Face's custom to stand chatting with strangers to the city around the railroad stations and ferryboat landings, and smiling very genially at them, and in this way Big False Face learns much about other parts of the country. But it seems that while he is chatting with these strangers, friends of Big False Face search the strangers' pockets, sometimes removing articles from these pockets such as watches, and lucky pieces, and keepsakes of one kind and another, including money.

Of course it is all in fun, but it seems that some of the strangers become greatly annoyed when they find their pockets empty, and go out of their way to mention the matter to the gendarmes. Well, after the gendarmes hear some little mention from strangers about their pockets being searched while they are chatting with a guy with a large, smiling kisser, the gendarmes take to looking around for such a guy. .

Naturally, they finally come upon Big False Face, for at the time I am speaking of, it is by no means common to find guys with smiles on their kissers on the Lower East Side, and, especially, large smiles. So what happens but Big False Face is sent to college in his youth by the gendarmes, and the place where the college is located is Auburn, N. Y., where they teach him that it is very, very wrong to smile at strangers while their pockets are being searched.

After Big False Face is in college for several years, the warden sends for him one day and gives him a new suit of clothes, and a railroad ticket, and a few bobs, and plenty of sound advice, and tells him to go back home again, and afterwards Big False Face says he is only sorry he can never remember the advice, as he has no doubt it will be of great value to him in his subsequent career.

Well, later on Big False Face takes a postgraduate

course at Ossining, and also at Dannemora, and by the time he is through with all this, he finds that conditions change throughout the country, and that his former occupation is old-fashioned, and by no means genteel, so Big False Face has to think up something else to do. And while he is thinking, he drives a taxicab and has his station in front of the Pekin restaurant on Broadway, which is a real hot spot at this time.

Then one night a sailor off a U. S. battleship hires Big False Face to take him riding in Central Park, and it seems that somewhere on this ride the sailor loses his leather containing a month's salary, and he hops out of the taxicab and starts complaining to a gendarme, making quite a mountain out of nothing but a molehill, for anybody knows that if the sailor does not lose his leather in the taxicab, he is bound to spend it at ten cents a clip dancing with the dolls in the Flowerland dance hall, or maybe taking boat rides on the lagoon in the park.

Well, Big False Face can see an argument coming up, and rather than argue, he retires from the taxicab business at once, leaving his taxicab right there in the park, and going over into New Jersey, and Big False Face always says that one of the regrets of his life is he never collects the taxi fare off the sailor.

In New Jersey, Big False Face secures a position with the late Crowbar Connolly, riding loads down out of Canada, and then he is with the late Hands McGovern, and the late Dark Tony de More, and also the late Lanky-lank Watson, and all this time Big False Face is advancing step by step in the business world, for he has a great personality, and is well liked by one and all.

Naturally, many citizens are jealous of Big False Face, and sometimes when they are speaking of him they speak of the days of his youth when he is on the whizz, as if this is something against him, but I always say it is very creditable of Big False Face to rise from such a humble beginning to a position of affluence in the business world.

Personally, I consider Big False Face a remarkable

character, especially when he takes over the idle breweries, because it is at a time when everybody is going
around saying that if they can only have beer everything will be all right. So Big False Face starts turning
out beer that tastes very good, indeed, and if everything
is not all right, it is by no means his fault.

You must remember that at the time he starts turning out his beer, and for years afterwards, Big False
Face is being most illegal and quite against the law, and
I claim that the way he is able to hide several breweries,
each covering maybe half a block of ground, from the
gendarmes all these years is practically magical, and
proves that what I say about Big False Face being a
remarkable character is very true.

Well, when Congress finally gets around to saying that
beer is all right again, Big False Face is a well-estab-
lished, going concern, and has a fair head-start on the
old-fashioned brewers who come back into the business
again, but Big False Face is smart enough to know that
he will be able to keep ahead of them only by great
enterprise and industry, because it seems that certain
parties are bound and determined to make it tough on
the brewers who supply this nation with beer when beer
is illegal, such as Big False Face, forgetting all the hardships and dangers that these brewers face through the
years to give the American people their beer, and all
the bother they are put to in hiding breweries from the
gendarmes.

In fact, these certain parties are making it so tough
that Big False Face himself has to write twice before
he can get permits for his breweries, and naturally this
annoys Big False Face no little, as he hates to write
letters.

Furthermore, he hears this condition prevails all over
the country, so Big False Face gets to thinking things
over, and he decides that the thing to do is to organize
the independent brewers like himself into an association
to protect their interests. So he calls a meeting in Newark, N. J., of all these brewers, and this is how it comes

that The Humming Bird is present, for The Humming Bird represents certain interests around Cleveland, O., and furthermore The Humming Bird is personally regarded as a very able young guy when it comes to breweries.

Well, the only reason I am in Newark, N. J., at this time is because a guy by the name of Abie Schumtzenheimer is a delegate representing a New York brewery, and this Abie is a friend of mine, and after the meeting lasts three days he sends for me to come over and play pinochle with him, because he cannot make heads or tails of what they are all talking about.

And anyway Abie does not care much, because the brewery he represents is going along for nearly twelve years, and is doing all the business it can handle, and any time it fails to do all the business it can handle, Abie will be around asking a lot of people why.

So Abie's brewery does not care if it enters any association or not, but of course Abie cannot disregard an invitation from such a guy as Big False Face. So there he is, and by and by there I am, and in this way I meet up with The Humming Bird, and after watching the way he goes darting around and about, especially if a doll happens to pop up in his neighborhood, I can understand why they call him The Humming Bird.

But, personally, I do not mind seeing a young guy displaying an interest in dolls, and in fact if a young guy does not display such an interest in dolls, I am apt to figure there is something wrong with him. And anyway what is the use of being young if a guy does not display an interest in dolls?

Well, there are delegates to the meeting from as far west as Chicago, and most of them seem to be greatly interested in Big False Face's proposition, especially a delegate from South Chicago who keeps trying to introduce a resolution to sue the government for libel for speaking of brewers who supply the nation with beer after prohibition sets in, as racket guys and wildcatters.

The reason the meeting lasts so long is partly because

Big False Face keeps making motions for recesses so he
can do a little entertaining, for if there is one thing Big
False Face loves, it is to entertain, but another reason is
that not all the delegates are willing to join Big False
Face's association, especially certain delegates who are
operating in Pennsylvania.

These delegates say it is nothing but a scheme on the
part of Big False Face to nab the business on them, and
in fact it seems that there is much resentment among
these delegates against Big False Face, and especially on
the part of a guy by the name of Cheeks Sheracki, who
comes from Philadelphia, Pa., and I wish to state that
if there is one guy in the United States I will not care to
have around resenting me, it is Cheeks Sheracki, for
nobody knows how many guys Cheeks cools off in his
time, not even himself.

But Big False Face does not seem to notice anybody
resenting him, and he is putting on entertainment for
the delegates right and left, including a nice steak dinner on the evening of the day I am speaking of, and it
is at this dinner I state to Big False Face that I hear he
is taking The Humming Bird out in society.

"Yes," Big False Face says, "I am going to take The
Humming Bird to call on the brakeman's daughter."

Well, when I hear this, I wish to say I am somewhat
surprised, because the brakeman's daughter is nothing
but a practical joke, and furthermore it is a practical
joke that is only for rank suckers, and The Humming
Bird does not look to be such a sucker to me.

In fact, when Big False Face speaks of the brakeman's
daughter, I take a gander at The Humming Bird, figuring to see some expression on his kisser that will show
he knows what the brakeman's daughter is, but instead
The Humming Bird is only looking quite eager, and
then I get to thinking about what he tells me in the
afternoon about Big False Face taking him to see a doll
who is daffy to meet him, and I can see that Big False
Face is working on him with the brakeman's daughter
for some time.

And I also get to thinking that a lot of smarter guys than The Humming Bird will ever be, no matter how smart he gets, fall for the brakeman's daughter joke, including Big False Face himself. In fact, Big False Face falls for it in the spring of 1928 at Hot Springs, Ark., and ever since it is his favorite joke, and it becomes part of his entertainment of all visitors to Newark, N. J., unless of course they happen to be visitors who are jerry to the brakeman's daughter. In fact, Big False Face builds up the brakeman's daughter into quite a well-known institution in Newark, N. J., and the way the brakeman's daughter joke goes is as follows:

The idea is Big False Face picks out some guy that he figures is a little doll-dizzy, and the way Big False Face can rap to a doll-dizzy guy is really quite remarkable. Then he starts telling this guy about the brakeman's daughter, who is the most beautiful doll that ever steps in shoe leather, to hear Big False Face tell it. In fact, I once hear Big False Face telling a sucker about how beautiful the brakeman's daughter is, and I find myself wishing to see her, although of course I know there is no such thing as the brakeman's daughter.

Furthermore, everybody around Big False Face starts putting in a boost for the brakeman's daughter, stating to the sucker that she is so lovely that guys are apt to go silly just looking at her. But it seems that the brakeman's daughter has a papa who is a brakeman on the Central, and who is the orneriest guy in the world when it comes to his daughter, and who will not let anybody get close enough to her to hand her a slice of fruit cake.

In fact, this brakeman is so ornery he will shoot you setting if he catches you fooling around his daughter, the way Big False Face and other citizens of Newark, N. J., state the situation to the sucker, and everybody is afraid of the brakeman, including guys who are not supposed to be afraid of anything in this world.

But it seems that Big False Face is acquainted with the brakeman's daughter, and knows the nights the brakeman has to be out on his run, and on these nights

the brakeman's daughter is home alone, and on such a
night Big False Face occasionally calls on her, and sometimes takes a friend. But Big False Face and everybody
else says that it is a dangerous proposition, because if
the brakeman ever happens to come home unexpectedly
and find callers with his daughter, he is pretty sure to
hurt somebody.

Well, the chances are the sucker wishes to call on the
brakeman's daughter, no matter what, especially as Big
False Face generally lets on that the brakeman's daughter sees the sucker somewhere and is very anxious to
meet him, just as he lets on to The Humming Bird, so
finally some night Big Falsy takes the sucker to the
house where the brakeman's daughter lives, making their
approach to the house very roundabout, and mysterious,
and sneaky.

Then the minute Big Falsy knocks on the door, out
pops a guy from somewhere roaring at them in a large
voice, and Big False Face yells that it is the brakeman's
daughter's papa himself, and starts running, telling the
sucker to follow, although as a rule this is by no means
necessary. And when the sucker starts running, he commences to hear shots, and naturally he figures that the
old brakeman is popping at him with a Betsy, but what
he really hears is incandescent light bulbs going off
around him and sometimes they hit him if the bulb-
thrower has good control.

Now, the house Big False Face generally uses is an
old empty residence pretty well out in a suburb of
Newark, N. J., and it sits away off by itself in a big yard
near a piece of woods, and when he starts running, Big
False Face always runs into this woods, and naturally
the sucker follows him. And pretty soon Big False Face
loses the sucker in the woods, and doubles back and
goes on downtown and leaves the sucker wandering
around in the woods for maybe hours.

Then when the sucker finally makes his way back to
his hotel, he always finds many citizens gathered to give
him the ha-ha, and to make him buy refreshments for

one and all, and the sucker tries to make out that he is greatly amused himself, although the chances are he is so hot you can fry an egg on any part of him.

The biggest laugh that Big False Face ever gets out of the brakeman's daughter joke is the time he leaves a guy from Brooklyn by the name of Rocco Scarpati in the woods one cold winter night, and Rocco never does find his way out, and freezes as stiff as a starched shirt. And of course Big False Face has quite a time explaining to Rocco's Brooklyn friends that Rocco is not cooled off by other means than freezing.

Well, now the way I tell it, you say to yourself how can anybody be sucker enough to fall for such a plant at this? But Big False Face's record with the brakeman's daughter joke in Newark, N. J., includes a congressman, a justice of the peace, three G-guys, eighteen newspaper scribes, five prize fighters, and a raft of guys from different parts of the country, who are such guys as the ordinary citizens will hesitate about making merry with.

In fact, I hear Big False Face is putting the feel on Cheeks Sheracki with reference to the brakeman's daughter until he finds out Cheeks knows this joke as well as he does himself, and then Big False Face discovers The Humming Bird, and no one is talking stronger for the brakeman's daughter with The Humming Bird than Cheeks.

Well, anyway, along about nine o'clock on the night in question, Big False Face tells The Humming Bird that the brakeman is now well out on his run on the Central, so they get in Big False Face's car and start out, and I notice that as they get in the car, Big False Face gives The Humming Bird a quick fanning, as Big False Face does not care to take chances on a sucker having that certain business on him.

The Humming Bird is all sharpened up for this occasion, and furthermore he is quite excited, and one and all are telling him what a lucky guy he is to get to call on the brakeman's daughter, but anybody can see from the way The Humming Bird acts that he feels that it is really the brakeman's daughter who is having the luck.

It seems that Cheeks Sheracki and a couple of his guys from Philadelphia go out to the house in advance to heave the incandescent bulbs and do the yelling, and personally I sit up playing pinochle with Abie Schumtzenheimer waiting to hear what comes off, although Abie says it is all great foolishness, and by no means worthy of grown guys. But Abie admits he will be glad to see the brakeman's daughter himself if she is as beautiful as Big False Face claims.

Well, when they come within a couple of blocks of the empty house in the suburbs of Newark, N. J., Big False Face tells his driver, a guy by the name of Ears Acosta, who afterwards informs me on several points in this transaction, to pull up and wait there, and then Big False Face and The Humming Bird get out of the car and Big False Face leads the way up the street and into the yard.

This yard is filled with big trees and shrubbery, but the moon is shining somewhat, and it is easy enough to make out objects around and about, but there are no lights in the house, and it is so quiet you can hear your watch tick in your pocket, if you happen to have a watch.

Well, Big False Face has The Humming Bird by the coat sleeve, and he tiptoes through the gate and up a pathway, and The Humming Bird tiptoes right with him, and every now and then Big False Face stops and listens, and the way Big False Face puts this on is really wonderful, because he does it so often he can get a little soul into his work.

Now, The Humming Bird has plenty of moxie from all I hear, but naturally seeing the way Big False Face is acting makes him feel a little nervous, because The Humming Bird knows that Big False Face is as game as they come, and he figures that any situation that makes Big False Face act as careful as all this must be a very dangerous situation, indeed.

When they finally get up close to the house, The Humming Bird sees there is a porch, and Big False Face tiptoes up on this porch, still leading The Humming Bird by the coat sleeve, and then Big False Face knocks softly on the door, and lets out a little low whistle, and just as The Humming Bird is commencing to notice that this place seems to be somewhat deserted, all of a sudden a guy comes busting around the corner of the house.

This guy is making a terrible racket, what with yelling and swearing, and among other things he yells as follows:

"Ah-ha!" the guy yells, "now I have you dead to rights!"

And with this, something goes pop, and then something goes pop-pop, and Big False Face says to The Humming Bird like this:

"My goodness," Big False Face says, "it is the brakeman! Run!" he says. "Run for your life!"

Then Big False Face turns and runs, and The Humming Bird is about to turn and run with him, because The Humming Bird figures if a guy like Big False Face can afford to run there can be no percentage in standing still himself, but before he can move the door of the house flies open and The Humming Bird feels himself being yanked inside the joint, and he puts up his dukes and gets ready to do the best he can until he is overpowered. Then he hears a doll's voice going like this:

"Sh-h-h-h!" the doll's voice goes. "Sh-h-h-h!"

So The Humming Bird sh-h-h-h's, and the racket goes on outside a while with a guy still yelling, and much pop-pop-popping away. Then the noise dies out, and all is still, and by the moonlight that is coming through a window on which there is no curtain, The Humming Bird can see a lot of furniture scattered around and about the room, but some of it is upside down, and none of it is arranged in any order.

Furthermore, The Humming Bird can now also see that the doll who pulls him into the house and gives him the sh-h-h-h is nobody but the black-haired doll he hauls out of the way of the beer truck in the afternoon, and naturally The Humming Bird is somewhat surprised to see her at this time.

Well, the black-haired doll smiles at The Humming Bird, and finally he forgets his nervousness to some extent, and in fact drops his dukes which he still has up ready to sell his life dearly, and by and by the black-haired doll says to him like this:

"I recognize you through the window in the moonlight," she says. "As I see you coming up on the porch, I also see some parties lurking in the shrubbery, and," she says, "I have a feeling they are seeking to do you harm, so I pull you inside the house. I am glad to see you again," she says.

Well, Big False Face does not show up in his accustomed haunts to laugh at the joke on The Humming Bird, but Ears Acosta returns with disquieting news such as causes many citizens to go looking for Big False Face, and they find him face downward on the path just inside the gateway, and when they turn him over the old castor-oil smile is still on his kisser, and even larger than ever, as if Big False Face is greatly amused by some thought that hits him all of a sudden.

And Big False Face is extremely dead when they find him, as it seems that some of the incandescent bulbs that go pop-popping around him are really sawed-off shot-guns, and it also seems that Cheeks Sheracki and his guys from Philadelphia are such careless shots that they tear off half the gate with their slugs, so it is pretty lucky for The Humming Bird that he is not running with Big False Face for this gate at the moment, or in fact anywhere near him.

And back in the house while they are lugging Big False Face away, The Humming Bird and the black-haired doll are sitting on an overturned sofa in the parlor with the moonlight streaming through the window on which there is no curtain and spilling all over them as The Humming Bird is telling her how much he loves her, and how he hopes and trusts she feels the same towards him, for they are young, and it is spring in Newark, N. J.

"Well," The Humming Bird says, "so you are the brakeman's daughter, are you? Well," he says, "I wish to state that they do not overboost you a nickel's worth when they tell me you are the most beautiful doll in all this world, and I am certainly tickled to find you."

"But how do you learn my new address so soon?" the black-haired doll says. "We just move in here this morning, although," she says, "I guess it is a good thing for you we do not have time to put up any window shades. And what do you mean," the black-haired doll says, "by calling me the brakeman's daughter? My papa is one of the oldest and best known conductors anywhere on the Erie," she says.

Little Miss Marker

One evening along toward seven o'clock, many citizens are standing out on Broadway in front of Mindy's restaurant, speaking of one thing and another, and particularly about the tough luck they have playing the races in the afternoon, when who comes up the street with a little doll hanging onto his right thumb but a guy by the name of Sorrowful.

This guy is called Sorrowful because this is the way he always is about no matter what, and especially about the way things are with him when anybody tries to put the bite on him. In fact, if anybody who tries to put the bite on Sorrowful can listen to him for two minutes about how things are with him and not bust into tears, they must be very hard-hearted, indeed.

Regret, the horse player, is telling me that he once tries to put the bite on Sorrowful for a sawbuck, and by the time Sorrowful gets through explaining how things are with him, Regret feels so sorry for him that he goes out and puts the bite on somebody else for the saw and gives it to Sorrowful, although it is well known to one and all that Sorrowful has plenty of potatoes hid away somewhere.

He is a tall, skinny guy with a long, sad, mean-looking kisser, and a mournful voice. He is maybe sixty years old, give or take a couple of years, and for as long as I can remember he is running a handbook over in Forty-ninth Street next door to a chop-suey joint. In fact, Sorrowful is one of the largest handbook makers in this town.

Any time you see him he is generally by himself, because being by himself is not apt to cost him anything, and it is therefore a most surprising scene when he comes along Broadway with a little doll.

And there is much speculation among the citizens as to how this comes about, for no one ever hears of Sorrowful having any family, or relations of any kind, or even any friends.

The little doll is a very little doll indeed, the top of her noggin only coming up to Sorrowful's knee, although of course Sorrowful has very high knees, at that. Moreover, she is a very pretty little doll, with big blue eyes and fat pink cheeks, and a lot of yellow curls hanging down her back, and she has fat little legs and quite a large smile, although Sorrowful is lugging her along the street so fast that half the time her feet are dragging the sidewalk and she has a license to be bawling instead of smiling.

Sorrowful is looking sadder than somewhat, which makes his face practically heart-rending as he pulls up in front of Mindy's and motions us to follow him in. Anybody can see that he is worried about something very serious, and many citizens are figuring that maybe he suddenly discovers all his potatoes are counterfeit, because nobody can think of anything that will worry Sorrowful except money.

Anyway, four or five of us gather around the table where Sorrowful sits down with the little doll beside him, and he states a most surprising situation to us.

It seems that early in the afternoon a young guy who is playing the races with Sorrowful for several days pops into his place of business next door to the chop-suey joint, leading the little doll, and this guy wishes to know how much time he has before post in the first race at Empire.

Well, he only has about twenty-five minutes, and he seems very down-hearted about this, because he explains to Sorrowful that he has a sure thing in this race, which he gets the night before off a guy who is a pal of a close friend of Jockey Workman's valet.

The young guy says he is figuring to bet himself about a deuce on this sure thing, but he does not have such a sum as a deuce on him when he goes to bed, so he plans to get up bright and early in the morning and hop down to a spot on Fourteenth Street where he knows a guy who will let him have the deuce.

But it seems he oversleeps, and here it is almost post time, and it is too late for him to get to Fourteenth Street and back before the race is run off, and it is all quite a sad story indeed, although of course it does not make much impression on Sorrowful, as he is already sadder than somewhat himself just from thinking that somebody may beat him for a bet during the day, even though the races do not start anywhere as yet.

Well, the young guy tells Sorrowful he is going to try to get to Fourteenth Street and back in time to bet on the sure thing, because he says it will be nothing short of a crime if he has to miss such a wonderful opportunity.

"But," he says to Sorrowful, "to make sure I do not miss, you take my marker for a deuce, and I will leave the kid here with you as security until I get back."

Now, ordinarily, asking Sorrowful to take a marker will be considered great foolishness, as it is well known to one and all that Sorrowful will not take a marker from Andrew Mellon. In fact, Sorrowful can almost break your heart telling you about the poorhouses that are full of bookmakers who take markers in their time.

But it happens that business is just opening up for the day, and Sorrowful is pretty busy, and besides the young guy is a steady customer for several days, and has an honest pan, and Sorrowful figures a guy is bound to take a little doll out of hock for a deuce. Furthermore, while Sorrowful does not know much about kids, he can see the little doll must be worth a deuce, at least, and maybe more.

So he nods his head, and the young guy puts the little doll on a chair and goes tearing out of the joint to get the dough, while Sorrowful marks down a deuce bet on Cold Cuts, which is the name of the sure thing. Then he forgets all about the proposition for a while, and all the time the little doll is sitting on the chair as quiet as a mouse, smiling at Sorrowful's customers, including the Chinks from the chop-suey joint who come in now and then to play the races.

Well, Cold Cuts blows, and in fact is not even fifth, and along late in the afternoon Sorrowful suddenly realizes that the young guy never shows up again, and that the little doll is still sitting in the chair, although she is now playing with a butcher knife which one of the Chinks from the chop-suey joint gives her to keep her amused.

Finally it comes on Sorrowful's closing time, and the little doll is still there, so he can think of nothing else to do in this situation, but to bring her around to Mindy's and get a little advice from different citizens, as he does not care to leave her in his place of business alone, as Sorrowful will not trust anybody in there alone, not even himself.

"Now," Sorrowful says, after giving us this long spiel, "what are we to do about this proposition?"

Well, of course, up to this minute none of the rest of us know we are being cut in on any proposition, and personally I do not care for any part of it, but Big Nig, the craps shooter, speaks up as follows:

"If this little doll is sitting in your joint all afternoon," Nig says, "the best thing to do right now is to throw a feed into her, as the chances are her stomach thinks her throat is cut."

Now this seems to be a fair sort of an idea, so Sorrowful orders up a couple of portions of ham hocks and sauerkraut, which is a very tasty dish in Mindy's at all times, and the little doll tears into it very enthusiastically, using both hands, although a fat old doll who is sitting at the next table speaks up and says this is terrible fodder to be tossing into a child at such an hour and where is her mamma?

"Well," Big Nig says to the old doll, "I hear of many people getting a bust in the snoot for not minding their own business in this town, but you give off an idea, at that. Listen," Big Nig says to the little doll, "where is your mamma?"

But the little doll does not seem to know, or maybe she does not wish to make this information public, because she only shakes her head and smiles at Big Nig, as her mouth is too full of ham hocks and sauerkraut for her to talk.

"What is your name?" Big Nig asks, and she says something that Big Nig claims sounds like Marky, although personally I think she is trying to say Martha. Anyway, it is from this that she gets the name we always call her afterward, which is Marky.

"It is a good monicker," Big Nig says. "It is short for marker, and she is certainly a marker unless Sorrowful is telling us a large lie. Why," Big Nig says, "this is a very cute little doll, at that, and pretty smart. How old are you, Marky?"

She only shakes her head again, so Regret, the horse player, who claims he can tell how old a horse is by its teeth, reaches over and sticks his finger in her mouth to get a peek at her crockery, but she seems to think Regret's finger is a hunk of ham hock and shuts down on it so hard Regret lets out an awful squawk. But he says

that before she tries to cripple him for life he sees enough
of her teeth to convince him she is maybe three, rising
four, and this seems reasonable, at that. Anyway, she
cannot be much older.

Well, about this time a guinea with a hand organ stops
out in front of Mindy's and begins grinding out a tune
while his ever-loving wife is passing a tambourine around
among the citizens on the sidewalk and, on hearing this
music, Marky slides off of her chair with her mouth still
full of ham hock and sauerkraut, which she swallows so
fast she almost chokes, and then she speaks as follows:

"Marky dance," she says.

Then she begins hopping and skipping around among
the tables, holding her little short skirt up in her hands
and showing a pair of white panties underneath. Pretty
soon Mindy himself comes along and starts putting up a
beef about making a dance hall of his joint, but a guy by
the name of Sleep-out, who is watching Marky with much
interest, offers to bounce a sugar bowl off of Mindy's
sconce if he does not mind his own business.

So Mindy goes away, but he keeps muttering about
the white panties being a most immodest spectacle, which
of course is great nonsense, as many dolls older than
Marky are known to do dances in Mindy's, especially
on the late watch, when they stop by for a snack on
their way home from the night clubs and the speaks,
and I hear some of them do not always wear white panties, either.

Personally, I like Marky's dancing very much, although of course she is no Pavlowa, and finally she trips
over her own feet and falls on her snoot. But she gets up
smiling and climbs back on her chair and pretty soon
she is sound asleep with her head against Sorrowful.

Well, now there is much discussion about what Sorrowful ought to do with her. Some claim he ought to
take her to a police station, and others say the best thing
to do is to put an ad in the Lost and Found columns of
the morning bladders, the same as people do when they

find Angora cats, and Pekes, and other animals which they do not wish to keep, but none of these ideas seems to appeal to Sorrowful.

Finally he says he will take her to his own home and let her sleep there while he is deciding what is to be done about her, so Sorrowful takes Marky in his arms and lugs her over to a fleabag in West Forty-ninth Street where he has a room for many years, and afterwards a bellhop tells me Sorrowful sits up all night watching her while she is sleeping.

Now what happens but Sorrowful takes on a great fondness for the little doll, which is most surprising, as Sorrowful is never before fond of anybody or anything, and after he has her overnight he cannot bear the idea of giving her up.

Personally, I will just as soon have a three-year-old baby wolf around me as a little doll such as this, but Sorrowful thinks she is the greatest thing that ever happens. He has a few inquiries made around and about to see if he can find out who she belongs to, and he is tickled silly when nothing comes of these inquiries, although nobody else figures anything will come of them anyway, as it is by no means uncommon in this town for little kids to be left sitting in chairs, or on doorsteps, to be chucked into orphan asylums by whoever finds them.

Anyway, Sorrowful says he is going to keep Marky, and his attitude causes great surprise, as keeping Marky is bound to be an expense, and it does not seem reasonable that Sorrowful will go to any expense for anything. When it commences to look as if he means what he says, many citizens naturally figure there must be an angle, and soon there are a great many rumors on the subject.

Of course one of these rumors is that the chances are Marky is Sorrowful's own offspring which is tossed back on him by the wronged mamma, but this rumor is started by a guy who does not know Sorrowful, and after he gets a gander at Sorrowful, the guy apologizes, saying he realizes that no wronged mamma will be daffy enough to permit herself to be wronged by Sorrowful. Personally, I always say that if Sorrowful wishes to keep Marky it is his own business, and most of the citizens around Mindy's agree with me.

But the trouble is Sorrowful at once cuts everybody else in on the management of Marky, and the way he talks to the citizens around Mindy's about her, you will think we are all personally responsible for her. As most of the citizens around Mindy's are bachelors, or are wishing they are bachelors, it is most inconvenient to them to suddenly find themselves with a family.

Some of us try to explain to Sorrowful that if he is going to keep Marky it is up to him to handle all her play, but right away Sorrowful starts talking so sad about all his pals deserting him and Marky just when they need them most that it softens all hearts, although up to this time we are about as pally with Sorrowful as a burglar with a copper. Finally every night in Mindy's is meeting night for a committee to decide something or other about Marky.

The first thing we decide is that the fleabag where Sorrowful lives is no place for Marky, so Sorrowful hires a big apartment in one of the swellest joints on West Fifty-ninth Street, overlooking Central Park, and spends plenty of potatoes furnishing it, although up to this time Sorrowful never sets himself back more than about ten bobs per week for a place to live and considers it extravagance, at that. I hear it costs him five G's to fix up Marky's bedroom alone, not counting the solid gold toilet set that he buys for her.

Then he gets her an automobile and he has to hire a guy to drive it for her, and finally when we explain to Sorrowful that it does not look right for Marky to be living with nobody but him and a chauffeur, Sorrowful hires a French doll with bobbed hair and red cheeks by the name of Mam'selle Fifi as a nurse for Marky, and this seems to be quite a sensible move, as it insures Marky plenty of company.

In fact, up to the time that Sorrowful hires Mam'selle Fifi, many citizens are commencing to consider Marky something of a nuisance and are playing the duck for her and Sorrowful, but after Mam'selle Fifi comes along you can scarcely get in Sorrowful's joint of Fifty-ninth Street, or around his table in Mindy's when he brings Marky and Mam'selle Fifi in to eat. But one night Sorrowful goes home early and catches Sleep-out guzzling Mam'selle Fifi, and Sorrowful makes Mam'selle Fifi take plenty of breeze, claiming she will set a bad example to Marky.

Then he gets an old tomato by the name of Mrs. Clancy to be Marky's nurse, and while there is no doubt Mrs. Clancy is a better nurse than Mam'selle Fifi and there is practically no danger of her setting Marky a bad example, the play at Sorrowful's joint is by no means as brisk as formerly.

You can see that from being closer than a dead heat with his potatoes, Sorrowful becomes as loose as ashes. He not only spends plenty on Marky, but he starts picking up checks in Mindy's and other spots, although up to this time picking up checks is something that is most repulsive to Sorrowful.

He gets so he will hold still for a bite, if the bite is not too savage and, what is more, a great change comes over his kisser. It is no longer so sad and mean-looking, and in fact it is almost a pleasant sight at times, especially as Sorrowful gets so he smiles now and then, and has a big hello for one and all, and everybody says the Mayor ought to give Marky a medal for bringing about such a wonderful change.

Now Sorrowful is so fond of Marky that he wants her with him all the time, and by and by there is much criticism of him for having her around his hand-book joint among the Chinks and the horse players, and especially the horse players, and for taking her around night clubs and keeping her out at all hours, as some people do not consider this a proper bringing-up for a little doll.

We hold a meeting in Mindy's on this proposition one night, and we get Sorrowful to agree to keep Marky out of his joint, but we know Marky is so fond of night clubs, especially where there is music, that it seems a sin and a shame to deprive her of this pleasure altogether, so we finally compromise by letting Sorrowful take her out one night a week to the Hot Box in Fifty-fourth Street, which is only a few blocks from where Marky lives, and Sorrowful can get her home fairly early. In fact, after this Sorrowful seldom keeps her out any later than 2 A.M.

The reason Marky likes night clubs where there is music is because she can do her dance there, as Marky is practically daffy on the subject of dancing, especially by herself, even though she never seems to be able to get over winding up by falling on her snoot, which many citizens consider a very artistic finish, at that.

The Choo-Choo Boys' band in the Hot Box always play a special number for Marky in between the regular dances, and she gets plenty of applause, especially from the Broadway citizens who know her, although Henri, the manager of the Hot Box, once tells me he will just as soon Marky does not do her dancing there, because one night several of his best customers from Park Avenue, including two millionaires and two old dolls, who do not understand Marky's dancing, bust out laughing when she falls on her snoot, and Big Nig puts the slug on the guys, and is trying to put the slug on the old dolls, too, when he is finally headed off.

Now one cold, snowy night, many citizens are sitting around the tables in the Hot Box, speaking of one thing and another and having a few drams, when Sorrowful drops in on his way home, for Sorrowful has now become a guy who is around and about, and in and out. He does not have Marky with him, as it is not her night out and she is home with Mrs. Clancy.

A few minutes after Sorrowful arrives, a party by the name of Milk Ear Willie from the West Side comes in, this Milk Ear Willie being a party who is once a prize fighter and who has a milk ear, which is the reason he is called Milk Ear Willie, and who is known to carry a

John Roscoe in his pants pocket. Furthermore, it is well known that he knocks off several guys in his time, so he is considered rather a suspicious character.

It seems that the reason he comes into the Hot Box is to shoot Sorrowful full of little holes, because he has a dispute with Sorrowful about a parlay on the races the day before, and the chances are Sorrowful will now be very dead if it does not happen that, just as Milk Ear outs with the old equalizer and starts taking dead aim at Sorrowful from a table across the room, who pops into the joint but Marky.

She is in a long nightgown that keeps getting tangled up in her bare feet as she runs across the dance floor and jumps into Sorrowful's arms, so if Milk Ear Willie lets go at this time he is apt to put a slug in Marky, and this is by no means Willie's intention. So Willie puts his rod back in his kick, but he is greatly disgusted and stops as he is going out and makes a large complaint to Henri about allowing children in a night club.

Well, Sorrowful does not learn until afterward how Marky saves his life, as he is too much horrified over her coming four or five blocks through the snow bare-footed to think of anything else, and everybody present is also horrified and wondering how Marky finds her way there. But Marky does not seem to have any good explanation for her conduct, except that she wakes up and discovers Mrs. Clancy asleep and gets to feeling lonesome for Sorrowful.

About this time, the Choo-Choo Boys start playing Marky's tune, and she slips out of Sorrowful's arms and runs out on the dance floor.

"Marky dance," she says.

Then she lifts her nightgown in her hands and starts hopping and skipping about the floor until Sorrowful collects her in his arms again, and wraps her in an overcoat and takes her home.

Now what happens, but the next day Marky is sick from being out in the snow bare-footed and with nothing on but her nightgown, and by night she is very sick indeed, and it seems that she has pneumonia, so Sorrowful takes her to the Clinic hospital, and hires two nurses and two croakers, and wishes to hire more, only they tell him these will do for the present.

The next day Marky is no better, and the next night she is worse, and the management of the Clinic is very much upset because it has no place to put the baskets of fruit and candy and floral horseshoes and crates of dolls and toys that keep arriving every few minutes. Furthermore, the management by no means approves of the citizens who are tiptoeing along the hall on the floor where Marky has her room, especially such as Big Nig, and Sleep-out, and Wop Joey, and the Pale Face Kid and Guinea Mike and many other prominent characters, especially as these characters keep trying to date up the nurses.

Of course I can see the management's point of view, but I wish to say that no visitor to the Clinic ever brings more joy and cheer to the patients than Sleep-out, as he goes calling in all the private rooms and wards to say a pleasant word or two to the inmates, and I never take any stock in the rumor that he is looking around to see if there is anything worth picking up. In fact, an old doll from Rockville Center, who is suffering with yellow jaundice, puts up an awful holler when Sleep-out is heaved from her room, because she says he is right in the middle of a story about a traveling salesman and she wishes to learn what happens.

There are so many prominent characters in and around the Clinic that the morning bladders finally get the idea that some well-known mob guy must be in the hospital full of slugs, and by and by the reporters come buzzing around to see what is what. Naturally they find out that all this interest is in nothing but a little doll, and while you will naturally think that such a little doll as Marky can scarcely be worth the attention of the reporters, it seems they get more heated up over her when they hear the story than if she is Jack Diamond.

In fact, the next day all the bladders have large stories

about Marky, and also about Sorrowful and about how all these prominent characters of Broadway are hanging around the Clinic on her account. Moreover, one story tells about Sleep-out entertaining the other patients in the hospital, and it makes Sleep-out sound like a very large-hearted guy.

It is maybe three o'clock on the morning of the fourth day Marky is in the hospital that Sorrowful comes into Mindy's looking very sad, indeed. He orders a sturgeon sandwich on pumpernickel, and then he explains that Marky seems to be getting worse by the minute and that he does not think his doctors are doing her any good, and at this Big Nig, the crap shooter, speaks up and states as follows:

"Well," Big Nig says, "if we are only able to get Doc Beerfeldt, the great pneumonia specialist, the chances are he will cure Marky like breaking sticks. But of course," Nig says, "it is impossible to get Doc Beerfeldt unless you are somebody like John D. Rockfeller, or maybe the President."

Naturally, everybody knows that what Big Nig says is very true, for Doc Beerfeldt is the biggest croaker in this town, but no ordinary guy can get close enough to Doc Beerfeldt to hand him a ripe peach, let alone get him to go out on a case. He is an old guy, and he does not practice much any more, and then only among a few very rich and influential people. Furthermore, he has plenty of potatoes himself, so money does not interest him whatever, and anyway it is great foolishness to be talking of getting Doc Beerfeldt out at such an hour as this.

"Who do we know who knows Doc Beerfeldt?" Sorrowful says. "Who can we call up who may have influence enough with him to get him to just look at Marky? I will pay any price," he says. "Think of somebody," he says.

Well, while we are all trying to think, who comes in but Milk Ear Willie, and he comes in to toss a few slugs at Sorrowful, but before Milk Ear can start blasting

Sleep-out sees him and jumps up and takes him off to a corner table, and starts whispering in Milk Ear's good ear.

As Sleep-out talks to him Milk Ear looks at Sorrowful in great surprise, and finally he begins nodding his head, and by and by he gets up and goes out of the joint in a hurry, while Sleep-out comes back to our table and says like this:

"Well," Sleep-out says, "let us stroll over to the Clinic. I just send Milk Ear Willie up to Doc Beerfeldt's house on Park Avenue to get the old Doc and bring him to the hospital. But, Sorrowful," Sleep-out says, "if he gets him, you must pay Willie the parlay you dispute with him, whatever it is. The chances are," Sleep-out says, "Willie is right. I remember once you out-argue me on a parlay when I know I am right."

Personally, I consider Sleep-out's talk about sending Milk Ear Willie after Doc Beerfeldt just so much nonsense, and so does everybody else, but we figure maybe Sleep-out is trying to raise Sorrowful's hopes, and anyway he keeps Milk Ear from tossing these slugs at Sorrowful, which everybody considers very thoughtful of Sleep-out, at least, especially as Sorrowful is under too great a strain to be dodging slugs just now.

About a dozen of us walk over to the Clinic, and most of us stand around the lobby on the ground floor, although Sorrowful goes up to Marky's floor to wait outside her door. He is waiting there from the time she is first taken to the hospital, never leaving except to go over to Mindy's once in a while to get something to eat, and occasionally they open the door a little to let him get a peek at Marky.

Well, it is maybe six o'clock when we hear a taxi stop outside the hospital and pretty soon in comes Milk Ear Willie with another character from the West Side by the name of Fats Finstein, who is well known to one and all as a great friend of Willie's, and in between them they have a little old guy with a Vandyke beard, who does not seem to have on anything much but a silk dressing gown and who seems somewhat agitated, especially as Milk Ear Willie and Fats Finstein keep prodding him from behind.

Now it comes out that this little old guy is nobody but Doc Beerfeldt, the great pneumonia specialist, and personally I never see a madder guy, although I wish to say I never blame him much for being mad when I learn how Milk Ear Willie and Fats Finstein boff his butler over the noggin when he answers their ring, and how they walk right into old Doc Beerfeldt's bedroom and haul him out of the hay at the point of their Roscoes and make him go with them.

In fact, I consider such treatment most discourteous to a prominent croaker, and if I am Doc Beerfeldt I will start hollering copper as soon as I hit the hospital, and for all I know maybe Doc Beerfeldt has just such an idea, but as Milk Ear Willie and Fats Finstein haul him into the lobby who comes downstairs but Sorrowful. And the minute Sorrowful sees Doc Beerfeldt he rushes up to him and says like this:

"Oh, Doc," Sorrowful says, "do something for my little girl. She is dying, Doc," Sorrowful says. "Just a little bit of a girl, Doc. Her name is Marky. I am only a gambler, Doc, and I do not mean anything to you or to anybody else, but please save the little girl."

Well, old Doc Beerfeldt sticks out his Vandyke beard and looks at Sorrowful a minute, and he can see there are large tears in old Sorrowful's eyes, and for all I know maybe the doc knows it has been many and many a year since there are tears in these eyes, at that. Then the doc looks at Milk Ear Willie and Fats Finstein and the rest of us, and at the nurses and internes who are commencing to come running up from every which way. Finally he speaks as follows:

"What is this?" he says. "A child? A little child? Why," he says, "I am under the impression that these gorillas are kidnapping me to attend to some other sick or wounded gorilla. A child? This is quite different. Why do you not say so in the first place? Where is the child?"

Doc Beerfeldt says, "and," he says, "somebody get me some pants."

We all follow him upstairs to the door of Marky's room and we wait outside when he goes in, and we wait there for hours, because it seems that even old Doc Beerfeldt cannot think of anything to do in this situation no matter how he tries. And along toward ten-thirty in the morning he opens the door very quietly and motions Sorrowful to come in, and then he motions all the rest of us to follow, shaking his head very sad.

There are so many of us that we fill the room around a little high narrow bed on which Marky is lying like a flower against a white wall, her yellow curls spread out over her pillow. Old Sorrowful drops on his knees beside the bed and his shoulders heave quite some as he kneels there, and I hear Sleep-out sniffing as if he has a cold in his head. Marky seems to be asleep when we go in, but while we are standing around the bed looking down at her, she opens her eyes and seems to see us and, what is more, she seems to know us, because she smiles at each guy in turn and then tries to hold out one of her little hands to Sorrowful.

Now very faint, like from far away, comes a sound of music through a half-open window in the room, from a jazz band that is rehearsing in a hall just up the street from the hospital, and Marky hears this music because she holds her head in such a way that anybody can see she is listening, and then she smiles again at us and whispers very plain, as follows: "Marky dance."

And she tries to reach down as if to pick up her skirt as she always does when she dances, but her hands fall across her breast as soft and white and light as snowflakes, and Marky never again dances in this world.

Well, old Doc Beerfeldt and the nurses make us go outside at once, and while we are standing there in the hall outside the door, saying nothing whatever, a young guy and two dolls, one of them old, and the other not so old, come along the hall, much excited. The young guy seems to know Sorrowful, who is sitting down again in his chair just outside the door, because he rushes up to Sorrowful and says to him like this:

"Where is she?" he says. "Where is my darling child? You remember me?" he says. "I leave my little girl with you one day while I go on an errand, and while I am on this errand everything goes blank, and I wind up back in my home in Indianapolis with my mother and sister here, and recall nothing about where I leave my child, or anything else."

"The poor boy has amnesia," the old doll says. "The stories that he deliberately abandons his wife in Paris and his child in New York are untrue."

"Yes," the doll who is not old puts in. "If we do not see the stories in the newspapers about how you have the child in this hospital we may never learn where she is. But everything is all right now. Of course we never approve of Harold's marriage to a person of the stage, and we only recently learn of her death in Paris soon after their separation there and are very sorry. But everything is all right now. We will take full charge of the child."

Now while all this gab is going on, Sorrowful never glances at them. He is just sitting there looking at Marky's door. And now as he is looking at the door a very strange thing seems to happen to his kisser, for all of a sudden it becomes the sad, mean-looking kisser that it is in the days before he ever sees Marky, and furthermore it is never again anything else.

"We will be rich," the young guy says. "We just learn that my darling child will be sole heiress to her maternal grandpapa's fortune, and the old guy is only a hop ahead of the undertaker right now. I suppose," he says, "I owe you something?"

And then Sorrowful gets up off his chair, and looks at the young guy and at the two dolls, and speaks as follows:

"Yes," he says, "you owe me a two-dollar marker for the bet you blow on Cold Cuts, and," he says, "I will trouble you to send it to me at once, so I can wipe you off my books."

Now he walks down the hall and out of the hospital,

never looking back again, and there is a very great silence behind him that is broken only by the sniffing of
Sleep-out, and by some first-class sobbing from some of
the rest of us, and I remember now that the guy who is
doing the best job of sobbing of all is nobody but Milk
Ear Willie.

Princess O'Hara

Now of course Princess O'Hara is by no means a regular
princess, and in fact she is nothing but a little red-headed
doll, with plenty of freckles, from over in Tenth Avenue,
and her right name is Maggie, and the only reason she is
called Princess O'Hara is as follows:

She is the daughter of King O'Hara, who is hacking
along Broadway with one of these old-time victorias for
a matter of maybe twenty-five years, and every time
King O'Hara gets his pots on, which is practically every
night, rain or shine, he is always bragging that he has
the royal blood of Ireland in his veins, so somebody
starts calling him King, and this is his monicker as long
as I can remember, although probably what King O'Hara
really has in his veins is about ninety-eight per cent al-
cohol.

Well, anyway, one night about seven or eight years
back, King O'Hara shows up on his stand in front of
Mindy's restaurant on Broadway with a spindly-legged
little doll about ten years of age on the seat beside him,
and he says that this little doll is nobody but his daughter, and he is taking care of her because his old lady is
not feeling so good, and right away Last Card Louie, the
gambler, reaches up and dukes the little doll and says to
her like this:

"If you are the daughter of the King, you must be the

princess," Last Card Louie says. "How are you, Princess?"

So from this time on, she is Princess O'Hara and afterwards for several years she often rides around in the early evening with the King, and sometimes when the King has his pots on more than somewhat, she personally drives Goldberg, which is the King's horse, although Goldberg does not really need much driving as he knows his way along Broadway better than anybody. In fact, this Goldberg is a most sagacious old pelter, indeed, and he is called Goldberg by the King in honor of a Jewish friend by the name of Goldberg, who keeps a delicatessen store in Tenth Avenue.

At this time, Princess O'Hara is as homely as a mud fence, and maybe homelier, what with the freckles, and the skinny gambs, and a few buck teeth, and she does not weigh more than sixty pounds, sopping wet, and her red hair is down her back in pigtails, and she giggles if anybody speaks to her, so finally nobody speaks to her much, but old King O'Hara seems to think well of her, at that.

Then by and by she does not seem to be around with the King any more, and when somebody happens to ask about her, the King says his old lady claims the Princess is getting too grown-up to be shagging around Broadway, and that she is now going to public school. So after not seeing her for some years, everybody forgets that King O'Hara has a daughter, and in fact nobody cares a cuss.

Now King O'Hara is a little shriveled-up old guy with a very red beezer, and he is a most familiar spectacle to one and all on Broadway as he drives about with a stovepipe hat tipped so far over to one side of his noggin that it looks as if it is always about to fall off, and in fact the King himself is always tipped so far over to one side that it seems to be a sure thing that he is going to fall off.

The way the King keeps himself on the seat of his victoria is really most surprising, and one time Last Card Louie wins a nice bet off a gambler from St. Louis by the name of Olive Street Oscar, who takes eight to five off of Louie that the King cannot drive them through Central Park without doing a Brodie off the seat. But of course Louie is betting with the best of it, which is the way he always dearly loves to bet, because he often rides through Central Park with King O'Hara, and he knows the King never falls off, no matter how far over he tips.

Personally, I never ride with the King very much, as his victoria is so old I am always afraid the bottom will fall out from under me, and that I will run myself to death trying to keep up, because the King is generally so busy singing Irish-come-all-yeez up on his seat that he is not apt to pay much attention to what his passengers are doing.

There are quite a number of these old victorias left in this town, a victoria being a low-neck, four-wheeled carriage with seats for four or five people, and they are very popular in the summertime with guys and dolls who wish to ride around and about in Central Park taking the air, and especially with guys and dolls who may wish to do a little offhand guzzling while taking the air.

Personally, I consider a taxicab much more convenient and less expensive than an old-fashioned victoria if you wish to get to some place, but of course guys and dolls engaged in a little offhand guzzling never wish to get any place in particular, or at least not soon. So these victorias, which generally stand around the entrances to the Park, do a fair business in the summertime, because it seems that no matter what conditions are, there are always guys and dolls who wish to do a little offhand guzzling.

But King O'Hara stands in front of Mindy's because he has many regular customers among the citizens of Broadway, who do not go in for guzzling so very much, unless a case of guzzling comes up, but who love to ride around in the Park on hot nights just to cool themselves out, although at the time I am now speaking of, things are so tough with one and all along Broadway that King O'Hara has to depend more on strangers for his trade.

Well, what happens one night, but King O'Hara is

seen approaching Mindy's, tipping so far over to one side of his seat that Olive Street Oscar, looking to catch even on the bet he loses before, is offering to take six to five off of Last Card Louie that this time the King goes plumb off, and Louie is about to give it to him, when the old King tumbles smack-dab into the street, as dead as last Tuesday, which shows you how lucky Last Card Louie is, because nobody ever figures such a thing to happen to the King, and even Goldberg, the horse, stops and stands looking at him very much surprised, with one hind hoof in the King's stovepipe hat. The doctors state that King O'Hara's heart just naturally hauls off and quits working on him, and afterwards Regret, the horse player, says the chances are the King probably suddenly remembers refusing a drink somewhere.

A few nights later, many citizens are out in front of Mindy's, and Big Nig, the crap shooter, is saying that things do not look the same around there since King O'Hara puts his checks back in the rack, when all of a sudden up comes a victoria that anybody can see is the King's old rattletrap, especially as it is being pulled by Goldberg.

And who is on the driver's seat, with King O'Hara's bunged-up old stovepipe hat sitting jack-deuce on her noggin but a red-headed doll of maybe eighteen or nineteen with freckles all over her pan, and while it is years since I see her, I can tell at once that she is nobody but Princess O'Hara, even though it seems she changes quite some.

In fact, she is now about as pretty a little doll as anybody will wish to see, even with the freckles, because the buck teeth seem to have disappeared, and the gambs are now filled out very nicely, and so has the rest of her. Furthermore, she has a couple of blue eyes that are most delightful to behold, and a smile like six bits, and all in all, she is a pleasing scene.

Well, naturally, her appearance in this manner causes some comment, and in fact some citizens are disposed to criticize her as being unladylike, until Big Nig, the crap

shooter, goes around among them very quietly stating
that he will knock their ears down if he hears any more
cracks from them, because it seems that Big Nig learns
that when old King O'Hara dies, all he leaves in this
world besides his widow and six kids is Goldberg, the
horse, and the victoria, and Princess O'Hara is the eldest
of these kids, and the only one old enough to work, and
she can think of nothing better to do than to take up her
papa's business where he leaves off.

After one peek at Princess O'Hara, Regret, the horse
player, climbs right into the victoria, and tells her to
ride him around the Park a couple of times, although it
is well known to one and all that it costs two bobs per
hour to ride in anybody's victoria, and the only dough
Regret has in a month is a pound note that he just borrows off of Last Card Louie for eating money. But from
this time on, the chances are Regret will be Princess
O'Hara's best customer if he can borrow any more pound
notes, but the competition gets too keen for him, especially from Last Card Louie, who is by this time quite a
prominent character along Broadway, and in the money,
although personally I always say you can have him, as
Last Card Louie is such a guy as will stoop to very sharp
practice, and in fact he often does not wait to stoop.

He is called Last Card Louie because in his youth he
is a great hand for riding the tubs back and forth between here and Europe and playing stud poker with
other passengers, and the way he always gets much
strength from the last card is considered quite abnormal,
especially if Last Card Louie is dealing. But of course
Last Card Louie no longer rides the tubs as this occupation is now very old-fashioned, and anyway Louie has
more profitable interests that require his attention, such
as a crap game, and one thing and another.

There is no doubt but what Last Card Louie takes
quite a fancy to Princess O'Hara, but naturally he cannot
spend all his time riding around in a victoria, so other
citizens get a chance to patronize her now and then, and
in fact I once take a ride with Princess O'Hara myself,

and it is a very pleasant experience, indeed, as she likes to sing while she is driving, just as old King O'Hara does in his time.

But what Princess O'Hara sings is not Irish-come-all-yeez but "Kathleen Mavourneen," and "My Wild Irish Rose," and "Asthore," and other such ditties, and she has a loud contralto voice, and when she lets it out while driving through Central Park in the early hours of the morning, the birds in the trees wake up and go tweet-tweet, and the coppers on duty for blocks around stand still with smiles on their kissers, and the citizens who live in the apartment houses along Central Park West and Central Park South come to their windows to listen.

Then one night in October, Princess O'Hara does not show up in front of Mindy's, and there is much speculation among one and all about this absence, and some alarm, when Big Nig, the crap shooter, comes around and says that what happens is that old Goldberg, the horse, is down with colic, or some such, so there is Princess O'Hara without a horse.

Well, this news is received with great sadness by one and all, and there is some talk of taking up a collection to buy Princess O'Hara another horse, but nobody goes very far with this idea because things are so tough with everybody, and while Big Nig mentions that maybe Last Card Louie will be glad to do something large in this matter, nobody cares for this idea, either, as many citizens are displeased with the way Last Card Louie is pitching to Princess O'Hara, because it is well known that Last Card Louie is nothing but a wolf when it comes to young dolls, and anyway about now Regret, the horse player, speaks up as follows:

"Why," Regret says, "it is great foolishness to talk of wasting money buying a horse, even if we have any money to waste, when the barns up at Empire City are packed at this time with crocodiles of all kinds. Let us send a committee up to the track," Regret says, "and borrow a nice horse for Princess O'Hara to use until Goldberg is back on his feet again."

"But," I say to Regret, "suppose nobody wishes to lend us a horse?"

"Why," Regret says, "I do not mean to ask anybody to lend us a horse. I mean let us borrow one without asking anybody. Most of these horse owners are so very touchy that if we go around asking them to lend us a horse to pull a hack, they may figure we are insulting their horses, so let us just get the horse and say nothing whatever."

Well, I state that this sounds to me like stealing, and stealing is something that is by no means upright and honest, and Regret has to admit that it really is similar to stealing, but he says what of it, and as I do not know what of it, I discontinue the argument. Furthermore, Regret says it is clearly understood that we will return any horse we borrow when Goldberg is hale and hearty again, so I can see that after all there is nothing felonious in the idea, or anyway, not much.

But after much discussion, it comes out that nobody along Broadway seems to know anything about stealing a horse. There are citizens who know all about stealing diamond necklaces, or hot stoves, but when it comes to horses, everybody confesses themselves at a loss. It is really amazing the amount of ignorance there is on Broadway about stealing horses.

Then finally Regret has a bright idea. It seems that a rodeo is going on at Madison Square Garden at this time, a rodeo being a sort of wild west show with bucking bronchos, and cowboys, and all this and that, and Regret seems to remember reading when he is a young squirt that stealing horses is a very popular pastime out in the Wild West.

So one evening Regret goes around to the Garden and gets to talking to a cowboy in leather pants with hair on them, and he asks this cowboy, whose name seems to be Laramie Pink, if there are any expert horse stealers connected with the rodeo. Moreover, Regret explains to Laramie Pink just why he wants a good horse stealer, and Pink becomes greatly interested and wishes to know if the loan of a nice bucking broncho, or a first-class cow pony will be of any assistance, and when Regret says he is afraid not, Laramie Pink says like this:

"Well," he says, "of course horse stealing is considered a most antique custom out where I come from, and in fact it is no longer practiced in the best circles, but," he says, "come to think of it, there is a guy with this outfit by the name of Frying Pan Joe, who is too old to do anything now except mind the cattle, but who is said to be an excellent horse stealer out in Colorado in his day. Maybe Frying Pan Joe will be interested in your proposition," Laramie Pink says.

So he hunts up Frying Pan Joe, and Frying Pan Joe turns out to be a little old pappy guy with a chin whisker, and a sad expression, and a wide-brimmed cowboy hat, and when they explain to him that they wish him to steal a horse, Frying Pan Joe seems greatly touched, and his eyes fill up with tears, and he speaks as follows:

"Why," Frying Pan Joe says, "your idea brings back many memories to me. It is a matter of over twenty-five years since I steal a horse, and the last time I do this it gets me three years in the calabozo. Why," he says, "this is really a most unexpected order, and it finds me all out of practice, and with no opportunity to get myself in shape. But," he says, "I will put forth my best efforts on this job for ten dollars, as long as I do not personally have to locate the horse I am to steal. I am not acquainted with the ranges hereabouts, and will not know where to go to find a horse."

So Regret, the horse player, and Big Nig, the crap shooter, and Frying Pan Joe go up to Empire this very same night, and it turns out that stealing a horse is so simple that Regret is sorry he does not make the tenner himself, for all Frying Pan Joe does is to go to the barns where the horses live at Empire, and walk along until he comes to a line of stalls that do not seem to have any watchers around in the shape of stable hands at the moment. Then Frying Pan Joe just steps into a stall and comes out leading a horse, and if anybody sees him, they are bound to figure he has a right to do this, because of course not even Sherlock Holmes is apt to think of anybody stealing a horse around this town.

Well, when Regret gets a good peek at the horse, he sees right away it is not just a horse that Frying Pan Joe steals. It is Gallant Godfrey, one of the greatest handicap horses in this country, and the winner of some of the biggest stakes of the year, and Gallant Godfrey is worth twenty-five G's if he is worth a dime, and when Regret speaks of this, Frying Pan Joe says it is undoubtedly the most valuable single piece of horseflesh he ever steals, although he claims that once when he is stealing horses along the Animas River in Colorado, he steals two hundred horses in one batch that will probably total up more.

They take Gallant Godfrey over to Eleventh Avenue, where Princess O'Hara keeps Goldberg in a little stable that is nothing but a shack, and they leave Gallant Godfrey there alongside old Goldberg, who is groaning and carrying on in a most distressing manner, and then Regret and Big Nig shake hands with Frying Pan Joe and wish him goodby.

So there is Princess O'Hara with Gallant Godfrey hitched up to her victoria the next night, and the chances are it is a good thing for her that Gallant Godfrey is a nice tame old dromedary, and does not mind pulling a victoria at all, and in fact he seems to enjoy it, although he likes to go along at a gallop instead of a slow trot, such as the old skates that pull these victorias usually employ.

And while Princess O'Hara understands that this is a borrowed horse, and is to be returned when Goldberg is well, nobody tells her just what kind of a horse it is, and when she gets Goldberg's harness on Gallant Godfrey, his appearance changes so that not even the official starter is apt to recognize him if they come face to face.

Well, I hear afterwards that there is great consternation around Empire when it comes out that Gallant Godfrey is missing, but they keep it quiet as they figure he

just wanders away, and as he is engaged in certain large
stakes later on, they do not wish it made public that he
is absent from his stall. So they have guys looking for
him high and low, but of course nobody thinks to look
for a high-class race horse pulling a victoria.

When Princess O'Hara drives the new horse up in
front of Mindy's, many citizens are anxious to take the
first ride with her, but before anybody has time to think
who steps up but Ambrose Hammer, the newspaper
scribe who has a foreign-looking young guy with him,
and Ambrose states as follows:

"Get in, Georges," Ambrose says. "We will take a spin
through the Park and wind up at the Casino."

So away they go, and from this moment begins one of
the greatest romances ever heard of on Broadway, for it
seems that the foreign-looking young guy that Ambrose
Hammer calls Georges takes a wonderful liking to Princess O'Hara right from taw, and the following night I
learn from Officer Corbett, the motorcycle cop who is
on duty in Central Park, that they pass him with Ambrose Hammer in the back seat of the victoria, but with
Georges riding on the driver's seat with Princess O'Hara.

And moreover, Officer Corbett states that Georges is
wearing King O'Hara's old stovepipe hat, while Princess
O'Hara is singing "Kathleen Mavourneen" in her loud
contralto in such a way as nobody ever hears her sing
before.

In fact, this is the way they are riding along a little
later in the week, and when it is coming on four bells in
the morning. But this time, Princess O'Hara is driving
north on the street that is called Central Park West because it borders the Park on the west, and the reason she
is taking this street is because she comes up Broadway
through Columbus Circle into Central Park West, figuring to cross over to Fifth Avenue by way of the transverse at Sixty-sixth Street, a transverse being nothing but
a roadway cut through the Park from Central Park West
to the Avenue.

There are several of these transverses, and why they

do not call them roads, or streets, instead of transverses, I do not know, except maybe it is because transverse sounds more fancy. These transverses are really like tunnels without any roofs, especially the one at Sixty-sixth Street, which is maybe a quarter of a mile long and plenty wide enough for automobiles to pass each other going in different directions, but once a car is in the transverse there is no way it can get out except at one end or the other. There is no such thing as turning off to one side anywhere between Central Park West and the Avenue, because the Sixty-sixth Street transverse is a deep cut with high sides, or walls.

Well, just as Princess O'Hara starts to turn Gallant Godfrey into the transverse, with the foreign-looking young guy beside her on the driver's seat, and Ambrose Hammer back in the cushions, and half asleep, and by no means interested in the conversation that is going on in front of him, a big beer truck comes rolling along Central Park West, going very slow.

And of course there is nothing unusual in the spectacle of a beer truck at this time, as beer is now very legal, but just as this beer truck rolls alongside Princess O'Hara's victoria, a little car with two guys in it pops out of no-where, and pulls up to the truck, and one of the guys requests the jockey of the beer truck to stop.

Of course Princess O'Hara and her passengers do not know at the time that this is one of the very first cases of histing a truckload of legal beer that comes off in this country, and that they are really seeing history made, although it all comes out later. It also comes out later that one of the parties committing this historical deed is nobody but a guy by the name of Fats O'Rourke, who is considered one of the leading characters over on the west side, and the reason he is histing this truckload of beer is by no means a plot against the brewing industry, but because it is worth several C's, and Fats O'Rourke can use several C's very nicely at the moment.

It comes out that the guy with him is a guy by the name of Joe the Blow Fly, but he is really only a fink in every respect, a fink being such a guy as is extra nothing, and many citizens are somewhat surprised when they learn that Fats O'Rourke is going around with finks.

Well, if the jockey of the beer truck does as he is re-quested without any shilly-shallying, all that will happen is he will lose his beer. But instead of stopping the truck, the jockey tries to keep right on going, and then all of a sudden Fats O'Rourke becomes very impatient and outs with the old thing, and gives it to the jockey, as follows: bang, bang.

By the time Fats O'Rourke lets go, The Fly is up on the seat of the truck and grabs the wheel just as the jockey turns it loose and falls back on the seat, and Fats O'Rourke follows The Fly up there, and then Fats O'Rourke seems to see Princess O'Hara and her cus-tomers for the first time, and he also realizes that these parties witness what comes off with the jockey, although otherwise Central Park West is quite deserted, and if anybody in the apartment houses along there hears the shots the chances are they figure it must be nothing but an automobile backfiring.

And in fact The Fly has the beer truck backfiring quite some at this moment as Fats O'Rourke sees Prin-cess O'Hara and her customers, and only somebody who happens to observe the flashes from Fats O'Rourke's duke, or who hears the same buzzes that Princess O'Hara, and the foreign-looking young guy, and Ambrose Ham-mer hear, can tell that Fats is emptying that old thing at the victoria.

The chances are Fats O'Rourke will not mind anybody witnessing him histing a legal beer truck, and in fact he is apt to welcome their testimony in later years when somebody starts disputing his claim to being the first guy to hist such a truck, but naturally Fats does not wish to have spectators spying on him when he is giving it to somebody, as very often spectators are apt to go around gossiping about these matters, and cause dissension.

So he takes four cracks at Princess O'Hara and her

customers, and it is a good thing for them that Fats O'Rourke is never much of a shot. Furthermore, it is a good thing for them that he is now out of ammunition, because of course Fats O'Rourke never figures that it is going to take more than a few shots to hist a legal beer truck, and afterwards there is little criticism of Fats' judgment, as everybody realizes that it is a most unprecedented situation.

Well, by now, Princess O'Hara is swinging Gallant Godfrey into the transverse, because she comes to the conclusion that it is no time to be loitering in this neighborhood, and she is no sooner inside the walls of the transverse than she knows this is the very worst place she can go, as she hears a rumble behind her, and when she peeks back over her shoulder she sees the beer truck coming lickity-split, and what is more, it is coming right at the victoria.

Now Princess O'Hara is no chump, and she can see that the truck is not coming right at the victoria by accident, when there is plenty of room for it to pass, so she figures that the best thing to do is not to let the truck catch up with the victoria if she can help it, and this is very sound reasoning, indeed, because Joe the Blow Fly afterwards says that what Fats O'Rourke requests him to do is to sideswipe the victoria with the truck and squash it against the side of the transverse, Fats O'Rourke's idea being to keep Princess O'Hara and her customers from speaking of the transaction with the jockey of the truck.

Well, Princess O'Hara stands up in her seat, and tells Gallant Godfrey to giddap, and Gallant Godfrey is giddapping very nicely, indeed, when she looks back and sees the truck right at the rear wheel of the victoria, and coming like a bat out of what-is-this. So she grabs up her whip and gives Gallant Godfrey a good smack across the vestibule, and it seems that if there is one thing Gallant Godfrey hates and despises it is a whip. He makes a lunge that pulls the victoria clear of the truck, just as The Fly drives it up alongside the victoria and is bearing over for the squash, with Fats O'Rourke yelling directions at him, and from this lunge, Gallant Godfrey settles down to running.

While this is going on, the foreign-looking young guy is standing up on the driver's seat of the victoria beside Princess O'Hara, whooping and laughing, as he probably figures it is just a nice, friendly little race. But Princess O'Hara is not laughing, and neither is Ambrose Hammer.

Now inside the next hundred yards, Joe the Blow Fly gets the truck up alongside again and this time it looks as if they are gone goslings when Princess O'Hara gives Gallant Godfrey another smack with the whip, and the chances are Gallant Godfrey comes to the conclusion that Westrope is working on him in a stretch run, as he turns on such a burst of speed that he almost runs right out of his collar and leaves the truck behind by anyway a length and a half.

And it seems that just as Gallant Godfrey turns on, Fats O'Rourke personally reaches over and gives the steering wheel of the beer truck a good twist, figuring that the squashing is now a cinch, and the next thing anybody knows the truck goes smack-dab into the wall with a loud kuh-boom, and turns over all mussed up, with beer kegs bouncing around very briskly, and some of them popping open and letting the legal beer leak out.

In the meantime, Gallant Godfrey goes tearing out of the transverse into Fifth Avenue and across Fifth Avenue so fast that the wheels of Princess O'Hara's victoria are scarcely touching the ground, and a copper who sees him go past afterwards states that what Gallant Godfrey is really doing is flying, but personally I always consider this an exaggeration.

Anyway, Gallant Godfrey goes two blocks beyond Fifth Avenue before Princess O'Hara can get him to whoa-up, and there is still plenty of run in him, although by this time Princess O'Hara is plumb worn out, and Ambrose Hammer is greatly fatigued, and only the foreign-looking young guy seems to find any enjoyment in the experience, although he is not so jolly when b learns that the coppers take two dead guys out of the truck, along with Joe the Blow Fly, who lives just long enough to relate the story.

Fats O'Rourke is smothered to death under a stack of kegs of legal beer, which many citizens consider a most gruesome finish, indeed, but what kills the jockey of the truck is the bullet in his heart, so the smash-up of the truck does not make any difference to him one way or the other, although of course if he lives, the chances are his employers will take him to task for losing the beer.

I learn most of the details of the race through the transverse from Ambrose Hammer, and I also learn from Ambrose that Princess O'Hara and the foreign-looking young guy are suffering from the worst case of love that Ambrose ever witnesses, and Ambrose Hammer witnesses some tough cases of love in his day. Furthermore, Ambrose says they are not only in love but are planning to get themselves married up as quickly as possible.

"Well," I say, "I hope and trust this young guy is all right, because Princess O'Hara deserves the best. In fact," I say, "a prince is none too good for her."

"Well," Ambrose says, "a prince is exactly what she is getting. I do not suppose you can borrow much on it in a hock shop in these times, but the title of Prince Georges Latour is highly respected over in France, although," he says, "I understand the proud old family does not have as many potatoes as formerly. But he is a nice young guy, at that, and anyway, what is money compared to love?"

Naturally, I do not know the answer to this, and neither does Ambrose Hammer, but the very same day I run into Princess O'Hara and the foreign-looking young guy on Broadway, and I can see the old love light shining so brightly in their eyes that I get to thinking that maybe money does not mean so much alongside of love, at that, although personally, I will take a chance on the money.

I stop and say hello to Princess O'Hara, and ask her how things are going with her, and she says they are going first class.

"In fact," she says, "it is a beautiful world in every respect. Georges and I are going to be married in a few days now, and are going to Paris, France, to live. At first I fear we will have a long wait, because of course I cannot leave my mamma and the rest of the children unprovided for. But," Princess O'Hara says, "what happens but Regret sells my horse to Last Card Louie for a thousand dollars, so everything is all right.

"Of course," Princess O'Hara says, "buying my horse is nothing but an act of great kindness on the part of Last Card Louie as my horse is by no means worth a thousand dollars, but I suppose Louie does it out of his old friendship for my papa. I must confess," she says, "that I have a wrong impression of Louie, because the last time I see him I slap his face thinking he is trying to get fresh with me. Now I realize it is probably only his paternal interest in me, and I am very sorry."

Well, I know Last Card Louie is such a guy as will give you a glass of milk for a nice cow, and I am greatly alarmed by Princess O'Hara's statement about the sale, for I figure Regret must sell Gallant Godfrey, not remembering that he is only a borrowed horse and must be returned in good order, so I look Regret up at once and mention my fears, but he laughs and speaks to me as follows:

"Do not worry," he says. "What happens is that Last Card Louie comes around last night and hands me a G note and says to me like this: 'Buy Princess O'Hara's horse off of her for me, and you can keep all under this G that you get it for.'

"Well," Regret says, "of course I know that old Last Card is thinking of Gallant Godfrey, and forgets that the only horse that Princess O'Hara really owns is Goldberg, and the reason he is thinking of Gallant Godfrey is because he learns last night about us borrowing the horse for her. But as long as Last Card Louie refers just to her horse, and does not mention any names, I do not see that it is up to me to go into any details with him. So I get him a bill of sale for Princess O'Hara's horse, and I am waiting ever since to hear what he says when he goes to collect the horse and finds it is nothing but old Goldberg."

"Well," I say to Regret, "it all sounds most confusing to me, because what good is Gallant Godfrey to Last Card Louie when he is only a borrowed horse, and is apt to be recognized anywhere except when he is hitched to a victoria? And I am sure Last Card Louie is not going into the victoria business."

"Oh," Regret says, "this is easy. Last Card Louie undoubtedly sees the same ad in the paper that the rest of us see, offering a reward of ten G's for the return of Gallant Godfrey and no questions asked, but of course Last Card Louie has no way of knowing that Big Nig is taking Gallant Godfrey home long before Louie comes around and buys Princess O'Hara's horse."

Well, this is about all there is to tell, except that a couple of weeks later I hear that Ambrose Hammer is in the Clinic Hospital very ill, and I drop around to see him because I am very fond of Ambrose Hammer no matter if he is a newspaper scribe.

He is sitting up in bed in a nice private room, and he has on blue silk pajamas with his monogram embroidered over his heart, and there is a large vase of roses on the table beside him, and a nice-looking nurse holding his hand, and I can see that Ambrose Hammer is not doing bad, although he smiles very feebly at me when I come in.

Naturally I ask Ambrose Hammer what ails him, and after he takes a sip of water out of a glass that the nice-looking nurse holds up to his lips, Ambrose sighs, and in a very weak voice he states as follows:

"Well," Ambrose says, "one night I get to thinking about what will happen to us in the transverse if we have old Goldberg hitched to Princess O'Hara's victoria instead of one of the fastest race horses in the world, and I am so overcome by the thought that I have what my doctor claims is a nervous breakdown. I feel terrible," Ambrose says.

A Light in France

In the summer of 1936, a personality by the name of Blond Maurice is found buried in a pit of quicklime up in Sullivan County, or, anyway, what is found is all that is left of Maury, consisting of a few odds and ends in the way of bones, and a pair of shoes which have Brown the shoemaker's name in them, and which Brown identifies as a pair of shoes he makes for Maury some months before, when Maury is in the money and is able to have his shoes made to order.

It is common gossip in all circles along Broadway that Maury is placed in this quicklime by certain parties who do not wish him well, and it is also the consensus of opinion that placing him there is by no means a bad idea, at that, as Maury is really quite a scamp and of no great credit to the community. In fact, when it comes out that there is nothing left of him but a pair of shoes, it is agreed by one and all that it is two shoes too many.

Well, knowing that Maury is quicklimed, it is naturally something of a surprise to me to come upon him in Mindy's restaurant one evening in the spring of 1943, partaking of cheese blintzes. At first I think I am seeing a ghost, but, of course, I know that ghosts never come in Mindy's, and, if they do, they never eat cheese blintzes, so I realize that it is nobody but Maury himself.

Consequently I step over to his table and give him a medium hello, and he looks up and gives me a medium hello right back, for, to tell the truth, Maury and I are never bosom friends. In fact, I always give him plenty of the back of my neck because I learn long ago that it is best not to associate with such harum-scarum personalities unless, of course, you need them.

But naturally I am eager to hear of his experiences in the quicklime as I never before meet a guy who returns from being buried in this substance, so I draw up a chair and speak to him as follows:

"Well, Maury," I say, "where are you all this time that I do not see you around and about?"

"I am in a place called France," Maury says. "I leave there on account of the war. Perhaps you hear of the war?"

"Yes," I say, "I hear rumors of it from time to time."

"It is a great nuisance," Maury says.

"But, Maury," I say, "how do you come to go to a place where there is a war?"

"Oh," Maury says, "there is no war when I go there. The war is here in New York. This city is very unsettled at the time, what with the unpleasantness between my employer, the late Little Kishke, and Sammy Downtown developing cases for the medical examiner all over the layout. I am pleased to find on my return that law and order now prevail."

"But, Maury," I say, "how do you stand with reference to law and order?"

"I·am in favor of both," Maury says. "Oh, I am all right. Immediately upon my return, I call on the D.A. in Manhattan to see if he has anything he wishes me to plead guilty to, and he cannot find a thing, although he seems somewhat regretful, at that.

"Then," Maury says, "I go over to Brooklyn and call on the D.A. there, and he consults the books of Murder, Incorporated, and he states that all he can find entered under my name is that I am deceased, and that he hopes and trusts I will remain so. I am as clean as a whistle, and," Maury says, "maybe cleaner."

"Well," I say, "I am glad to hear this, Maury. I always know you are sound at bottom. By the way, do you run into Girondel on your travels? We hear that he is over there also. At least, he is absent quite a spell. Girondel is always a great one for going around and about in foreign lands."

"No," Maury says, "I do not see him there. But if you care to listen, I will now relate to you my adventures in France."

Well [Maury says] I go to France when things come up that convince me that I am not as popular as formerly with Sammy Downtown and his associates, and, furthermore, I am tired out and feel that I can use a little rest and peace.

And the reason I pick this France as a place to go to is because I take a fancy to the country when I am there once on a pleasure trip all over Europe as a guest of the late Drums Capello, who is in the importing business, and what he imports is such merchandise as morphine and heroin and sometimes a little opium.

But I wish to state that I have no part of Drums' play in this respect and no part of his fall when the Brush finally catches up with him. And, furthermore, I wish to state that I never approve of his enterprise in any way whatever, but I must say he is a fine host and takes me all over England and Germany, and introduces me to many of his friends and business associates, and you can have them.

Now, the exact spot in France to which I go is a sleepy little town on the seacoast, but I cannot reveal the name at this time as it is a military secret and, anyway, I am unable to pronounce it. The main drag of this town faces a small harbor, and you can stand in front of any place of business along the stem and almost flip a dime into the water—if you happen to have a dime to spare.

It is an old fishing spot, and when I first go there, it is infested by fishermen with hay on their chins, and while most of them inhabit dinky little houses in the town, others live on farms about the size of napkins just outside the burg, and they seem to divide their time between chasing fish and cows. But it is quiet and peaceful there, and very restful after you get used to not hearing the Broadway traffic.

I reside in a tiny gaff that is called a hotel on the main street, and this gaff is run by a French bim by the name of Marie. In fact, all bims in France seem to be named Marie when they are not named Yvonne. I occasionally notice an old sack in the background who may be Marie's mamma or her aunt or some such, but Marie is strictly the boss of the trap and operates it in first-class style. She is the chief clerk and the headwaiter and she is also the bartender in the little smoky barroom that opens directly on the street, so, if the door is left open, you get herring with your cognac.

I know she makes the beds and dusts up the three tiny bedrooms in the joint, so you can see she is an all-around personality. She is maybe twenty years old, and I will not attempt to describe her except to say that if I am interested in the hugging and kissing department, I will most certainly take my business to Marie, especially as she speaks English, and you will not have to waste time with the sign language.

Well, it is very pleasant, to be sure, strolling around the little town talking to the fishermen or wandering out into the country and observing the agriculturists, who seem to be mostly female personalities who are all built in such a way that they will never be able to sit down in a washtub with comfort, and who really have very little glamor.

It is also very pleasant to nuzzle a dram or two in the cool of the evening at a little table in front of Marie's hotel and it is there I make the acquaintance of the only other roomer in the hotel. He is a fat old guy who is nobody but Thaddeus T. Blackman, a rich zillionaire from the city of New York and a lam-master from the Brush boys back home for over twenty years on an income-tax beef.

It seems that Thaddeus T. is mixed up in a large scandal about oil lands, and a grand jury hands out readers right and left among some of the best people in the U.S.A., although all they do is swindle the government, and it is a great shock to them to learn that this is against the law.

Anyway, Thaddeus T. starts running as soon as he

gets wind of the beef and does not pause for breath until he arrives in this little town in France, and there he lives all these years. It seems the Brush cannot touch him there, and why this is I do not know, but I suppose it is because he is smart enough to take his zillions with him, and naturally this kind of moolouw is protection on land or sea.

He discusses his case with me once and gives me to understand that it is a bum beef as far as he is concerned and that he only takes the fall for others, but of course this is by no means an unfamiliar tale to me, and, as he never mentions why he does not try to chill the beef by paying the government the dough, I do not consider it tactful to bring the matter up.

He is up in the paint-cards in age when I meet him, being maybe close to seventy, and he is a fashion plate of the fashion of about 1922. Moreover, he seems to be a lonely old gee, though how anybody can be lonely with all his zillions is a great mystery to me. He always has a short briar pipe in his mouth and is generally lighting it with little wax matches, and, in fact, I never see a pipe man who is not generally lighting his pipe, and if ever I get time I will invent a pipe that stays lit and make a fortune.

Anyway, Thaddeus T. and I become good friends over the little table in front of the hotel, and then one day who shows up but an old pal of mine out of the city of Boston, Mass., who is also an absentee from a small charge of homicide in his home town.

He is called by the name of Mike the Mugger because it seems his occupation is reaching out of doorways on dark nights and taking passers-by by the neck and pulling them in close to him with one hand and examining into their pockets with the other hand, the idea of the hand around the neck being to keep them from complaining aloud until he is through with them.

Personally, I do not consider this occupation at all essential or even strictly ethical, but I always say every guy to his own taste and naturally I have to respect Mike as the very top guy in his profession who never makes a mistake except the one time he clasps a customer too tight and too long and becomes involved in this difficulty I mention.

He is about thirty-odd and is a nifty-drifty in his dress and very good company, except that he is seldom holding anything and is generally leaning on me. However, I am personally loaded at this time and I am not only pleased to okay Mike with Marie for the last of her three rooms, but I stake him to walk-about money, which is money for his pocket, and he is grateful to me in every respect.

Naturally, Mike joins out with Thaddeus T. and me in strolling here and there and in sitting at the little table in front of the hotel or in the barroom, talking and playing cards, and what we generally talk about, of course, is the good old U.S.A., which is a subject of great interest to all three of us.

A few fishermen and small merchants of the town are also usually in the barroom, and Marie is always behind the bar, and it is not long before I notice that both Thaddeus T. and Mike the Mugger are paying considerable attention to her. In fact, Mike tells me he is in love with her and is surprised that I am not in the same condition.

"But," Mike says, "of course I will never mention my love to Marie because I am undoubtedly a low-class personality with a tough beef against me and am unfit to associate with a nice lady saloonkeeper."

As far as I can see, Thaddeus T.'s interest in Marie is more fatherly than anything else, which is very nice if you like an old wolf for a father. He tells me he wishes he has her for his daughter because, he says, the one of his own back in the U.S.A. is a dingbat and so is her mamma, and from the way he carries on about them, I can see that Thaddeus T.'s former home life is far from being a plug for matrimony.

Now it comes on 1939 and with it the war, and Thaddeus T., who can gabble the frog language quite fluently and is always around on the Ear-ie finding out what is going on, tells me that the people of the town are pretty much worked up and that some of the guys are going away to join the army, but it makes little difference in our lives, as we seem to be outside the active war zone, and all we know about any actual fighting is what we hear.

We still sit out in front of the hotel in the afternoon and in the barroom at night, though I observe Marie now pays more attention to other customers than she does to us and is always chattering to them in a most excited manner, and Thaddeus T. says it is about the war. He says Marie is taking it to heart no little and quite some.

But it is not until the summer of 1940 that Thaddeus T. and me and even Mike really notice the war, because overnight the little town fills up with German soldiers and other German guys who are not soldiers but seem to be working gees, and it is plain to be seen that something big is doing. Thaddeus T. says he hears they are making a submarine base of the harbor because it is a very handy spot for the subs to sneak out of and knock off the British ships, and in fact after a while we see many subs and other shipping along the quays.

Anyway, the Germans pay very little attention to us at first except to examine our papers, and the officers who come into Marie's bar for drinks are quite polite and nod to us and sometimes talk to Thaddeus T., who speaks German better than he does French. Presently we are practically ignoring the presence of the Germans in our midst, although naturally Marie has no fancy for them whatever and is always making faces at them behind their backs and spitting on the ground when they pass, until I tell her that this is unlady like.

Well, on coming home one night from a little stroll, I hear a commotion in the kitchen, which is just off the barroom, and on entering I observe Marie wrestling with a big blubber in civilian clothes who is wearing a small scrubby mustache and a derby hat and who has practically no neck whatever.

They are knocking kitchen utensils right and left, in-

cluding a pot of spaghetti which I know Marie prepares
for my dinner and which vexes me no little. Marie is
sobbing and I can see that the blubber is outwrestling
her and in fact has a strangle hold on her that figures to
win him the fall very shortly. I am standing there, ad-
miring his technique in spite of my vexation over the
spaghetti, when Marie sees me and calls to me as follows:

"Please help me, Chauncey," which, as I forget to tell
you before, is at this time my monicker, and I am then
in possession of passports and other papers to prove
same.

Naturally, I pay no attention to her, as I do not know
on what terms she is wrestling the blubber, but finally I
see she is in some distress, so I step forward and tap the
bloke on the shoulder and say to him like this:

"I beg your pardon," I say, "but the strangle hold is
illegal. If you are going to wrestle, you must obey the
rules."

At this, the guy lets go of Marie and steps back and I
say to her in English, "Who is this plumber?"

"He is Herr Klauber," Marie says back to me in English. "He is the head of the Gestapo in this district."

Well, then I get a good glaum at the gee and I see
that he is nobody but the same Klauber that Drums Capello does business with in Hamburg the time I am
Drums' guest, only in those days he is not usually called
by the name of Klauber. He is called the Vasserkopf,
which is a way of saying "waterhead" in German, because he has an extra large sconce piece that is practically
a deformity and as the Vasserkopf he is known far and
wide on two continents, and especially here in New
York, where he once operates, as a very sure-footed
merchant in morphine, heroin, opium and similar com-
modities.

Naturally, it is a great pleasure to me to behold a
familiar puss in a strange place, even if it is only the
Vasserkopf's puss, so I give him a sizable hello and speak
to him as follows:

"Well, Vasser," I say, "this is an unexpected privilege,

to be sure. There you are and here I am, and much water runs over the dam since last we met, and how are you anyway?"

"Who are you?" the Vasserkopf says in English and in a most unfriendly manner.

"Come, come, Vasser," I say. "Let us not waste time in shadowboxing. Do you know our old pal Drums finally takes a fall in Milwaukee, Wis., for a sixer?"

Then the Vasserkopf comes close to me and speaks to me in a low voice like this: "Listen," he says, "it is in my mind to throw you in the jail house."

"Tut-tut, Vass," I say, "if you throw me in the jail house, I will be compelled to let out a bleat. I will be compelled to remember the time you ship the cargo of Santa Clauses out of Nuremburg and each Santa contains enough of the white to junk up half of the good old U.S.A. I hear your Fuehrer is a strait-laced gee, and what will he say if he hears one of his big coppers peddles junk and maybe uses it?"

I can see the Vasserkopf turns a little pale around the guzzle at this statement and he says: "Come outside. We will talk."

So I go outside the gaff with him, and we stand in the street in the darkness and have quite a chat and the Vasserkopf becomes more friendly and tells me that he is now a real high-muck-a-muck with the Gestapo and the greatest spy catcher in the racket. Then he wishes to know what I am doing in these parts, and I tell him quite frankly that I am there for my health and explain my ailment to him. I also tell him why Thaddeus T. and Mike the Mugger are there because I know that, as a former underworld personality, the Vasserkopf is apt to be understanding and sympathetic in such situations, especially when he knows my hole card is my knowledge of his background in junk.

"Now, Vass," I say, "all we wish is to be let alone, and if you can assist us in any way, I will personally be much obliged. What is more," I say, "I will see that you are well rewarded, if a member of the Gestapo takes."

"Sure," the Vasserkopf says. "Only let us understand one thing right off the reel. The broad belongs to me. I am crazy about her. But there is talk today at headquarters of closing this place and putting her out of business because of her attitude, and because one of our officers becomes ill after drinking cognac in here last night.

"I will tell the dumb military he probably has a touch of ptomaine," he continues. "I will tell them I need this hotel as a listening post to find out what is going on among the people around here. I will advise them not to molest you, as you are neutrals, and it may make trouble with your government, although," the Vasserkopf says, "I can see that the only trouble your government may make will be for you. But the Reich is not interested in American lammeroos, and neither am I as long as you remember the dame is mine and see that I collect a hundred a week in your money. I can scarcely sleep nights thinking of her."

Now this seems to me to be a very reasonable proposition all the way around, except for the hundred a week. The way I look at it, the Vasserkopf is at least entitled to Marie for his trouble because, to tell the truth, it will be most inconvenient for Thaddeus T. and Mike the Mugger and me to leave this spot at the moment, as there is no other place we can go and no way of getting there if there is such a place.

So I shave the Vasserkopf to half a C every week, and then I go back into the hotel to find Marie in the bar with Thaddeus T. and Mike, and I can see that she is quite agitated by her recent experience with the Vasserkopf. I also learn from her that it is not his first visit.

"He is here several times before," Marie says. "He comes to me first with news of my brother who is a prisoner in a camp near Hamburg. Herr Klauber tells me he can make things easier for Henri and perhaps get him released. He comes again and again on different excuses. I am frightened because I fear his motive." Then all of a sudden Marie puts her finger to her lips and says, "Hark!"

We hark, and I hear away off somewhere a sound that I know must come from a lot of planes, and as this sound grows louder and louder, and then dies away again, Marie says:

"English bombers," she says. "Every night they pass over here and go on up the coast to drop their bombs. They do not know what is going on here. Oh, if we can only show a light here to let them know this is a place to strike—this nest of snakes."

"A light?" I say. "Why, if you show a light around here, these squareheads will settle you in no time. Besides," I say, "it may get me and my friends in a jam, and we are Americans and very neutral. Let us not even think of showing a light and, Marie," I say, "kindly cease sizzling every time you serve a German, and, Mike, if you have any more Mickey Finns on your person, please take them yourself instead of dropping them in officers' drinks."

"Who? Me?" Mike the Mugger says.

Well, I see the Vasserkopf in the hotel almost every day after this talking to Marie, and he always gives me an E-flat hello and I give him the same, and, while I can see that Marie is afraid of him, she says he is now very polite to her and does not try to show her any more holds.

Of course, I do not tell Marie about my deal with the Vasserkopf and I do not tell Mike either, though I inform Thaddeus T., as I expect him to kick with some of the dough, and he says okay and that he is glad to learn that the Vasserkopf is on the take, only he thinks the half a C is enough without throwing in Marie. But he says a deal is a deal, and I can count on his co-operation.

From now on as far as we are concerned, everything seems to be almost the same as before there is any war whatever, except that we cannot go near the water front where the Germans are working and everything has to be blacked out good after dark, and you cannot as much as strike a match in the street, which is a great nuisance to Thaddeus T., as he is always striking matches. In fact, he almost gets his toupée blown off by sentries before he can break himself of the habit of striking matches outdoors at night.

I can see that the Vasserkopf must be keeping his agreement to front for us at headquarters, all right, and I am greasing him every week per our arrangement, but I find myself bored by the place, and I have a feeling that it is time for Mike the Mugger and maybe Thaddeus T., too, to leave, especially as the Vasserkopf accidentally drops a hint one day that he finds himself impeded in his progress with Marie by our constant presence in the hotel and that he thinks he is getting the short end of the deal. Finally, I have a conference with Thaddeus T., and state my views to him.

"Yes," Thaddeus T. says, "you are a hundred per cent right. But," he says, "leaving here is not a simple matter for us now. I am reliably informed that the military is likely to oppose our departure for the present, because the sub base here is a great secret and they do not care to run the risk of having us noise it about.

"In fact," he says, "I am told that they are sorry they do not chase us when they first come here, but now that they make this mistake, they are not going to make another by letting us depart, and other information that I hesitate to credit is that they may wind up clapping us in a detention camp somewhere."

"Thaddeus T.," I say, "I am an American and so is Mike and so are you, and our country is not concerned in this war. No one can hold us here against our wishes."

Well, at this, Thaddeus T. lets out a large laugh, and I can see his point and laugh with him, and then he informs me that for some days he is personally laying plans for our departure and that he buys a slightly tubercular motorboat from a certain personality and has it hidden at this very moment in a little cove about a mile up the coast and that all he now needs is a little petrol, which is a way of saying gasoline, to run the boat with the three of us in it out to sea, where we will have the chance of being picked up.

Thaddeus T. explains to me that all the petrol in this vicinity is in the hands of the Germans, but he says that where there is a will, there is a way. Consequently, he makes arrangements with the same personality who sells him the boat for a supply of gasoline, and who is this personality but the Vasserkopf, and Thaddeus is paying him more per gill for the gas than the old Vass ever gets per ounce for his hop, and, as I am personally paying him regularly, I can see that he is getting his coming and going and, naturally, I have to admire his enterprise.

However, Thaddeus states that the Vasserkopf is really most co-operative in every respect, and that he is to deliver the gas at the hotel the following night, and moreover that he is going to escort us to the cove so we will not be molested by any sentries we may encounter in that vicinity, which I say is very nice of the Vasserkopf though I seem to remember that there are never any sentries in that vicinity anyway, as it is part of the coast that does not seem to interest the Germans in any manner.

Then I get to meditating more and more on the Vasserkopf and on what a big heart he has, to be sure, and as I am meditating I am also sauntering late the next evening in a roundabout way up the coast as I wish to confirm the presence of the boat in the cove because, of course, there is the possibility of it getting away after the Vasserkopf has it placed there.

My roundabout saunter carries me across the fields of the little farms beyond the town that in some places run almost down to the sea, and it is a route that the Germans are not apt to suspect as taking me on any considerable journey, even if they notice me sauntering, which I take care they do not.

Finally, I saunter through a field to a slight rise of ground that overlooks the little cove, and there is just enough daylight left by now for me to see a boat floating just offshore, and at this same moment, I am surprised to scent the odor of fresh-turned earth near at hand, and the reason I am surprised is because it is now winter and by no means plowing time.

Consequently, I look around and I am further surprised to observe on this rise a newly made trench in the ground of a size and shape that brings back many memories to me. So I saunter back in a more roundabout way still meditating no little and quite some on the Vasserkopf.

But, sure enough, he shows up this very night around nine o'clock after Marie closes her place, and he brings with him two five-gallon cans of gasoline which he delivers to Thaddeus T. in the bar where Thaddeus and me and Mike the Mugger are waiting to receive the gas. Then, after handing over the cans, the Vass goes looking for Marie, saying he wishes to speak to her before escorting us to the boat.

As soon as he leaves the bar, Mike the Mugger outs with his pocketknife and stabs holes in two corners of the can and speaks as follows, "It smells like gasoline on the outside, but we smear the outside of cans with booze in the old bootleg days for the liquor smell when there is only water inside the cans. I hear the Vasserkopf is an old booter and he may remember the trick, and, besides, I do not trust him on general principles."

Now Mike lifts the can up as if it is no more than a demitasse and he holds it to his mouth so he can get a swig of the contents through one of the holes, when all of a sudden who comes into the bar all out of breath but Marie, and who is right behind her but the Vasserkopf, and there is no doubt that Marie is greatly flustered, and the Vasserkopf is much perturbed.

"So," he says to me, "you are double-crossing me and are going to take this omelet with you, hey? Well, it is a good thing I walk in on her as she is packing a keister, and I am now arresting her as a dangerous spy."

Marie begins to weep and wail and to carry on as bims will do when they are flustered, and naturally Thaddeus T. and me and Mike the Mugger are quite perplexed by this situation and, in fact, Mike is so perplexed that he is still holding the can in his hands and his cheeks are bulged out on each side from the gasoline in his mouth as if he has the mumps.

I am about to say something to cool the Vasserkopf off, for, to tell the truth, up to this minute I have no idea Marie is going with us, though I can see from the way Thaddeus T. and Mike the Mugger look that it is undoubtedly their idea. And, before I can say anything, Mike steps up to the Vasserkopf and gives a huge ploo-oo-oo-oo and spews his mouthful of gasoline right in the Vasserkopf's kisser and, as he gets his mouth clear, Mike says, "Why, you muzzler, it is somewhat watered, just as I suspect."

Well, naturally, the gasoline runs off the Vasserkopf's face and down over his clothes and he is standing there looking quite nonplused, and, as Mike the Mugger sees me gazing at him disapprovingly, he becomes embarrassed and self-conscious and, maybe to cover his confusion, he lifts the can of gasoline and holds it over the Vasserkopf's head, and the gas pours out and splashes off the old Vass' derby hat and splatters over his shoulders while he just stands there nonplused.

Thaddeus T. Blackman is leaning against the bar and, as usual, he is lighting his pipe with a little wax match and watching the Vasserkopf, and Marie has stopped crying and is laughing, and I am just standing there, when we again hear the sound of the planes high overhead and Thaddeus T. speaks as follows:

"A light you say, Marie?" he says. "A light for the English?"

Then he flips the lighted match on the Vasserkopf, whose clothes burst into flames at once and, almost as if they plan it all out beforehand, Mike jumps to the front door and opens it, and Thaddeus T. pushes the Vasserkopf, all ablaze, out the door into the street and yells at him:

"Run for the water!" he yells. "Run, run, run!"

The Vasserkopf seems to see what he means and starts

galloping lickity-split toward the water front with Thaddeus T. puffing along behind him and giving him a shove whenever he shows signs of lagging, and Mike the Mugger runs up behind the Vasserkopf and keeps throwing little spurts of gasoline on him by jerking the can at him and, from the way it burns on the Vasserkopf, I think Mike's statement of its dilution may be a slight exaggeration.

As he runs and burns, the Vasserkopf is letting out loud cries which bring soldiers from every which way, and presently they start shooting off their rifles in different directions. He is really quite a bonfire there in the darkness, and now I hear once more far overhead the drone of planes and I figure the English bombers see the light and turn back over the town.

All of a sudden, there is a whistling sound and then a big *ker-bloom,* and then more whistling and more *ker-blooms,* and there is no doubt in my mind that it is Katie-bar-the-door for the water front and the subs lying along the quays.

I can see the Vasserkopf still blazing and I can hear Thaddeus T. still urging him to run, and now the bombs are shellacking the surrounding buildings, and presently I hear, in between the blasts of the bombs, some rifle shots, and I know the soldiers are firing at Thaddeus T. and Mike the Mugger and maybe at the Vasserkopf, too, for making the light.

In fact, by the glow shed by the Vasserkopf, I see old Thaddeus stumble and fall, and Mike the Mugger go down right afterward with his can of gasoline blazing over him, but the Vasserkopf continues on still in flames until he falls off the quay into the water and, the chances are, goes out with a zizz.

Well, when I think of Marie, I turn from these unusual scenes to the little hotel, but it is no longer there, because a bomb flattens it, too, and it is now nothing but a pile of miscellany. I do not have much time to look for Marie, as the German soldiers are all over the layout, trying to learn what happens, but I finally locate her

with a big beam across her chest, and I can see that there
is nothing I can do for her except kiss her and say goodby,
and when I do this, she murmurs, "Thanks," but I am
sure it is only for Thaddeus T. and Mike the Mugger
and the light.

You will scarcely believe the difficulty I experience in
getting away from this unpleasant situation and out of
the country. In fact, I have only a vague recollection of
my adventures now, but I will always remember very
clearly how neatly I slip past four German soldiers sitting in the new-made trench on the rise of ground above
the cove, with a machine gun covering the cove itself,
and how I get in the boat and cut it loose and work it,
with my hands for paddles, to open water, before they
realize what is going on.

And I can never again have any respect for the memory of the Vasserkopf when I take to meditating on his
unsportsmanlike conduct in trying to double-cinch a sure
thing with a machine gun, although there are times before I am picked up at sea by an English destroyer that
I find myself wishing that Mike the Mugger does not
waste all the gasoline on the Vass, even if it is watered.

And this is all there is to the story [Maury says].

"But, Maury," I say, "do you not know that some
remainders found in a pit of quicklime up in Sullivan
County are supposed to be yours? They have on your
shoes, which are identified by Brown the shoemaker.
Are you ever in a quicklime pit in Sullivan County and,
if so, what is it like?"

"Oh," Maury says, "I am in Sullivan County, all right,
but never in a quicklime pit. I go to Sullivan County at
the invitation of Girondel, and the purpose of his invitation is to discuss ways and means of getting me straight-
ened out with his chief, Sammy Downtown.

"But one day," Maury says, "Girondel invites me to
a stroll in the woods with him and, while we are strolling,
he is talking about the beauties of the landscape and
calling my attention to the flowers and the birds, which is
ull very interesting, to be sure, but something tells me

that Girondel is by no means the nature lover he seems.

"Finally," Maury says, "he strolls me to a spot in the deep, tangled wildwood, and all of a sudden I catch an odor of something I never scent but once before in my life but will never again forget, and that is the time we lay the late Bugs Wonder to rest in Greenvale Cemetery. It is the odor of the fresh-turned earth from Bugs' last resting place.

"And as I catch this again in the woods," Maury says, "I realize that somebody does some digging around there lately, so I quietly give Girondel a boff over his pimple with a blackjack and flatten him like a welcome mat. Then I examine my surroundings and, sure enough, there, hidden by the shrubbery, I find a deep freshmade hole lined with quicklime, and I place Girondel in it and cover him up and leave him with my best wishes.

"But, first," Maury says, "I change shoes with him because my own are badly worn and, besides, I know that if ever he is found, the shoes will outlast the quicklime and be traced as mine, and I wish Girondel's connection to think I am no more. By the way," he says, "the odor I mention is the same I notice on the rise of ground at the cove in France which causes me to distrust the Vasserkopf. I guess I am just naturally allergic to the odor of newmade graves."

Romance in the Roaring Forties

Only a rank sucker will think of taking two peeks at Dave the Dude's doll, because while Dave may stand for the first peek, figuring it is a mistake, it is a sure thing he will get sored up at the second peek, and Dave the Dude is certainly not a man to have sored up at you.

But this Waldo Winchester is one hundred per cent

sucker, which is why he takes quite a number of peeks at Dave's doll. And what is more, she takes quite a number of peeks right back at him. And there you are. When a guy and a doll get to taking peeks back and forth at each other, why, there you are indeed.

This Waldo Winchester is a nice-looking young guy who writes pieces about Broadway for the *Morning Item*. He writes about the goings-on in night clubs, such as fights, and one thing and another, and also about who is running around with who, including guys and dolls.

Sometimes this is very embarrassing to people who may be married and are running around with people who are not married, but of course Waldo Winchester cannot be expected to ask one and all for their marriage certificates before he writes his pieces for the paper.

The chances are if Waldo Winchester knows Miss Billy Perry is Dave the Dude's doll, he will never take more than his first peek at her, but nobody tips him off until his second or third peek, and by this time Miss Billy Perry is taking her peeks back at him and Waldo Winchester is hooked.

In fact, he is plumb gone, and being a sucker, like I tell you, he does not care whose doll she is. Personally, I do not blame him much, for Miss Billy Perry is worth a few peeks, especially when she is out on the floor of Miss Missouri Martin's Sixteen Hundred Club doing her tap dance. Still, I do not think the best tap dancer that ever lives can make me take two peeks at her if I know she is Dave the Dude's doll, for Dave somehow thinks more than somewhat of his dolls.

He especially thinks plenty of Miss Billy Perry, and sends her fur coats, and diamond rings, and one thing and another, which she sends back to him at once, because it seems she does not take presents from guys. This is considered most surprising all along Broadway, but people figure the chances are she has some other angle.

Anyway, this does not keep Dave the Dude from liking her just the same, and so she is considered his doll by one and all, and is respected accordingly until this Waldo Winchester comes along.

It happens that he comes along while Dave the Dude is off in the Modoc on a little run-down to the Bahamas to get some goods for his business, such as Scotch and champagne, and by the time Dave gets back, Miss Billy Perry and Waldo Winchester are at the stage where they sit in corners between her numbers and hold hands.

Of course nobody tells Dave the Dude about this, because they do not wish to get him excited. Not even Miss Missouri Martin tells him, which is most unusual because Miss Missouri Martin, who is sometimes called "Mizzoo" for short, tells everything she knows as soon as she knows it, which is very often before it happens.

You see, the idea is when Dave the Dude is excited he may blow somebody's brains out, and the chances are it will be nobody's brains but Waldo Winchester's, although some claim that Waldo Winchester has no brains or he will not be hanging around Dave the Dude's doll.

I know Dave is very, very fond of Miss Billy Perry, because I hear him talk to her several times, and he is most polite to her and never gets out of line in her company by using cuss words, or anything like this. Furthermore, one night when One-eyed Solly Abrahams is a little stewed up he refers to Miss Billy Perry as a broad, meaning no harm whatever, for this is the way many of the boys speak of the dolls.

But right away Dave the Dude reaches across the table and bops One-eyed Solly right in the mouth, so everybody knows from then on that Dave thinks well of Miss Billy Perry. Of course Dave is always thinking fairly well of some doll as far as this goes, but it is seldom he gets to bopping guys in the mouth over them.

Well, one night what happens but Dave the Dude walks into the Sixteen Hundred Club, and there in the entrance, what does he see but this Waldo Winchester and Miss Billy Perry kissing each other back and forth friendly. Right away Dave reaches for the old equalizer to shoot Waldo Winchester, but it seems Dave does not happen to have the old equalizer with him, not expecting to have to shoot anybody this particular evening.

So Dave the Dude walks over and, as Waldo Winchester hears him coming and lets go his strangle hold on Miss Billy Perry, Dave nails him with a big right hand on the chin. I will say for Dave the Dude that he is a fair puncher with his right hand, though his left is not so good, and he knocks Waldo Winchester bowlegged. In fact, Waldo folds right up on the floor.

Well, Miss Billy Perry lets out a screech you can hear clear to the Battery and runs over to where Waldo Winchester lights, and falls on top of him squalling very loud. All anybody can make out of what she says is that Dave the Dude is a big bum, although Dave is not so big, at that, and that she loves Waldo Winchester.

Dave walks over and starts to give Waldo Winchester the leather, which is considered customary in such cases, but he seems to change his mind, and instead of booting Waldo around, Dave turns and walks out of the joint looking very black and mad, and the next anybody hears of him he is over in the Chicken Club doing plenty of drinking.

This is regarded as a very bad sign indeed, because while everybody goes to the Chicken Club now and then to give Tony Bertazzola, the owner, a friendly play, very few people care to do any drinking there, because Tony's liquor is not meant for anybody to drink except the customers.

Well, Miss Billy Perry gets Waldo Winchester on his pegs again, and wipes his chin off with her handkerchief, and by and by he is all okay except for a big lump on his chin. And all the time she is telling Waldo Winchester what a big bum Dave the Dude is, although afterwards Miss Missouri Martin gets hold of Miss Billy Perry and puts the blast on her plenty for chasing a two-handed spender such as Dave the Dude out of the joint.

"You are nothing but a little sap," Miss Missouri Martin tells Miss Billy Perry. "You cannot get the right time off this newspaper guy, while everybody knows Dave the Dude is a very fast man with a dollar."

"But I love Mr. Winchester," says Miss Billy Perry. "He's so romantic. He is not a bootlegger and a gunman like Dave the Dude. He puts lovely pieces in the paper about me, and he is a gentleman at all times."

Now of course Miss Missouri Martin is not in a position to argue about gentlemen, because she meets very few in the Sixteen Hundred Club and anyway, she does not wish to make Waldo Winchester mad as he is apt to turn around and put pieces in his paper that will be a knock to the joint, so she lets the matter drop.

Miss Billy Perry and Waldo Winchester go on holding hands between her numbers, and maybe kissing each other now and then, as young people are liable to do, and Dave the Dude plays the chill for the Sixteen Hundred Club and everything seems to be all right. Naturally we are all very glad there is no more trouble over the proposition, because the best Dave can get is the worst of it in a jam with a newspaper guy.

Personally, I figure Dave will soon find himself another doll and forget all about Miss Billy Perry, because now that I take another peek at her, I can see where she is just about the same as any other tap dancer, except that she is red-headed. Tap dancers are generally blackheads, but I do not know why.

Moosh, the doorman at the Sixteen Hundred Club, tells me Miss Missouri Martin keeps plugging for Dave the Dude with Miss Billy Perry in a quiet way, because he says he hears Miss Missouri Martin make the following crack one night to her: "Well, I do not see any Simple Simon on your lean and linger."

This is Miss Missouri Martin's way of saying she sees no diamond on Miss Billy Perry's finger, for Miss Missouri Martin is an old experienced doll, who figures if a guy loves a doll he will prove it with diamonds. Miss Missouri Martin has many diamonds herself, though how any guy can ever get himself heated up enough about

Miss Missouri Martin to give her diamonds is more than I can see.

I am not a guy who goes around much, so I do not see Dave the Dude for a couple of weeks, but late one Sunday afternoon little Johnny McGowan, who is one of Dave's men, comes and says to me like this: "What do you think? Dave grabs the scribe a little while ago and is taking him out for an airing!"

Well, Johnny is so excited it is some time before I can get him cooled out enough to explain. It seems that Dave the Dude gets his biggest car out of the garage and sends his driver, Wop Joe, over to the *Item* office where Waldo Winchester works, with a message that Miss Billy Perry wishes to see Waldo right away at Miss Missouri Martin's apartment on Fifty-ninth Street.

Of course this message is nothing but the phonus bolonus, but Waldo drops in for it and gets in the car. Then Wop Joe drives him up to Miss Missouri Martin's apartment, and who gets in the car there but Dave the Dude. And away they go.

Now this is very bad news indeed, because when Dave the Dude takes a guy out for an airing the guy very often does not come back. What happens to him I never ask, because the best a guy can get by asking questions in this man's town is a bust in the nose.

But I am much worried over this proposition, because I like Dave the Dude, and I know that taking a newspaper guy like Waldo Winchester out for an airing is apt to cause talk, especially if he does not come back. The other guys that Dave the Dude takes out for airings do not mean much in particular, but here is a guy who may produce trouble, even if he is a sucker, on account of being connected with a newspaper.

I know enough about newspapers to know that by and by the editor or somebody will be around wishing to know where Waldo Winchester's pieces about Broadway are, and if there are no pieces from Waldo Winchester, the editor will wish to know why. Finally it will get around to where other people will wish to know, and after a while many people will be running around saying: "Where is Waldo Winchester?"

And if enough people in this town get to running around saying where is So-and-so, it becomes a great mystery and the newspapers hop on the cops and the cops hop on everybody, and by and by there is so much heat in town that it is no place for a guy to be.

But what is to be done about this situation I do not know. Personally, it strikes me as very bad indeed, and while Johnny goes away to do a little telephoning, I am trying to think up some place to go where people will see me, and remember afterwards that I am there in case it is necessary for them to remember.

Finally Johnny comes back, very excited, and says: "Hey, the Dude is up at the Woodcock Inn on the Pelham Parkway, and he is sending out the word for one and all to come at once. Good Time Charley Bernstein just gets the wire and tells me. Something is doing. The rest of the mob are on their way, so let us be moving."

But here is an invitation which does not strike me as a good thing at all. The way I look at it, Dave the Dude is no company for a guy like me at this time. The chances are he either does something to Waldo Winchester already, or is getting ready to do something to him which I wish no part of.

Personally, I have nothing against newspaper guys, not even the ones who write pieces about Broadway. If Dave the Dude wishes to do something to Waldo Winchester, all right, but what is the sense of bringing outsiders into it? But the next thing I know, I am in Johnny McGowan's roadster, and he is zipping along very fast indeed, paying practically no attention to traffic lights or anything else.

As we go busting out the Concourse, I get to thinking the situation over, and I figure that Dave the Dude probably keeps thinking about Miss Billy Perry, and drinking liquor such as they sell in the Chicken Club, until finally he blows his topper. The way I look at it, only a guy who is off his nut will think of taking a newspaper guy out for an airing over a doll, when dolls are a dime a dozen in this man's town.

Still, I remember reading in the papers about a lot of different guys who are considered very sensible until they get tangled up with a doll, and maybe loving her, and the first thing anybody knows they hop out of windows, or shoot themselves, or somebody else, and I can see where even a guy like Dave the Dude may go daffy over a doll.

I can see that little Johnny McGowan is worried, too, but he does not say much, and we pull up in front of the Woodcock Inn in no time whatever, to find a lot of other cars there ahead of us, some of which I recognize as belonging to different parties.

The Woodcock Inn is what is called a roadhouse, and is run by Big Nig Skolsky, a very nice man indeed, and a friend of everybody's. It stands back a piece off the Pelham Parkway and is a very pleasant place to go to, what with Nig having a good band and a floor show with a lot of fair-looking dolls, and everything else a man can wish for a good time. It gets a nice play from nice people, although Nig's liquor is nothing extra.

Personally, I never go there much, because I do not care for roadhouses, but it is a great spot for Dave the Dude when he is pitching parties, or even when he is only drinking single-handed. There is a lot of racket in the joint as we drive up, and who comes out to meet us but Dave the Dude himself with a big hello. His face is very red, and he seems heated up no little, but he does not look like a guy who is meaning any harm to anybody, especially a newspaper guy.

"Come in, guys!" Dave the Dude yells. "Come right in!"

So we go in, and the place is full of people sitting at tables, or out on the floor dancing, and I see Miss Missouri Martin with all her diamonds hanging from her in different places, and Good Time Charley Bernstein, and Feet Samuels, and Tony Bertazzola, and Skeets Boliver, and Nick the Greek, and Rochester Red, and a lot of other guys and dolls from around and about.

In fact, it looks as if everybody from all the joints on Broadway are present, including Miss Billy Perry, who is all dressed up in white and is lugging a big bundle of orchids and so forth, and who is giggling and smiling and shaking hands and going on generally. And finally I see Waldo Winchester, the scribe, sitting at a ringside table all by himself, but there is nothing wrong with him as far as I can see. I mean, he seems to be all in one piece so far.

"Dave," I say to Dave the Dude, very quiet, "what is coming off here? You know a guy cannot be too careful what he does around this town, and I will hate to see you tangled up in anything right now."

"Why," Dave says, "what are you talking about? Nothing is coming off here but a wedding, and it is going to be the best wedding anybody on Broadway ever sees. We are waiting for the preacher now."

"You mean somebody is going to be married?" I ask, being somewhat confused.

"Certainly," Dave the Dude says. "What do you think? What is the idea of a wedding, anyway?"

"Who is going to be married?" I ask.

"Nobody but Billy and the scribe," Dave says. "This is the greatest thing I ever do in my life. I run into Billy the other night and she is crying her eyes out because she loves this scribe and wishes to marry him, but it seems the scribe has nothing he can use for money. So I tell Billy to leave it to me, because you know I love her myself so much I wish to see her happy at all times, even if she has to marry to be that way.

"So I frame this wedding party, and after they are married I am going to stake them to a few G's so they can get a good running start," Dave says. "But I do not tell the scribe and I do not let Billy tell him as I wish it to be a big surprise to him. I kidnap him this afternoon and bring him out here and he is scared half to death thinking I am going to scrag him.

"In fact," Dave says, "I never see a guy so scared. He is still so scared nothing seems to cheer him up. Go over and tell him to shake himself together, because nothing but happiness for him is coming off here."

Well, I wish to say I am greatly relieved to think that Dave intends doing nothing worse to Waldo Winchester than getting him married up, so I go over to where Waldo is sitting. He certainly looks somewhat alarmed. He is all in a huddle with himself, and he has what you call a vacant stare in his eyes. I can see that he is indeed frightened, so I give him a jolly slap on the back and I say: "Congratulations, pal! Cheer up, the worst is yet to come!"

"You bet it is," Waldo Winchester says, his voice so solemn I am greatly surprised.

"You are a fine-looking bridegroom," I say. "You look as if you are at a funeral instead of a wedding. Why do you not laugh ha-ha, and maybe take a dram or two and go to cutting up some?"

"Mister," says Waldo Winchester, "my wife is not going to care for me getting married to Miss Billy Perry."

"Your wife?" I say, much astonished. "What is this you are speaking of? How can you have any wife except Miss Billy Perry? This is great foolishness."

"I know," Waldo says, very sad. "I know. But I got a wife just the same, and she is going to be very nervous when she hears about this. My wife is very strict with me. My wife does not allow me to go around marrying people. My wife is Lola Sapola, of the Rolling Sapolas, the acrobats, and I am married to her for five years. She is the strong lady who juggles the other four people in the act. My wife just gets back from a year's tour of the Interstate time, and she is at the Marx Hotel right this minute. I am upset by this proposition."

"Does Miss Billy Perry know about this wife?" I ask.

"No," he says. "No. She thinks I am single-o."

"But why do you not tell Dave the Dude you are already married when he brings you out here to marry you

off to Miss Billy Perry?" I ask. "It seems to me a newspaper guy must know it is against the law for a guy to
marry several different dolls unless he is a Turk, or some
such."

"Well," Waldo says, "if I tell Dave the Dude I am
married after taking his doll away from him, I am quite
sure Dave will be very much excited, and maybe do
something harmful to my health."

Now there is much in what the guy says, to be sure. I
am inclined to think, myself, that Dave will be somewhat
disturbed when he learns of this situation, especially
when Miss Billy Perry starts in being unhappy about it.
But what is to be done I do not know, except maybe to
let the wedding go on, and then when Waldo is out of
reach of Dave, to put in a claim that he is insane, and
that the marriage does not count. It is a sure thing I do
not wish to be around when Dave the Dude hears Waldo
is already married.

I am thinking that maybe I better take it on the lam
out of there, when there is a great row at the door and I
hear Dave the Dude yelling that the preacher arrives. He
is a very nice-looking preacher, at that, though he seems
somewhat surprised by the goings-on, especially when
Miss Missouri Martin steps up and takes charge of him.
Miss Missouri Martin tells him she is fond of preachers,
and is quite used to them, because she is twice married
by preachers, and twice by justices of the peace, and
once by a ship's captain at sea.

By this time one and all present, except maybe myself
and Waldo Winchester, and the preacher and maybe Miss
Billy Perry, are somewhat corned. Waldo is still sitting at
his table looking very sad and saying "Yes" and "No" to
Miss Billy Perry whenever she skips past him, for Miss
Billy Perry is too much pleasured up with happiness to
stay long in one spot.

Dave the Dude is more corned than anybody else, because he has two or three days' running start on everybody. And when Dave the Dude is corned I wish to say

that he is a very unreliable guy as to temper, and he is apt to explode right in your face any minute. But he' seems to be getting a great bang out of the doings.

Well, by and by Nig Skolsky has the dance floor cleared, and then he moves out on the floor a sort of arch of very beautiful flowers. The idea seems to be that Miss Billy Perry and Waldo Winchester are to be married under this arch. I can see that Dave the Dude must put in several days planning this whole proposition, and it must cost him plenty of the old do-re-mi, especially as I see him showing Miss Missouri Martin a diamond ring as big as a cough drop.

"It is for the bride," Dave the Dude says. "The poor loogan she is marrying will never have enough dough to buy her such a rock, and she always wishes a big one. I get it off a guy who brings it in from Los Angeles. I am going to give the bride away myself in person, so how do I act, Mizzo? I want Billy to have everything according to the book."

Well, while Miss Missouri Martin is trying to remember back to one of her weddings to tell him, I take another peek at Waldo Winchester to see how he is making out. I once see two guys go to the old warm squativoo up in Sing Sing, and I wish to say both are laughing heartily compared to Waldo Winchester at this moment.

Miss Billy Perry is sitting with him and the orchestra leader is calling his men dirty names because none of them can think of how "Oh, Promise Me" goes, when Dave the Dude yells: "Well, we are all set! Let the happy couple step forward!"

Miss Billy Perry bounces up and grabs Waldo Winchester by the arm and pulls him up out of his chair. After a peek at his face I am willing to lay six to five he does not make the arch. But he finally gets there with everybody laughing and clapping their hands, and the preacher comes forward, and Dave the Dude looks happier than I ever see him look before in his life as they all get together under the arch of flowers.

Well, all of a sudden there is a terrible racket at the

front door of the Woodcock Inn, with some doll doing a lot of hollering in a deep voice that sounds like a man's, and naturally everybody turns and looks that way. The doorman, a guy by the name of Slugsy Sachs, who is a very hard man indeed, seems to be trying to keep somebody out, but pretty soon there is a heavy bump and Slugsy Sachs falls down, and in comes a doll about four feet high and five feet wide.

In fact, I never see such a wide doll. She looks all hammered down. Her face is almost as wide as her shoulders, and makes me think of a great big full moon. She comes in bounding-like, and I can see that she is all churned up about something. As she bounces in, I hear a gurgle, and I look around to see Waldo Winchester slumping down to the floor, almost dragging Miss Billy Perry with him.

Well, the wide doll walks right up to the bunch under the arch and says in a large bass voice: "Which one is Dave the Dude?"

"I am Dave the Dude," says Dave the Dude, stepping up. "What do you mean by busting in here like a walrus and gumming up our wedding?"

"So you are the guy who kidnaps my ever-loving husband to marry him off to this little red-headed pancake here, are you?" the wide doll says, looking at Dave the Dude, but pointing at Miss Billy Perry.

Well now, calling Miss Billy Perry a pancake to Dave the Dude is a very serious proposition, and Dave the Dude gets very angry. He is usually rather polite to dolls, but you can see he does not care for the wide doll's manner whatever.

"Say, listen here," Dave the Dude says, "you better take a walk before somebody clips you. You must be drunk," he says. "Or daffy," he says. "What are you talking about, anyway?"

"You will see what I am talking about," the wide doll yells. "The guy on the floor there is my lawful husband. You probably frighten him to death, the poor dear. You kidnap him to marry this red-headed thing, and I am going to get you arrested as sure as my name is Lola Sapola, you simple-looking tramp!"

Naturally, everybody is greatly horrified at a doll using such language to Dave the Dude, because Dave is known to shoot guys for much less, but instead of doing something to the wide doll at once, Dave says: "What is this talk I hear? Who is married to who? Get out of here!" Dave says, grabbing the wide doll's arm.

Well, she makes out as if she is going to slap Dave in the face with her left hand, and Dave naturally pulls his kisser out of the way. But instead of doing anything with her left, Lola Sapola suddenly drives her right fist smack-dab into Dave the Dude's stomach, which naturally comes forward as his face goes back.

I wish to say I see many a body punch delivered in my life, but I never see a prettier one than this. What is more, Lola Sapola steps in with the punch, so there is plenty on it.

Now a guy who eats and drinks like Dave the Dude does cannot take them so good in the stomach, so Dave goes "oof," and sits down very hard on the dance floor, and as he is sitting there he is fumbling in his pants pockets for the old equalizer, so everybody around tears for cover except Lola Sapola, and Miss Billy Perry, and Waldo Winchester.

But before he can get his pistol out, Lola Sapola reaches down and grabs Dave by the collar and hoists him to his feet. She lets go her hold on him, leaving Dave standing on his pins, but teetering around somewhat, and then she drives her right hand to Dave's stomach a second time.

The punch drops Dave again, and Lola steps up to him as if she is going to give him the foot. But she only gathers up Waldo Winchester from off the floor and slings him across her shoulder like he is a sack of oats, and starts for the door. Dave the Dude sits up on the floor again and by this time he has the old equalizer in his duke.

"Only for me being a gentleman I will fill you full of slugs," he yells.

Lola Sapola never even looks back, because by this time she is petting Waldo Winchester's head and calling him loving names and saying what a shame it is for bad characters like Dave the Dude to be abusing her precious one. It all sounds to me as if Lola Sapola thinks well of Waldo Winchester.

Well, after she gets out of sight, Dave the Dude gets up off the floor and stands there looking at Miss Billy Perry, who is out to break all crying records. The rest of us come out from under cover, including the preacher, and we are wondering how mad Dave the Dude is going to be about the wedding being ruined. But Dave the Dude seems only disappointed and sad.

"Billy," he says to Miss Billy Perry, "I am mighty sorry you do not get your wedding. All I wish for is your happiness, but I do not believe you can ever be happy with this scribe if he also has to have his lion tamer around. As Cupid I am a total bust. This is the only nice thing I ever try to do in my whole life, and it is too bad it does not come off. Maybe if you wait until he can drown her, or something—"

"Dave," says Miss Billy Perry, dropping so many tears that she seems to finally wash herself right into Dave the Dude's arms, "I will never, never be happy with such a guy as Waldo Winchester. I can see now you are the only man for me."

"Well, well, well," Dave the Dude says, cheering right up. "Where is the preacher? Bring on the preacher and let us have our wedding anyway."

I see Mr. and Mrs. Dave the Dude the other day, and they seem very happy. But you never can tell about married people, so of course I am never going to let on to Dave the Dude that I am the one who telephones Lola Sapola at the Marx Hotel, because maybe I do not do Dave any too much of a favor, at that.

Dream Street Rose

Of an early evening when there is nothing much doing anywhere else, I go around to Good Time Charley's little speak in West Forty-seventh Street that he calls the Gingham Shoppe, and play a little klob with Charley, because business is quiet in the Gingham Shoppe at such an hour, and Charley gets very lonesome.

He once has a much livelier spot in Forty-eighth Street that he calls the Crystal Room, but one night a bunch of G-guys step into the joint and bust it wide open, besides confiscating all of Charley's stock of merchandise. It seems that these G-guys are members of a squad that comes on from Washington, and being strangers in the city they do not know that Good Time Charley's joint is not supposed to be busted up, so they go ahead and bust it, just the same as if it is any other joint.

Well, this action causes great indignation in many quarters, and a lot of citizens advise Charley to see somebody about it. But Charley says no. Charley says if this is the way the government is going to treat him after the way he walks himself bow-legged over in France with the Rainbow Division, making the Germans hard to catch, why, all right. But he is not going to holler copper about it, although Charley says he has his own opinion of Mr. Hoover, at that.

Personally, I greatly admire Charley for taking the disaster so calmly, especially as it catches him with very few potatoes. Charley is a great hand for playing the horses with any dough he makes out of the Crystal Room, and this particular season the guys who play the horses are being murdered by the bookies all over the country, and are in terrible distress.

So I know if Charley is not plumb broke that he has a terrible crack across his belly, and I am not surprised that I do not see him for a couple of weeks after the government guys knock off the Crystal Room. I hear rumors that he is at home reading the newspapers very carefully every day, especially the obituary notices, for it seems that Charley figures that some of the G-guys may be tempted to take a belt or two at the merchandise they confiscate, and Charley says if they do, he is even for life.

Finally I hear that Charley is seen buying a bolt of gingham in Bloomington's one day, so I know he will be in action again very soon, for all Charley needs to go into action is a bolt of gingham and a few bottles of Golden Wedding. In fact, I know Charley to go into action without the gingham, but as a rule he likes to drape a place of business with gingham to make it seem more homelike to his customers, and I wish to say that when it comes to draping gingham, Charley can make a sucker of Joseph Urban, or anybody else.

Well, when I arrive at the Gingham Shoppe this night I am talking about, which is around ten o'clock, I find Charley in a very indignant state of mind, because an old tomato by the name of Dream Street Rose comes in and tracks up his floor, just after Charley gets through mopping it up, for Charley does his mopping in person, not being able as yet to afford any help.

Rose is sitting at a table in a corner, paying no attention to Charley's remarks about wiping her feet on the welcome mat at the door before she comes in, because Rose knows there is no welcome mat at Charley's door, anyway, but I can see where Charley has a right to a few beefs, at that, as she leaves a trail of black hoofprints across the clean floor as if she is walking around in mud somewhere before she comes in, although I do not seem to remember that it is raining when I arrive.

Now this Dream Street Rose is an old doll of maybe fifty-odd, and is a very well-known character around and about, as she is wandering through the Forties for many a year, and especially through West Forty-seventh Street between Sixth and Seventh Avenues, and this Block is called Dream Street. And the reason it is called Dream Street is because in this block are many characters of one kind and another who always seem to be dreaming of different matters.

In Dream Street there are many theatrical hotels, and rooming houses, and restaurants, and speaks, including Good Time Charley's Gingham Shoppe, and in the summer time the characters I mention sit on the stoops or lean against the railings along Dream Street, and the gab you hear sometimes sounds very dreamy indeed. In fact, it sometimes sounds very pipe-dreamy.

Many actors, male and female, and especially vaudeville actors, live in the hotels and rooming houses, and vaudeville actors, both male and female, are great hands for sitting around dreaming out loud about how they will practically assassinate the public in the Palace if ever they get a chance.

Furthermore, in Dream Street are always many hand bookies and horse players, who sit on the church steps on the cool side of Dream Street in the summer and dream about big killings on the races, and there are also nearly always many fight managers, and sometimes fighters, hanging out in front of the restaurants, picking their teeth and dreaming about winning championships of the world, although up to this time no champion of the world has yet come out of Dream Street.

In this street you see burlesque dolls, and hoofers, and guys who write songs, and saxophone players, and newsboys, and newspaper scribes, and taxi drivers, and blind guys, and midgets, and blondes with Pomeranian pooches, or maybe French poodles, and guys with whiskers, and night-club entertainers, and I do not know what all else. And all of these characters are interesting to look at, and some of them are very interesting to talk to, although if you listen to several I know long enough, you may get the idea that they are somewhat daffy, especially the horse players.

But personally I consider all horse players more or less daffy anyway. In fact, the way I look at it, if a guy is not daffy he will not be playing the horses.

Now this Dream Street Rose is a short, thick-set, square-looking old doll, with a square pan, and square shoulders, and she has heavy iron-gray hair that she wears in a square bob, and she stands very square on her feet. In fact, Rose is the squarest-looking doll I ever see, and she is as strong and lively as Jim Londos, the wrestler. In fact, Jim Londos will never be any better than six to five in my line over Dream Street Rose, if she is in any kind of shape. Nobody in this town wishes any truck with Rose if she has a few shots of grog in her, and especially Good Time Charley's grog, for she can fight like the dickens when she is grogged up. In fact, Rose holds many a decision in this town, especially over coppers, because if there is one thing she hates and despises more than somewhat it is a copper, as coppers are always heaving her into the old can when they find her jerking citizens around and cutting up other didoes.

For many years Rose works in the different hotels along Dream Street as a chambermaid. She never works in any one hotel very long, because the minute she gets a few bobs together she likes to go out and enjoy a little recreation, such as visiting around the speaks, although she is about as welcome in most speaks as a G-guy with a search warrant. You see, nobody can ever tell when Rose may feel like taking the speak apart, and also the customers.

She never has any trouble getting a job back in any hotel she ever works in, for Rose is a wonderful hand for making up beds, although several times, when she is in a hurry to get off, I hear she makes up beds with guests still in them, which causes a few mild beefs to the management, but does not bother Rose. I speak of this matter only to show you that she is a very quaint character indeed, and full of zest.

Well, I sit down to play klob with Good Time Charley, but about this time several customers come into the

Gingham Shoppe, so Charley has to go and take care of them, leaving me alone. And while I am sitting there alone I hear Dream Street Rose mumbling to herself over in the corner, but I pay no attention to her, although I wish to say I am by no means unfriendly with Rose.

In fact, I say hello to her at all times, and am always very courteous to her, as I do not wish to have her bawling me out in public, and maybe circulating rumors about me, as she is apt to do, if she feels I am snubbing her.

Finally I notice her motioning to me to come over to her table, and I go over at once and sit down, because I can see that Rose is well grogged up at this time, and I do not care to have her attracting my attention by chucking a cuspidor at me. She offers me a drink when I sit down, but of course I never drink anything that is sold in Good Time Charley's, as a personal favor to Charley. He says he wishes to retain my friendship.

So I just sit there saying nothing much whatever, and Rose keeps on mumbling to herself, and I am not able to make much of her mumbling, until finally she looks at me and says to me like this:

"I am now going to tell you about my friend," Rose says.

"Well, Rose," I say, "personally I do not care to hear about your friend, although," I say, "I have no doubt that what you wish to tell me about this friend is very interesting. But I am here to play a little klob with Good Time Charley, and I do not have time to hear about your friend."

"Charley is busy selling his poison to the suckers," Rose says. "I am now going to tell you about my friend. It is quite a story," she says. "You will listen."

So I listen.

It is a matter of thirty-five years ago [Dream Street Rose says] and the spot is a town in Colorado by the name of Pueblo, where there are smelters and one thing and another. My friend is at this time maybe sixteen or seventeen years old, and a first-class looker in every respect. Her papa is dead, and her mamma runs a boardinghouse for the guys who work in the smelters, and who are very hearty eaters. My friend deals them off the arm for the guys in her mamma's boardinghouse to save her mamma the expense of a waitress.

Now among the boarders in this boardinghouse are many guys who are always doing a little pitching to my friend, and trying to make dates with her to take her places, but my friend never gives them much of a tumble, because after she gets through dealing them off the arm all day her feet generally pain her too much to go anywhere on them except to the hay.

Finally, however, along comes a tall, skinny young guy from the East by the name of Frank something, who has things to say to my friend that are much more interesting than anything that has ever been said to her by a guy before, including such things as love and marriage, which are always very interesting subjects to any young doll.

This Frank is maybe twenty-five years old, and he comes from the East with the idea of making his fortune in the West, and while it is true that fortunes are being made in the West at this time, there is little chance that Frank is going to make any part of a fortune, as he does not care to work very hard. In fact, he does not care to work at all, being much more partial to playing a little poker, or shooting a few craps, or maybe hustling a sucker around Mike's poolroom on Santa Fe Avenue, for Frank is an excellent pool player, especially when he is playing a sucker.

Now my friend is at this time a very innocent young doll, and a good doll in every respect, and her idea of love includes a nice little home, and children running here and there and around and about, and she never has a wrong thought in her life, and believes that everybody else in the world is like herself. And the chances are if this Frank does not happen along, my friend will marry a young guy in Pueblo by the name of Higginbottom, who is very fond of her indeed, and who is a decent young guy and afterwards makes plenty of potatoes in the grocery dodge.

But my friend goes very daffy over Frank and cannot see anybody but him, and the upshot of it all is she runs away with him one day to Denver, being dumb enough to believe that he means it when he tells her that he loves her and is going to marry her. Why Frank ever bothers with such a doll as my friend in the first place is always a great mystery to one and all, and the only way anybody can explain it is that she is young and fresh, and he is a heel at heart.

"Well, Rose," I say, "I am now commencing to see the finish of this story about your friend, and," I say, "it is such a story as anybody can hear in a speak at any time in this town, except," I say, "maybe your story is longer than somewhat. So I will now thank you, and excuse myself, and play a little klob with Good Time Charley."

"You will listen," Dream Street Rose says, looking me slap-dab in the eye.

So I listen.

Moreover, I notice now that Good Time Charley is standing behind me, bending in an ear, as it seems that his customers take the wind after a couple of slams of Good Time Charley's merchandise, a couple of slams being about all that even a very hardy customer can stand at one session.

Of course [Rose goes on] the chances are Frank never intends marrying my friend at all, and she never knows until long afterward that the reason he leads her to the parson is that the young guy from Pueblo by the name of Higginbottom catches up with them at the old Windsor Hotel where they are stopping and privately pokes a six-pistol against Frank's ribs and promises faithfully to come back and blow a hole in Frank you can throw a watermelon through if Frank tries any phenagling around with my friend.

Well, in practically no time whatever, love's young dream is over as far as my friend is concerned. This Frank turns out to be a most repulsive character indeed, especially if you are figuring him as an ever-loving husband. In fact, he is no good. He mistreats my friend in every way any guy ever thought of mistreating a doll, and besides the old established ways of mistreating a doll, Frank thinks up quite a number of new ways, being really quite ingenious in this respect.

Yes, this Frank is one-hundred-per-cent heel.

It is not so much that he gives her a thumping now and then, because, after all, a thumping wears off, and hurts heal up, even when they are such hurts as a broken nose and fractured ribs, and once an ankle cracked by a kick. It is what he does to her heart, and to her innocence. He is by no means a good husband, and does not know how to treat an ever-loving wife with any respect, especially as he winds up by taking my friend to San Francisco and hiring her out to a very loose character there by the name of Black Emanuel, who has a dance joint on the Barbary Coast, which, at the time I am talking about, is hotter than a stove. In this joint my friend has to dance with the customers, and get them to buy beer for her and one thing and another, and this occupation is most distasteful to my friend, as she never cares for beer.

It is there Frank leaves her for good after giving her an extra big thumping for a keepsake, and when my friend tries to leave Black Emanuel's to go looking for her ever-loving husband, she is somewhat surprised to hear Black Emanuel state that he pays Frank three C's for her to remain there and continue working. Furthermore, Black Emanuel resumes the thumpings where Frank leaves off, and by and by my friend is much bewildered and down-hearted and does not care what happens to her.

Well, there is nothing much of interest in my friend's life for the next thirty-odd years, except that she finally gets so she does not mind the beer so much, and, in fact, takes quite a fondness for it, and also for light wines and Bourbon whisky, and that she comes to realize that Frank does not love her after all, in spite of what he says. Furthermore, in later years, after she drifts around the country quite some, in and out of different joints, she

realizes that the chances are she will never have a nice
little home, with children running here and there, and
she often thinks of what a disagreeable influence Frank
has on her life.

In fact, this Frank is always on her mind more than
somewhat. In fact, she thinks of him night and day, and
says many a prayer that he will do well. She manages to
keep track of him, which is not hard to do, at that, as
Frank is in New York, and is becoming quite a guy in
business, and is often in the newspapers. Maybe his success is due to my friend's prayers, but the chances are
it is more because he connects up with some guy who
has an invention for doing something very interesting to
steel, and by grabbing an interest in this invention Frank
gets a shove toward plenty of potatoes. Furthermore, he
is married, and is raising up a family.

About ten or twelve years ago my friend comes to
New York, and by this time she is getting a little faded
around the edges. She is not so old, at that, but the air
of the Western and Southern joints is bad on the complexion, and beer is no good for the figure. In fact, my
friend is now quite a haybag, and she does not get any
better-looking in the years she spends in New York as
she is practically all out of the old sex appeal, and has to
do a little heavy lifting to keep eating. But she never forgets to keep praying that Frank will continue to do well,
and Frank certainly does this, as he is finally spoken of
everywhere very respectfully as a millionaire and a high-
class guy.

In all the years she is in New York my friend never
runs into Frank, as Frank is by no means accustomed to
visiting the spots where my friend hangs out, but my
friend goes to a lot of bother to get acquainted with a
doll who is a maid for some time in Frank's town house
in East Seventy-fourth Street, and through this doll my
friend keeps a pretty fair line on the way Frank lives. In
fact, one day when Frank and his family are absent, my
friend goes to Frank's house with her friend, just to see

what it looks like, and after an hour there my friend has the joint pretty well cased.

And now my friend knows through her friend that on very hot nights such as tonight Frank's family is bound to be at their country place at Port Washington, but that Frank himself is spending the night at this town house, because he wishes to work on a lot of papers of some kind. My friend knows through her friend that all of Frank's servants are at Port Washington, too, except my friend's friend, who is in charge of the town house, and Frank's valet, a guy by the name of Sloggins.

Furthermore, my friend knows through her friend that both her friend and Sloggins have a date to go to a movie at eight-thirty, to be gone a couple of hours, as it seems Frank is very big-hearted about giving his servants time off for such a purpose when he is at home alone; although one night he squawks no little when my friend is out with her friend drinking a little beer, and my friend's friend loses her door key and has to ring the bell of the servants' entrance, and rousts Frank out of a sound sleep.

Naturally, my friend's friend will be greatly astonished if she ever learns that it is with this key that my friend steps into Frank's house along about nine o'clock to-night. An electric light hangs over the servants' entrance, and my friend locates the button that controls this light just inside the door and turns it off, as my friend figures that maybe Frank and his family will not care to have their high-class neighbors, or anyone else, see an old doll who has no better hat than she is wearing, entering or leaving their house at such an hour.

It is an old-fashioned sort of house, four or five stories high, with the library on the third floor in the rear, looking out through French windows over a nice little garden, and my friend finds Frank in the library where she expects to find him, because she is smart enough to figure that a guy who is working on papers is not apt to be doing this work in the cellar.

But Frank is not working on anything when my friend moves in on him. He is dozing in a chair by the window, and, looking at him after all these years, she finds something of a change, indeed. He is much heavier than he is thirty-five years back, and his hair is white, but he looks pretty well to my friend, at that, as she stands there for maybe five minutes watching him. Then he seems to realize somebody is in the room, as sleeping guys will do, for his regular breathing stops with a snort, and he opens his eyes, and looks into my friend's eyes, but without hardly stirring. And finally my friend speaks to Frank as follows:

"Well, Frank," she says, "do you know me?"

"Yes," he says, after a while, "I know you. At first I think maybe you are a ghost, as I once hear something about your being dead. But," he says, "I see now the report is a canard. You are too fat to be a ghost."

Well, of course, this is a most insulting crack, indeed, but my friend passes it off as she does not wish to get in any arguments with Frank at this time. She can see that he is upset more than somewhat and he keeps looking around the room as if he hopes he can see somebody else he can cut in on the conversation. In fact, he acts as if my friend is by no means a welcome visitor.

"Well, Frank," my friend says, very pleasant, "there you are, and here I am. I understand you are now a wealthy and prominent citizen of this town. I am glad to know this, Frank," she says. "You will be surprised to hear that for years and years I pray that you will do well for yourself and become a big guy in every respect, with a nice family, and everything else. I judge my prayers are answered," she says. "I see by the papers that you have two sons at Yale, and a daughter in Vassar, and that your ever-loving wife is getting to be very high mucky-mucky in society. Well, Frank," she says, "I am very glad. I pray something like all this will happen to you."

Now, at such a speech, Frank naturally figures that my

friend is all right, at that, and the chances are he also figures that she still has a mighty soft spot in her heart for him, just as she has in the days when she deals them off the arm to keep him in gambling and drinking money. In fact, Frank brightens up somewhat, and he says to my friend like this:

"You pray for my success?" he says. "Why, this is very thoughtful of you, indeed. Well," he says, "I am sitting on top of the world, I have everything to live for."

"Yes," my friend says, "and this is exactly where I pray I will find you. On top of the world," she says, "and with everything to live for. It is where I am when you take my life. It is where I am when you kill me as surely as if you strangle me with your hands. I always pray you will not become a bum," my friend says, "because a bum has nothing to live for, anyway. I want to find you liking to live, so you will hate so much to die."

Naturally, this does not sound so good to Frank, and he begins all of a sudden to shake and shiver and to stutter somewhat.

"Why," he says, "what do you mean? Are you going to kill me?"

"Well," my friend says, "that remains to be seen. Personally," she says, "I will be much obliged if you will kill yourself, but it can be arranged one way or the other. However, I will explain the disadvantages of me killing you.

"The chances are," my friend says, "if I kill you I will be caught and a very great scandal will result, because," she says, "I have on my person the certificate of my marriage to you in Denver, and something tells me you never think to get a divorce. So," she says, "you are a bigamist."

"I can pay," Frank says. "I can pay plenty."

"Furthermore," my friend says, paying no attention to his remark, "I have a sworn statement from Black Emanuel about your transaction with him, for Black Emanuel gets religion before he dies from being shivved by Johnny

Mizzoo, and he tries to round himself up by confessing all the sins he can think of, which are quite a lot. It is a very interesting statement," my friend says.

"Now then," she says, "if you knock yourself off you will leave an unsullied, respected name. If I kill you, all the years and effort you have devoted to building up your reputation will go for nothing. You are past sixty," my friend says, "and any way you figure it, you do not have so very far to go. If I kill you," she says, "you will go in horrible disgrace, and everybody around you will feel the disgrace, no matter how much dough you leave them. Your children will hang their heads in shame. Your ever-loving wife will not like it," my friend says.

"I wait on you a long time, Frank," my friend says. "A dozen times in the past twenty years I figure I may as well call on you and close up my case with you, but," she says, "then I always persuade myself to wait a little longer so you would rise higher and higher and life will be a bit sweeter to you. And there you are, Frank," she says, "and here I am."

Well, Frank sits there as if he is knocked plumb out, and he does not answer a word; so finally my friend outs with a large John Roscoe which she is packing in the bosom of her dress, and tosses it in his lap, and speaks as follows:

"Frank," she says, "do not think it will do you any good to pot me in the back when I turn around, because," she says, "you will be worse off than ever. I leave plenty of letters scattered around in case anything happens to me. And remember," she says, "if you do not do this job yourself, I will be back. Sooner or later, I will be back."

So [Dream Street Rose says] my friend goes out of the library and down the stairs, leaving Frank sprawled out in his chair, and when she reaches the first floor she hears what may be a shot in the upper part of the house, and then again may be only a door slamming. My friend never knows for sure what it is, because a little later as she nears the servants' entrance she hears quite a commotion outside, and a guy cussing a blue streak, and a doll tee-heeing, and pretty soon my friend's friend, the maid, and Sloggins, the valet, come walking in.

Well, my friend just has time to scroonch herself back in a dark corner, and they go upstairs, the guy still cussing and the doll still giggling, and my friend cannot make out what it is all about except that they come home earlier than she figures. So my friend goes tippy-toe out of the servants' entrance, to grab a taxi not far from the house and get away from this neighborhood, and now you will soon hear of the suicide of a guy who is a millionaire, and it will be all even with my friend.

"Well, Rose," I say, "it is a nice long story, and full of romance and all this and that, and," I say, "of course I will never be ungentlemanly enough to call a lady a liar, but," I say, "if it is not a lie, it will do until a lie comes along."

"All right," Rose says. "Anyway, I tell you about my friend. Now," she says, "I am going where the liquor is better, which can be any other place in town, because," she says, "there is no chance of liquor anywhere being any worse."

So she goes out, making more tracks on Good Time Charley's floor, and Charley speaks most impolitely of her after she goes, and gets out his mop to clean the floor, for one thing about Charley, he is as neat as a pin, and maybe neater.

Well, along toward one o'clock I hear a newsboy in the street outside yelling something I cannot make out, because he is yelling as if he has a mouthful of mush, as newsboys are bound to do. But I am anxious to see what goes in the first race at Belmont, on account of having a first-class tip, so I poke my noggin outside Good Time Charley's and buy a paper, and across the front page, in large letters, it states that the wealthy Mr. Frank Billingsworth McQuiggan knocks himself off by putting a slug through his own noggin.

It says Mr. McQuiggan is found in a chair in his library as dead as a doornail with the pistol in his lap with which he knocks himself off, and the paper states that nobody can figure what causes Mr. McQuiggan to do such a thing to himself as he is in good health and has plenty of potatoes and is at the peak of his career. Then there is a lot about his history.

When Mr. McQuiggan is a young fellow returning from a visit to the Pacific Coast with about two hundred dollars in his pocket after paying his railroad fare, he meets in the train Jonas Calloway, famous inventor of the Calloway steel process. Calloway also then young, is desperately in need of funds and he offers Mr. McQuiggan a third interest in his invention for what now seems the paltry sum of one hundred dollars. Mr. McQuiggan accepts the offer and thus paves the way to his own fortune.

I am telling all this to Good Time Charley while he is mopping away at the floor, and finally I come on a paragraph down near the finish which goes like this: "The body was discovered by Mr. McQuiggan's faithful valet, Thomas Sloggins, at eleven o'clock. Mr. McQuiggan was then apparently dead a couple of hours. Sloggins returned home shortly before ten o'clock with another servant after changing his mind about going to a movie. Instead of going to see his employer at once, as is his usual custom, Sloggins went to his own quarters and changed his clothes.

" 'The light over the servants' entrance was out when I returned home,' the valet said, 'and in the darkness I stumbled over some scaffolding and other material left near this entrance by workmen who are to regravel the roof of the house tomorrow, upsetting all over the entranceway a large bucket of tar, much of which got on my apparel when I fell, making a change necessary before going to see Mr. McQuiggan.' "

Well, Good Time Charley keeps on mopping harder than ever, though finally he stops a minute and speaks to me as follows:

"Listen," Charley says, "understand I do not say the guy does not deserve what he gets, and I am by no means hollering copper, but," Charley says, "if he knocks himself off, how does it come the rod is still in his lap where Dream Street Rose says her friend tosses it? Well, never mind," Charley says, "but can you think of something that will remove tar from a wood floor? It positively will not mop off."

All Horse Players Die Broke

It is during the last race meeting at Saratoga, and one evening I am standing out under the elms in front of the Grand Union Hotel thinking what a beautiful world it is, to be sure, for what do I do in the afternoon at the track but grab myself a piece of a ten-to-one shot. I am thinking what a beautiful moon it is, indeed, that is shining down over the park where Mr. Dick Canfield once deals them higher than a cat's back, and how pure and balmy the air is, and also what nice-looking Judys are wandering around and about, although it is only the night before that I am standing in the same spot wondering where I can borrow a Betsy with which to shoot myself smack-dab through the pimple.

In fact, I go around to see a character I know by the name of Solly something, who owns a Betsy, but it seems he has only one cartridge to his name for this Betsy and he is thinking some of either using the cartridge to shoot his own self smack-dab through the pimple, or of going out to the race course and shooting an old catfish by the name of Pair of Jacks that plays him false in the fifth race, and therefore Solly is not in a mood to lend his Betsy to anybody else. So we try to figure out a way we can make one cartridge do for two pimples, and in the meantime Solly outs with a bottle of applejack, and after a couple of belts at this bottle we decide that the sensible thing to do is to take the Betsy out and peddle it for whatever we can, and maybe get a taw for the next day.

Well, it happens that we run into an Italian party from Passaic, N. J., by the name of Guiseppe Palladino, who is called Joe for short, and this Joe is in the money very good at the moment, and he is glad to lend us a pound note on the Betsy, because Joe is such a character as never knows when he may need an extra Betsy, and anyway it is the first time in his experience around the race tracks that anybody ever offers him collateral for a loan. So there Solly and I are with a deuce apiece after we spend the odd dollar for breakfast the next day, and I run my deuce up to a total of twenty-two slugs on the ten-to-one shot in the last heat of the day, and everything is certainly all right with me in every respect.

Well, while I am standing there under the elms, who comes along but a raggedy old Dutchman by the name of Unser Fritz, who is maybe seventy-five years old, come next grass, and who is following the giddyaps since the battle of Gettysburg, as near as anybody can figure out. In fact, Unser Fritz is quite an institution around the race tracks, and is often written up by the newspaper scribes as a terrible example of what a horse player comes to, although personally I always say that what Unser Fritz comes to is not so tough when you figure that he does not do a tap of work in all these years. In his day, Unser Fritz is a most successful handicapper, a handicapper being a character who can dope out from the form what horses ought to win the races, and as long as his figures turn out all right, a handicapper is spoken of most respectfully by one and all, although of course when he begins missing out for any length of time as handicappers are bound to do, he is no longer spoken of respectfully, or even as a handicapper. He is spoken of as a bum.

It is a strange thing how a handicapper can go along for years doing everything right, and then all of a sudden he finds himself doing everything wrong, and this

is the way it is with Unser Fritz. For a long time his figures on the horse races are considered most remarkable,
indeed, and as he will bet till the cows come home on
his own figures, he generally has plenty of money, and
a fiancée by the name of Emerald Em. She is called
Emerald Em because she has a habit of wearing a raft
of emeralds in rings, and pins, and bracelets, and one
thing and another, which are purchased for her by
Unser Fritz to express his love, an emerald being a
green stone that is considered most expressive of love,
if it is big enough. It seems that Emerald Em is very
fond of emeralds, especially when they are surrounded
by large, coarse diamonds. I hear the old timers around
the race tracks say that when Emerald Em is young,
she is a tall, good-looking Judy with yellow hair that is
by no means a phony yellow, at that, and with a shape
that does not require a bustle such as most Judys always
wear in those days.

But then nobody ever hears an old timer mention any
Judy that he remembers from back down the years who
is not good-looking, and in fact beautiful. To hear the
old-timers tell it, every pancake they ever see when they
are young is a double Myrna Loy, though the chances
are, figuring in the law of averages, that some of them
are bound to be rutabagas, the same as now. Anyway,
for years this Emerald Em is known on every race track
from coast to coast as Unser Fritz's fiancée, and is considered quite a remarkable scene, what with her emeralds, and not requiring any bustle, and everything else.

Then one day Unser Fritz's figures run plumb out on
him, and so does his dough, and so does Emerald Em,
and now Unswer Fritz is an old pappy guy, and it is
years since he is regarded as anything but a crumbo
around the race tracks, and nobody remembers much of
his story, or cares a cuss about it, for if there is anything that is a drug on the market around the tracks it
is the story of a broker. How he gets from place to
place, and how he lives after he gets there, is a very
great mystery to one and all, although I hear he often

rides in the horsecars with the horses, when some owner or trainer happens to be feeling tenderhearted, or he hitchhikes in automobiles, and sometimes he even walks, for Unser Fritz is still fairly nimble, no matter how old he is.

He always has under his arm a bundle of newspapers that somebody throws away, and every night he sits down and handicaps the horses running the next day according to his own system, but he seldom picks any winners and even if he does pick any winners, he seldom has anything to bet on them. Sometimes he promotes a stranger, who does not know he is bad luck to a good hunting dog, to put down a few dibs on one of his picks, and once in a while the pick wins, and Unser Fritz gets a small stake, and sometimes an old timer who feels sorry for him will slip him something. But whatever Unser Fritz gets hold of, he bets off right away on the next race that comes up, so naturally he never is holding anything very long.

Well, Unser Fritz stands under the elms with me a while, speaking of this and that, and especially of the races, and I am wondering to myself if I will become as disheveled as Unser Fritz if I keep on following the races, when he gazes at the Grand Union Hotel, and says to me like this:

"It looks nice," he says. "It looks cheery-like, with the lights, and all this and that. It brings back memories to me. Emma always lives in this hotel whenever we make Saratoga for the races back in the days when I am in the money. She always has a suite of two or three rooms on this side of the hotel. Once she has four. I often stand here under these trees," Unser Fritz says, "watching her windows to see what time she puts out her lights, because, while I trust Emma implicitly, I know she has a restless nature, and sometimes she cannot resist returning to scenes of gaiety after I bid her good night, especially," he says, "with a party by the name of Pete Shovelin, who runs the restaurant where she once deals them off the arm."

"You mean she is a biscuit shooter?" I say.

"A waitress," Unser Fritz says. "A good waitress. She comes of a family of farm folks in this very section, although I never know much about them," he says. "Shovelin's is a little hole-in-the-wall up the street here somewhere which long since disappears. I go there for my morning java in the old days. I will say one thing for Shovelin," Unser Fritz says, "he always has good java. Three days after I first clap eyes on Emma, she is wearing her first emerald, and is my fiancée. Then she moves into a suite in the Grand Union. I only wish you can know Emma in those days," he says. "She is beautiful. She is a fine character. She is always on the level, and I love her dearly."

"What do you mean—always on the level?" I say. "What about this Shovelin party you just mention?"

"Ah," Unser Fritz says, "I suppose I am dull company for a squab, what with having to stay in at night to work on my figures, and Emma likes to go around and about. She is a highly nervous type, and extremely restless, and she cannot bear to hold still very long at a time. But," he says, "in those days it is not considered proper for a young Judy to go around and about without a chaperon, so she goes with Shovelin for her chaperon. Emma never goes anywhere without a chaperon," he says.

Well, it seems that early in their courtship, Unser Fritz learns that he can generally quiet her restlessness with emeralds, if they have diamonds on the side. It seems that these stones have a very soothing effect on her, and this is why he purchases them for her by the bucket. "Yes," Unser Fritz says, "I always think of Emma whenever I am in New York City, and look down Broadway at night with the go lights on."

But it seems from what Unser Fritz tells me that even with the emeralds her restless spells come on her very bad, and especially when he finds himself running short of ready, and is unable to purchase more emeralds for her at the moment, although Unser Fritz claims this is nothing unusual. In fact, he says anybody with any experience with nervous female characters knows that it becomes very monotonous for them to be around people who are short of ready. "But," he says, "not all of them require soothing with emeralds. Some require pearls," he says.

Well, it seems that Emma generally takes a trip without Unser Fritz to break the monotony of his running short of ready, but she never takes one of these trips without a chaperon, because she is very careful about her good name, and Unser Fritz's, too. It seems that in those days Judys have to be more careful about such matters than they do now.

He remembers that once when they are in San Francisco she takes a trip through the Yellowstone with Jockey Gus Kloobus as her chaperon, and is gone three weeks and returns much refreshed, especially as she gets back just as Unser Fritz makes a nice score and has a seidel of emeralds waiting for her. He remembers another time she goes to England with a trainer by the name of Blootz as her chaperon and comes home with an English accent that sounds right cute, to find Unser Fritz going like a house afire at Belmont. "She takes a lot of other trips without me during the time we are engaged," Unser Fritz says, "but," he says, "I always know Emma will return to me as soon as she hears I am back in the money and can purchase more emeralds for her. In fact," he says, "this knowledge is all that keeps me struggling now."

"Look, Fritz," I say, "what do you mean, keeps you going? Do you mean you think Emma may return to you again?"

"Why, sure," Unser Fritz says. "Why, certainly, if I get my rushes again. Why not?" he says. "She knows there will be a pail of emeralds waiting for her. She knows I love her and always will," he says.

Well, I ask him when he sees Emerald Em last, and he says it is 1908 in the old Waldorf-Astoria the night he blows a hundred and sixty thousand betting on a hide called Sir Martin to win the Futurity, and it is all the dough Unser Fritz has at the moment. In fact, he is cleaner than a jay bird, and he is feeling somewhat discouraged. It seems he is waiting on his floor for the elevator, and when it comes down Emerald Em is one of the several passengers, and when the door opens, and Unser Fritz starts to get in, she raises her foot and plants it in his stomach, and gives him a big push back out the door and the elevator goes on down without him.

"But, of course," Unser Fritz says, "Emma never likes to ride in the same elevator with me, because I am not always tidy enough to suit her in those days, what with having so much work to do on my figures, and she claims it is a knock to her socially. Anyway," he says, "this is the last I see of Emma."

"Why, Fritz," I say, "nineteen-eight is nearly thirty years back, and if she ever thinks of returning to you, she will return long before this."

"No," Unser Fritz says. "You see, I never make a scratch since then. I am never since in the money, so there is no reason for Emma to return to me. But," he says, "wait until I get going good again and you will see."

Well, I always figure Unser Fritz must be more or less of an old screwball for going on thinking there is still a chance for him around the tracks, and now I am sure of it, and I am about to bid him good evening, when he mentions that he can use about two dollars if I happen to have a deuce on me that is not working, and I will say one thing for Unser Fritz, he seldom comes right out and asks anybody for anything unless things are very desperate with him, indeed. "I need it to pay something on account of my landlady," he says. "I room with old Mrs. Crob around the corner for over twenty years, and," he says, "she only charges me a finnif a week, so I try to keep from getting too far to the rear with her. I will return it to you the first score I make."

Well, of course I know this means practically never, but I am feeling so good about my success at the track that I slip him a deucer, and it is half an hour later before I fully realize what I do, and go looking for Fritz to get anyway half of it back. But by this time he disappears, and I think no more of the matter until the next day out at the course when I hear Unser Fritz bets two dollars on a thing by the name of Speed Cart, and it bows down at fifty to one, so I know Mrs. Crob is still waiting for hers.

Now there is Unser Fritz with one hundred slugs, and this is undoubtedly more money than he enjoys since Hickory Slim is a two-year-old. And from here on the story becomes very interesting, and in fact remarkable, because up to the moment Speed Cart hits the wire, Unser Fritz is still nothing but a crumbo, and you can say it again, while from now on he is somebody to point out and say can you imagine such a thing happening? He bets a hundred on a centipede called Marchesa, and down pops Marchesa like a trained pig at twenty to one. Then old Unser Fritz bets two hundred on a caterpillar by the name of Merry Soul, at four to one, and Merry Soul just laughs his way home. Unser Fritz winds up the day betting two thousand more on something called Sharp Practice, and when Sharp Practice wins by so far it looks as if he is a shoo-in, Fritz finds himself with over twelve thousand slugs, and the way the bookmakers in the betting ring are sobbing is really most distressing to hear.

Well, in a week Unser Fritz is a hundred thousand dollars in front, because the way he sends it in is quite astonishing to behold, although the old timers tell me it is just the way he sends it when he is younger. He is betting only on horses that he personally figures out, and what happens is that Unser Fritz's figures suddenly come to life again, and he cannot do anything wrong. He wins so much dough that he even pays off a few old touches, including my two, and he goes so far as to lend Joe Palladino three dollars on the Betsy that Solly and I hock with Joe for the pound note, as it seems that by this time Joe himself is practically on his way to

the poorhouse, and while Unser Fritz has no use whatsoever for a Betsy he cannot bear to see a character
such as Joe go to the poorhouse.

But with all the dough Unser Fritz carries in his pockets, and plants in a safe-deposit box in the jug downtown, he looks just the same as ever, because he claims
he cannot find time from working on his figures to buy
new clothes and dust himself off, and if you tell anybody who does not know who he is that this old crutch
is stone rich, the chances are they will call you a liar.

In fact, on a Monday around noon, the clerk in the
branch office that a big Fifth Avenue jewelry firm keeps
in the lobby of the States Hotel is all ready to yell for
the constables when Unser Fritz leans up against the
counter and asks to see some jewelry on display in a
showcase, as Unser Fritz is by no means the clerk's idea
of a customer for jewelry. I am standing in the lobby of
the hotel on the off chance that some fresh money may
arrive in the city on the late trains that I may be able
to connect up with before the races, when I notice Unser
Fritz and observe the agitation of the clerk, and presently I see Unser Fritz waving a fistful of bank notes
under the clerk's beak, and the clerk starts setting out
the jewelry with surprising speed.

I go over to see what is coming off, and I can see that
the jewelry Unser Fritz is looking at consists of a neck-
lace of emeralds and diamonds, with a centerpiece the
size of the home plate, and some eardrops, and bracelets, and clips of same, and as I approach the scene I
hear Unser Fritz ask how much for the lot as if he is
dickering for a basket of fish.

"One hundred and one thousand dollars, sir," the
clerk says. "You see, sir, it is a set, and one of the finest
things of the kind in the country. We just got it in from
our New York store to show a party here, and," he says,
"she is absolutely crazy about it, but she states she cannot give us a final decision until five o'clock this afternoon. Confidentially, sir," the clerk says, "I think the
real trouble is financial, and doubt that we will hear from

her again. In fact," he says, "I am so strongly of this opinion that I am prepared to sell the goods without waiting on her. It is really a bargain at the price," he says.

"Dear me," Unser Fritz says to me, "this is most unfortunate as the sum mentioned is just one thousand dollars more than I possess in all this world. I have twenty thousand on my person, and eighty thousand over in the box in the jug, and not another dime. But," he says, "I will be back before five o'clock and take the lot. In fact," he says, "I will run in right after the third race, and pick it up." Well, at this, the clerk starts putting the jewelry back in the case, and anybody can see that he figures he is on a lob and that he is sorry he wastes so much time, but Unser Fritz says to me like this: "Emma is returning to me," he says.

"Emma who?" I say.

"Why," Unser Fritz says, "my Emma. The one I tell you about not long ago. She must hear I am in the money again, and she is returning just as I always say she will."

"How do you know?" I say. "Do you hear from her, or what?"

"No," Unser Fritz says, "I do not hear from her direct, but Mrs. Crob knows some female relative of Emma's that lives at Ballston Spa a few miles from here, and this relative is in Saratoga this morning to do some shopping, and she tells Mrs. Crob and Mrs. Crob tells me. Emma will be here tonight. I will have these emeralds waiting for her." Well, what I always say is that every guy knows his own business best, and if Unser Fritz wishes to toss his dough off on jewelry, it is none of my put-in, so all I remark is that I have no doubt Emma will be very much surprised, indeed. "No," Unser Fritz says. "She will be expecting them. She always expects emeralds when she returns to me. I love her," he says. "You have no idea how I love her. But let us hasten to the course," he says. "Cara Mia is a right good thing in the third, and I will make just one bet today to win the thousand I need to buy these emeralds."

"But, Fritz," I say, "you will have nothing left for operating expenses after you invest in the emeralds."

"I am not worrying about operating expenses now," Unser Fritz says. "The way my figures are standing up, I can run a spool of thread into a pair of pants in no time. But I can scarcely wait to see the expression on Emma's face when she sees her emeralds. I will have to make a fast trip into town after the third to get my dough out of the box in the jug and pick them up," he says. "Who knows but what this other party that is interested in the emeralds may make her mind up before five o'clock and pop in there and nail them?"

Well, after we get to the race track, all Unser Fritz does is stand around waiting for the third race. He has his figures on the first two races, and ordinarily he will be betting himself a gob on them, but he says he does not wish to take the slightest chance on cutting down his capital at this time, and winding up short of enough dough to buy the emeralds. It turns out that both of the horses Unser Fritz's figures make on top in the first and second races bow down, and Unser Fritz will have his thousand if he only bets a couple of hundred on either of them, but Unser Fritz says he is not sorry he does not bet. He says the finishes in both races are very close, and prove that there is an element of risk in these races. And Unser Fritz says he cannot afford to tamper with the element of risk at this time.

He states that there is no element of risk whatever in the third race, and what he states is very true, as everybody realizes that this mare Cara Mia is a stick-out. In fact, she is such a stick-out that it scarcely figures to be a contest. There are three other horses in the race, but it is the opinion of one and all that if the owners of these horses have any sense they will leave them in the barn and save them a lot of unnecessary lather.

The opening price offered by the bookmakers on

Cara Mia is two to five, which means that if you wish
to wager on Cara Mia to win you will have to put up five
dollars to a bookmaker's two dollars, and everybody
agrees that this is a reasonable thing to do in this case
unless you wish to rob the poor bookmaker. In fact,
this is considered so reasonable that everybody starts
running at the bookmakers all at once, and the bookmakers can see if this keeps up they may get knocked
off their stools in the betting ring and maybe seriously
injured, so they make Cara Mia one to six, and out, as
quickly as possible to halt the rush and give them a
chance to breathe.

This one to six means that if you wish to wager on
Cara Mia to win, you must wager six of your own dollars to one of the bookmaker's dollars, and means that
the bookies are not offering any prices whatsoever on
Cara Mia running second, or third. You can get almost
any price you can think of right quick against any of the
other horses winning the race, and place and show
prices, too, but asking the bookmakers to lay against
Cara Mia running second or third will be something like
asking them to bet that Mr. Roosevelt is not President
of the United States. Well, I am expecting Unser Fritz
to step in and partake of the two to five on Cara Mia
for all the dough he has on his person the moment it is
offered, because he is very high indeed on this mare,
and in fact I never see anybody any higher on any horse,
and it is a price Unser Fritz will not back off from when
he is high on anything.

Moreover, I am pleased to think he will make such a
wager, because it will give him plenty over and above
the price of the emeralds, and as long as he is bound to
purchase the emeralds, I wish to see him have a little
surplus, because when anybody has a surplus there is
always a chance for me. It is when everybody runs out
of surpluses that I am handicapped no little. But instead
of stepping in and partaking, Unser Fritz keeps hesitat-
ing until the opening price gets away from him, and
finally he says to me like this:

"Of course," he says, "my figures show Cara Mia cannot possibly lose this race, but," he says, "to guard against any possibility whatever of her losing, I will make an absolute cinch of it. I will bet her third."

"Why, Fritz," I say, "I do not think there is anybody in this world outside of an insane asylum who will give you a price on the peek. Furthermore," I say, "I am greatly surprised at this sign of weakening on your part on your figures."

"Well," Unser Fritz says, "I cannot afford to take a chance on not having the emeralds for Emma when she arrives. Let us go through the betting ring, and see what we can see," he says. So we walk through the betting ring, and by this time it seems that many of the books are so loaded with wagers on Cara Mia to win that they will not accept any more under any circumstances, and I figure that Unser Fritz blows the biggest opportunity of his life in not grabbing the opening. The bookmakers who are loaded are now looking even sadder than somewhat, and this makes them a pitiful spectacle, indeed.

Well, one of the saddest-looking is a character by the name of Slow McCool, but he is a character who will usually give you a gamble and he is still taking Cara Mia at one to six, and Unser Fritz walks up to him and whispers in his ear, and what he whispers is he wishes to know if Slow McCool cares to lay him a price on Cara Mia third. But all that happens is that Slow McCool stops looking sad a minute and looks slightly perplexed, and then he shakes his head and goes on looking sad again. Now Unser Fritz steps up to another sad-looking bookmaker by the name of Pete Phozzler and whispers in his ear, and Pete also shakes his head and after we leave him I look back and see that Pete is standing up on his stool watching Unser Fritz, and still shaking his head. Well, Unser Fritz approaches maybe a dozen other sad-looking bookmakers, and whispers to them, and all he gets is the old head shake, but none of them seem to become angry with Unser Fritz, and I always say that this proves that bookmakers are better than some people think, because, personally, I claim they have a right to get angry with Unser Fritz for insulting their intelligence, and trying to defraud them, too, by asking a price on Cara Mia third.

Finally we come to a character by the name of Willie the Worrier, who is called by this name because he is always worrying about something, and what he is generally worrying about is a short bank roll, or his everloving wife, and sometimes both, though mostly it is his wife. Personally, I always figure she is something to worry about, at that, though I do not consider details necessary. She is a red-headed Judy about half as old as Willie the Worrier, and this alone is enough to start any guy worrying, and what is more she is easily vexed, especially by Willie. In fact, I remember Solly telling me that she is vexed with Willie no longer ago than about 11 A.M. this very day, and gives him a public reprimanding about something or other in the telegraph office downtown when Solly happens to be in there hoping maybe he will receive an answer from a mark in Pittsfield, Mass., that he sends a tip on a horse. Solly says the last he hears Willie the Worrier's wife say is that she will leave him for good this time, but I just see her over on the clubhouse lawn wearing some right classy-looking garments, so I judge she does not leave him as yet, as the clubhouse lawn is not a place to be waiting for a train.

Well, when Unser Fritz sees that he is in front of Willie's stand, he starts to move on, and I nudge him and motion at Willie, and ask him if he does not notice that Willie is another bookmaker, and Unser Fritz says he notices him all right, but that he does not care to offer him any business, because Willie insults him ten years ago. He says Willie calls him a dirty old Dutch bum, and while I am thinking what a wonderful memory Unser Fritz has to remember insults from bookmakers for ten years, Willie the Worrier, sitting there on his stool looking out over the crowd, spots Unser Fritz and yells at him as follows:

"Hellow, Dirty Dutch," he says. "How is the soap market? What are you looking for around here, Dirty Dutch? Santa Claus?"

Well, at this, Unser Fritz pushes his way through the crowd around Willie the Worrier's stand, and gets close to Willie, and says:

"Yes," he says, "I am looking for Santa Claus. I am looking for a show price on number two horse, but," he says, "I do not expect to get it from the shoemakers who are booking nowadays."

Now the chances are Willie the Worrier figures Unser Fritz is just trying to get sarcastic with him for the benefit of the crowd around his stand in asking for such a thing as a price on Cara Mia third, and in fact the idea of anybody asking a price third on a horse that some bookmakers will not accept any more wagers on first, or even second, is so humorous that many characters laugh right out loud. "All right," Willie the Worrier says. "No one can ever say he comes to my store looking for a market on anything and is turned down. I will quote you a show price, Dirty Dutch," he says. "You can have one to one hundred." This means that Willie the Worrier is asking Unser Fritz for one hundred dollars to the book's one dollar, if Unser Fritz wishes to bet on Cara Mia dropping in there no worse than third, and of course Willie has no idea Unser Fritz or anybody else will ever take such a price, and the chances are if Willie is not sizzling a little at Unser Fritz, he will not offer such a price, because it sounds foolish.

Furthermore, the chances are if Unser Fritz offers Willie a comparatively small bet at this price, such as may enable him to chisel just a couple of hundred out of Willie's book, Willie will find some excuse to wiggle off, but Unser Fritz leans over and says in a low voice to Willie the Worrier: "A hundred thousand."

Willie nods his head and turns to a clerk alongside him, and his voice is as low as Unser Fritz's as he says to the clerk: "A thousand to a hundred thousand, Cara Mia third."

The clerk's eyes pop open and so does his mouth, but he does not say a word. He just writes something on a pad of paper in his hand, and Unser Fritz offers Willie the Worrier a package of thousand-dollar bills, and says:

"Here is twenty," he says. "The rest is in the jug."

"All right, Dutch," Willie says. "I know you have it, although," he says, "this is the first crack you give me at it. You are on, Dutch," he says. "P. S.," Willie says, "the Dirty does not go any more."

Well, you understand Unser Fritz is betting one hundred thousand dollars against a thousand dollars that Cara Mia will run in the money, and personally I consider this wager a very sound business proposition, indeed, and so does everybody else, for all it amounts to is finding a thousand dollars in the street. There is really nothing that can make Cara Mia run out of the money, the way I look at it, except what happens to her, and what happens is she steps in a hole fifty yards from the finish when she is on top by ten, and breezing, and down she goes all spread out, and of course the other three horses run on past her to the wire, and all this is quite a disaster to many members of the public, including Unser Fritz

am standing with him on the rise of the grandstand lawn watching the race, and it is plain to be seen that he is slightly surprised at what happens, and personally, I am practically dumfounded because, to tell the truth, I take a nibble at the opening price of two to five on Cara Mia with a total of thirty slugs, which represents all my capital, and I am thinking what a great injustice it is for them to leave holes in the track for horses to step in, when Unser Fritz says like this:

"Well," he says, "it is horse racing."

And this is all he ever says about the matter, and then he walks down to Willie the Worrier, and tells Willie if he will send a clerk with him, he will go to the jug and get the balance of the money that is now due Willie. "Dutch," Willie says, "it will be a pleasure to accompany you to the jug in person." As Willie is getting down off his stool, somebody in the crowd who hears of the wager gazes at Unser Fritz, and remarks that he is really a game guy, and Willie says:

"Yes," he says, "he is a game guy at that. But," he says, "what about me?" And he takes Unser Fritz by the arm, and they walk away together, and anybody can see that Unser Fritz picks up anyway twenty years or more, and a slight stringhalt, in the last few minutes.

Then it comes on night again in Saratoga, and I am standing out under the elms in front of the Grand Union, thinking that this world is by no means as beautiful as formerly, when I notice a big, fat old Judy with snow-white hair and spectacles standing near me, looking up and down the street. She will weigh a good two hundred pounds, and much of it is around her ankles, but she has a pleasant face, at that, and when she observes me looking at her, she comes over to me, and says:

"I am trying to fix the location of a restaurant where I work many years ago," she says. "It is a place called Shovelin's. The last thing my husband tells me is to see if the old building is still here, but," she says, "it is so long since I am in Saratoga I cannot get my bearings."

"Ma'am," I say, "is your name Emma by any chance, and do they ever call you Emerald Em?"

Well, at this the old Judy laughs, and says:

"Why, yes," she says. "That is what they call me when I am young and foolish. But how do you know?" she says. "I do not remember ever seeing you before in my life."

"Well," I say, "I know a party who once knows you. A party by the name of Unser Fritz."

"Unser Fritz?" she says. "Unser Fritz? Oh," she says, "I wonder if you mean a crazy Dutchman I run around with many years ago? My gracious," she says, "I just barely remember him. He is a great hand for giving me little presents, such as emeralds. When I am young, I think emeralds are right pretty, but," she says, "otherwise I cannot stand him."

"Then you do not come here to see him?" I say.

"Are you crazy, too?" she says. "I am on my way to Ballston Spa to see my grandchildren. I live in Macon, Georgia. If ever you are in Macon, Georgia, drop in at Shovelin's restaurant and get some real Southern fried chicken. I am Mrs. Joe Shovelin," she says. "By the way," she says, "I remember more about that crazy Dutchman. He is a horse player. I always figure he must die long ago and that the chances are he dies broke, too. I remember I hear people say all horse players die broke."

"Yes," I say, "he dies all right, and he dies as you suggest, too," for it is only an hour before that they find old Unser Fritz in a vacant lot over near the railroad station with the Betsy he gets off Joe Palladino in his hand and a bullet hole smack-dab through his pimple.

Nobody blames him much for taking this out, and in fact I am standing there thinking long after Emerald Em goes on about her business that it will be a good idea if I follow his example, only I cannot think where I can find another Betsy, when Solly comes along and stands there with me. I ask Solly if he knows anything new. "No," Solly says, "I do not know anything new, except," he says, "I hear Willie the Worrier and his ever-loving make up again, and she is not going to leave him after all. I hear Willie takes home a squarer in the shape of a batch of emeralds and diamonds that she orders sent up here when Willie is not looking, and that they are fighting about all day. Well," Solly says, "maybe this is love."

Lonely Heart

It seems that one spring day, a character by the name of Nicely-Nicely Jones arrives in a ward in a hospital in the city of Newark, N. J., with such a severe case of pneumonia that the attending physician, who is a horse player at heart, and very absent-minded, writes 100, 40 and 10 on the chart over Nicely-Nicely's bed. It comes out afterward that what the physician means is that it is one hundred to one in his line that Nicely-Nicely does not recover at all, forty to one that he will not last a week, and ten to one that if he does get well he will never be the same again. Well, Nicely-Nicely is greatly discouraged when he sees this price against him, because he is personally a chalk eater when it comes to price, a chalk eater being a character who always plays the short-priced favorites, and he can see that such a long shot as he is has very little chance to win. In fact, he is so discouraged that he does not even feel like taking a little of the price against him to show.

Afterward there is some criticism of Nicely-Nicely among the citizens around Mindy's restaurant on Broadway, because he does not advise them of this market, as these citizens are always willing to bet that what Nicely-Nicely dies of will be overfeeding and never anything small like pneumonia, for Nicely-Nicely is known far and wide as a character who dearly loves to commit eating. But Nicely-Nicely is so discouraged that he does not as much as send them word that he is sick, let alone anything about the price. He just pulls the covers up over his head and lies there waiting for the finish and thinking to himself what a tough thing it is to pass away of pneumonia, and especially in Newark, N. J., and nobody along Broadway knows of his predicament until Nicely-Nicely appears in person some months later and relates this story to me.

So now, I will tell you about Nicely-Nicely Jones, who is called Nicely-Nicely because any time anybody asks him how he is feeling, or how things are going with him, he always says nicely, nicely, in a very pleasant tone of voice, although generally this is by no means the gospel truth, especially about how he is going. He is a character of maybe forty-odd, and he is short, and fat, and very good-natured, and what he does for a livelihood is the best he can, which is an occupation that is greatly overcrowded at all times along Broadway.

Mostly, Nicely-Nicely follows the races, playing them whenever he has anything to play them with, but anyway following them, and the reason he finds himself in Newark, N. J., in the first place is because of a business proposition in connection with the races. He hears of a barber in Newark, N. J., who likes to make a wager on a sure thing, now and then, and Nicely-Nicely goes over there to tell him about a sure thing that is coming up at Pimlico the very next Tuesday. Nicely-Nicely figures that the barber will make a wager on this sure thing and cut him in on the profits, but it seems that somebody else gets to the barber the week before with a sure thing that is coming up a Monday, and the barber bets on this sure thing, and the sure thing blows, and now the barber will have to shave half of Newark, N. J., to catch even.

Nicely-Nicely always claims that the frost he meets when he approaches the barber with his sure thing gives him a cold that results in the pneumonia I am speaking of, and furthermore that his nervous system is so disorganized by the barber chasing him nine blocks with a razor in his hand that he has no vitality left to resist the germs. But at that it seems that he has enough vitality left to beat the pneumonia by so far the attending physician is somewhat embarrassed, although afterwards he claims that he makes a mistake in chalking up the 100, 40 and 10 on Nicely-Nicely's chart. The attending physician claims he really means the character in the bed next to Nicely-Nicely, who passes away of lockjaw the second day after Nicely-Nicely arrives.

Well, while he is convalescing in the hospital of this pneumonia, Nicely-Nicely has a chance to do plenty of thinking, and what he thinks about most is the uselessness of the life he leads all these years, and how he has nothing to show for same except some high-class knowledge of race horses, which at this time is practically a drug on the market.

There are many other patients in the same ward with Nicely-Nicely, and he sees their ever-loving wives, and daughters, and maybe their sweet peas visiting them, and hears their cheerful chatter, and he gets to thinking that here he is without chick or child, and no home to to go, and it just about breaks his heart. He gets to thinking of how he will relish a soft, gentle, loving hand on his brow at this time, and finally he makes a pass at one of the nurses, figuring she may comfort his lonely hours, but what she lays on his brow is a beautiful straight right cross, and furthermore she hollers watch, murder, police, and Nicely-Nicely has to pretend he has a relapse and is in a delirium to avoid being mistreated by the internes.

As Nicely-Nicely begins getting some of his strength back, he takes to thinking, too, of such matters as food, and when Nicely-Nicely thinks of food it is generally very nourishing food, such as a nice double sirloin, smothered with chops, and thinking of these matters, and of hamburgers, and wiener schnitzel and goulash with noodles, and lamb stew, adds to his depression, especially when they bring him the light diet provided for invalids by the hospital. He takes to reading to keep himself from thinking of his favorite dishes, and of his solitary life, and one day in a bundle of old magazines and newspapers that they give him to read, he comes upon a bladder that is called the *Matrimonial Tribune,* which seems to be all about marriage, and in this *Matrimonial Tribune* Nicely-Nicely observes an advertisement that reads as follows:

Widow of middle age, no children, cheerful companion, neat, excellent cook, owner of nice farm in Central New Jersey, wishes to meet home-loving gentleman of not more than fifty who need not necessarily be possessed of means but who will appreciate warm, tender companionship and pleasant home. Object, matrimony. Address Lonely Heart, this paper.

Well, Nicely-Nicely feels romance stirring in his bosom as he reads these lines, because he is never married, and has no idea that marriage is as described in this advertisement. So what does he do but write a letter to Lonely Heart in care of the Matrimonial Tribune stating that he is looking for a warm, tender companionship, and a pleasant home, and an excellent cook, especially an excellent cook, all his life, and the next thing he knows he is gazing into what at first seems to be an old-fashioned round cheese, but which he finally makes out as the face of a large Judy seated at his bedside. She is anywhere between forty and fifty-five years of age, and she is as big and raw-boned as a first baseman, but she is by no means a crow. In fact, she is rather nice-looking, except that she has a pair of eyes as pale as hens' eggs, and these eyes never change expression.

She asks Nicely-Nicely as many questions as an assistant district attorney, and especially if he has any money, and does he have any relatives, and Nicely-Nicely is able to state truthfully that he is all out of both, although she does not seem to mind. She wishes to know about his personal habits, and Nicely-Nicely says they are all good, but of course he does not mention his habit of tapping out any time a four-to-five shot comes along, which is as bad a habit as anybody can have, and finally she says she is well satisfied with him and will be pleased to marry him when he is able to walk. She has a short, sharp voice that reminds Nicely-Nicely of a tough starter talking to the jockeys at the post, and she never seems to smile, and, take her all around, the chances are she is not such a character as Nicely-Nicely will choose as his ever-loving wife if he has the pick of a herd, but he figures that she is not bad for an offhand draw.

So Nicely-Nicely and the Widow Crumb are married, and they go to live on her farm in Central New Jersey, and it is a very nice little farm, to be sure, if you care for farms, but it is ten miles from the nearest town, and in a very lonesome country, and furthermore there are no neighbors handy, and the Widow Crumb does not have a telephone or even a radio in her house. In fact, about all she has on this farm are a couple of cows, and a horse, and a very old joskin with a chin whisker and rheumatism and a mean look, whose name seems to be Harley something, and who also seems to be the Widow Crumb's hired hand. Nicely-Nicely can see at once that Harley has no use for him, but afterward he learns that Harley has no use for anybody much, not even himself.

Well, it comes on suppertime the first night. Nicely-Nicely is there and he is delighted to observe that the Widow Crumb is making quite an uproar in the kitchen with the pots and pans, and this uproar is music to Nicely-Nicely's ears as by now he is in the mood to put on the hot meat very good, and he is wondering if the Widow Crumb is as excellent a cook as she lets on in her advertisement. It turns out that she is even better. It turns out that she is as fine a cook as ever straddles a skillet, and the supper she spreads for Nicely-Nicely is too good for a king. There is round steak hammered flat and fried in a pan, with thick cream gravy, and hot biscuits, and corn on the cob, and turnip greens, and cottage fried potatoes, and lettuce with hot bacon grease poured over it, and apple pie, and coffee, and I do not know what all else, and Nicely-Nicely almost founders himself, because it is the first time since he leaves the hospital that he gets a chance to move into real food.

Harley, the old joskin, eats with them, and Nicely-Nicely notices that there is a fourth place set at the table, and he figures that maybe another hired hand is going to show up, but nobody appears to fill the vacant chair, and at first Nicely-Nicely is glad of it, as it gives him more room in which to eat. But then Nicely-Nicely notices that the Widow Crumb loads the plate at the vacant place with even more food than she does any of the others, and all through the meal Nicely-Nicely keeps expecting someone to come in and knock off these victuals. Nobody ever appears, however, and when they are through eating, the Widow Crumb clears up the extra

place the same as the others, and scrapes the food off
the plate into a garbage pail. Well, of course, Nicely-
Nicely is somewhat perplexed by this proceeding, but
he does not ask any questions, because where he comes
from only suckers go around asking questions. The next
morning at breakfast, and again at dinner, and in fact
at every meal put on the table the extra place is fixed,
and the Widow Crumb goes through the same perform-
ance of serving the food to this place, and afterward
throwing it away, and while Nicely-Nicely commences
thinking it is a great waste of excellent food, he keeps
his trap closed.

Now being the Widow Crumb's husband is by no
means a bad dodge, as she is anything but a gabby Judy,
and will go all day long without saying more than a few
words, and as Nicely-Nicely is a character who likes to
chat this gives him a chance to do all the talking, although she never seems to be listening to him much.
She seldom asks him to do any work, except now and
then to help the old joskin around the barn, so Nicely-
Nicely commences to figure this is about as soft a
drop-in as anybody can wish. The only drawback is that
sometimes the Widow Crumb likes to sit on Nicely-
Nicely's lap of an evening, and as he does not have
much lap to begin with, and it is getting less every day
under her feeding, this is quite a handicap, but he can
see that it comes of her affectionate nature, and he bears
up the best he can.

One evening after they are married several months,
the Widow Crumb is sitting on what is left of Nicely-
Nicely's lap, and she puts her arms around his neck,
and speaks to him as follows:

"Nicely," she says, "do you love me?"

"Love you?" Nicely-Nicely says. "Why, I love you
like anything. Maybe more. You are a wonderful cook.
How can I help loving you?" he says.

"Well," the Widow Crumb says, "do you ever stop to
consider that if anything happens to you, I will be left

here lone and lorn, because you do not have any means with which to provide for me after you are gone?"

"What do you mean after I am gone?" Nicely-Nicely says. "I am not going anywhere."

"Life is always a very uncertain proposition," the Widow Crumb says. "Who can say when something is apt to happen to you and take you away from me, leaving me without a cent of life insurance?"

Naturally, Nicely-Nicely has to admit to himself that what she says is very true, and of course he never gives the matter a thought before, because he figures from the way the Widow Crumb feeds him that she must have some scratch of her own stashed away somewhere, although this is the first time the subject of money is ever mentioned between them since they are married. "Why," Nicely-Nicely says, "you are quite right, and I will get my life insured as soon as I get enough strength to go out and raise a few dibs. Yes, indeed," Nicely-Nicely says, "I will take care of this situation promptly."

Well, the Widow Crumb says there is no sense in waiting on a matter as important as this, and that she will provide the money for the payment of the premiums herself, and for Nicely-Nicely to forget about going out to raise anything, as she cannot bear to have him out of her sight for any length of time, and then she gets to telling Nicely-Nicely what she is going to give him for breakfast, and he forgets about the insurance business. But the next thing Nicely-Nicely knows, a thin character with a nose like a herring comes out from town, and there is another character with him who has whiskers that smell of corn whisky, but who seems to be a doctor, and in practically no time at all Nicely-Nicely's life is insured for five thousand dollars, with double indemnity if he gets used up by accident, and Nicely-Nicely is greatly pleased by this arrangement because he sees that he is now worth something for the first time in his career, although everybody on Broadway claims it is a terrible overlay by the insurance company when they hear the story.

Well, several months more go by, and Nicely-Nicely finds life on the farm very pleasant and peaceful as there is nothing much for him to do but eat and sleep, and he often finds himself wondering how he ever endures his old life, following the races and associating with the low characters of the turf. He gets along first class with the Widow Crumb and never has a cross word with her, and he even makes friends with the old joskin, Harley, by helping him with his work, although Nicely-Nicely is really not fitted by nature for much work, and what he likes best at the farm is the eating and sleeping, especially the eating. For a while he finds it difficult to get as much sleep as he requires, because the Widow Crumb is a great hand for staying up late reading books in their bedroom by kerosene lamp, and at the same time eating molasses candy which she personally manufactures, and sometimes she does both in bed, and the molasses candy bothers Nicely-Nicely no little until he becomes accustomed to it.

Once he tries reading one of her books to put himself to sleep after she dozes off ahead of him, but he discovers that it is all about nothing but spiritualism, and about parties in this life getting in touch with characters in the next world, and Nicely-Nicely has no interest whatever in matters of this nature, although he personally knows a character by the name of Spooks McGurk who claims to be a spiritualist, and who makes a nice thing of it in connection with tips on the races, until a race-track fuzz catches up with him. Nicely-Nicely never discusses the books with the Widow Crumb, because in the first place he figures it is none of his business, and in the second place, the more she reads the better chance he has of getting to sleep before she starts snoring, because it seems that as a snorer the Widow Crumb is really all-America material, although of course Nicely-Nicely is too much of a gentleman to make an issue of this.

She gives him three meals every day, and every meal is better than the last, and finally Nicely-Nicely is as fat as a goose, and can scarcely wobble. But he notices that

the Widow Crumb never once fails to set the fourth place
that nobody ever fills, and furthermore he suddenly commences to notice that she always puts the best cuts of
meat, and the best of everything else on the plate at this
place, even though she throws it all away afterward.
Well, this situation preys on Nicely-Nicely's mind, as he
cannot bear to see all this good fodder going to waste, so
one morning he gets hold of old Harley and puts the
siphon on him, because by this time Harley talks freely
with Nicely-Nicely, although Nicely-Nicely can see that
Harley is somewhat simple in spots and his conversation
seldom makes much sense.

Anyway, he asks Harley what the Widow Crumb's
idea is about the extra place at the table, and Harley says
like this:

"Why," he says, "the place is for Jake."

"Jake who?" Nicely-Nicely says.

"I do not recall his other name," Harley says. "He is
her third or fourth husband, I do not remember which.
Jake is the only one the Widow Crumb ever loves, although she does not discover this until after Jake departs. So," Harley says, "in memory of Jake she always
sets his place at the table, and gives him the best she has.
She misses Jake and wishes to feel that he is still with
her."

"What happens to Jake?" Nicely-Nicely says.

"Arsenic," Harley says. "Jake departs ten years ago."

Well, of course all this is news to Nicely-Nicely, and
he becomes very thoughtful to be sure, because in all
the time he is married to her the Widow Crumb does not
crack to him about her other husbands, and in fact
Nicely-Nicely has no idea there is ever more than one.
"What happens to the others?" he says. "Do they depart
the same as Jake?"

"Yes," Harley says, "they all depart. One by one. I remember number two well. In fact, you remind me of
him. Carbon monoxide," Harley says. "A charcoal stove
in his room. It is most ingenious. The coroner says number three commits suicide by hanging himself with a

rope in the barn loft. Number three is small and weak, and it is no trouble whatever to handle him. Then comes Jake," Harley says, "unless Jake is number three and the hanging item is number four. I do not remember exactly. But the Widow Crumb never employs arsenic or other matters of this nature again. It is too slow. Jake lingers for hours. Besides," Harley says, "she realizes it may leave traces if anybody happens to get nosey. Jake is a fine-looking character," Harley says. "But a ne'er-do-well. He is a plumber from Salt Lake City, Utah, and has a hearty laugh. He is always telling funny stories. He is a great eater, even better than you, and he loves beans the way the Widow Crumb cooks them, with bacon and tomatoes. He suffers no little from the arsenic. He gets it in his beans. Number five comes upon a black widow spider in his bed. He is no good. I mean number five."

Well, by this time, Nicely-Nicely is very thoughtful to be sure, because what Harley says is commencing to sound somewhat disquieting.

"Number six steps on a plank in the doorway of the house that drops a two hundred-pound keystone on his head," Harley says. "The Widow Crumb personally figures this out herself. She is very bright. It is like a figure-four trap, and has to be very accurate. An inch one way or the other, and the stone misses number six. I remember he has a big wen on the back of his neck. He is a carpenter from Keokuk, Iowa," Harley says.

"Why," Nicely-Nicely says, "do you mean to say that the Widow Crumb purposely arranges to use up husbands in the manner you describe?"

"Oh, sure," Harley says. "Why do you suppose she marries them? It is a good living to her because of the insurance," he says, "although," he says, "to show you how bright she is, she does not insure number five for a dime, so people can never say she is making a business of the matter. He is a total loss to her, but it quiets talk. I am wondering," Harley says, "what she will think up for you."

Well, Nicely-Nicely now commences to wonder about this, too, and he hopes and trusts that whatever she thinks up it will not be a black widow spider, because if there is one thing Nicely-Nicely despises, it is insects. Furthermore, he does not approve of hanging, or of dropping weights on people. After giving the matter much thought, he steps into the house and mentions to the Widow Crumb that he will like to pay a little visit to town, figuring that if he can get to town, she will never see him again for heel dust. But he finds that the Widow Crumb is by no means in favor of the idea of him visiting the town. In fact, she says it will bring great sorrow to her if he absents himself from her side more than two minutes, and moreover, she points out that it is coming on winter, and that the roads are bad, and she cannot spare the horse for such a trip just now.

Well, Nicely-Nicely says he is a fair sort of walker and, in fact, he mentions that he once walks from Saratoga Springs to Albany to avoid a bookmaker who claims there is a slight difference between them, but the Widow Crumb says she will not hear of him trying to walk to town because it may develop varicose veins in his legs. In fact, Nicely-Nicely can see that the subject of his leaving the farm is very distasteful to her in every respect, and the chances are he will feel quite flattered by her concern for him if he does not happen to go into the house again a little later this same afternoon, and find her cleaning a double-barreled shotgun.

She says she is thinking of going rabbit hunting, and wishes him to keep her company, saying it may take his mind off the idea of a visit to town; but she goes out of the room for a minute, and Nicely-Nicely picks up one of the shotgun shells she lays out on a table, and notices that it is loaded with buckshot. So he tells her he guesses he will not go, as he is not feeling so good, and in fact he is not feeling so good, at that, because it seems that Nicely-Nicely is a rabbit hunter from infancy, and he never before hears of anyone hunting these creatures with buckshot. Then the Widow Crumb says all right, she will postpone her hunting until he feels better, but Nicely-Nicely cannot help noticing that she loads the shotgun and stands it in a corner where it is good and handy.

Well, Nicely-Nicely now sits down and gives this general situation some serious consideration, because he is now convinced that the Widow Crumb is unworthy of his companionship as a husband. In fact, Nicely-Nicely makes up his mind to take steps at his earliest convenience to sue her for divorce on the grounds of incompatibility, but in the meantime he has to think up a means of getting away from her, and while he is thinking of this phase of the problem, she calls him to supper. It is now coming on dark, and she has the lamps lit and the table set when Nicely-Nicely goes into the dining room, and a fire is going in the base burner, and usually this is a pleasant and comforting scene to Nicely-Nicely, but tonight he does not seem to find it as attractive as usual.

As he sits down at the table he notices that Harley is not present at the moment, though his place at the table is laid, and as a rule Harley is Johnny-at-the-rat-hole when it comes time to scoff, and moreover he is a pretty good doer, at that. The fourth place that nobody ever occupies is also laid as usual, and now that he knows who this place is for, Nicely-Nicely notes that it is more neatly laid than his own, and that none of the china at this place is chipped, and that the bread and butter, and the salt and pepper, and the vinegar cruet and the bottle of Worcestershire sauce are handier to it than to any other place, and naturally his feelings are deeply wounded.

Then the Widow Crumb comes out of the kitchen with two plates loaded with spareribs and sauerkraut, and she puts one plate in front of Nicely-Nicely, and the other at Jake's place, and she says to Nicely-Nicely like this:

"Nicely," she says, "Harley is working late down at the barn, and when you get through with your supper, you go down and call him. But," she says, "go ahead and eat first."

Then she returns to the kitchen, which is right next to the dining room with a swinging door in between, and Nicely-Nicely now observes that the very choicest spareribs are on Jake's plate, and also the most kraut, and this is really more than Nicely-Nicely can bear, for if there is one thing he adores it is spareribs, so he gets to feeling very moody to be sure about this discrimination, and he turns to Jake's place, and in a very sarcastic tone of voice he speaks out loud as follows:

"Well," he says, "it is pretty soft for you, you big lob, living on the fat of the land around here."

Now, of course what Nicely-Nicely is speaking is what he is thinking, and he does not realize that he is speaking out loud until the Widow Crumb pops into the dining room carrying a bowl of salad, and looking all around and about. "Nicely," she says, "do I hear you talking to someone?"

Well, at first Nicely-Nicely is about to deny it, but then he takes another look at the choice spareribs on Jake's plate, and he figures that he may as well let her know that he is on to her playing Jake for a favorite over him, and maybe cure her of it, for by this time Nicely-Nicely is so vexed about the spareribs that he almost forgets about leaving the farm, and is thinking of his future meals, so he says to the Widow Crumb like this:

"Why, sure," he says. "I am talking to Jake."

"Jake?" she says. "What Jake?" And with this she starts looking all around and about again, and Nicely-Nicely can see that she is very pale, and that her hands are shaking so that she can scarcely hold the bowl of salad, and there is no doubt but what she is agitated no little, and quite some. "What Jake?" the Widow Crumb says again.

Nicely-Nicely points to the empty chair, and says:

"Why, Jake here," he says. "You know Jake. Nice fellow, Jake." Then Nicely-Nicely goes on talking to the empty chair as follows:

"I notice you are not eating much tonight, Jake," Nicely-Nicely says. "What is the matter, Jake? The food cannot disagree with you, because it is all picked out and cooked to suit you, Jake. The best is none too good for you around here, Jake," he says. Then he lets on that he is listening to something Jake is saying in reply, and Nicely-Nicely says is that so, and I am surprised, and what do you think of that, and tut-tut, and my-my, just as if Jake is talking a blue streak to him, although of course, Jake is by no means present.

Now Nicely-Nicely is really only being sarcastic in this conversation for the Widow Crumb's benefit, and naturally he does not figure that she will take it seriously, because he knows she can see Jake is not there, but Nicely-Nicely happens to look at her while he is talking, and he observes that she is still standing with the bowl of salad in her hands, and looking at the empty chair with a most unusual expression on her face, and in fact, it is such an unusual expression that it makes Nicely-Nicely feel somewhat uneasy, and he readies himself up to dodge the salad bowl at any minute.

He commences to remember the loaded shotgun in the corner, and what Harley gives him to understand about the Widow Crumb's attitude toward Jake, and Nicely-Nicely is sorry he ever brings Jake's name up, but it seems that Nicely-Nicely now finds that he cannot stop talking to save his life with the Widow Crumb standing there with the unusual expression on her face, and then he remembers the books she reads in bed at night, and he goes on as follows:

"Maybe the pains in your stomach are just indigestion, Jake," he says. "I have stomach trouble in my youth myself. You are suffering terribly, eh, Jake? Well, maybe a little of the old bicarb will help you, Jake. Oh," Nicely-Nicely says, "there he goes."

And with this he jumps up and runs to Jake's chair and lets on that he is helping a character up from the floor, and as he stoops over and pretends to be lifting this character, Nicely-Nicely grunts no little, as if the character is very heavy, and the grunts are really on the level with Nicely-Nicely as he is now full of spareribs, because he never really stops eating while he is talking, and stooping is not easy for him. At these actions the Widow Crumb lets out a scream and drops the bowl of salad on the floor.

"I will help you to bed, Jake," he says. "Poor Jake. I know your stomach hurts, Jake. There now, Jake," he says, "take it easy. I know you are suffering horribly, but I will get something for you to ease the pain. Maybe it is the sauerkraut," Nicely-Nicely says. Then when he seems to get Jake up on his legs, Nicely-Nicely pretends to be assisting him across the floor toward the bedroom and all the time he is talking in a comforting tone to Jake, although you must always remember that there really is no Jake.

Now, all of a sudden, Nicely-Nicely hears the Widow Crumb's voice, and it is nothing but a hoarse whisper that sounds very strange in the room, as she says like this:

"Yes," she says. "It is Jake. I see him. I see him as plain as day."

Well, at this Nicely-Nicely is personally somewhat startled, and he starts looking around and about himself, and it is a good thing for Jake that Nicely-Nicely is not really assisting Jake or Jake will find himself dropped on the floor, as the Widow Crumb says:

"Oh, Jake," she says, "I am so sorry. I am sorry for you in your suffering. I am sorry you ever leave me. I am sorry for everything. Please forgive me, Jake," she says. "I love you."

Then the Widow Crumb screams again and runs through the swinging door into the kitchen and out the kitchen door and down the path that leads to the barn about two hundred yards away, and it is plain to be seen that she is very nervous. In fact, the last Nicely-Nicely sees of her before she disappears in the darkness down the path, she is throwing her hands up in the air, and letting out little screams, as follows: eee-eee-eee, and calling out old Harley's name.

Then Nicely-Nicely hears one extra loud scream, and

after this there is much silence, and he figures that now is the time for him to take his departure, and he starts down the same path toward the barn, but figuring to cut off across the fields to the road that leads to the town when he observes a spark of light bobbing up and down on the path ahead of him, and presently he comes upon old Harley with a lantern in his hand. Harley is down on his knees at what seems to be a big, round hole in the ground, and this hole is so wide it extends clear across the path, and Harley is poking his lantern down the hole, and when he sees Nicely-Nicely, he says:

"Oh," he says. "There you are. I guess there is some mistake here," he says. "The Widow Crumb tells me to wait in the barn until after supper and she will send you out after me, and," Harley says, "she also tells me to be sure and remove the cover of this old well as soon as it comes on dark. And," Harley says, "of course, I am expecting to find you in the well at this time, but who is in there but the Widow Crumb. I hear her screech as she drops in. I judge she must be hastening along the path and forgets about telling me to remove the cover of the well," Harley says. "It is most confusing," he says.

Then he pokes his lantern down the well again, and leans over and shouts as follows:

"Hello, down there," Harley shouts. "Hello, hello, hello." But all that happens is an echo comes out of the well like this: Hello. And Nicely-Nicely observes that there is nothing to be seen down the well but a great blackness. "It is very deep, and dark, and cold down there," Harley says. "Deep, and dark, and cold and half full of water. Oh, my poor baby," he says. Then Harley busts out crying as if his heart will break, and in fact he is so shaken by his sobs that he almost drops the lantern down the well.

Naturally Nicely-Nicely is somewhat surprised to observe these tears because personally he is by no means greatly distressed by the Widow Crumb being down the well, especially when he thinks of how she tries to put him down the well first, and finally he asks Harley why he is so downcast, and Harley speaks as follows:

"I love her," Harley says. "I love her very, very very much. I am her number one husband, and while she divorces me thirty years ago when it comes out that I have a weak heart, and the insurance companies refuse to give me a policy, I love her just the same. And now," Harley says, "here she is down a well." And with this he begins hollering into the hole some more, but the Widow Crumb never personally answers a human voice in this life again and when the story comes out, many citizens claim this is a right good thing, to be sure.

So Nicely-Nicely returns to Broadway, and he brings with him the sum of eleven hundred dollars, which is what he has left of the estate of his late ever-loving wife from the sale of the farm, and one thing and another, after generously declaring old Harley in for fifty per cent of his bit when Harley states that the only ambition he has left in life is to rear a tombstone to the memory of the Widow Crumb, and Nicely-Nicely announces that he is through with betting on horses, and other frivolity, and will devote his money to providing himself with food and shelter, and maybe a few clothes. Well, the chances are Nicely-Nicely will keep his vow, too, but what happens the second day of his return, but he observes in the entries for the third race at Jamaica a horse by the name of Apparition, at ten to one in the morning line, and Nicely-Nicely considers this entry practically a message to him, so he goes for his entire bundle on Apparition.

And it is agreed by one and all along Broadway who knows Nicely-Nicely's story, that nobody in his right mind can possibly ignore such a powerful hunch as this, even though it loses, and Nicely-Nicely is again around doing the best he can.

Cemetery Bait

One pleasant morning in early April, a character by the name of Gentleman George wakes up to find himself in a most embarrassing predicament. He wakes up to find himself in a cell in the state penitentiary at Trenton, N. J., and while a cell in a state penitentiary is by no means a novelty to George, and ordinarily will cause him no confusion whatever, the trouble is this particular cell is in what is known as the death house. Naturally, George is very self-conscious about this, as it is only the second time in his life he ever finds himself in such a house, and the first time is so far back in his youth that it leaves scarcely any impression on him, especially as he is commuted out of it in less than sixty days. Well, George sits there on the side of the cot in his cell this pleasant April morning, thinking what a humiliating circumstance this is to a proud nature such as his, when all of a sudden he remembers that on the morrow he is to be placed in Mister Edison's rocking chair in the room adjoining his cell, and given a very severe shock in the seat of his breeches.

On remembering this, George becomes very thoughtful, to be sure, and sighs to himself as follows: Heigh-ho, heigh-ho, heigh-ho. And then he sends for me to come and see him, although George is well aware that I have no use for penitentiaries, or their environs, and consider them a most revolting spectacle. In fact, I have such a repugnance for penitentiaries that I never even glance at them in passing, because I am afraid that peepings may be catchings, but of course in a situation such as this I can scarcely deny the call of an old friend. They let me talk to George through the bars of his cell, and naturally I am somewhat perturbed to observe him in this plight, although I can see that his surroundings are clean and sanitary, and that the hacks seem kindly disposed toward him, except one big doorknob who is inclined to be somewhat churlish because George just beats him in a game of two-handed pinochle.

Furthermore, I can see that George is in pretty fair physical condition, although a little stouter than somewhat, and that he looks as if he is getting some rest. He is at this time about forty-five years of age, and is still as good-looking as in the days when he is known far and wide as the handsomest and most genteel character on Broadway. His brown hair now has some gray in it along the edges, and there are lines of care in his face, and, of course, George is not dressed as fashionably as usual. In fact, his clothes need pressing, and he can stand a haircut, and a shave, and when I mention this to George he says he understands they are going to give him all the haircutting he requires before morning, and maybe a close shave, too.

In the old days, Gentleman George is very prominent in the jewelry trade with Tommy Entrata, and his associates, and anybody will tell you that Tommy and his crowd are the best in the country, because they pursue strictly business methods, and are very high principled. They generally work with a character by the name of Lou Adolia, who is a private fuzz often employed by big insurance companies that make a specialty of insuring jewelry for wealthy female parties, a fuzz being a way of saying a detective, although the chances are Lou Adolia cannot really find his hip pocket with both hands.

But when Tommy Entrata and his associates come into possession of jewelry belonging to these wealthy female parties, they notify Lou Adolia, and he arranges with the insurance companies to pay a certain sum for the return of the merchandise, and no beefs, and everybody is satisfied, especially the insurance companies, because, of course, if they do not get the goods back, the companies will have to pay the full amount of the in-

surance. As Tommy Entrata is generally very reasonable
in his fees on jewelry that comes into his possession, it
really is a most economical arrangement for the insurance companies, and for everybody else concerned, and
it is also very nice for Lou Adolia, as he always gets a
reward from the companies, and sometimes a piece of
what Tommy Entrata collects. Then a piece always goes
to the stout fellow in the city in which Tommy Entrata
and his associates are operating, the stout fellow being
the local fix, because, of course, you understand that in a
business as large as this carried on by Tommy Entrata
it is necessary to take care of all angles. So the stout fellow looks after the local law to see that it does not interfere with Tommy Entrata any more than is absolutely
necessary.

To tell the truth, when Tommy Entrata and his associates go into a town, it is generally as well organized
from top to bottom as Standard Oil, and Tommy not
only has a complete roster of all the local jewelry owners,
and what they are insured for, from Lou Adolia, but also
a few diagrams as to where this jewelry is located, and
Tommy never fails to make ample provision for one and
all in the town who may be concerned before he turns a
wheel. In fact, I hear that in a spot up in the Northwest
Tommy once even declares the mayor and the com-
missioner of public safety in on one of his transactions,
just out of the goodness of his heart, and this unselfish-
ness in his business operations makes Tommy highly
respected far and wide.

Anyway, Gentleman George is one of Tommy Entrata's experts in the matter of coming into possession of
jewelry, and Tommy appreciates George no little, as
George is strictly a lone hand at his work, and he never
carries that thing on him, and considers all forms of violence most revolting, so he never gets into trouble, or at
least not much. I am telling you all this so you will understand that Tommy Entrata conducts his business in a
high-class, conservative manner, and personally I con-

sider him a great boon to a community, because he teaches people the value of insurance, and now I will return to Gentleman George in his cell in the death house in Trenton, N. J.

"Well," George says, "there you are, and here I am, and you are the only friend that comes to see me since the judge mentions the date that now becomes of some importance in my life, and which is in fact tomorrow. And now I wish to tell you a story, which will be the truth, the whole truth, and nothing but the truth, and the object of this story is to show that I once perform a great service to the public." At this, I become uneasy, because I am afraid it may be a tedious story, and I do not care to remain in such surroundings listening to reminiscence, so I request George to epitomize as much as possible, and to omit all reference to low characters and sordid situations, and then George states as follows, and to wit, viz.:

In the winter of 1935, I am going southward by train on business bent, and the reason I do not reveal my destination at this time is because I do not wish to be recalled as ever hollering copper, even on a city, but I will say that it is a certain winter resort spot about as far below the Mason and Dixon's line as you can get before you start swimming, and a very pleasant spot it is, at that. The first night out on the train, I go into the diner and partake of a fish that is on the menu, because the steward of the diner weighs in with a strong shill for this fish, and the next thing I know I am back in my compartment as sick as anything, and maybe a little bit sicker. To tell the truth, I am so sick that I think I am going to pass away, and this thought disturbs me no little, as Tommy Entrata is looking forward to my arrival with keen interest, and I know that he is apt to take my passing away as a personal affront.

Well, while I am lying in my berth as sick as stated, all of a sudden the door of my compartment opens, and a pair of specs and a short, scrubby, gray tash appear, and behind the specs and the tash is a stern-looking character of maybe fifty-odd, who speaks to me in a gruff voice, as follows:

"See here, now," he says, "what is all this runting and grunting about? Are you sick?"

"Well," I say, "if I am not sick, I will do until an invalid comes along." And then I start retching again, and in between retches, I mention the dining-car fish, and I tell the stern-looking character that if he will kindly get the dining-car steward to step into my compartment for just one minute I will die happy.

"You speak great nonsense," the stern-looking character says. "You are not going to die, although, he says, who knows but what you may be better off if you do? Not enough people know when to die. What ails you is ptomaine poisoning, and I will take charge of this situation myself because I will be unable to sleep in this car with you scrooning and mooning all night. I once get the same thing myself in Gloucester, Mass.," he says. "You will expect the fish to be all right in Gloucester, Mass. If I remember," he says, "it is mackerel in my case."

Then he rings for the porter, and pretty soon he has the train secretary, and the Pullman conductor, and even a couple of other passengers running in and out of my compartment getting him this, and that, and one thing and another, and dosing me with I do not know what, and sick as I am, I can see that this stern-looking character is accustomed to having people step around when he speaks. Well, for a while I am thinking that the best break I can get is to pass away without any further lingering; then, by and by, I commence feeling better, and finally I doze off to sleep. But I seem to remember the stern-looking character mentioning that he is going to the same place that I am, and that he is just returning from a hunting trip in Canada, and I also seem to recall him telling me what a wonderful shot he is with any kind of firearms.

Afterward, however, I figure I must dream all this be-

cause the next morning the stern-looking character just
glances in on me once and asks how I feel in a tone of
voice that indicates he does not care much one way or
the other, and after this I do not see hide or hair of him,
and I can see that he does not mean to make a friendship of the matter. In fact, when I am getting off the
train at my destination, I suddenly remember that I do
not even know the stern-looking character's name, and
I am sorry about this, as so few people in the world are
ever good to me that I wish to cherish the names of
those who are. But, of course, I now have no time for
sentiment, as duty calls me, and I do not bother to in-
quire around and about with reference to the stern-looking character.

I telephone Tommy Entrata, and make a meet with
him for dinner in a night club that is called by the name
of the Bath and Sail Club, although there is no bathing
connected with it whatever, and no sailing either, for
that matter, and while I am waiting there for Tommy, I
observe at another table the most beautiful Judy I see in
many a day, and you know very well that few better
judges of beauty ever live than yours sincerely, G.
George. She is young, and has hair the color of straw,
and she is dressed in a gorgeous white evening gown,
and she has plenty of junk on her in the way of diamonds,
and she seems to be waiting for someone and I find myself regretting that it is not me. I am so impressed by her
that I call Emil, the headwaiter, and question him, because Emil is an old friend of mine, and I know he always has a fund of information on matters such as this.
"Emil," I say, "who is the lovely pancake over there by
the window?"

"Cemetery bait," Emil says, so I know he means she
is married, and has a husband who is selfish about her,
and naturally I cast no sheep's eyes in her direction, especially as Tommy Entrata comes in about now and
takes me to a private room where we have a nice dinner,
and discuss my business in this city.

It is in pursuit of this business, at the hour of 1 A.M.

on a warm Sunday morning, that I am making a call at the residence of a character by the name of Colonel Samuel B. Venus, and am in the boudoir of his everloving wife, and a beautiful room it is, at that, with the windows on one side looking out over the sea waves, and the windows on the other side overlooking a patio of whispering palm trees. The moon is shining down on this scene, and it is so lovely that I stand at the front windows a few moments looking out over the water before I start seeking the small can, or safe, that I know is concealed in a clothes closet in the room unless the butler in the Venus house is telling a terrible falsehood and accepting money from us under false pretenses for this information and for admitting me to the premises. Of course, Colonel Samuel B. Venus' ever-loving wife is not present in her boudoir at this hour, and neither is Colonel Samuel B. Venus, and in fact I afterward learn that the only way Colonel Samuel B. Venus can get in there is on a writ of habeas corpus, but this has nothing to do with my story.

My information is that Colonel Samuel B. Venus is a very wealthy character of maybe sixty years of age, come next grass, and that his ever-loving wife is less than half of that, and has some of the finest jewelry in this country, including pearls, diamonds, star rubies, emeralds, and I do not know what all else, and I am given to understand that Colonel Samuel B. Venus leaves the night before on a fishing trip, and that Mrs. Colonel Samuel B. Venus is out somewhere wearing only a couple of pounds of her jewels, so the rest of her stuff is bound to be in the little can in her boudoir. Well, the little can is in the closet just where the butler reports, and I observe that it is such a can as I will be able to open with a toothpick if necessary, although, of course, I bring along my regular can opener, which is a tool for cutting open safes that I personally invent, as you perhaps remember, although I never think to get a patent on it from the government, and I am about to start operations when I hear voices, and two characters, male and female, enter the boudoir.

So there I am in the closet among a lot of dresses and coats, and all this and that, and, what is more, I leave the closet door open a little when I go in, as I figure I may require a little air, and I am now afraid to close the door for fear of making a noise, and the best I can make of this situation is that I am a gone gosling. To tell the truth, it is one of the few times in my life that I regret I do not have that thing on me, just for self-defense. I can see right away from the way she talks that the female character must be Mrs. Colonel Samuel B. Venus, but the character with her is by no means her husband, and naturally I am greatly scandalized to think that a married broad will bring a party not her husband into her boudoir with her at such an hour, and I am wondering what on earth the world is coming to. But although I listen keenly, there seems to be no goings-on, and in fact all they are doing is talking, so I figure the character with Mrs. Colonel Samuel B. Venus must be a character without any imagination whatever.

Finally, when I judge from their conversation that they are looking at the view of the sad sea waves, I cop a quick peek, and I see that Mrs. Colonel Samuel B. Venus is nobody but the blonde I admire at the Bath and Sail Club, and while this surprises me no little, it does not surprise me half as much as the fact that the character with her is a party by the name of Count Tomaso, who is known far and wide as a most unworthy character. In fact, Count Tomaso is regarded in some circles as a 22-carat fink, a fink being a character who is lower than a mudcat's vest pocket. He is a small, slim-built character, with dark hair greased down on his head, and he wears a monocle, and seems very foreign in every respect. In fact, Count Tomaso claims to belong to the Italian nobility, but he is no more a count than I am, and to tell the truth, he is nothing but a ginzo out of Sacramento, and his right name is Carfarelli.

For a matter of twenty years or more, this Count Tomaso is on the socket, which is a way of saying his dodge is blackmail, and of course there is little or no class to such a dodge as this. He generally pitches to foolish old married Judys, and gets them wedged in with letters, and one thing and another, and then puts the shake on them. Personally, I rarely criticize anybody else's methods of earning a livelihood, but I can never approve of the shake, although I must admit that from what I hear of Count Tomaso, he really is an artist in his line, and can nine those old phlugs in first-class style when he is knuckling.

I only hope and trust that his presence in Mrs. Colonel Samuel B. Venus' boudoir does not mean that Count Tomaso is trespassing in any way upon my affairs, as I can see where this will produce complications, and it is always my policy to avoid complications, so I remain very quiet, with a firm grip on my can opener in case Mrs. Colonel Samuel B. Venus or Count Tomaso happens to come to the closet. But it seems to be nothing but a social visit, as I can hear her getting out some liquor, and after a couple of drinks they begin speaking of nothing much in particular, including the weather. Presently the conversation becomes quite dull, for it is all about love, and conversation about love always bores me no little unless I am making the conversation myself, although I can see that Mrs. Colonel Samuel B. Venus is better than a raw hand in conversation of this nature.

I am so bored that I put down my can opener and am about to doze off among the dresses, when all of a sudden the conversation takes a very unusual turn, to be sure, for Mrs. Colonel Samuel B. Venus says to Count Tomaso like this:

"I know you love me," she says, "and I love you madly in return, but what good will it do us? I am married to a character old enough to be my father, and although he does not know it, I hate and despise him. But even if I tell him this, I know he will never give me a divorce, and, besides, if I do get a divorce, he is sure to put me off with a mere pittance. I am bound to him as long as he lives," she says. "As long as he lives, Tomaso."

Well, Count Tomaso says this is certainly a sad state of affairs, and seems to be taking another drink, and she goes on as follows:

"Of course," she says, "if he passes away, Tomaso, I will marry you the next day, or anyway," she says, "as soon as my mourning goes out of style. Then we can go all over the world and enjoy our love, because I know his will leaves me all his vast fortune. I am afraid it is wicked," she says, "but sometimes I wish an accident will befall him."

Now I can see that what is coming off here is that Mrs. Colonel Samuel B. Venus is giving Count Tomaso a hint in a roundabout way to cause an accident to befall Colonel Samuel B. Venus, and thinks I to myself there in the closet, it is a pretty how-do-you-do if such goings-on are tolerated in society circles, and I am glad I am not in society. To tell the truth, I consider Mrs. Colonel Samuel B. Venus' attitude most unbecoming.

Well, they converse at some length about various forms of accidents that they hear of, but they seem unable to arrive at any definite conclusion, and I am almost sorry I am unable to join in the discussion and offer a few original ideas of my own, when Mrs. Colonel Samuel B. Venus says:

"Well," she says, "we are sailing next week on the Castilla for New York, and you can come on the same ship. New York is a better place for accidents than down here, because they are not apt to attract so much attention there. But, Tomaso," she says, "be very careful the colonel does not see you on the trip, as he has been hearing things here, and he is terribly jealous, and has a violent temper, and, furthermore, he always has deadly weapons around, and he claims he is a wonderful marksman. "Oh, Tomaso," she says, "is it not awful to be yoked to an old character who thinks of nothing but hunting, and fishing, and business, when I love you so much?"

Well, Tomaso says it is, indeed, and does she have a few dibs on her to tide him over the week end, and it

seems she has, and then there is a little offhand billing
and cooing that I consider very bad taste in her under
her own roof, and finally they go out of the boudoir. As
soon as they depart, I turn to my own business of opening the little can and removing the jewelry, which I deliver to Tommy Entrata, who gives it to Lou Adolia,
and this is the time that Lou Adolia gets eighty thousand
dollars from the insurance companies for the return of
the goods, and then disappears with all the sugar, and
without as much as saying aye, yes or no to anybody.

But I am getting ahead of my story.

A couple of days later, I am reclining on the beach
with Tommy Entrata, taking a little sun for my complexion, when who comes along in a bathing suit which dis-
plays a really remarkable shape but Mrs. Colonel Samuel
B. Venus, and who is with her but the stern-looking
character who doctors me up on the train, and at first
I have half a notion to jump up and say hello to him and
thank him for his kindness to me about the fish, but he
looks right through me as if he never sees me before in
his life, and I can see that he does not remember me, or
if he does, he does not care to make anything of it.

So I do not give him a blow, because the way I look at
it, the fewer people you know in this world, the better
you are off. But I ask Tommy Entrata who the stern-
looking character is, and I am somewhat surprised when
Tommy says: "Why," he says, "he is Colonel Samuel B.
Venus, the party you knock off the other night, but,"
Tommy says, "let us not speak of that now. Colonel
Samuel B. Venus is a most irascible character, and he is
making quite a chirp about matters, and it is very for-
tunate for us that he and his wife are sailing for New
York, because the stout fellow is getting nervous about
the outcry. By the way," Tommy says, "I do not wish to
seem inhospitable in suggesting your departure from
these pleasant scenes, but it may be a good idea for you
to take it on the Jesse Owens until the beef is chilled.
There are many nightingales in these parts," he says,

"and they will sing to the law on very slight provocation, for instance such a character as Count Tomaso. I notice him around here nuzzling up to Mrs. Colonel Samuel B. Venus, and while the chances are he is on a business mission of his own, Count Tomaso knows you, and it is always my opinion that he is a singer, at heart."

Well, I do not mention the incident in Mrs. Colonel Samuel B. Venus' boudoir to Tommy Entrata, because in the first place I do not consider it any of his business, and in the second place I know Tommy is not apt to be interested in such a matter, but I get to thinking about the conversation between Mrs. Colonel Samuel B. Venus and Count Tomaso, and I also get to thinking about Colonel Samuel B. Venus being so nice to me in connection with the bad fish. And thinks I, as long as I must take my departure anyway, a little sea voyage may be beneficial to my health, and I will go on the Castilla myself, and will look up Count Tomaso and admonish him that I will hold him personally responsible if any accident happens to Colonel Samuel B. Venus, as I feel that it is only fair to do what I can to discharge my debt of gratitude to Colonel Samuel B. Venus concerning the fish.

So when the Castilla sails a few days later, I am a passenger, and, furthermore, I have a nice cabin on the same deck as Colonel Samuel B. Venus and his everloving wife, because I always believe in traveling with the best people, no matter what. I see Colonel Samuel B. Venus, and I also see Mrs. Colonel Samuel B. Venus on the first day out, and I observe that Colonel Samuel B. Venus is looking sterner than ever, and also that Mrs. Colonel Samuel B. Venus is growing lovelier by the hour, but never do I see Count Tomaso, although I am pretty sure he does not miss the boat. I figure that he is taking Mrs. Colonel Samuel B. Venus' advice about keeping out of sight of Colonel Samuel B. Venus.

I do not bother to go looking for Count Tomaso on the Castilla to admonish him about Colonel Samuel B. Venus, because I figure I am bound to catch up with him getting off the boat in New York, and that in the meantime Colonel Samuel B. Venus is safe from accident, especially as it comes up stormy at sea after we are a few hours out, and Colonel Samuel B. Venus and his ever-loving wife seem to be keeping close to their cabin, and in fact so is everybody else.

Well, the storm keeps getting worse, and it is sleety and cold all around and about, and the sea is running higher than somewhat, and now one night off the Jersey coast when I am sleeping as peacefully as anything, I am awakened by a great to-do and it seems that the Castilla is on fire. Naturally, I do not care to be toasted in my cabin, so I don my clothes, and pop out into the passageway and start for the nearest exit, when I remember that in moments of confusion many characters, male and female, are apt to forget articles of one kind and another that may come in handy to somebody such as me later on, for instance bits of jewelry, and other portable merchandise. So I try various doors as I go along the passageway, and all of them are open and unoccupied, as the Castilla is an old-time vessel with cabin doors that lock with keys, and not with snap locks, and, just as I suspect, I find numerous odds and ends in the way of finger rings, and bracelets and clips and pins and necklaces, and watches, and gold cigarette cases, and even a few loose bundles of ready scratch, so I am very glad, indeed, that I am gifted with foresight.

Finally I come to one door that seems to be locked, and I remember that this is the cabin occupied by Colonel Samuel B. Venus and his ever-loving wife, and after first knocking at the door and receiving no reply, I figure they hastily depart and carelessly lock the door after them, and I also figure that I am bound to garner something of more than ordinary value there. So I kick the door in, and who is in the cabin on a bed, all trussed up like a goose, with a towel tied across his mouth to keep him from hollering out loud, but Colonel Samuel B. Venus, in person. Naturally, I am somewhat surprised at this spectacle, and also somewhat embarrassed to have Colonel Samuel B. Venus find me kicking in his door, but of course this is no time for apologies, so I take a quick swivel about the cabin to see if there are any articles lying around that I may be able to use. I am slightly disappointed to note that there appears to be nothing, and I am about to take my departure, when all of a sudden I remember my debt of gratitude to Colonel Samuel B. Venus, and I realize that it will be most unkind to leave him in this predicament to be barbecued like a steer without being able to move hand or foot.

So I out with my pocket shiv, and cut him loose, and I also remove the towel, and as soon as he can talk, Colonel Samuel B. Venus issues a statement to me in a most severe tone of voice, as follows:

"They try to murder me," he says. "My own wife, Cora, and a character in a white polo coat with a little cap to match. When the alarm of fire is sounded," Colonel Samuel B. Venus says, "she starts screaming, and he comes banging up against our door, and she unlocks it and lets him in before I have time to think, and then he knocks me down with something, I do not know what."

"The chances are," I say, "it is a blunt instrument."

"You may be right," Colonel Samuel B. Venus says. "Anyway, after he knocks me down, my own wife, Cora, picks up one of my shoes and starts belting me over the head with the heel, and then she helps the character in the polo coat and the little cap to match tie me up as you find me."

"It is a scurvy trick," I say.

"I am half unconscious," Colonel Samuel B. Venus says, "but I remember hearing my own wife, Cora, remark that the fire is a wonderful break for them, and will save them a lot of bother in New York. And then before they leave, she hits me another belt on the head with the shoe. I fear," Colonel Samuel B. Venus says, "that my own wife, Cora, is by no means the ever-loving helpmeet I think. In fact," he says, "I am now wondering about the overdose of sleeping powders she gives me in London, England, in 1931, and about the bomb in my automobile in Los Angeles, Cal., in 1933."

"Well, well, well," I say, "let us let bygones be bygones, and get off this tub, as it seems to be getting hotter than a ninth-inning finish around here."

But Colonel Samuel B. Venus remains very testy about the incident he just describes, and he fumbles around under a pillow on the bed on which I find him, and outs with that thing, and opens the cylinder as if to make sure it is loaded, and says to me like this:

"I will shoot him down like a dog," he says. "I mean the character in the white polo coat and the little cap to match. He undoubtedly leads my poor little wife, Cora, astray in this, although," he says, "I do not seem to recall him anywhere in the background of the overdose and the bomb matters. But she is scarcely more than a child and does not know right from wrong. He is the one who must die," Colonel Samuel B. Venus says. "I wonder who he is?" he says.

Well, of course I know Colonel Samuel B. Venus must be talking about Count Tomaso, but I can see that Count Tomaso is a total stranger to him, and while I am by no means opposed to Colonel Samuel B. Venus' sentiments with reference to Count Tomaso, I do not approve of his spirit of forgiveness toward Mrs. Colonel Samuel B. Venus, because I figure that as long as she is around and about, Colonel Samuel B. Venus will always be in danger of accidents. But I do not feel that this is a time for argument, so I finally get him to go up on the deck with me, and as soon as we are on deck, Colonel Samuel B. Venus leaves me and starts running every which way as if he is looking for somebody.

There seems to be some little agitation on deck, what with smoke and flame coming out of the Castilla amidships, and many characters, male and female, running up and down, and around and about, and small children crying. Some of the crew are launching lifeboats, and then getting into these boats themselves, and pulling

away from the burning ship without waiting for any
passengers, which strikes me as most discourteous on the
part of the sailors and which alarms many passengers so
they start chucking themselves over the rail into the sea
trying to catch up with the boats.

Well, this scene is most distasteful to me, so I retire
from the general melee, and go looking elsewhere about
the ship, figuring I may find an opportunity to ease myself quietly into a boat before all the seats are taken by
sailors, and finally I come upon a group trying to launch
a big life raft over the rail, and about this time I observe
Colonel Samuel B. Venus standing against the rail with
that thing in his hand, and peering this way and that.
And then I notice a boat pulling away from the ship, and
in the stern of the boat I see a character in a white polo
coat, and a little cap to match, and I call the attention of
Colonel Samuel B. Venus to same.

The boat is so overcrowded that it is far down in the
water, but the waves, which are running very high, are
carrying it away in long lunges, and it is fully one hundred yards off, and is really visible to the naked eye by
the light of the flames from the Castilla only when it
rises a moment to the top of a wave, and Colonel Samuel
B. Venus looks for some time before he sees what I
wish him to see. "I spot him now," he says. "I recognize
the white polo coat and the little cap to match." And
with this, he ups with that thing and goes rooty-toot-toot
out across the water three times, and the last I see of the
white polo coat and the little cap to match they are fold-
ing up together very gently just as a big wave washes the
boat off into the darkness beyond the light of the burning
ship.

By this time the raft is in the water, and I take Colonel
Samuel B. Venus and chuck him down onto the raft,
and then I jump after him, and as the raft is soon overcrowded, I give the foot to a female character who is on
the raft before anybody else and ease her off into the
water. As this female character disappears in the raging
sea, I am not surprised to observe that she is really no-

body but Count Tomaso, as I seem to remember seeing Count Tomaso making Mrs. Colonel Samuel B. Venus change clothes with him at the point of a knife.

Well, some of the boats get ashore, and some do not, and in one that does arrive, they find the late Mrs. Colonel Samuel B. Venus, and everybody is somewhat surprised to note that she is in male garments with a white polo coat and a little cap to match. I wish to call attention to the public service I render in easing Count Tomaso off the raft, because here is a character who is undoubtedly a menace to the sanctity of the American home.

And I take pride in the fact that I discharge my debt of gratitude to Colonel Samuel B. Venus, and it is not my fault that he permits himself to be so overcome by his experience on the ship and on the raft that he turns out to be a raving nut, and never has the pleasure of learning that his aim is still so good that he can put three slugs in a moving target within the span of a baby's hand.

"Why, George," I say to Gentleman George, "then you are the victim of a great wrong, and I will see the governor, or somebody, in your behalf at once. They cannot do this to you, when, according to your own story, you are not directly connected with the matter of Mrs. Colonel Samuel B. Venus, and it is only a case of mistaken identity, at best."

"Oh, pshaw!" Gentleman George says. "They are not taking the severe measures they contemplate with me because of anything that happens to Mrs. Colonel Samuel B. Venus.

"They are vexed with me," George says, "because one night I take Lou Adolia's automobile out on the salt meadows near Secaucus, N. J., and burn it to a crisp, and it seems that I forget to remove Lou Adolia first from same."

"Well, George," I say, "bon voyage."

"The same to you," George says, "and many of them."

Baseball Hattie

It comes on springtime, and the little birdies are singing in the trees in Central Park, and the grass is green all around and about, and I am at the Polo Grounds on the opening day of the baseball season, when who do I behold but Baseball Hattie. I am somewhat surprised at this spectacle, as it is years since I see Baseball Hattie, and for all I know she long ago passes to a better and happier world. But there she is, as large as life, and in fact twenty pounds larger, and when I call the attention of Armand Fibleman, the gambler, to her, he gets up and tears right out of the joint as if he sees a ghost, for if there is one thing Armand Fibleman loathes and despises, it is a ghost. I can see that Baseball Hattie is greatly changed, and to tell the truth, I can see that she is getting to be nothing but an old bag. Her hair that is once as black as a yard up a stovepipe is gray, and she is wearing gold-rimmed cheaters, although she seems to be pretty well dressed and looks as if she may be in the money a little bit, at that.

But the greatest change in her is the way she sits there very quiet all afternoon, never once opening her yap, even when many of the customers around her are claiming that Umpire William Klem is Public Enemy No. 1 to 16 inclusive, because they think he calls a close one against the Giants. I am wondering if maybe Baseball Hattie is stricken dumb somewhere back down the years, because I can remember when she is usually making speeches in the grandstand in favor of hanging such characters as Umpire William Klem when they call close ones against the Giants. But Hattie just sits there as if she is in a church while the public clamor goes on about

her, and she does not as much as cry out robber, or even
you big bum at Umpire William Klem. I see many a
baseball bug in my time, male and female, but without
doubt the worst bug of them all is Baseball Hattie, and
you can say it again. She is most particularly a bug about
the Giants, and she never misses a game they play at the
Polo Grounds, and in fact she sometimes bobs up watching them play in other cities, which is always very embarrassing to the Giants, as they fear the customers in
these cities may get the wrong impression of New York
womanhood after listening to Baseball Hattie awhile.

The first time I ever see Baseball Hattie to pay any
attention to her is in Philadelphia, a matter of twenty-
odd years back, when the Giants are playing a series
there, and many citizens of New York, including Armand
Fibleman and myself, are present, because the Philadelphia customers are great hands for betting on baseball
games in those days, and Armand Fibleman figures he
may knock a few of them in the creek. Armand Fibleman is a character who will bet on baseball games from
who-laid-the-chunk, and in fact he will bet on anything
whatever, because Armand Fibleman is a gambler by
trade and has been such since infancy. Personally, I will
not bet you four dollars on a baseball game, because in
the first place I am not apt to have four dollars, and in
the second place I consider horse races a much sounder
investment, but I often go around and about with Armand
Fibleman, as he is a friend of mine, and sometimes he
gives me a little piece of one of his bets for nothing.

Well, what happens in Philadelphia but the umpire
forfeits the game in the seventh inning to the Giants by a
score of nine to nothing when the Phillies are really leading by five runs, and the reason the umpire takes this
action is because he orders several of the Philadelphia
players to leave the field for calling him a scoundrel and
a rat and a snake in the grass, and also a baboon, and
they refuse to take their departure, as they still have
more names to call him. Right away the Philadelphia customers become infuriated in a manner you will scarcely

believe, for ordinarily a Philadelphia baseball customer
is as quiet as a lamb, no matter what you do to him, and
in fact in those days a Philadelphia baseball customer is
only considered as somebody to do something to.

But these Philadelphia customers are so infuriated
that they not only chase the umpire under the stand,
but they wait in the street outside the baseball orchard
until the Giants change into their street clothes and come
out of the clubhouse. Then the Philadelphia customers
begin pegging rocks, and one thing and another, at the
Giants, and it is a most exciting and disgraceful scene
that is spoken of for years afterwards. Well, the Giants
march along toward the North Philly station to catch a
train for home, dodging the rocks and one thing and another the best they can, and wondering why the Philadelphia gendarmes do not come to the rescue, until somebody notices several gendarmes among the customers
doing some of the throwing themselves, so the Giants
realize that this is a most inhospitable community, to be
sure.

Finally all of them get inside the North Philly station
and are safe, except a big, tall, left-handed pitcher by
the name of Haystack Duggeler, who just reports to the
club the day before and who finds himself surrounded
by quite a posse of these infuriated Philadelphia customers, and who is unable to make them understand that
he is nothing but a rookie, because he has a Missouri
accent, and besides, he is half paralyzed with fear. One
of the infuriated Philadelphia customers is armed with a
brickbat and is just moving forward to maim Haystack
Duggeler with this instrument, when who steps into the
situation but Baseball Hattie, who is also on her way to
the station to catch a train, and who is greatly horrified
by the assault on the Giants.

She seizes the brickbat from the infuriated Philadelphia customer's grasp, and then tags the customer smack-
dab between the eyes with his own weapon, knocking
him so unconscious that I afterwards hear he does not
recover for two weeks, and that he remains practically

an imbecile the rest of his days. Then Baseball Hattie cuts loose on the other infuriated Philadelphia customers with language that they never before hear in those parts, causing them to disperse without further ado, and after the last customer is beyond the sound of her voice, she takes Haystack Duggeler by the pitching arm and personally escorts him to the station.

Now out of this incident is born a wonderful romance between Baseball Hattie and Haystack Duggeler, and in fact it is no doubt love at first sight, and about this period Haystack Duggeler begins burning up the league with his pitching, and at the same time giving Manager Mac plenty of headaches, including the romance with Baseball Hattie, because anybody will tell you that a left-hander is tough enough on a manager without a romance, and especially a romance with Baseball Hattie. It seems that the trouble with Hattie is she is in business up in Harlem, and this business consists of a boarding and rooming house where ladies and gentlemen board and room, and personally I never see anything out of line in the matter, but the rumor somehow gets around, as rumors will do, that in the first place, it is not a boarding and rooming house, and in the second place that the ladies and gentlemen who room and board there are by no means ladies and gentlemen, and especially ladies.

Well, this rumor becomes a terrible knock to Baseball Hattie's social reputation. Furthermore, I hear Manager Mac sends for her and requests her to kindly lay off his ballplayers, and especially off a character who can make a baseball sing high C like Haystack Duggeler. In fact, I hear Manager Mac gives her such a lecture on her civic duty to New York and to the Giants that Baseball Hattie sheds tears, and promises she will never give Haystack another tumble the rest of the season. "You know me, Mac," Baseball Hattie says. "You know I will cut off my nose rather than do anything to hurt your club. I sometimes figure I am in love with this big bloke, but," she says, "maybe it is only gas pushing up around my heart.

I will take something for it. To hell with him, Mac!" she says.

So she does not see Haystack Duggeler again, except at a distance, for a long time, and he goes on to win fourteen games in a row, pitching a no-hitter and four two-hitters among them, and hanging up a reputation as a great pitcher, and also as a hundred-per-cent heel.

Haystack Duggeler is maybe twenty-five at this time, and he comes to the big league with more bad habits than anybody in the history of the world is able to acquire in such a short time. He is especially a great rumpot, and after he gets going good in the league, he is just as apt to appear for a game all mulled up as not. He is fond of all forms of gambling, such as playing cards and shooting craps, but after they catch him with a deck of readers in a poker game and a pair of tops in a crap game, none of the Giants will play with him any more, except of course when there is nobody else to play with. He is ignorant about many little things, such as reading and writing and geography and mathematics, as Haystack Duggeler himself admits he never goes to school any more than he can help, but he is so wise when it comes to larceny that I always figure they must have great tutors back in Haystack's old home town of Booneville, Mo.

And no smarter jobbie ever breathes than Haystack when he is out there pitching. He has so much speed that he just naturally throws the ball past a batter before he can get the old musket off his shoulder, and along with his hard one, Haystack has a curve like the letter Q. With two ounces of brains, Haystack Duggeler will be the greatest pitcher that ever lives. Well, as far as Baseball Hattie is concerned, she keeps her word about not seeing Haystack, although sometimes when he is mulled up he goes around to her boarding and rooming house, and tries to break down the door.

On days when Haystack Duggeler is pitching, she is always in her favorite seat back of third, and while she roots hard for the Giants no matter who is pitching, she puts on extra steam when Haystack is bending them over, and it is quite an experience to hear her crying lay them in there, Haystack, old boy, and strike this big tramp out, Haystack, and other exclamations of a similar nature, which please Haystack quite some, but annoy Baseball Hattie's neighbors back of third base, such as Armand Fibleman, if he happens to be betting on the other club.

A month before the close of his first season in the big league, Haystack Duggeler gets so ornery that Manager Mac suspends him, hoping maybe it will cause Haystack to do a little thinking, but naturally Haystack is unable to do this, because he has nothing to think with. About a week later, Manager Mac gets to noticing how he can use a few ball games, so he starts looking for Haystack Duggeler, and he finds him tending bar on Eighth Avenue with his uniform hung up back of the bar as an advertisement. The baseball writers speak of Haystack as eccentric, which is a polite way of saying he is a screwball, but they consider him a most unique character and are always writing humorous stories about him, though any one of them will lay you plenty of nine to five that Haystack winds up an umbay. The chances are they will raise their price a little, as the season closes and Haystack is again under suspension with cold weather coming on and not a dime in his pants pockets.

It is sometime along in the winter that Baseball Hattie hauls off and marries Haystack Duggeler, which is a great surprise to one and all, but not nearly as much of a surprise as when Hattie closes her boarding and rooming house and goes to live in a little apartment with Haystack Duggeler up on Washington Heights.

It seems that she finds Haystack one frosty night sleeping in a hallway, after being around slightly mulled up for several weeks, and she takes him to her home and gets him a bath and a shave and a clean shirt and two boiled eggs and some toast and coffee and a shot or two of rye whisky, all of which is greatly appreciated by Haystack, especially the rye whisky. Then Haystack proposes marriage to her and takes a paralyzed oath that if she becomes his wife he will reform, so what with loving Haystack anyway, and with the fix commencing to request more dough off the boarding-and-rooming-house business than the business will stand, Hattie takes him at his word, and there you are. The baseball writers are wondering what Manager Mac will say when he hears these tidings, but all Mac says is that Haystack cannot possibly be any worse married than he is single-o, and then Mac has the club office send the happy couple a little paper money to carry them over the winter. Well, what happens but a great change comes over Haystack Duggeler. He stops bending his elbow and helps Hattie cook and wash the dishes, and holds her hand when they are in the movies, and speaks of his love for her several times a week, and Hattie is as happy as nine dollars' worth of lettuce. Manager Mac is so delighted at the change in Haystack that he has the club office send over more paper money, because Mac knows that with Haystack in shape he is sure of twenty-five games, and maybe the pennant.

In late February, Haystack reports to the training camp down South still as sober as some judges, and the other ballplayers are so impressed by the change in him that they admit him to their poker game again. But of course it is too much to expect a man to alter his entire course of living all at once, and it is not long before Haystack discovers four nines in his hand on his own deal and breaks up the game.

He brings Baseball Hattie with him to the camp, and this is undoubtedly a slight mistake, as it seems the old rumor about her boarding-and-rooming-house business gets around among the ever-loving wives of the other players, and they put on a large chill for her. In fact, you will think Hattie has the smallpox. Naturally, Baseball Hattie feels the frost, but she never lets on, as it seems she runs into many bigger and better frosts than this in her time. Then Haystack Duggeler notices it, and it seems that it makes him a little peevish toward Baseball Hattie, and in fact it is said that he gives her a slight pasting one night in their room, partly because she has no better social standing and partly because he is commencing to cop a few sneaks on the local corn now and then, and Hattie chides him for same.

Well, about this time it appears that Baseball Hattie discovers that she is going to have a baby, and as soon as she recovers from her astonishment, she decides that it is to be a boy who will be a great baseball player, maybe a pitcher, although Hattie admits she is willing to compromise on a good second baseman. She also decides that his name is to be Derrill Duggeler, after his paw, as it seems Derrill is Haystack's real name, and he is only called Haystack because he claims he once makes a living stacking hay, although the general opinion is that all he ever stacks is cards. It is really quite remarkable what a belt Hattie gets out of the idea of having this baby, though Haystack is not excited about the matter. He is not paying much attention to Baseball Hattie by now, except to give her a slight pasting now and then, but Hattie is so happy about the baby that she does not mind these pastings.

Haystack Duggeler meets up with Armand Fibleman along in midsummer. By this time, Haystack discovers horse racing and is always making bets on the horses, and naturally he is generally broke, and then I commence running into him in different spots with Armand Fibleman, who is now betting higher than a cat's back on baseball games.

It is late August, and the Giants are fighting for the front end of the league, and an important series with Brooklyn is coming up, and everybody knows that Haystack Duggeler will work in anyway two games of the series, as Haystack can generally beat Brooklyn just by throwing his glove on the mound. There is no doubt but what he has the old Indian sign on Brooklyn, and the night before the first game, which he is sure to work, the gamblers along Broadway are making the Giants two-to-one favorites to win the game.

This same night before the game, Baseball Hattie is home in her little apartment on Washington Heights waiting for Haystack to come in and eat a delicious dinner of pigs' knuckles and sauerkraut, which she personally prepares for him. In fact, she hurries home right after the ball game to get this delicacy ready, because Haystack tells her he will surely come home this particular night, although Hattie knows he is never better than even money to keep his word about anything. But sure enough, in he comes while the pigs' knuckles and sauerkraut are still piping hot, and Baseball Hattie is surprised to see Armand Fibleman with him, as she knows Armand backwards and forwards and does not care much for him, at that. However, she can say the same thing about four million other characters in this town, so she makes Armand welcome, and they sit down and put on the pigs' knuckles and sauerkraut together, and a pleasant time is enjoyed by one and all. In fact, Baseball Hattie puts herself out to entertain Armand Fibleman, because he is the first guest Haystack ever brings home.

Well, Armand Fibleman can be very pleasant when he wishes, and he speaks very nicely to Hattie. Naturally, he sees that Hattie is expecting, and in fact he will have to be blind not to see it, and he seems greatly interested in this matter and asks Hattie many questions, and Hattie is delighted to find somebody to talk to about what is coming off with her, as Haystack will never listen to any of her remarks on the subject. So Armand Fibleman gets to hear all about Baseball Hattie's son, and how he is to be a great baseball player, and Armand says is that so, and how nice, and all this and that, until Haystack Duggeler speaks up as follows, and to wit:

"Oh, dag-gone her son!" Haystack says. "It is going to be a girl, anyway, so let us dismiss this topic and get down to business. Hat," he says, "you fan yourself into the kitchen and wash the dishes, while Armand and me talk."

So Hattie goes into the kitchen, leaving Haystack and Armand sitting there talking, and what are they talking about but a proposition for Haystack to let the Brooklyn club beat him the next day so Armand Fibleman can take the odds and clean up a nice little gob of money, which he is to split with Haystack. Hattie can hear every word they say, as the kitchen is next door to the dining room where they are sitting, and at first she thinks they are joking, because at this time nobody ever even as much as thinks of skulduggery in baseball, or anyway, not much. It seems that at first Haystack is not in favor of the idea, but Armand Fibleman keeps mentioning money that Haystack owes him for bets on the horse races, and he asks Haystack how he expects to continue betting on the races without fresh money, and Armand also speaks of the great injustice that is being done Haystack by the Giants in not paying him twice the salary he is getting, and how the loss of one or two games is by no means such a great calamity.

Well, finally Baseball Hattie hears Haystack say all right, but he wishes a thousand dollars then and there as a guarantee, and Armand Fibleman says this is fine, and they will go downtown and he will get the money at once, and now Hattie realizes that maybe they are in earnest, and she pops out of the kitchen and speaks as follows:

"Gentlemen," Hattie says, "you seem to be sober, but I guess you are drunk. If you are not drunk, you must both be daffy to think of such a thing as phenagling around with a baseball game."

"Hattie," Haystack says, "kindly close your trap and go back in the kitchen, or I will give you a bust in the nose."

And with this he gets up and reaches for his hat, and Armand Fibleman gets up, too, and Hattie says like this:

"Why, Haystack," she says, "you are not really serious in this matter, are you?"

"Of course I am serious," Haystack says. "I am sick and tired of pitching for starvation wages, and besides, I will win a lot of games later on to make up for the one I lose tomorrow. Say," he says, "these Brooklyn bums may get lucky tomorrow and knock me loose from my pants, anyway, no matter what I do, so what difference does it make?"

"Haystack," Baseball Hattie says, "I know you are a liar and a drunkard and a cheat and no account generally, but nobody can tell me you will sink so low as to purposely toss off a ball game. Why, Haystack, baseball is always on the level. It is the most honest game in all this world. I guess you are just ribbing me, because you know how much I love it."

"Dry up!" Haystack says to Hattie. "Furthermore, do not expect me home again tonight. But anyway, dry up."

"Look, Haystack," Hattie says, "I am going to have a son. He is your son and my son, and he is going to be a great ballplayer when he grows up, maybe a greater pitcher than you are, though I hope and trust he is not left-handed. He will have your name. If they find out you toss off a game for money, they will throw you out of baseball and you will be disgraced. My son will be known as the son of a crook, and what chance will he have in baseball? Do you think I am going to allow you to do this to him, and to the game that keeps me from going nutty for marrying you?"

Naturally, Haystack Duggeler is greatly offended by Hattie's crack about her son being maybe a greater pitcher than he is, and he is about to take steps, when Armand Fibleman stops him. Armand Fibleman is commencing to be somewhat alarmed at Baseball Hattie's attitude, and he gets to thinking that he hears that people in her delicate condition are often irresponsible, and he fears that she may blow a whistle on this enterprise without realizing what she is doing. So he undertakes a few soothing remarks to her. "Why, Hattie," Armand Fibleman says, "nobody can possibly find out about this little matter, and Haystack will have enough money to send your son to college, if his markers at the race track do not take it all. Maybe you better lie down and rest awhile," Armand says.

But Baseball Hattie does not as much as look at Armand, though she goes on talking to Haystack. "They always find out thievery, Haystack," she says, "especially when you are dealing with a fink like Fibleman. If you deal with him once, you will have to deal with him again and again, and he will be the first to holler copper on you, because he is a stool pigeon in his heart."

"Haystack," Armand Fibleman says, "I think we better be going."

"Haystack," Hattie says, "you can go out of here and stick up somebody or commit a robbery or a murder, and I will still welcome you back and stand by you. But if you are going out to steal my son's future, I advise you not to go."

"Dry up!" Haystack says. "I am going."

"All right, Haystack," Hattie says, very calm. "But just step into the kitchen with me and let me say one little word to you by yourself, and then I will say no more."

Well, Haystack Duggeler does not care for even just one little word more, but Armand Fibleman wishes to get this disagreeable scene over with, so he tells Haystack to let her have her word, and Haystack goes into the kitchen with Hattie, and Armand cannot hear what is said, as she speaks very low, but he hears Haystack laugh heartily and then Haystack comes out of the kitchen, still laughing, and tells Armand he is ready to go.

As they start for the door, Baseball Hattie outs with a long-nosed .38-caliber Colt's revolver, and goes root-a-toot-toot with it, and the next thing anybody knows, Haystack is on the floor yelling bloody murder, and Armand Fibleman is leaving the premises without bothering to open the door. In fact, the landlord afterwards talks some of suing Haystack Duggeler because of the damage Armand Fibleman does to the door. Armand himself afterwards admits that when he slows down for a breather a couple of miles down Broadway he finds splinters stuck all over him.

Well, the doctors come, and the gendarmes come, and there is great confusion, especially as Baseball Hattie is sobbing so she can scarcely make a statement, and Haystack Duggeler is so sure he is going to die that he cannot think of anything to say except oh-oh-oh, but finally the landlord remembers seeing Armand leave with his door, and everybody starts questioning Hattie about this until she confesses that Armand is there all right, and that he tries to bribe Haystack to toss off a ball game, and that she then suddenly finds herself with a revolver in her hand, and everything goes black before her eyes, and she can remember no more until somebody is sticking a bottle of smelling salts under her nose. Naturally, the newspaper reporters put two and two together, and what they make of it is that Hattie tries to plug Armand Fibleman for his rascally offer, and that she misses Armand and gets Haystack, and right away Baseball Hattie is a great heroine, and Haystack is a great hero, though nobody thinks to ask Haystack how he stands on the bribe proposition, and he never brings it up himself.

And nobody will ever offer Haystack any more bribes, for after the doctors get through with him he is shy a left arm from the shoulder down, and he will never pitch a baseball again, unless he learns to pitch right-handed. The newspapers make quite a lot of Baseball Hattie protecting the fair name of baseball. The National League plays a benefit game for Haystack Duggeler and presents him with a watch and a purse of twenty-five thousand dollars, which Baseball Hattie grabs away from him, saying it is for her son, while Armand Fibleman is in bad with one and all.

Baseball Hattie and Haystack Duggeler move to the Pacific Coast, and this is all there is to the story, except that one day some years ago, and not long before he passes away in Los Angeles, a respectable grocer, I run into Haystack when he is in New York on a business trip, and I say to him like this:

"Haystack," I say, "it is certainly a sin and a shame that Hattie misses Armand Fibleman that night and puts you on the shelf. The chances are that but for this little accident you will hang up one of the greatest pitching records in the history of baseball. Personally," I say, "I never see a better left-handed pitcher."

"Look," Haystack says. "Hattie does not miss Fibleman. It is a great newspaper story and saves my name, but the truth is she hits just where she aims. When she calls me into the kitchen before I start out with Fibleman, she shows me a revolver I never before know she has, and says to me, 'Haystack,' she says, 'if you leave with this weasel on the errand you mention, I am going to fix you so you will never make another wrong move with your pitching arm. I am going to shoot it off for you.'

"I laugh heartily," Haystack says. "I think she is kidding me, but I find out different. By the way," Haystack says, "I afterwards learn that long before I meet her, Hattie works for three years in a shooting gallery at Coney Island. She is really a remarkable broad," Haystack says.

I guess I forget to state that the day Baseball Hattie is at the Polo Grounds she is watching the new kid sensation of the big leagues, Derrill Duggeler, shut out Brooklyn with three hits.

He is a wonderful young left-hander.

A Call on the President

When I got home from work the other night my wife Ethel ses O Joe, an awful thing has happened. Jim the mailman got fired. I ses who fired him? She ses why, the Government fired him. Somebody told the Government that they saw him take a letter out of his mail sack and burn it. The Government ses Jim, why did you do such a thing, and Jim would not tell so they fired him.

She ses Joe, you go and see some politicians and have them make the Government put Jim the mailman back to work right away because he is too old to do anything else but carry the mail and he would starve to death in no time. It is not justice to fire a man who has carried the mail for over thirty years, she ses. I ses Ethel sweets, I do not know no politicians that have got anything to do with the Government or justice. I ses anyway we are only little people and they are big people and what is the use of talking to them? I ses they would only give me a pushing around because that is what big people always do to little people.

Well, Ethel ses, who runs the Government? I ses the President of the United States runs the Government and she ses I bet anything the President of the United States would give Jim the mailman back his job if we tell him about it. Lets us go see the President of the United States. I ses Ethel sugar plum, the President of the United States lives in Washington and he is a busy fellow and I do not think he would have time to see us even if we went there, and she ses now there you go rooting against yourself like you always do. We will go to Washington and see the President of the United States because it is important that Jim the mailman gets his job back. Why, she ses Jim the mailman would simply lay down and die if he could not keep on carrying the mail.

So the next day I got a day's layoff and then we climbed in the old bucket and drove to Washington and my wife Ethel wore her best dress and her new hat, and I put on my gray suit and a necktie and when we arrived in Washington about noon, I ses to a cop, look cop, where do you find the President of the United States? He ses I never find him.

O, I ses, a wise guy, hay? I ses cop, I am a citizen of the United States of America and this is my wife Ethel and she is a citizen too and I asked you a question like a gentleman and you have a right to answer me like a gentleman. Yes, my wife Ethel ses, we are from Brooklyn and we do not like to have hick cops get fresh with us. O, the cop ses, I am a hick am I, and she ses well you look like one to me. I ses pipe down Ethel honey, and let me do the talking will you, and the cop ses Buddy I have got one of those too, and I sympathize with you.

He ses you have to go to the White House to find the President of the United States. You follow this street a ways he ses, and you cannot miss. Give him my regards when you see him, the cop ses. I ses what name will I tell him. The cop ses George, and I ses George what? My wife Ethel ses drive on Joe, that hick cop is just trying to kid people.

So we followed the street like the cop ses and pretty soon we came to a big building in a yard and I ses well, Ethel, I guess that is the White House all right. Then I parked the old bucket up against the curb and we got out and walked into the yard and up to the door of this building and at the door was another cop. He ses what do you want? I ses who wants to know? He ses I do. I ses all right, we want to see the President of the United States and he ses so does a hundred million other people. He ses what do you want to see him about anyway? My wife Ethel ses Joe, why do you waste your time talking to hick cops? I never saw so many hick cops in my life. She ses in Brooklyn people do not have to go around answering questions from cops.

Well, go back to Brooklyn the cop ses. Anyway, get away from here. I do not like to look at you he ses. Your faces make me tired. I ses cop, you are no rose geranium yourself when it comes to looks. I ses I am a citizen of the United States of America and I know my rights. I do not have to take no lip off of cops. I ses it is a good thing for you that you have got that uniform on, and that I have respect for the law or I would show you something.

He ses you and who else? I ses I do not need nobody else and my wife Ethel ses show him something anyway, Joe, and I might have showed him something all right but just then a fellow with striped pants on came out of the door and ses what is the trouble here? I ses there is no trouble, just a fresh cop. I ses my wife Ethel and me want to see the President of the United States and this jerk here ses we cannot do so. I ses that is always the way it is with cops, when they get that uniform on they want to start pushing people around.

I ses I am a citizen of the United States of America and it is a fine note if a citizen cannot see the President of the United States when he wants to without a lot of cops horning in. I ses it is not justice for cops to treat a citizen that way. I ses what is the President of the United States for if a citizen cannot see him? My wife Ethel ses yes, we are not going to eat him, and I ses Ethel baby, you better let me handle this situation.

The fellow in the striped pants ses what do you want to see the President of the United States about? I ses look Mister, we came all the way from Brooklyn to see the President of the United States and I have got to be back to work on my job tomorrow and if I stop and tell everybody what I want to see him about I won't have no time left. I ses Mister, what is so tough about seeing the President of the United States? When he was after this job he was glad to see anybody. I ses is he like those politicians in Brooklyn now or what?

Wait a minute, the fellow in the striped pants ses, and he went back into the building and after awhile he came out again and ses the President of the United States will see you at once. What is your name? I ses my name is Joe Turp and this is my wife Ethel. He ses I am pleased to meet you and I ses the same to you. Then he took us into the building and finally into a big office, and there was the President of the United States all right. I could tell him from his pictures.

He smiled at us and the fellow in the striped pants who took us in ses this is Joe Turp of Brooklyn and his wife Ethel, and the President of the United States shook hands with us and ses I am glad to see you, and I ses likewise. He ses how are things in Brooklyn? Rotten, I ses. They always are. The Dodgers are doing better but they need more pitching, I ses. How are things in Washington? He ses not so good. He ses I guess we need more pitching here too. He told us to set down and then he ses, what is on your mind Joe, but there was some other fellows in the office and I ses Your Honor, what my wife Ethel and me want to see you about is strictly on the q t and he laughed and motioned at the other fellows and they went out of the room laughing too and my wife Ethel ses what is so funny around here anyway? I ses nix Ethel. I ses nix now. Kindly let me handle this situation.

Then I ses to the President of the United States, Your Honor, you do not know me and I do not know you so we start even. I know you are a busy fellow and I will not waste your time any more than I have to so I better come to the point right away, I ses. My wife Ethel and me want to talk to you about Jim the mailman. Yes, Ethel ses, he got fired from his job. I ses Ethel sugar plum, please do not butt in on this. I will tell the President of the United States all about it. Your Honor, I ses, when women start to tell something they always go about it

the wrong end to, and he ses yes but they mean well.
Who is Jim the mailman?

I ses Your Honor, Jim the mailman is a fellow over
sixty years old and he has been carrying the mail in our
neighborhood for thirty some odd years. My wife Ethel
and me were little kids when Jim the mailman started
carrying the mail. Your Honor, I ses, you may not believe it but my wife Ethel was a good looking little squab
when she was a kid. I can well believe it, the President
of the United States ses. Well, Your Honor, I ses, you
would think Jim the mailman was a grouchy old guy
until you got to know him. He is a tall thin fellow with
humped over shoulders from carrying that mail sack
around and he has long legs like a pair of scissors and
gray hair and wears specs. He is no where near as
grouchy as he looks. The reason he looks grouchy is
because his feet always hurt him.

Yes, my wife Ethel ses, I gave him some lard to rub on
his feet one day and Jim the mailman ses he never had
anything help him so much. My mother used to rub my
pops feet with lard when he came home with them ach-
ing. My pops was a track walker in the subway she ses.
I ses look Ethel, the President of the United States is
not interested in your pops feet and she ses well that is
how I thought of the lard for Jim the mailman.

I ses Your Honor, Jim the mailman was always real
nice to kids. I remember one Christmas he brought me
a sack of candy and a Noahs ark. Yes, my wife Ethel
ses, and once he gave me a doll that ses mama when
you punched it in the stomach. I ses Ethel, honey, the
President of the United States does not care where you
punched it. Well, she ses you punched it in the stomach
if you wanted it to say mama.

Your Honor, I ses, old Missus Crusper lived a couple
of doors from us and she was about the same age as Jim
the mailman. She was a little off her nut. My wife Ethel
ses Your Honor, she was not so. She was just peculiar.
You should not say such things about Missus Crusper
the poor old thing Joe, she ses. You ought to be ashamed

of yourself to say such things. All right, Ethel baby, I ses. She was peculiar Your Honor. I mean Missus Crusper. She was a little old white-haired lady with a voice like a canary bird and she had not been out of her house in twenty-five years and most of the time not out of bed. Something happened to her when her son Johnny was born.

I had to stop my story a minute because I noticed Ethel at a window acting very strange and I ses Ethel, what is the idea of looking out that window and screwing up your face the way you are doing and she ses I am making snoots at that hick cop. He is right under this window and I have got him half crazy. I ses Your Honor, kindly excuse my wife Ethel, but she is getting even with a cop who tried to keep us from seeing you and the President of the United States laughed and ses well, what about Missus Crusper?

I ses well, Missus Crusper's name before she got married was Kitten O'Brien, Your Honor, and her old man ran a gin mill in our neighborhood but very respectable. She married Henry Crusper when she was eighteen and the old folks in our neighborhood ses it broke Jim the mailman's heart. He went to school with her and Henry Crusper and Jim the mailman used to follow Kitten O'Brien around like a pup but he never had no chance.

Henry Crusper was a good-looking kid, I ses, and Jim the mailman was as homely as a mule and still is. Besides he was an orphan and Henry Crusper's old man had a nice grocery store. He gave the store to Henry when he married Kitten O'Brien. But Jim the mailman did not get mad about losing Missus Crusper like people do nowadays. He ses he did not blame her and he ses he certainly did not blame Henry Crusper. He stayed good friends with them both and used to be around with them a lot but he never looked at another broad again. The President of the United States ses another what? Another broad I ses. Another woman I ses. O, he ses. I see.

Yes, my wife Ethel ses, I bet you would not be the way Jim the mailman was, Joe Turp. I bet you would

have been as sore as a goat if I had married Linky
Moses but I bet you would have found somebody else
in no time. I ses please, Ethel. Please now. Anyway, I
ses, look how Linky Moses turned out. How did Linky
Moses turn out, the President of the United States ses,
and I ses he turned out a bum.

Your Honor, I ses, Missus Crusper married Henry
Crusper when she was about eighteen. Henry was a good
steady-going fellow and he made her a fine husband
from what everybody ses and in our neighborhood if
anybody does not make a fine husband it gets talked
around pretty quick. She was crazy about him but she
was crazier still about her son Johnny especially after
Henry died. That was when Johnny was five or six
years old. Henry got down with pneumonia during a
tough winter.

Yes, my wife Ethel ses, my mother ses he never would
wear an overcoat no matter how cold it was. My mother
ses not wearing overcoats is why lots of people get
pneumonia and die. I always try to make Joe wear his
overcoat and a muffler too, Ethel ses. I ses Ethel, never
mind what you make me wear, and she ses well Joe, I
only try to keep you healthy.

Missus Crusper must have missed Henry a lot, Your
Honor, I ses. Henry used to carry her up and down
stairs in his arms. He waited on her hand and foot. Of
course much of this was before my time and what I tell
you is what the old people in our neighborhood told me.
After Henry died it was Jim the mailman who carried
Missus Crusper up and down stairs in his arms until she
got so she could not leave her bed at all and then Jim
the mailman spent all his spare time setting there talking to her and waiting on her like she was a baby.

I ses I did not know Missus Crusper until I was about
ten years old and got to running around with Johnny.
He was a tough kid, Your Honor, and I had him marked
stinko even then and so did all the other kids in the
neighborhocd. His mother could not look out after him
much and he did about as he pleased. He was a natural-

born con artist and he could always salve her into believing whatever he wanted her to believe. She thought he was the smartest kid in the world and that he was going to grow up to be a big man. She was proud of Johnny and what he was going to be. Nobody in our neighborhood wanted to tell her that he was no good. I can see her now, Your Honor, a little lady with a lace cap on her head leaning out of the window by her bed and calling Johnny so loud you could hear her four blocks away because she always called him like she was singing.

My wife Ethel had quit making snoots at the cop and was sitting in a chair by the window and she jumped out of the chair and ses yes, Your Honor, Missus Crusper sing-sanged O hi, Johnny, and a hey Johnny, and a ho, Johnny, just like that.

The fellow in the striped pants stuck his head in the door but the President of the United States waggled a finger at him and he closed the door again and I ses look Ethel, when you holler like that you remind me of your mother. She ses what is the matter with my mother, and I ses nothing that being deaf and dumb will not cure. I ses Ethel, it is not dignified to holler like that in the presence of the President of the United States. Why, Ethel ses, I was only showing how Missus Crusper used to call Johnny by sing-sanging O hi Johnny, and a hey Johnny, and a ho, Johnny. I ses Ethel, that will do. I ses do you want to wake the dead?

Your Honor, I ses, Jim the mailman was around Missus Crusper's house a lot and he was around our neighborhood a good deal too and he knew what Johnny was doing. As Johnny got older Jim the mailman tried to talk to him and make him behave but that only made Johnny take to hating Jim the mailman. The old folks ses Jim the mailman wanted to marry Missus Crusper after she got over being so sorry about Henry but one day she told him she could never have anything to do with a man who spoke disrespectfully of her late husband and ordered him out of her house. Afterwards Jim the mailman found out that Johnny had told her Jim had said something bad about Henry Crusper around the neighborhood and nothing would make her believe any different until long later. Your Honor, I ses, Johnny Crusper was one of the best liars in the world even when he was only a little kid.

The fellow in the striped pants came in the room about now and he bent over and said something in a whisper to the President of the United States but the President waved his hand and ses tell him I am busy with some friends from Brooklyn and the fellow went out again.

Your Honor, I ses, this Johnny Crusper got to running with some real tough guys when he was about seventeen and pretty soon he was in plenty of trouble with the cops but Jim the mailman always managed to get him out without letting his mother know. The old folks ses it used to keep Jim the mailman broke getting Johnny out of trouble. Finally one day Johnny got in some real bad trouble that Jim the mailman could not square or nobody else and Johnny had to leave town in a big hurry. He did not stop to say good-by to his mother. The old folks ses Jim the mailman hocked his salary with a loan shark to get Johnny the dough to leave town on and some ses he sent Johnny more dough afterwards to keep going. But Jim the mailman never ses a word himself about it one way or the other so nobody but him and Johnny knew just what happened about that.

Your Honor, I ses, Johnny going away without saying good-by made Missus Crusper very sick and this was when she commenced being peculiar. Old Doc Steele ses she was worrying herself to death because she never heard from Johnny. He ses he would bet if she knew where Johnny was and if he was all right it would save her life and her mind too but nobody knew where Johnny was so there did not seem to be anything anybody could do about that.

Then one day Jim the mailman stopped at Missus Crusper's house and gave her a letter from Johnny. It

was not a long letter and it was from some place like
Vancouver and it ses Johnny was working and doing
well and that he loved her dearly and thought of her all
the time. I know it ses that, Your Honor, because Jim
the mailman wrote it all out himself and read it to me
and ses how does it sound? I ses it sounded great. It
looked great too because Jim the mailman had fixed up
the envelope at the post office so it looked as if it had
come through the mail all right and he had got hold of
one of Johnny's old school books and made a good stab
at imitating Johnny's handwriting. It was not a hard job
to do that. Johnny never let himself get past the fourth
grade and his handwriting was like a child would do.

Missus Crusper never bothered about the handwriting anyway, Your Honor. She was so glad to hear from
Johnny she sent for everybody in the neighborhood and
read them the letter. It must have sounded genuine because Jennie Twofer went home and told her old man
that Mrs. Crusper had got a letter from Johnny and her
old man told his brother Fred who was a plain-clothes
cop and Fred went around to see Missus Crusper and
find out where Johnny was. Jim the mailman got hold of
Fred first and they had a long talk and Fred went away
without asking Missus Crusper anything.

Yes, my wife Ethel ses, that Jennie Twofer always
was a two-face meddlesome old thing and nobody ever
had any use for her. I ses look, Ethel, kindly do not
knock our neighbors in public. I ses wait until we get
back home and she ses all right but Jennie Twofer is
two face just the same.

Your Honor, I ses, every week for over ten years old
Missus Crusper got a letter from Johnny and he was always doing well although he seemed to move around a
lot. He was in Arizona California Oregon and everywhere else. Jim the mailman made him a mining engi-
neer so he could have a good excuse for moving around.
On Missus Crusper's birthdays and on Christmas she
always got a little present from him. Jim the mailman
took care of that. She kept the letters in a box under her

bed and she would read them to all her old friends when they called and brag about the way Johnny was doing and what a good boy he was to his mother. Your Honor, old chromos in our neighborhood whose sons were bums and who had a pretty good idea the letters were phony would set and listen to Missus Crusper read them and tell her Johnny surely was a wonderful man.

About a month ago the only legitimate letter that came to Missus Crusper since Johnny went away bobbed up in Jim the mailman's sack, I ses. It was a long thin envelope and Jim the mailman opened it and read it and then he touched a match to it and went on to Missus Crusper's house and delivered a letter to her from Johnny in Australia. This letter ses he was just closing a deal that would make him a millionaire and that he would then come home and bring her a diamond breastpin and never leave her again as long as he lived.

But Your Honor, I ses, Jim the mailman knew that it would be the last letter he would ever deliver to Missus Crusper because old Doc Steele told him the day before that she had only a few hours more to go and she died that night. Jim the mailman was setting by her bed. He ses that at the very last she tried to lean out the window and call Johnny.

Well I ses, some louse saw Jim the mailman burn that letter and turned him in to the Government and got him fired from his job but Jim could not do anything else but burn it because it was a letter from the warden of the San Quentin prison where Johnny had been a lifer for murder all those years, telling Missus Crusper her son had been killed by the guards when he was trying to escape and saying she could have his body if she wanted it.

Your Honor, I ses, I guess we have got plenty of gall coming to you with a thing like this when you are so busy. I ses my wife Ethel wanted me to go to some politicians about it but I told her the best we would get from politicians would be a pushing around and then she ses we better see you and here we are. But I ses it is only fair to tell you that if you do anything to help Jim the mailman we cannot do anything for you in return because we are just very little people and all we can do is say much obliged and God bless you and that is what everybody in our neighborhood would say.

Well, my wife Ethel ses, Jim the mailman has got to have his job back because I would hate to have anybody else bring me my mail. I ses Ethel baby, the only mail I ever knew you to get was a Valentine from Linky Moses four years ago and I told him he better not send you any more and she ses yes, that is the mail I mean.

The President of the United States ses Joe and Missus Turp think no more of it. You have come to the right place. I will take good care of the matter of Jim the mailman. Then he pushes a button on his desk and the man in the striped pants came in and the President ses tell them I will have two more for luncheon. The fellow ses who are they and the President ses my friends Joe and Missus Turp of Brooklyn and my wife Ethel ses it is a good job I wore my new hat.

We drove back home in the old bucket after we had something to eat and I got back to work the next day on time all right and a couple of days later I saw Jim the mailman around delivering mail so I knew he was okay too.

I never gave the trip to Washington any more thought and my wife did not say anything about it either for a couple of weeks then one night she woke me up out of a sound sleep by jabbing me in the back with her elbow and ses Joe, I have been thinking about something. I ses look Ethel, you do your thinking in the day time please and let me sleep. But she ses no, listen Joe. She ses if ever I go back to Washington again I will give that hick cop a piece of my mind because I have just this minute figured out what he meant when he said he had one of those too and sympathized with you.

Nice and Quiet, She Was

Brooklyn

Dear Sir: The other night I took my wife Ethel to the movies and when we were on our way home she ses Joe, are nice people uninteresting? I ses baby, I think you are one of the most interesting people I ever saw in my whole life and that goes double in spades.

She ses no, I am serious Joe although I thank you just the same. You are a very fine fellow to tell me that but I wish you would answer my question. Are nice people uninteresting? I ses why I suppose they are but you will have to explain what you mean. I ses it sounds to me like one of those trick questions of yours.

Ethel ses well, we have seen three pictures in the past two weeks and all of them were about nasty people like murderers and dopers and ladies who like fellows who are not their husbands and mean policemen. There were no nice people in any of them but only unnice ones. Well, the movies are supposed to be interesting to those who pay to see them and I am sure those who make the movies put in the people they think would be most interesting to the customers.

Well, Ethel ses, as there were no nice people in all those pictures we saw I was just wondering if it is because nice people are not interesting to any one. I mean nice people like my moms and Mrs. Crutcher and all the others in our neighborhood who go to church and do their best to be good to everybody.

I ses, well Ethel, I guess maybe nice people don't lead very exciting lives like the unnice ones in the pictures. I ses all they do is work hard all day long and go home and just sit around until it is time to go to bed although of course some of them go to the movies like

351

us once in awhile and see those pictures you are beefing about. Ethel ses I am not beefing Joe, I am just asking.

I ses well, you know yourself nobody would pay a dime to see a picture about people like the ones we know in our neighborhood. I ses I guess I will have to answer yes to your question and say nice people are uninteresting and that is why you do not see any pictures about them. I ses that is why you see pictures about bad people who are really quite interesting, especially if they commit a murder.

Ethel ses there has not been a murder in our neighborhood for over thirty years. Not since you and I were born, Joe. The last murder around our neighborhood was when old Miss Julia killed her fiancé by locking him up in her cellar and starving him to death. I ses what are you talking about Ethel? She ses I am talking about Miss Julia. I ses do you mean that nice quiet old lady that lives across the street from your mom's house?

Ethel ses yes Joe, she is the one. She is one of my mom's best friends. She was in love with a policeman named Brown many years ago and when she found out that he was keeping company with another girl she got them both to come and see her to talk things over and somehow got them to go down in the cellar and locked them in. They starved to death because she wouldn't give them anything to eat or drink and nobody could hear the noise they made because she made her old father fix the cellar up with stone and cement in advance so it was soundproof.

I ses I never heard that story in my life and I thought I knew everything that ever happened around here. Ethel ses well of course it was a long time and they had Miss Julia in the asylum for many years. I ses my goodness and I never saw anybody nicer than she is and Ethel ses isn't she nice? But I don't think you will ever see nice people like she is in the movies Joe, they are so uninteresting.

Yours truly,

JOE TURP

One of Those Things

Brooklyn

Dear Sir: My wife Ethel's Uncle Ben called me up one afternoon not long ago and ses Joe, a friend of mine from Scranton is in town and he bought two duckets to the fight at Madison Square Garden tonight and all of a sudden he finds he can't go so he has given them to me and I want you to go with me.

I ses why sure and thanks for thinking of me, Ben. He ses okay meet me at Fiftieth and Broadway at seven o'clock and we will have a nice Italian dinner somewheres and go. So I telephoned my wife Ethel that I would not be home and I met her Uncle Ben right on the dot and we went to the Progressivo restaurant in West Fifty-fifth and had some real nice spaghetti.

While we was eating Uncle Ben looked all around and then dropped his voice almost to a whisper and ses Joe, did you bring any dough with you? I ses O, so that is it, is it? I ses I suppose you are clean and I will have to pay for this spread? He ses no, no, Joe. It is all on me because I am really loaded tonight. I am there with over a hundred fish but I want to give you a chance to pick up a few seeds.

I ses how? Ben ses well, I have found out that this fight tonight is one of those things. It is a do-se-do. It is a rumba, with music by Cugat. Joe, the guy who is the one to three favorite is going to blow the duke to the other gee and all you have to do to pick up a nice bundle is to bet on the short-ender. I have already bet myself fifty and I will get you on for whatever you feel like going for.

353

I ses Uncle Ben, I do not feel like going for anything. I ses now that I am a partner in our business I have to be more careful with my dough than ever before and besides I do not think it is dignified for a business man to be betting on prize fights. Uncle Ben ses suit yourself Joe, but don't get jealous when you see me with a hundred and fifty bills that I haven't got now.

I ses what makes you so sure this is one of those things? I ses I have seen many a one of those things go wrong in my time at the old Ridgewood Grove. He ses why everybody in town knows it. A fellow standing on the sidewalk in front of the Forrest Hotel that I never saw before in my life told me. A shoeshine kid on Eighth avenue told me. A guy who runs one of the newsstands at Fiftieth and Broadway told me while I was waiting there for you. The whole town is hep, Joe.

I ses well, Uncle Ben, I haven't paid much attention to fights since the war but if everybody knows like you ses, the price ought to be shorter than three to one because everybody would be betting on the short-ender. Uncle Ben ses well, of course I am speaking of the early betting. I expect it to be something like even money at ring time. Anyway, I will give you a piece of my bet at three if you like, Joe, but I ses thanks, but I am keeping my money in my kick.

When we got to the Garden, I went right to my seat but Uncle Ben hung out in the lobby awhile and when he came in I ses is it still one of those things? Uncle Ben ses sure. Everybody out there knows it. The favorite is to pull to the other gee from start to finish. The price is still three so I bet all the rest of the dough I had on me. I only hope there isn't too much of a scandal about it.

I ses Uncle Ben, I would be worried about that price if I was you. I ses it ought to be shorter and he ses the price makes no difference and just then the bell rang and the favorite walked over to the other gee and belted him on the chin with a big right hand and the short-end fellow went down and plumb out.

I turned around to say something to Uncle Ben but he had disappeared and he didn't come back for ten minutes when nearly everybody was out of the building and he ses I went around to see what happened. Do you know what happened, Joe? They forget to tell the favorite this was to be one of those things.

Yours truly,
JOE TURP

Home-Cooking

Brooklyn

Dear Sir: The other night my wife Ethel was reading the evening paper and she ses strike, strike, strike, strike. That is all you can read nowadays. Strike, strike, strike, strike. Everybody is on a strike. I don't know what the world is coming to.

I ses well, don't worry, beautiful. I ses the world always comes out all right and Ethel's moms who was setting there sewing ses out of a clear sky, I was on a strike once. Ethel's pops got up and ses I think I will go down to Schultze's for a beer before I turn in. Ethel's moms ses he doesn't like to hear this story. Don't stay too late, pops.

Ethel ses, why, moms, I never knew you worked at anything besides keeping house for pops and her moms ses Oh, I did a few things besides that. I worked quite a little before I got married and Ethel ses what union did you belong to? Her moms ses I didn't belong to any union. Ethel ses then how could you go on a strike?

Moms ses I went on a strike against cooking for your pops and that didn't call for any union. I found out he played a kind of trick on me and while it was years ago before you was even born I haven't got over it to this day. But whenever I bring it up, your pops thinks of an excuse to leave the house like he did just now.

I ses I should think he would, moms. I ses a subject can get a little tiresome after it has been used for years but why did the cooking for pops cause you to strike? I ses you are the greatest cook I ever saw in my life and Ethel would be second best if she would only concentrate. Ethel ses I hate cooking. Her moms ses, daughter, you keep hating it and never mind what Joe ses about concentrating.

She ses I hated cooking, too, and the only reason I did it when I first married your pops was because we was very poor and could not hire anyone to do it or go out to meals. Your pops loved my cooking and he was always telling me that it was almost as good as his sister Martha's cooking. She was married to a police inspector over in the Bronx and I never saw her very often but your pops was always telling me what a wonderful cook she was and how her cooking was probably responsible for her husband's success.

Moms ses your pops talked about Martha's cooking so much that I was very jealous of her and I made a regular study of cooking. I almost lived in the kitchen because I wanted to become a better cook than Martha. After your pops commenced to do very well he would sometimes take me to a restaurant for a meal but he always criticized the food and told me it couldn't compare with my cooking and of course that made me feel nice.

Once in a while I would ask him if I wasn't getting better than Martha and one day he ses maybe I wasn't better but that it was surely a dead heat and that pleased me so much I forgot about suggesting that we could afford to hire a woman to come in and help me with the cooking because it had really become quite a job as your pops was quite a heavy feeder.

Then one day when your pops was at work his sister Martha came to this very house to see me and she was really a very fine-looking woman with a big hat and a nice fur coat and when I told her your pops ses I was a tie with her on cooking she looked at me in a funny way and ses I can't cook a lick. I can't even boil water. I never cooked a meal in my whole life and I hope I never have to start.

Moms ses that is when I went on a strike because I could see that your pops had made up a story to keep me steaming in that hot kitchen learning to cook and I guess I would be on a strike to this day only after about a week of going to restaurants for meals I couldn't stand their cooking any longer.

Yours truly,

JOE TURP

A Right Good-Looking Gal

It is a very hot day in the late eighties back in my old home town out West, when One-Arm Jack Maddox and his gang come a-cussing and a-shooting into town to hold up the Stockgrowers' National Bank.

I am not there myself, of course, but I get the story from my grandpap, who is sitting under the awning in front of the Greenlight saloon with his chair tilted back against the wall, when One-Arm Jack rides in.

This One-Arm Jack Maddox is a train robber and cattle thief, and an all-around no-good guy, generally, and every man in his gang is about the same, although some may be worse than others. He has riding with him this day Zeb Coultry, Bad Pete Jacobs, Chew-'em-up Charley Williams and the two Karrick boys, and they come galloping in on their horses raising the very dickens.

They all have six-pistols and Winchester rifles, and

as they go tearing along Santa Fe Ave. toward the Stockgrowers' National Bank, they take pot shots at everybody in sight, including my grandpap.

My grandpap says he gets up off his chair very quietly and steps into the Greenlight saloon as if he is just going in for a drink, because he does not wish to be a party to a holdup, even as a witness, but my Uncle Abner always tells the story a little different.

My Uncle Abner says he is inside the Greenlight playing a little stud poker with some of the boys, when all of a sudden something goes by him like a bat out of a cave, and the next thing he hears is a terrible crash of glass as my grandpap takes the window in the back of the joint.

But, of course, you never can believe my Uncle Abner, as he is always stretching things.

Well, anyway, people are very scarce in the streets, indeed, by the time One-Arm Jack Maddox and his gang reach the Stockgrowers' National Bank. The only one in sight is old Pat Dillon, the marshal, and he is stooped down behind an iron fireplug, and is cracking away at One-Arm Jack for all he is worth with a six-pistol. But old Pat is not much of a shot and One-Arm and his bunch do not pay much attention to him until the old boy sticks his noggin out a little too far around the fireplug and Sid Karrick clips him with a Winchester.

One-Arm Jack, Zeb Coultry and Bad Pete Jacobs hop off their horses when they reach the bank, and go inside, leaving the others outside to shoot at anybody that shows up.

One-Arm Jack walks up to the cashier's window, shoves his six-pistol in a face that he sees inside the cage, and says like this:

"Shell out that gravy in there," he says, "and be quick about it, too."

Well, the next thing One-Arm Jack knows, but the nozzle of the pistol is pushed aside, and he finds he is looking smack-dab into the face of a right good-looking gal, and the gal is saying to him like this: "Why, hello Jack! What is the matter!"

Well, sir, who is this gal but Daisy Bartfield, whose old man, Dan Bartfield, is cashier of the Stockgrowers' National Bank, and what is Daisy doing in the cashier's cage, as it comes out afterwards, but working for her dad, who is down with the rheumatism.

Well, One-Arm Jack stands there looking at her with his mouth open, not knowing much of anything to say, and Daisy Bartfield goes right on talking, as pleasant as a basket of chips.

"Where are you keeping yourself all these years, Jack Maddox?" she says to One-Arm Jack. "What are you looking at me that way for? Don't you remember me— Daisy Bartfield?"

Well, naturally, One-Arm Jack does not, for he never sees Daisy Bartfield before in his whole life, and, as a matter of fact, not many people back in my old home town ever see her, either, because she is just back for a summer vacation from a college in the East. She is only stalling One-Arm for time.

Now, naturally, all this gab takes a little time, maybe five or six minutes, maybe more, and a few minutes are very valuable when you are robbing a bank.

While One-Arm Jack is standing in there sort of petrified with surprise, the citizens of my old home town hump themselves and get their guns, and all of a sudden from every roof and window along the street comes a-boiling bullets.

Hearing all the shooting, One-Arm Jack and Zeb Coultry and Bad Pete comes bursting out of the bank, and old One-Arm goes over with his only other wing busted from a shot which nineteen of our best citizens afterwards claim.

Bad Pete, who is as game a guy as ever steps in shoeleather, picks up Chew-'em-up Charley and throws him over his horse and rides away, head up, and paying no attention, whatever, to the bullets whizzing around him.

Zeb Coultry tries to pick up One-Arm, but a bullet chips him in the shoulder and he has all he can do getting onto his horse alone.

Well, they all get away but One-Arm himself, and after Doc Wilcox patches up his arm some they take him off to the sneezer, which is a way of saying the jail. As they lock him up One-Arm is looking mighty puzzled, like a guy who is thinking of something to himself, and finally he says to Bob Davis, the sheriff, like this:

"Bob," he says, "I do not place this gal in the bank. I do not remember ever seeing her before. I am commencing to think she is mistaken 'about knowing me."

The Wooing of Nosey Gillespie

In all the world there is nothing so sweet as love, and we have plenty of this business going on back in my old home town out West at all times.

In fact, it is as good as an even money bet that we have as much love going on in my old home town as any other town in this country, population considered.

We have all kinds of romances, some of which are very lovely indeed, and others which are not so good, and among these romances is the romance between Nosey Gillespie, the editor of the Weekly Bee, and Miss Jo Eva Gildersleeve, the schoolteacher.

This Nosey Gillespie is called Nosey because he is nosey, but of course being nosey is largely his racket, being the editor of this *Weekly Bee*. This *Weekly Bee* is not much of a newspaper, being nothing like the *Pueblo Morning Chieftain,* but Nosey Gillespie does fairly well for himself with it, what with ads from the saloonkeepers, and contributions from the candidates at election times.

He is a little dried-up man, maybe fifty years old, with a goatee, and he is as quiet and mild as an old tomato. Nothing much ever happens to him in his whole life, except one time years ago when he first starts his paper, a Mexican drops in on him and shoots his right leg off, thinking he is shooting the editor of the Morning Chieftain for putting something dirty in the paper about him.

Anybody knows that the last thing Nosey Gillespie will ever think of is putting anything dirty in his paper about anybody, even a Mexican. There is no harm in Nosey, whatever. He is always ready to put something nice in his paper about people, and while not many are apt to see it after it is in the paper on account of the circulation of the Bee *being* very low, this shows Nosey has a good disposition anyway.

Well, for many years Nosey goes along on his one leg as an old bachelor, doing all right, and well satisfied with life, when Miss Jo Eva Gildersleeve lights on him. My old man claims that the reason Miss Jo Eva lights on Nosey is because he is the only man left in town she does not light on in thirty years, it being Miss Jo Eva's idea to catch herself a husband.

Well, of course, it is a tough break for Nosey, because Miss Jo Eva is homelier than a mud fence, and with a terrible disposition, but somehow poor old Nosey does not have the strength to resist her, what with being one-legged, and none too lively to begin with.

So it begins to look as if Miss Jo Eva will become Mrs. Nosey as sure as you are a foot high, especially when she takes to making old Nosey keep out of saloons, and change his collar more than somewhat, to say nothing of having himself shaved several times a week.

Furthermore, Miss Jo Eva hangs out in the office of the *Weekly Bee* more than is good for circulation, and she makes Nosey have the windows washed, and keep his desk tidied up, all of which is naturally very much against nature with Nosey.

But in general Nosey seems resigned to his fate, because he is not experienced enough to get away from such a crafty dame as Miss Jo Eva, when what happens but Miss Jo Eva commences to get romantic. Up to this time, her idea of marrying Nosey is strictly a business proposition with her, but Nosey is so easy that Miss Jo Eva gets to thinking maybe she ought to have a little romance in it, like other people before they get married.

So she gets to mooning to Nosey, and getting very soft, and by and by she tries to make Nosey act like a regular knight, or some such. But of course Nosey is no knight, except a Knight Templar, and there is no more romance in his system than there is in a crab apple.

But Miss Jo Eva keeps at him, trying to make him romantic, and poetic, and what not, like the guys in the novels who are in love, and one day they are out walking down by the Arkansaw River, watching the spring rise, which carries away all the bridges, as usual, and a few spare houses here and there.

Now during the spring rise, if the bridges go out down the river, the side Nosey and Miss Jo Eva happen to be on is cut off for a few days from the railroad depot on the other side, and this is the case the day Nosey and Miss Jo Eva stroll down to the river.

They are watching the old Arkansaw, with the spare houses from ranches up the river, and logs, and chicken coops, and dog kennels, and one thing and another floating past, when Miss Jo Eva lays her head on Nosey's shoulder, and says to Nosey like this:

"Gerald," she says, Gerald being Nosey's regular name, "Gerald," she says, "suppose I ask you to swim this raging torrent to prove your love for me, would you do it?"

"Would I?" Nosey says. "Well, just watch me!"

Before you can say Jack Robinson, he offs with his coat and hops into the river, and the next anybody sees of him he is crawling out on the opposite bank, half a mile below, near the railroad yards.

Well, Miss Jo Eva faints dead away when she sees

Nosey in the river, and so she does not see him when he comes out and hops on a freight train which is just pulling out of the yards, wet as he is, and everything.

Furthermore, Miss Jo Eva never sees Nosey again, and nobody else in my old home town does either, and this is the reason why the *Weekly Bee* is now edited by Miss Jo Eva Gildersleeve, and why it prints many boiler-plate stories of blighted love, and what not.

The Shooting of Dude McCoy

Nobody back in my old home town will ever forget the time my grandpap shoots Dude McCoy, and the great indignation which it causes Dude.

In fact, this is one of the most exciting things that ever comes off back in my old home town, and it is written up very big in *The Chieftain,* which is my home town paper.

This Dude McCoy is a ranchman down in the Arkansaw Valley, and he is called Dude because he always wears a white shirt and a white collar when he comes to town, but Dude is by no means stuck up, and is highly respected by one and all, especially as he is considered a bad guy to monkey with.

He carries a six-pistol in his pocket at all times, and when he is drinking it is a good idea to give Dude plenty of room, because sometimes he does not realize who he is shooting at.

As a general proposition he means no harm to no-body, but liquor seems to have a peculiar effect on his eyesight. So when Dude comes to town and starts drink-ing, traffic never gets clogged up in front of him.

Well, if there is anybody my grandpap has no use for it is this same Dude McCoy, but of course my grandpap is no chump, and he does not mention anything about his feelings to Dude when Dude is drinking.

But Dude knows pretty well what my grandpap thinks, because this business between them goes back to years and years ago when they are young squirts, and he is always trying to pick a quarrel with my grandpap. Well, of course, my grandpap tries to avoid such a thing, because he is a peace-loving man, but one day Dude sends word ahead of him that he is coming into town to knock my grandpap off, which is Dude's way of saying he will kill him.

Naturally this proposition worries my grandpap more than somewhat, as he is not the man he used to be, so he gets out a Winchester 30-30, loads her up, and goes down town to the First Chance Saloon, which is on the street that Dude generally hits first when he lands in town.

My grandpap's idea is to see Dude and argue things out with him peacefully, and he takes the 30-30 along more for company than anything else, as he is used to having a rifle around.

Well, when he gets to the First Chance Saloon, my grandpap stands the 30-30 up in a corner near the window, and he does not notice that right in that same corner is a little .22-caliber rifle, one of these little popguns which belongs to Joey Curtis, whose old man runs the First Chance Saloon. Joey is only about ten years old, and it seems he uses this .22-caliber thing to shoot rabbits, and so forth, with.

Well, Grandpap is standing up against the bar talking to old man Curtis, and he loses track of the time, when all of a sudden he hears a yell out in the street, and he knows Dude McCoy is coming.

So my grandpap hurries to the corner where he leaves his 30-30, grabs up the rifle, pokes the nozzle out the front door and turns it loose on Dude McCoy, who is outside on a horse yelling like blue blazes.

For all my grandpap not being the man he used to be, he pops Dude slap-dab in the gizzard the first shot, and

Dude falls off his horse, much surprised. Then my grand-pap comes on home, walking not too fast, and not too slow, and waits to have the coroner subpoena him for the inquest.

Well, the next thing we hear, Dude McCoy is in the hospital, by no means dead. In fact he is not close to dead, but he is very indignant, and what he is indignant about is my grandpap shooting him with a .22-caliber rifle.

It seems that Grandpap grabs the wrong gun and shoots Dude with Joey Curtis' popgun, and naturally Dude is very sore. He says he does not mind Grandpap shooting him, but he cannot see why he insults him by using a pea-shooter, instead of a man's gun.

Well, of course, my grandpap is much ashamed, and the upshot of it all is he walks right over to the hospital and apologizes to Dude for such actions. He promises Dude if he ever takes another shot at him it will be with a decent gun, but then they get to talking over old times, and finally fall on each other's necks.

The next thing we hear of them they are out and around with Joey Curtis' popgun, for which they trade him the 30-30 and what they are doing with it is to take turns shooting at other citizens, so it all comes out all right after all.

The Strange Story of Tough-Guy
Sammy Smith

My old home town out West may not be so much to look at, what with the smelters smoking it up some, and our citizens not being so very careful about what they throw in the streets, but it is a pretty first-rate town at that.

In fact, if anybody thinks it is not a good town, they had better keep it to themselves until they get out of the city limits, because our citizens are quite touchy, indeed, on this particular subject.

The people of my old home town are the finest people that the Lord ever lets live, which nobody can deny, not even my grandpap, who is not very much of a booster either when it comes to talking about people.

Maybe you read some of the stories my grandpap tells me about people, and also about himself, but this story has nothing to do with him. This story is about Sammy Smith, the toughest guy in my old home town, bar nobody.

Sammy Smith is the only son of the Widow Smith, and he grows up on the same block I do on Cottonwood Street. In fact, Sammy Smith and I run together more than somewhat, but when he starts getting tough I split out with him, because the way I look at it, being tough only breeds scabs on a guy's nose.

Sammy Smith's mother is a little old blind woman, no bigger than a minute, and I can see her now, leaning over the gate in front of their house, with a black shawl over her head, and I can hear her calling Sammy Smith. She always calls him in a funny kind of way, her voice high and singsongy, like this: "Hi, Sammy, and a ho, Sammy, and a hey, Sammy."

It sounds like music to hear the Widow Smith calling Sammy Smith, and Sammy Smith never fails to drop whatever he is doing, which is more apt to be some hellishness than not, and hurry to her. As near as I can figure, Sammy Smith loves his little old blind mother pretty much, and nobody blames him.

Well, as I am telling you, Sammy Smith grows up good and tough, what with hanging around saloons, and one thing and another, and everybody in my old home town is pretty much against him. He is always quarreling and fighting and some people do not put it past him to be doing even worse.

But always along toward evening Sammy Smith manages to get himself home somehow, for that is the time his little old blind mother comes to the gate and starts calling him the same as she does when he is a little boy, "Hi, Sammy, and a ho, Sammy, and a hey, Sammy."

Sometimes it is pretty tough going for Sammy Smith what with being full of liquor, but he always gets there, and no matter how bad off he is his little old blind mother is glad to feel his arms around her.

Well, everybody in my old home town feels sorry for the Widow Smith, and they put Sammy Smith's orneriness down to his old man, who dies when Sammy Smith is quite young of general cussedness. Everybody in my old home town tries to be nice to Sammy Smith and excuse him for his goings-on, but one day when he is about twenty years old he hauls off and kills Joe Follansbee over nothing at all, and everybody figures Sammy finally goes too far.

The killing comes off about noon and Sammy Smith makes his getaway out of town. He has two six-shooters on him, and everybody knows he will certainly endeavor to knock everybody off who fools with him, so he is not pursued so very much.

This Joe Follansbee is not a bad guy, and there is much indignation over his killing, especially in his own family, and Joe's old man and several brothers take to hunting for Sammy Smith.

One of these brothers, a fellow by the name of Bob, goes to school with Sammy Smith, and he knows all about Sammy Smith's little old blind mother, and what Sammy thinks of her.

So along toward evening, this Bob gets behind a tree in Cottonwood Street with a Winchester rifle in his hand, not far from Sammy Smith's house, and waits. Pretty soon the Widow Smith comes out of the house with a shawl over her head and goes down to the gate and begins calling: "Hi, Sammy, and a ho, Sammy, and a hey, Sammy."

Her voice is still echoing along the street when out of the shadows comes Sammy Smith, the guy everybody is looking for. There he comes hurrying to meet his mother, and back of the tree Bob Follansbee takes dead aim at him down the sights of the Winchester.

Well, sir, this Bob Follansbee is naturally pretty sore at Sammy Smith, and maybe he is justified if he pulls the trigger, but somehow he is not able to do it. No, sir, he does not shoot Sammy Smith at all, but leaves Sammy there with his arms around his little old blind mother, and comes back down town.

And this is all the story, except that Sammy Smith clears out, and takes his little old blind mother with him, and the committee which organizes to hang Bob Follansbee if he shoots Sammy Smith under such circumstances breaks up without Bob ever knowing anything about it.

At Dead Mule Crossing

"Things certainly look mighty bad for us this night," my grandpap is saying. "There we are, fifteen of us men with the women and children, behind the wagons and four thousand Injuns pressing in from all sides."

"What in time are you talking about, anyway?" my grandmaw says, as she comes into the room just as my grandpap makes this crack.

Well, my grandpap seems no little confused for a minute, but he says to my grandmaw like this:

"I am telling my grandson about the fight we have at Dead Mule Crossing with the Comanches back in the early days," he says.

"How many Injuns do you say are there?" my grandmaw says, looking at my grandpap over her specs.

"Well," my grandpap says, "I say there are four hundred," although, of course, what he really says is four thousand.

"Tell him the truth," my grandmaw says. "There are just four Injuns, and tell him what happens to these four Injuns."

"It is a very historical fight," my grandpap says, "anybody knows this."

"Historical fiddlesticks," my grandmaw says, "I will tell our grandson just what happens myself. I do not mind your lying to tourists, and the like, but do not corrupt the mind of our youth with misstatements of fact."

Then my grandmaw draws up a chair and sits down and says to me like this:

"Bub," she says, "it happens away back when we are coming from St. Joseph, Mo., in wagons, with the women doing all the work, as usual, and a passel of good-for-nothing men like your grandpap walking ahead and behind to keep a lookout for danger, and half scared to death they will find it.

"We come to Dead Mule Crossing on the Arkansaw one evening and make camp for the night. They are maybe a dozen wagons, and ten or fifteen men and twenty-five women and children, more or less, including the Wintergreen family from Fulton, Mo.

"Mis' Wintergreen has a young baby, Ella May, and Ella May is teething, and raising Ned all the trip. Mis' Wintergreen sits up with Ella May most of the way from St. Joseph, and any time Ella May dozes off it is a great blessing to poor Mis' Wintergreen.

"Well, along toward midnight there is a terrible whooping and hollering around the camp, and your grandpap, who is a very brave man, comes climbing into our wagon with his gun and says: " 'My goodness, maw, we are surrounded by Injuns! There are thousands of them outside, and we are gone goslings!'

"From the noise they are making I can tell there are not thousands, although it sounds as if there may be twenty or thirty, because one Injun is like one frog. He can make plenty of racket.

"All the other men are running every which way trying to find some place to hide, and maybe fight after they get hid good, when I hear Mis' Wintergreen's voice saying: 'Please stop the noise, it will wake up Ella May. I just get her to sleep, and I wish to catch a few winks myself.'

"Then somebody tells Mis' Wintergreen it is the Injuns making all the racket, so all of a sudden I see her run to a campfire where there is a big kettle of water which she is heating in case Ella May wakes up and needs medicine or what not.

"The next thing I see, Mis' Wintergreen has the kettle by the handle and is headed for the direction of the noises, and by and by we hear Injuns squalling louder than they are whooping a few minutes before. In two shakes of a lamb's tail these Injuns are tearing up the underbrush getting away, and Mis' Wintergreen is back looking to see if Ella May is awake.

"What she does to these Injuns is give them a good scalding," my grandmaw says. "I can show you one of them to this day. He is old Chief Tomato who sells hot tamales, and he has no more hair on his head than a bald eagle. Old Tomato tells me many times there are only four in the bunch, and they are just looking to steal a horse or mule when out hops a crazy woman throwing liquid fire around.

"This is the story of the terrible fight at Dead Mule Crossing which your grandpap tells about," my grandmaw says.

"It is a very historic battle," my grandpap insists.

"Ella May Wintergreen grows up and marries this Dods Campbell," my grandmaw says, paying no attention to my grandpap. "Come to think of it now, she will be a lot better off if the Injuns get her this night at Dead Mule Crossing.

"Furthermore," she says, looking at my grandpap, "maybe some of the rest of us poor women will be better off if the same thing happens to us."

The Old Men of the Mountain

Many a strange thing happens back in my old home town out West, but nothing stranger ever happens than the time old Zeb Griscom suddenly hauls off and drops out of sight, leaving his wife, Mrs. Griscom, mourning for him more than somewhat.

My grandmaw says that as far as she can see Mrs. Griscom gets a pretty good break one way and another, because old Zeb Griscom is not much husband. In fact, Old Zeb is a good deal of an old sot, going around getting his pots on very often, and only going home when there is no other place to go.

My grandpap says he does not blame old Zeb for this, because the best he gets when he does go home is plenty of cold shoulder and tongue, what with Mrs. Griscom being no rose geranium when it comes to temper, which is a crack that starts some little talking back and forth between my grandmaw and my grandpap.

But no matter what he is, old Zeb is too prominent as a pioneer to be allowed to haul off and disappear without somebody asking questions, especially as Mrs. Griscom is going down to see the authorities every day, and threatening to give them a good stirring up if they do not do something or other about it.

Finally, when it begins to look as if old Zeb is gone sure enough and it does not look as if he is coming back, the authorities get to snooping around on this proposition, and it comes out that the last seen of Zeb he is traveling on foot off in the direction of the Greenhorn Mountains with a pack of what seems to be supplies on his back.

The man who mentions this to the authorities is a

party by the name of Diggers, who keeps sheep, and is therefore very unreliable, so nobody pays any attention to him for a couple of weeks.

Then as old Zeb is still missing, and cannot be located any place, somebody decides that maybe the sheep party is partly telling the truth. In fact it commences to be the opinion back in my old home town that maybe something happens to old Zeb, because it does not stand to reason that a man rising sixty years old, will suddenly disappear from the earth leaving no word, even if he is married to Mrs. Griscom.

So three of old Zeb's best friends decide to go off toward the Greenhorn Mountains to see if they can find a clue of Zeb. These friends are old Joe Calkins, the horse trader, Mr. Hathaway, the banker and Weed McCullough, the dry-goods man. They are all pioneers of my old home town and highly respected by one and all.

I remember my grandpap saying at the time that he does not see how Joe Calkins ever gets his wife, Mrs. Calkins, to let him go on the search, and my Aunt Margaret says it is a sure thing that Mr. Hathaway chloroforms Mrs. Hathaway before she lets him out of her sight, because it is pretty well known in my old home town who wears the pants in these families.

It comes out after they leave that Weed McCullough never asks his wife, Mrs. McCullough, if he can go, and there is plenty of talk about what will happen to him when he comes back, because Mrs. McCullough is one of those women.

Well, sir, what happens but the searching party does not come back. When it is gone a week, with no word from anybody, there is plenty of excitement back in my old home town. Somebody figures that there must be a band of outlaws, or maybe Indians, out there toward the Greenhorn Mountains grabbing up these citizens and robbing and murdering them, and one thing and another.

So finally my grandpap goes around town and gets up

a posse of seven men, all of them old-time Indian fighters, and they get themselves a team and wagon which they load up with plenty of supplies, including food, although my grandmaw afterwards says she notices they do not forget to take more or less liquor with them.

In fact my grandmaw says it is more than less, and there is plenty of talk back and forth between her and my grandpap asking her if she has the heart to talk to him like that when his dear old comrades may be perishing out there in the hills, and my grandmaw saying yes she has.

But my grandmaw says she guesses she can spare him all right if old Pete Dillaway's wife, Mrs. Dillaway, can let Pete go; old Pete being one of my grandpap's posse, and a very much henpecked man. It comes out afterwards that as soon as the posse gets out of the city limits, old Pete lets out a big whoop, and when somebody asks him why he does this he explains it is because it is the first time in twenty-five years he dares raise his voice above a whisper.

Well, it is quite a sight to see this posse of old gentlemen loaded in the wagon and carrying rifles, and six-pistols, and one thing and another, driving to the rescue of their old comrades. My grandpap is in the front seat wearing the old coonskin cap he wears when he first comes up the Arkansaw Valley with Kit Carson, and Marshal Pat Dillon has a skinning knife in his belt with which he says he expects to scalp any hostile Indians they come across, and he hopes they will be Kiowas, these being the Indians he especially hates, because they run him knock-kneed back in the early days.

The last word of the rescue party comes from this same man Diggers who keeps the sheep, and he says when they pass his place they seem to be quite jolly, and that a man in a coonskin cap takes an off hand crack at him with a Winchester rifle from about two hundred yards off, but misses him quite some.

My grandmaw says when she hears this news that it confirms her suspicion about the liquor, because it does not stand to reason, she says, that my grandpap will miss a sheepman at two hundred yards if he is perfectly O.K., although my grandmaw admits when somebody calls her attention to the matter that my grandpap is not as young as he used to be.

Well, sir, a week goes by and no word comes from the rescue party, although they promise to let people know how they are getting along. Another week goes by, and there is talk of asking the governor to call out the state militia. Every morning you can see Mrs. Griscom, Mrs. McCullough and all the other wives of the missing, except my grandmaw, down in front of the mayor's office demanding that Mayor Joe Heintzman do something or other.

My grandmaw does not go visiting the mayor, because she says in the first place Joe Heintzman is an old fool and has been such for many years. In the second place she says she will go find those old scalawags herself if they do not show up pretty soon, and when she does find them they better make themselves mighty scarce, especially my grandpap.

My grandmaw will not believe anything very terrible happens to any of the lot, although everybody but her in my old home town is in pretty much of a sweat. Finally she commences to worry a little herself, because, say what you please, my grandmaw rather likes my grandpap.

Old Jake Warburton, one of grandpap's best friends, starts in organizing a new posse to go in search of the missing, and somebody notices that he is picking only old pioneers, and asking none of the young squirts of the town to go along, which old Jake explains by saying that this looks like a big fighting job, and he wants experienced fighting men.

When my grandmaw hears of old Jake's posse she says, "Uh-huh," like that, and the next thing anybody knows she makes me hitch up old Silver, our gray horse, and away she goes off toward the Greenhorn Mountains in our light buggy, all alone and looking very determined.

It is a good day's drive to the mountains in those days but my grandmaw knows the roads and the country well. Furthermore, she has many friends on the ranches out that way, and nobody will worry about her whatever, if it is not for what happens to the different missing parties.

Three days later my grandmaw comes driving back again, and who is with her but my grandpap looking none too brash. Furthermore, not far behind them comes all the parites who are missing, even old Zeb Griscom with a new set of whiskers, and looking very wild. In fact all of them look wild, and they look still wilder after my grandmaw tells their wives a thing or two.

It seems that what happens is as follows:

Old Zeb Griscom gets sick and tired listening to Mrs. Griscom after many years, and so he tells a few of his old friends that he is going out into the Greenhorn Mountains to live in a cave and have a good time the rest of his life.

Of course many wish to go with him, but Zeb shows them how it will look too suspicious if they all start off at once. So they figure out they can go searching for each other in bunches until they are all together in the cave, and living happy.

The scheme works out great until my grandmaw gets to worrying about my grandpap, which of course is something they do not figure possible. And it seems my grandmaw knows enough about Indian fighting to know that Indian fighters do not need as much liquor to do their fighting on as my grandpap and his searching party takes with them, and she judges that some dirty work is going on somewhere.

She is pretty sure of it when Jake Warburton starts picking out only old guys, and while she does not wish to spoil anybody's fun she decides that it goes far enough. So she starts searching herself, and the first thing she does when she hits the mountains is to find herself a Mexican who lives in those parts, and who naturally knows what is going on.

This Mexican leads my grandmaw to the cave, and she busts right into as jolly a party as anybody will wish to find with Mr. Hathaway, the banker, doing some cooking over a big fire, and my grandpap dealing out drinks, and everybody laying around looking very happy indeed, until they see my grandmaw.

Well, that is all there is to the great disappearance, except that old Jake Warburton is missing for several days after the lost ones return and it comes out that he is in the Greenhorn Mountains looking for the Mexican who guides my grandmaw. It seems that old Jake is so sore over losing out on the party that he wishes to cut the Mexican's ears off and keep them for souvenirs, but the Mexican outruns him through the Hardscrabble Canyon, and old Jake comes back to town to spend the rest of his life listening to the stories of the others about the good time they have, and feeling sore at the Mexican.

Marriage Counsel

Our old man said one time a charming young lady by the name of Miss Abagail Zuz came to him for advice on the subject of marriage. She was being courted by a young man named Clukey and also by Obadiah Envelope, a sod widower of several years' standing and twice her age. Our old man said she asked him which one he thought she should marry and that he advised her to take Obey.

He said he told her that he did not entirely agree with Benjamin Franklin's advice to young men to marry widows, but that he did think it was an excellent idea for young women to marry widowers. He said he explained to her that it had been his observation that second wives had all the best of it because their husbands tried to do for them all the things they had neglected to do for their first wives.

Our old man said he told her that a girl who caught a fellow who had been bereft of his helpmate after ten to twenty years of married life became the beneficiary of conscience payments by the husband to the memory of the first wife, although our old man said the husband was not always really to blame for inattention to the first wife. He said as a rule a first marriage comes in youth and a fellow is out hustling around to make a living and is too busy to remember the little amenities of matrimony, such as taking the wife places and buying her things.

He said that after a lapse of years marriage became a routine with the husband, and he did not notice how hard the wife worked at home or how tired she looked and in fact gave her presence scant consideration until one day she up and died, and then he got to remembering her only too well. Our old man said then the husband began thinking of the things he could have done and perhaps meant to do for her and was downright conscience-stricken, so when he got married a second time he was generally always on his toes trying to make up to the second wife for his derelictions in the case of the first. He said he told Miss Zuz that he had known Obadiah Envelope long enough to feel that he was that type and that she would be missing a right good thing if she failed to nail him.

So Miss Zuz became Mrs. Obadiah, but our old man said she was around in two weeks complaining that the advice given her was all wrong, especially with reference to Obadiah taking her places and buying her things. She said Obadiah was about as loose as the post office foundations with his money and that he was not conscience stricken enough to keep her from doing all the housework. Our old man said the former Miss Zuz was right put out and wanted to know what he advised now.

He said he suddenly remembered that Obadiah inclined a bit toward spiritualism, so he told Mrs. Obadiah to leave everything to him. Our old man said then one night he dropped in at the home of Mr. and Mrs. Obadiah and that he took with him a friend of his by the name of Mrs. Toober, who gave séances with a table and after a little social chat he got her to call up a few spirits and one of them was the spirit of the first Mrs. Obadiah.

Our old man said Mrs. Toober said this spirit wanted to talk with Obadiah, and what the spirit talked about was how it suffered thinking of the way Obadiah had neglected it in life and how it hoped he was showing the second Mrs. Obadiah every possible kindness and spending plenty of money on her. Our old man said he never heard a more convincing spirit than this one, although Mrs. Toober did all the talking for it, and Obadiah cried as if his heart would break and he promised the spirit he would do just as requested if it cost him the fifty thousand dollars he had saved up and for several months the second Mrs. Obadiah had a wonderful time.

Our old man said it would have gone on indefinitely, but one day Mrs. Toober told one of the neighbors that he had directed her what to say at the séance and the neighbor told Obadiah and Obadiah shut down on his generosity to his second wife until she was no better off than the first one was. Our old man said Obadiah wanted to fight him for interfering with his married life and the second Mrs. Obadiah hated him for advising her to marry Obadiah and on top of that Mrs. Toober persecuted him for years claiming he had promised her five dollars for the séance.

Our old man said it was remarkable the way his well-meant advice was always getting him into trouble.

On Good Turns

My old man used to have a motto that he had printed out himself in big letters pasted on the wall of his bedroom. It read: *Never Blame the Booster for What the Sucker Does.* It was one of his favorite sayings, too.

He said it meant that you should never hold a fellow responsible for the consequences of an effort to do you a nice turn. He said many of his own troubles in life had come from getting the blame from friends he was only trying to help, like the time he took the stranger to a poker room back in our old home town of Pueblo.

The poker room was run by one of my old man's closest pals, a fellow they called Poker Joe. The stranger got to talking to my old man down at the Union Depot and wanted to know if there was a poker room in town. He said that he was not much of a poker player, but he wanted to kill a few hours between trains.

My old man told the stranger he would be glad to take him to one of the nicest poker rooms he ever saw in his life. He personally vouched for the honesty and integrity of Poker Joe's. So he took the stranger there, and when the stranger pulled out a roll of money that would have choked four horses, Poker Joe was so grateful to my old man that he wanted to kiss him. It was not often that a stranger with a big roll came Poker Joe's way.

Well, the stranger won all the money in the house in such a short time that he still had to wait an hour at the depot, and Poker Joe hit my old man in the eye with his fist. He blamed my old man for bringing the stranger in, and that was when my old man went back to the *Chieftain* office and printed his motto.

Another time, my old man met a woman who was looking for a boarding house. He knew a fine place kept by a fellow and his wife who were great friends of his. My old man was anxious to see these friends do well.

He took the woman to the boarding house, and she proved such a good client that the fellow and his wife never seemed to get tired of thanking my old man for doing them the favor of bringing her there. Then one day the boarder ran off with the husband, and the wife went to the *Chieftain* office where my old man was busy setting type and gave him an awful bawling out.

She called him names nobody suspected she ever knew. She put all the blame on him for her husband skipping out, just because my old man had taken the woman to the boarding house. He sent the wife a copy of his motto: *Never Blame the Booster for What the Sucker Does.*

My old man said one of the worst enemies he had back in our old home town was a chap named Sam, to whom he introduced a girl Sam eventually married. My old man had often mentioned to Sam what a nice girl this girl was, and finally Sam insisted on meeting her. He even thanked my old man warmly for arranging the introduction, but, of course that was before they were married.

My old man said every time he met Sam after the marriage Sam would recall that my old man had told him she was a nice girl. He seemed to feel but for his recommendation he would never have married her. My old man said personally he continued to think she was a nice girl, but he was not so sure of Sam's niceness, only he never mentioned that thought out loud, as Sam was a touchy fellow.

However, he sent Sam a copy of his motto.

My old man said he guessed he had sent nearly everybody in town a copy of his motto. He said he never failed to send one to merchants to whom he introduced customers and who blamed him if the customers failed to meet their bills.

He said one time he sent out several thousand in the course of a single week on postal cards. That was the time a candidate for public office got him to go around town plugging his candidacy. My old man told the voters that this candidate was a wonderful man for the job, and apparently most people agreed with him, as the candidate was elected by a considerable majority.

He immediately became one of the worst officeholders our old home town had ever known, and then a lot of people began remembering my old man's work on behalf of the fellow, and started blaming him. So he just sat down and sent those postal cards to everybody he figured must have voted for the officeholder.

My old man once bought a hundred dollars' worth of gold mining stock from a friend of his named Chris, who said the stock was as good as wheat in the bin. Chris left town, and my old man learned that the stock was phony and was going to have Chris arrested.

Chris must have heard of the threat, and he sent my old man a letter that kept him at liberty, because all he put in the letter was my old man's motto: *Never Blame the Booster for What the Sucker Does.*

The Good Sport

My old man had great admiration and respect for women. Maybe that is where I get mine. He always contended that women are better sports than men in any situation.

"Even love?" someone might ask.

"Even love," my old man would say and then he would tell a story about a woman named Hattie who ran what was known in those days as a roadhouse outside Oldtown in Colorado. A roadhouse was a place where people went to drink and dance. We still have roadhouses under other titles.

Hattie's house was not considered a very nice place. In fact, the public prints in speaking of it generally referred to it as notorious and they spoke of Hattie the same way when occasion required that they speak of her at all.

Oldtown was also known as Colorado City. It is near Colorado Springs, the famous resort city in the shadow of Pike's Peak. Colorado City was the first capital of Colorado, if memory serves. We understand it is now part of Colorado Springs.

However, in the days of Hattie and her roadhouse, Oldtown was a separate municipality and gambling houses and saloons ran wide open there. Colorado Springs was supposed to be dry and the only places you could buy liquor were the drug stores where they sold whiskey that tasted like something a doctor prescribes for malaria. If a fellow wanted to really cut up, he had to go to Oldtown.

Well, this Hattie my old man used to tell about was a handsome woman of mature years, maybe forty, and had flashing, slashing black eyes and blue black hair and a swell figure. She fell in love with a young gambler named Dan something who was about ten years her junior and a tall, good-looking fellow, but rather shiftless. He may have reciprocated Hattie's love, though my old man was not sure about that.

Hattie was making a lot of money with her roadhouse and she bestowed plenty of it on Dan, giving him expensive presents like a fast buggy horse and a big diamond ring and a diamond stud for his shirt bosom and finally bank-rolling him in a gambling house of his own that was a success from the start.

Dan had a good business head, because he was soon investing in side lines of a sounder nature than gambling and finally one of these ventures took him east to New York City. Hattie's interest kept her in Oldtown and my old man says she seemed to mourn Dan's absence greatly, especially as Dan was no hand for writing letters.

Well, Dan discovered Wall Street on his trip east and presently he was setting himself up in business there and going great, and in fact if it would not be getting ahead of our story we would tell you that his name and fame eventually became nationwide—for this is a true yarn. But before that he met a young girl of highly respectable family and fell in love with her.

He was away from Oldtown a couple of years and one day he turned up back there to settle some business affairs in connection with his gambling enterprise and he was in town a couple of days before he went to see Hattie. She knew of his arrival but never said a word to anyone about it and my old man says there was speculation as to how she would receive Dan because everybody knew Hattie had a hot temper.

One evening Dan dropped in at the roadhouse and went into a private room and sent for Hattie. She came in quietly and greeted him with a handshake and said she was glad to see him. Dan, a little shamefaced, said: "Let's have a bottle of wine, Hattie, like old times."

So she rang for a waiter and they had a bottle of wine and sat there talking about how well each thought the other was looking and saying how are things, and all that with Dan wondering how he was going to explain certain matters. Finally Hattie said: "Well, Dan, I'm going to save you any embarrassment by telling you I know all about you—how well you've done, and the girl back East and your wanting to marry her, and everything else. You need not apologize to me because I understand thoroughly. All I can say is good luck to you always. We have had great times together and it's been swell knowing you and there are no hard feelings on my side."

Dan murmured something about the money she had invested in him and Hattie said: "It was my pleasure, and it's all wiped off the slate. Never mind about it."

Dan got up to go and said: "Thanks, Hattie. I always thought you were one of the finest women in the world and now I know it. Good-bye, Hattie, and God bless you."

"Much obliged, Dan, and the same to you," Hattie replied, then as he got to the door, she added: "By the way, Dan, don't forget you owe me for that bottle of wine."

* * *

My old man always contended that men were ten times greater gossips and tattletales than women. He said one big reason for this was that the men had more opportunities for gossiping than the women.

He said that the average married woman had to put in most of her time at home attending to her household duties and her children. She ordinarily had few social callers in the course of a working day and therefore no one to gossip with. That was before there was a telephone within anybody's reach, of course.

He said that while it was true a good many single women were on the loose, the majority of them also usually worked most of the day in the house or in offices and stores, where they did not get much chance to do any considerable gossiping.

On the other hand, my old man said, look at the clubs and saloons where men were to be found gabbing at all hours of the day. He said he had noticed that a raft of the busiest of business and professional men always seemed to be able to find time to spend in chewing the rag in clubs and saloons, or over a luncheon table, and generally much of their conversation took the form of gossip about their fellow citizens.

He said he would bet he could go through any business building right there in our old home town of Pueblo in the middle of a business day and discover any number of men with their feet up on their desks in their private offices swapping gossip with some chance caller. He said few women with the cares of a household on their shoulders could knock off work in the middle of the day and sit down to a prolonged gabfest but he had noticed that many supposedly very busy men could always find leisure for a little gossip.

My old man said that for every pair of women you could find standing gabbing on street corners, he could show you twenty pairs of men doing the same thing. He said the ratio was about the same for hotel lobbies and the corridors of the post office and courthouse and city hall.

When it came to sitting on steps, my old man said it ran a hundred men to no women. He said he could not recall ever seeing a woman sitting on steps except perhaps in her own yard, while he could take you out almost any pleasant day and show you steps of public buildings fairly festooned with men gossiping like mad.

He said he never recalled seeing any women standing watching men at work, either, though that was a popular pastime with many men. He said they liked to accompany their watching with a little offhand gossiping, perhaps about the fellow who was having the work done. He said some of the watchers could generally recall something to the fellow's discredit.

My old man said he had come to the conclusion that men were gabbier by nature than women, though through persistent propaganda across the years the men had pretty well established the women as the gabby and gossipy ones. He said since time began it had been a favorite trick of the men to make themselves out superior to women in every way. He said it always made him snicker when some fellow, that he knew had a tongue loose at both ends, spoke of women as gossipy.

He said as a matter of fact, nearly all gossip started with the men who picked it up downtown and carried it home to their wives and other members of their families who otherwise would never have heard it. He said just let every man who is honest with himself just sit down and figure how much gossip he had heard from his wife as compared to what he had taken home, and he would see the difference right away.

My old man said to tell the truth, he enjoyed a little

gossiping himself now and then. He said he had never found himself in a gathering in a club or saloon or Pullman car or hotel lobby but what he soon heard his own tongue wagging gossipily with the best of them. He said he would hear his own voice telling rumors he had heard about someone, or dissecting characters or speculating on motives.

He said of course the best gossip was always that which presented the subject of gossip in an unenviable light. My old man said he had noticed that gossipers did not usually linger long on gossip that was favorable to the subject. He said in fact, he had found that among men gossips one got much more eager attention with gossip of a scandalous nature.

My old man said he had probably lost more sleep than any man alive through gossip. He said many a time he had been in gatherings that were gossiping about everybody they knew practically in alphabetical order. He said sometimes he would get pretty tired and sleepy and would have liked to have gone to bed but that long experience had taught him to stick around because he knew they would gossip about him as soon as he was out of earshot.

He said he always waited until only one man besides himself was left and then he would retire. He said, however, he had known men who were such inveterate gossips that even when they were the last man left they would go on gossiping to themselves.

As Between Friends

Abimilech Fetcher sat upon the front stoop of the Parkins County courthouse, smoking a fretful pipe and paying no heed to the snow-lined breezes that searched his meager apparel. He gazed with eyes of gloom upon the frame houses and store buildings, standing like serrated teeth; his gaze traveled moodily on to the vast expanse of flat country which aproned the small but enthusiastic town of Advance, and against the far horizon he could see the windmills, flogged by a relentless eastern Colorado wind, waving wildly. Abimilech Fetcher, Sheriff of the County of Parkins aforesaid, was a study of gloom, done in heavy corpulent lines.

A tall, thin ragged young man, with a self-confident air and a lean, alert face, suddenly sketched himself into the picture and stood looking at Abimilech Fetcher, who returned the gaze morosely.

"Well," said the young man finally, "I may be wrong, but if I was guessin' and had just one guess, it'd be that there sits Chicago Fat, lookin' as sad and forlorn as a millionaire in jail."

The dull eye of Abimilech Fetcher slowly brightened. "It's me," he said. "And you might be Kid Switch."

He arose and extended a cheerless fat hand. "Set down, Kid, set down, and tell me how come you to git shoved offen the main line."

"You tell me what you're doin' here," said Kid Switch. "I heard you'd quit hoboin' some years back and had settled down somewheres, but this can't be the where?"

"Yes," replied Abimilech drearily, "this is it. I'm the sheriff. Also I'm a married man, with two children and a mortgage on my house, and I'm starvin' to death right now, Kid."

Kid Switch laughed uproariously.

"That's it—laugh!" said Abimilech bitterly. "I've gotta notion to vag you. You're the first feller that even looks like a possible prisoner I've seen in a year. Whatta you doin' here, anyway, Kid?"

"On my way to San Francisco," said Switch. "I didn't know this was a branch line until I got here. I snared a freight train at the junction, havin' been chased offen a varnished rattler, and I didn't know I wasn't pursuin' the main haulage-way until I peeked out and saw this wide place in the road. And to think I've scairt you up—Chicago Fat—who usta be one of the grandest hoboes in the world!"

"It's me, Kid," said Abimilech. "And I thank you for them words. Sometimes I wisht I'd stuck to the road, but I got remorse and fat and et cetery and here I be, starvin' to death. I was a good hobo—I was a good hobo when you was just a gay cat, and I might be a good one yet, barrin' the fat."

"Tell me what's the trouble," urged Switch, as he contemplated the stout figure and suppressed further hilarity.

"It's the cussed fee system," said Abimilech. "The sheriff has to make his livin' offen fees. If he's on the main line, like ole Tobias over here in the next county, he can arrest enough of you hoboes in the winter time to make money. We git paid a dollar a day for feedin' prisoners and we kin feed 'em for ten cents a day, if we use judgment—that's ninety cents profit. If you've got enough prisoners you kin git fat. If you ain't got no prisoners, you starve, or go to work. I been sheriff two years, come next month, and I ain't seen enough mallyfacters to keep me in kerosene and other delicacies."

"If you had, say twelve prisoners for, say, ten days each, would that help you any?" asked Kid Switch.

"Help?" said Abimilech. "Help? Say, Kid, it'd set me in swell! I'd perk up and take a reg'lar interest in life. But what's the use o' talkin'? How kin I git twelve prisoners? How kin I git any prisoners, when folks don't violate the law, or if they do they're friends o' yourn and you dassen't stick 'em?"

"I met Cleveland George yesterday and he tells me a bunch of the fellers are layin' out the cold spell with your neighbor, Tobias," said Switch.

"He's a mean guy, is Tobias," interrupted Abimilech. "Bein' prosperous, he's natchally mean."

"Well, he's all right to the tourists," said Kid Switch. "And a dozen or more of them are hangin' up with him for a coupla weeks. They're nearly all ole time pals o'

yourn and mine and'd be glad to help you out if it was
put to 'em right. We'll call my end just half, if that's
satisfactory to you."

"Talk sense, Kid," urged the bewildered Abimilech.
"I don't git you. How'm I goin' to git them fellers? Tobias ain't goin' to lend me any. He's too blame stingy."

"Listen," said the Kid mysteriously. "But let's find
some place where it ain't so crimpy around the edges."

2

Sheriff John Tobias, of Queever County, had at least a
nodding acquaintance with all the gentry of the break-
beams who traveled from east to west a few years ago.
The county seat of Queever County is a division point
on a transcontinental railroad and during the year hundreds of nomadic individuals pass that way.

The Queever County jail is a rickety, but fairly com-
fortable structure and during bad weather it was the custom for the human birds of passage to lodge with Sheriff
John Tobias and thus insure him, in return for good
food and treatment, a prosperous business under the
fee system.

He had a sort of gentleman's agreement with the vet-
erans of the rail that they might plead guilty to a charge
of vagrancy before the only justice of the peace in the
town and ten days was the limit of their sentences. Nov-
ices, who were sensitive in the matter of being called
vagrants, but who desired shelter over a stretch of un-
travelable weather, could plead to a charge of carrying
concealed weapons—a razor being a weapon in those
parts, and Sheriff John Tobias was obliging to the extent
of furnishing the razor.

No one really had to remain in the Queever County
jail; it was of such a frail texture that even a sparrow
might have escaped without great difficulty. Half a dozen
tunnels beneath the floor, leading to sunshine and liberty,
told of the passing, in days gone by, of many an itinerant
from the hands of less obliging officers than Sheriff John
Tobias. In his regime, if a prisoner happened to be in a

hurry, Tobias would permit him to go before the expira-
tion of his term, via the front door, and would speed
him on his way with words of cheer.

Through the years of his long tenure of office this
arrangement endured, an indictment against the fee
system, perhaps, but a source of comfort to those who
traveled the western trails in that day. The town of
Queever understood the situation, but when the jail was
filled, plenty of supplies had to be purchased of the local
merchants, for Tobias was content with small profits
and treated his patrons liberally; the local merchants
consequently favored the full county jail, particularly as
the burden of taxation fell upon the balance of the
county, which probably, did not fully understand.

Sheriff John Tobias was viewing the snowstorm from
the window of the jail office with deep satisfaction; snow
meant that his jail population would rest contented
against the coming of warmer weather. The darkened
skies, pinned down all around the horizon, foretold a
long continued storm.

The office bell jangled shrilly and Sheriff Tobias
opened the door to look upon the damp figure of Kid
Switch, who had found a ten-mile tramp across the snow
a bit more of a hardship than he had figured on. Only
freight trains ran to Advance and they were few and far
between.

"Well! Well!" said Sheriff Tobias heartily. "Come
right in, Switch! I haven't seen you in over a year. Come
in, boy, you'll find a lot of friends present, if you're plan-
nin' to stay, and they'll be mighty glad to see you."

"I hope so," said the Kid. "Stake me to some dry
clothes, Sheriff; I'm as wet as a fish. I'm goin' to hang up
with you until it clears a little."

"Yes, sir!" said the Sheriff, with the unction of a hotel
clerk greeting a wealthy guest and leading the way to a
big steel door, from behind which came a subdued mur-
mur of voices. "You'll find Red, and Gordon, and Kline,
and Kilgallon, and the Philadelphia Shine and a lot of

friends inside, Kid. Cleveland George left here yesterday. It's a good winter for me, son."

Kid Switch was familiar with the personnel of Tobias' guests, having been enlightened by Cleveland George. He was prepared for the roar of greeting which arose when he stepped into the "bullpen" of the none too commodious jail. After having changed his wet clothing for capacious garments loaned by the sheriff, Switch took a careful inventory of those present and found that, besides nine whom he knew personally, there were three subdued-looking individuals. He diagnosed them as "natives."

"They're holdovers to the next term of the district court," explained Kilgallon contemptuously. "Plain yaps charged with stealin' cattle or somethin'. They ain't even got sense enough to git out o' this pokey and we use 'em to do the cleanin' up. I thought you was on your way to the Coast, Kid?"

"I was," replied Switch. "But I've stopped over to do a friend a turn. Bring all the fellers except them rubes around me and I'll let you in on the play."

"You all know the old Chicago Fat?" was his introductory remark as he squatted upon the floor and nine choice gentlemen who had carved their initials on every water tank between the coasts gathered about him. Most of them nodded, Kilgallon with emphasis.

"Ain't he the guy that got up the hoboes' convention?" he demanded. "Well, he done me dirt—"

"Never mind!" interrupted the Kid. "That's past and gone. He's in hard lines now."

With vivid eloquence he painted a verbal picture of Abimilech Fetcher, once Chicago Fat, starving at his own hearthside, as it were; he etched in pathetic touches here and there which caused the inky face of Philadelphia Shine to wrinkle lugubriously.

"Fat was a good guy," said Kid Switch. "He was always helpin' someone else and now he's in distress it seems to me we oughta remember the mole ties—ties of brotherhood and such, I mean—and go over there and give him a play for ten days so he can make his fees offen us. We can step out through one of the ole tunnels tonight and hike over there in no time."

"No, sah!" dissented the Shine. "Ah ain't makin' no premedjutated changes. Dis hive suits me an' Ah ain' movin' till mah rent comes due!"

"Shut up!" said Kid Switch savagely. "You'll go if the rest do."

"It ain't a bad idea," said Kline, a pallid young man who was known to the police between the two coasts as a hotel sneak thief, but who was, withal, romantic-looking and interesting. "We've been pretty good to ole Tobias. And after we stay at Fat's for a week or so, if the weather is still bad, we can come back here and finish out with Tobe."

Kilgallon, Jack Gordon, the Cincinnati Skin, Red, Henry Hennessey, One-Thumb Cafferty, George, the Greek and Heine Barr nodded grave approval.

"We'd better take them felons, too," said Gordon. "They'll help swell the count."

"Them's vallyble felons and Tobias thinks as much of them as he does of his right arm," demurred Hennessey. "Supposin' they'd beat it?"

"They've got a fat chance!" said Kid Switch. "We'll take 'em right along and return 'em to Tobe when we git through. Set 'em to work cleanin' out one of them tunnels now."

3

Abimilech Fetcher doubted that Kid Switch would be able to carry out this plan successfully; long continued adversity had made Abimilech pessimistic, but he waited, nevertheless, in the rarely occupied bastille of Parkins County and amused himself playing solitaire as the night wore on. His teeth chattered as occasional wisps of wind sneaked through the chinks in the building and he shook his head dolefully as he looked about the bare quarters the thrifty commonwealth had designed for criminal habitation.

As compared to the county jail of Queever County, the Parkins place of incarceration was a shanty against a country villa. Queever County had at least provided heat and electric lights. Parkins County simply purchased a tier of steel cells, set them down upon the ground and walled them in with loosely laid brick. Lanterns were the source of whatever illumination was required.

"I never seen a worse one myself," mused Abimilech. "And I've seen some bad ones. I never thought it looked so fierce before until it comes to offerin' it to my friends."

A shout aroused him from his shivering reverie and he opened the door to admit a terrific gust of wind and an assemblage of chilled and profane men.

"We're here," said Kid Switch, shaking a blanket of snow from his shoulders. "Maybe you think it ain't some job herdin' three felons through ten miles of snow, specially when they know the country and have a yen to go home. And that coon there—" He turned a baleful eye upon Philadelphia Shine who snuffled damply in a corner.

"He bus' me in the nose," whined the Shine dolorously.

Abimilech Fetcher was engaged in shaking hands with friends of another day. A pang of remorse bit at his vitals as he found himself surrounded by faces he had been more than glad to see in times gone by, and Kilgallon almost forgot the discomfort of that long march over the snow as he held a passage in rough repartee with Abimilech.

"I suttinly appreciates your kindness, fellers," said the Sheriff. "I suttinly do. Now if you'll step into them cells two in each, I'll bed you down for the night."

"Ah doan lak dis place," sniffled the Shine. "Ah reckon Ah'll go back to Mista Tobe's."

"Second the motion!" said One-Thumb Cafferty, who had been investigating the tiny cells.

At that moment the front door again opened and admitted two stalwart individuals whose coats bulged ominously and who wore gleaming stars upon their bosoms. Abimilech was relieved. He had become slightly alarmed over the tardiness of these efficient farm hands whom e had impressed as deputies that afternoon and whom had instructed to hasten to the jail upon the arrival any strangers. His manner changed. He looked as ern as it is possible for a fat man to look.

"Silence!" he roared. "Jail rules prohibit talkin'. Officers, put 'em in their cells!" he added, turning to the newcomers.

Kid Switch looked at Abimilech, startled.

"You ain't goin' to double-cross me?" he whispered.

"Ah-h-h," said Abimilech. "Of course not."

He personally escorted Switch into a small cell near the door and locked him up by himself.

"You're a swell actor, 'bo," he whispered. "They ain't on."

As the locks clicked behind the prisoners, Gordon shouted, "Turn on some heat, will you?"

"Heat!" bellowed Abimilech. "They ain't no heat! Lessee, you're Gordon, ain't you? I know a man what looks like you who would interest some people in Oskaloosa."

Gordon subsided immediately.

"Hey, you!" bawled Red Hennessey bitterly. "What about that church door welcome mat that got lost in Sacramento when you was there last?"

Abimilech went close to the door of the cell and hissed: "Statoot of limentations, Red: statoot of limentations. But maybe I kin dig up some place where the statoot ain't run agin Henry Hennessey."

Whereupon Red became strangely silent.

"If these guys git to chewin' the rag with you, just git some pails o' cold water and throw it in on them," instructed Abimilech to his deputies, as he took his departure.

Then the night wore on in cold silence, broken only

by the intermittent comment of the guards upon the weather and the prospective crops. The prisoners sat hunched up in their chilly cells whispering schemes of vengeance not only upon Abimilech Fetcher, but upon that incarnation of misguided philanthropy, Kid Switch, who slept the sleep of the just and innocent beneath a large country quilt which Abimilech had thoughtfully left in his cell.

Morning brought a succession of incidents, including some underdone beans and an apology for coffee. Abimilech also arrived accompanied by an aged bewhiskered individual who wore an air of vast solemnity and carried an enormous book.

Abimilech called him "Judge." A table was placed in the narrow corridor before the cells and Abimilech seated the tottering judge thereat with much ceremony. Then the judge opened his book, scanned the pages through gigantic horn spectacles and read: "John Doe, alias George Kilgallon."

"That's this wicked-lookin' murderer here," said Abimilech, indicating the peaceful Kilgallon. "Stand up, you Doe, alias Kilgallon! This is your trial!"

"Who'd I resist and who'd I assault?" roared Kilgallon.

The judge was evidently deaf, as Abimilech bawled in his ear: "He says he's guilty and that you're a——ole fool."

"Hey!" howled Kilgallon, in wild remonstrance.

"Six months!" piped the judge, making an entry in his book.

"Richard Roe, alias the Philadelphia Shine," he read next. "Assault with a deadly weapon and attempt to commit arson."

"Ah wants a mouthpiece! Ah wants a lie-er!" yelled the Shine in a great dismay.

"He says he's guilty," bellowed Abimilech into the whiskers of the Court.

"Ninety days," said the judge.

Hennessey got three months on a charge of stealing chickens; One-Thumb Cafferty got sixty days on a charge of disturbance; the three felons were given twenty days each for vagrancy and all the others received varying sentences on various charges without having the opportunity of saying a word. Some turmoil arose, as they endeavoured to voice their protests, but the deputies secured buckets of water and quelled the incipient disturbance by a dumb show of throwing it over the already half-frozen prisoners.

"Kid Switch," said the judge finally. "You are charged with carrying concealed weapons!"

"Not guilty!" shouted the Kid from the depths of his cell, where he was still buried beneath the quilt.

"This man's a dangerous character," yelled Abimilech. "You'd better get rid of him."

"Two hours to leave town," squeaked the old man and then the procession filed out, while the prisoners babbled wildly. Abimilech stopped long enough to unlock Kid Switch's cell.

"You don't want to let dark ketch you here," he warned.

"You don't want to let me ketch you anywhere!" howled Gordon from his cell, regardless of the deputies, and there was a hoarse growling from the other prisoners.

Outside the jail door, Abimilech handed Kid Switch a package of yellow bills. "That represents every cent I could borry," he said. "It means a second mortgage on my house and everything else. I didn't like to hand it to the gang so hard, but I can't let this good thing get away from me. It'll never happen again. I wouldn't want to be in your shoes when them parties gits out."

"Don't worry," said the Kid lightly. "I can square it with them."

"Square it!" said Abimilech. "What a chance! You better beat it out o' town now, before some of the citizens take a shot at you on general principles. Square it! What a nerve!"

"Good-bye," said Kid Switch blithely. "You won't hear from me for quite a while."

And then he set off, kicking the snow before him in

little flurries and Sheriff Abimilech Fetcher looked at the jail with a complacent grin.

"Here's where I either git rich or bankrupt the county," he said. "I may have give it to 'em a little strong, but a feller has got to snatch his opportunities nowadays. I suppose I will have to give 'em some heat."

4

When Sheriff John Tobias found his jail depopulated he did not immediately notify the citizens. He sat down to think the matter over. By creating tumult, the people might become cognizant of a laxity of vigilance around the bastille which would hardly redound to the credit of the sheriff. Besides, Tobias felt that the strange exodus was no common jail break.

Fresh snow had fallen during the night and the ground gave no clue. No train had passed through since the preceding day, owing to blockades, and it was quite cold. Tobias was satisfied that his guests would not have undertaken travel in such weather simply because of a sudden desire for freedom.

"Them boys wouldn't a-took my felons," he argued. "They wouldn't let no ornery cattle thieves go with them."

So the old sheriff sat quiet and pondered the matter throughout the day. The light of information broke upon him along in the evening and the people were aroused by the clamor of a huge bell in the tower of the court-house, used to apprise the public of trouble and festivity. The citizens hurried to the courthouse, carrying lanterns, guns and pitchforks, to find Sheriff John Tobias waiting on the steps of the building.

As soon as he could secure order, the sheriff made public an address.

"My friends," he said, "they's been a jail burglary. My prisoners, including felons what stole cattle on the Piedras, was stole out of my jail by Abimilech Fetcher, Sheriff of Parkins County, who now holds them without warrant o' law in his jail. He larcenied my prisoners,

bag and baggage, including them felons, well knowin'
the same to be then and there my pussonel property and
the goods and chattels o' Queever County. He figgers to
collect fees offen his ill-gotten gains from the County o'
Parkins, which never has no prisoners, because no prisoner would ever become such thereabouts if he had any
sense. Shell this town stand for such injestice, my friends?
I don't think it shell. Shell it allow my jail to be burglar-
ized and my prisoners stolen away to fatten the fee account o' Abimilech Fetcher? I don't think it shell."

The crowd yelled: "No, no!"

"Then, my friends," said Sheriff John Tobias, "I want
volunteers to go with me and rescue them poor prisoners
from the clutches of the rapscallion Fetcher."

Forty or fifty men stepped forward with alacrity.

"Come on!" shouted Tobias.

In twenty minutes a weird procession of horsemen,
light buggies and footmen was streaming across the snow
towards Advance, clamoring for the blood of Abimilech
Fetcher.

Arriving at the county seat of Parkins County and
finding the town asleep, the citizens of Queever lost no
time in assailing the jail. The prisoners, who had put in
a wretched day, were vastly alarmed, fearing that they
were to be the victims of mob violence, but when they
saw Sheriff Tobias leading a charge through the shat-
tered door, they set up a cheer of welcome. Abimilech's
deputies disappeared with amazing rapidity.

A general reunion was in progress inside and outside
the jail, the three felons being the only persons present
not transported with joy at the turn of events, when
Abimilech Fetcher, in a state of great dishevelment,
rushed upon the scene.

"Hey! Whatta you doin' with my prisoners?" he roared
at Sheriff Tobias. "It's agin the law!"

"Your prisoners! I like your nerve!" said Tobias.
"Whose prisoners be you gents?" he asked of the assembled jailbirds.

"Yours!" they cried in chorus.

"Come on, then, let's go home," said Tobias.

The prisoners assembled with alacrity, Abimilech viewed the proceedings with a feeling of dismay. Then a thought occurred to him.

"Lemme ask you one thing, Tobias," he said. "How'd you find out where them people was?"

"Why," said Tobias, "Kid Switch, he told me. I give him fifty dollars for the information. He wouldn't let it out until I paid him the money, either. What's the matter, 'Bimilech!"

The Informal Execution of Soupbone Pew

What is it the Good Book says? I read it last night—it said:

That he who sheddeth another man's blood by man shall his blood be shed!
That's as fair as a man could ask it, who lives by the gun and knife—
But the Law don't give him an even break when it's taking away his life.
Ho, the Law's unfair when it uses a chair, and a jolt from an unseen Death;
Or it makes him flop to a six-foot drop and a rope shuts off his breath;
If he's got to die let him die by the Book, with a Death that he can see,
By a gun or knife, as he went through life, and both legs kicking free!

Songs of the "Shut-Ins"

The condemned man in the cell next to us laughed incessantly. He had been sentenced that morning, and they told us he had started laughing as soon as the words "May the Lord have mercy on your soul" were pronounced. He was to be taken to the penitentiary next day to await execution.

Chicago Red had manifested a lively interest in the case. The man had killed a railroad brakeman, so one of the guards told us; had killed him coldly, and without provocation. The trial had commenced since our arrival at the county jail and had lasted three days, during which time Red talked of little else.

From the barred windows of the jail corridor, when we were exercising, we could see the dingy old criminal court across the yard and Red watched the grim procession to and from the jail each day. He speculated on the progress of the trial; he knew when the case went to the jury, and when he saw the twelve men, headed by the two old bailiffs returning after lunch the third day, he announced: "They've got the verdict, and it's first degree murder. They ain't talking and not a one has ever grinned."

Then when the unfortunate was brought back, laughing that dismal laugh, Red said: "He's nutty. He was nutty to go. It ain't exactly right to swing that guy."

Red and I were held as suspects in connection with an affair which had been committed a full forty-eight hours before we landed in town. We had no particular fear of being implicated in the matter, and the officers had no idea that we had anything to do with it, but they were holding us as evidence to the public that they were working on the case. We had been "vagged" for ten days each.

It was no new experience for us in any respect—not even the condemned man, for we had frequently been under the same roof with men sentenced to die. The only unusual feature was Red's interest in the laughing man.

"Red," I asked, as we sat playing cards, "did you ever kill a man?"

He dropped a card calmly, taking the trick, and as he

contemplated his hand, considering his next lead, he answered:

"For why do you ask me that?"

"Oh, I don't know; I just wondered," I said. "You've seen and done so many things that I thought you might accidentally have met with something of the sort."

"It isn't exactly a polite question," he replied. "I've seen some murders. I've seen quite a few, in fact. I've seen some pulled off in a chief's private office, when they was sweating some poor stiff, and I've seen some, other places."

"Did you ever kill a man?" I insisted.

He studied my lead carefully.

"I never did," he finally answered. "That is to say, I never bumped no guy off personal. I never had nothing to do with no job from which come ghosts to wake me up at night and bawl me out. They say a guy that kills a man never closes his eyes again, even when he really sleeps. I go to the hay, and my eyes are shut tight, so I know I ain't to be held now or hereafter for nothing like that."

We finished the game in silence, and Red seemed very thoughtful. He laid the cards aside, rolled a cigarette, and said: "Listen! I never killed no guy personal, like I say; I mean for nothing he done to me. I've been a gun and crook for many years, like you know, but I'm always mighty careful about hurting anyone permanent. I'm careful about them pete jobs, so's not to blow up no harmless persons, and I always tell my outside men that, when they have to do shooting, not to try to hit anyone. If they did, accidental, that ain't my fault. One reason I took to inside work was to keep from having to kill anyone. I've been so close to being taken that I could hear the gates of the Big House slam, and one little shot would have saved me a lot of trouble, but I always did my best to keep from letting that shot go. I never wanted to kill no man. I've been in jams where guys were after me good and strong, and I always tried to get by without no killings.

"I said I never killed a guy. I helped once, but it wasn't murder. It's never worried me a ——— bit since, and I sleep good."

He walked to the window and peered out into the yard where a bunch of sparrows were fluttering about. Finally he turned and said: "I hadn't thought of that for quite a while, and I never do until I see some poor stiff that's been tagged to go away. Some of them make me nervous—especially this tee-hee guy next to us. I'll tell you about Soupbone Pew—some day you can write it, if you want to."

Soupbone Pew was a rat who trained years ago with Billy Coulon, the Honey Grove Kid, and a bunch of other old timers that you've never seen. It was before my time, too, but I've heard them talk about him. He was in the Sioux City bank tear-off, when they all got grabbed and were sent to the Big House for fifteen years each. In them days Soupbone was a pretty good guy. He had nerve, and was smart, and stood well with everybody, but a little stretch in the big stir got to him. He broke bad. Honey Grove laid a plan for a big spring—a get-away—while they were up yonder. It looked like it would go through, too, but just as they were about ready, Soupbone got cold feet and gave up his insides.

For that he got a pardon, and quit the road right off. He became a railroad brakeman, and showed up at a shack running between Dodge City and La Junta. And he became the orneriest white man that God ever let live, too.

To hoboes and guns he was like a reformed soak toward a drunk. He treated them something fierce. He was a big, powerful stiff, who could kill a man with a wallop of his hands, if he hit him right, and his temper soured on the world. Most likely it was because he was afraid that every guy on the road was out to get him because of what he'd done, or maybe it was because he knew that they knew he was yellow. Anyway, they never tried to do him, that job belonging to Coulon, Honey Grove and the others.

Soupbone cracked that no 'bo could ride his division, and he made it good, too. He beat them up when they tried it, and he made it so strong that the old heads wouldn't go against a try when he was the run. Once in a while some kid took a stab at it, but if he got caught by Soupbone he regretted it the rest of his life. I've heard of that little road into Hot Springs, where they say a reward used to be offered to any 'bo that rode it, and how a guy beat it by getting in the water tank; and I've personally met that Wyoming gent on the Union Pacific, and all them other guys they say is so tough, but them stories is only fairytales for children beside what could be told about Pew. He went an awful route.

I've known of him catching guys in the pilot and throwing scalding water in on them; I've heard tell of him shoveling hot cinders into empties on poor bums laying there asleep. That trick of dropping a coupling pin on the end of a wire down alongside a moving train, so that it would swing up underneath and knock a stiff off the rods, was about the mildest thing he did.

He was simply a devil. The other railroad men on the division wouldn't hardly speak to him. They couldn't stand his gaff, but they couldn't very well roar at him keeping 'boes off his trains because that was what he was there for.

His longest suit was beating guys up. He just loved to catch some poor old broken-down bum on his train and pound the everlasting stuffing out of him. He's sent many a guy to the hospital, and maybe he killed a few before my acquaintance with him, for all I know.

Once in a while he ran against some live one—some real gun, and not a bum—who'd give him a battle, but he was there forty ways with a sap and gat, and he'd shoot as quick as he'd slug. He didn't go so strong on the real guns, if he knew who they was, and I guess he was always afraid they might be friends of Honey Grove or Coulon.

He was on the run when I first heard of him, and some of the kids of my day would try to pot him from the road, when his train went by, but they never even come close. I've heard them talk of pulling a rail on him and letting his train go into the ditch, but that would have killed the other trainmen, and they was some good guys on that same run then. The best way to do was to fight shy of Soupbone, and keep him on ice for Honey Grove and Coulon.

Training with our mob in them days was a young kid called Manchester Slim—a real kid, not over eighteen, and as nice and quiet a youngster as I ever see. He wasn't cut out for the road. It seems he'd had some trouble at home and run away. Old man Muller, that Dutch prowler, used to have him on his staff, but he never let this kid in on any work for some reason. He was always trying to get Slim to go home.

"Der road is hell for der kits," he used to say. "Let der ole stiffs vork out dere string, und don't make no new vuns."

The Slim paid no attention to him. Still he had no great love for the life, and probably would have quit long before if he hadn't been afraid some one would think he was scared off.

They was a pete job on at La Junta, which me and 'Frisco Shine and Muller had laid out. We had jungled up—camped—in a little cottonwood grove a few miles out of town, and was boiling out soup—nitro-glycerine —from dynamite, you know—and Muller sent the Slim into town to look around a bit. It was winter and pretty cold. We had all come in from the west and was headed east. We was all broke bad, too, and needed dough the worst way.

Slim come back from town much excited. He was carrying a Denver newspaper in his hand.

"I've got to go home, Mull," he said, running up to the old man and holding out the paper. "Look at this ad."

Muller read it and called to me. He showed me a little want ad, reading that Gordon Keleher, who disappeared from his home in Boston two years before, was wanted at home because his mother was dying. It was signed Pelias Keleher, and I knew who he was, all right—president of the National Bankers' Association.

"Well, you go," I said, right off the reel, and I could see that was the word he was waiting for.

"For certainly he goes," said Muller. "Nail der next rattler."

"All the passengers are late, but there's a freight due out of here tonight; I asked," said Slim.

"How much dough iss dere in dis mob?" demanded Muller, frisking himself. We all shook ourselves down, but the most we could scare up was three or four dollars.

"If you could wait until after tonight," I says, thinking of the job, but Muller broke me off with: "Ve don't vant him to vait. Somedings might happens."

"I'd wire home for money, but I want to get to Kansas City first," said Slim. "That paper is a couple of days old, and there's no telling how long it may have been running that ad. I can stop over in K.C. long enough to get plenty of dough from some people I know there. I'm going to grab that freight."

"Soupbone on dat freight," said the 'Frisco Shine, a silent, wicked black.

"Ve'll see Soub," said Muller quietly. "I guess maybe he von't inderfere mit dis case."

We decided to abandon the job for the night, and all went uptown. The Slim was apparently very much worried, and he kept telling us that if he didn't get home in time he'd never forgive himself, so we all got dead-set on seeing him started.

We looked up the conductor of the freight due out that night and explained things to him. None of us knew him, but he was a nice fellow.

"I tell you, boys," he said. "I'd let the young fellow ride, but you'd better see my head brakeman, Soupbone

Pew. He's a tough customer, but in a case like this he ought to be all right. I'll speak to him myself."

Muller went after Pew. He found him in a saloon, drinking all by his lonesome, although there was a crowd of other railroad men in there at the time. Muller knew Pew in the old days, but there was no sign of recognition between them. The old Dutchman explained to Pew very briefly, winding with: "It vould pe a gread personal favour mit me, Soub; maype somedimes I return it."

"He can't ride my train!" said Pew shortly. "That's flat. No argument goes."

The Dutchman looked at him long and earnestly, murder showing in his eyes, and Pew slunk back close to the bar, and his hand dropped to his hip.

"Soub, der poy rides!" said Muller, his voice low but shaking with anger. "He rides your rattler. Und if anyding happens by dot poy, de Honey Grove Kit von't get no chance at you! Dot all, Soub!"

But when he returned to us, he was plainly afraid for the Slim.

"You don't bedder go tonid," he said. "Dot Soub is a defil, und he'll do you."

"I'm not afraid," said Slim. "He can't find me, anyhow."

The old man tried to talk him out of the idea, but Slim was determined, and finally Muller, in admiration of his spirit, said: "Vell, if you vill go, you vill. Vun man can hide besser as two, but der Shine must go mit you as far as Dodge."

That was the only arrangement he would consent to, and while the Slim didn't want the Shine, and I myself couldn't see what good he could do, Muller insisted so strong that we all gave in.

We went down to the yards that night to see them off, and the old man had a private confab with the Shine. The only time I ever saw Muller show any feeling was when he told the boy good-bye. I guess he really liked him.

The two hid back of a pile of ties, a place where the trains slowed down, and me and Muller got off a distance and watched them. We could see Soupbone standing on top of a boxcar as the train went by, and he looked like a tall devil. He was trying to watch both sides of the train at the same time, but I didn't think he saw either Slim or the Shine as they shot underneath the cars, one after the other, and nailed the rods. Then the train went off into the darkness, Soupbone standing up straight and stiff.

We went back to our camp to sleep, and the next morning before we were awake, the Shine came limping in, covered with blood and one arm hanging at his side.

I didn't have to hear his story to guess what had happened. Soupbone made them at the first stop. He hadn't expected two, but he did look for the kid. Instead of warning him off, he told him to get on top where he'd be safe. That was one of his old tricks. He didn't get to the Shine, who dodged off into the darkness, as soon as he found they were grabbed, and then caught the train after it started again. He crawled up between the cars to the deck, to tip the Slim off to watch out for Soupbone. Slim didn't suspect anything, and was thanking Soupbone, and explaining about his mother.

The moment the train got under way good, Soupbone says: "Now my pretty boy, you're such a—good traveler, let's see you jump off this train!"

The kid thought he was joshing, but there wasn't no josh about it. Soup pulled a gun. The Shine, with his own gun in hand, crawled clear on top and lay flat on the cars, trying to steady his aim on Soupbone. The kid was pleading and almost crying, when Soupbone suddenly jumped at him, smashed him in the jaw with the gun barrel, and knocked him off the train. The Shine shot Soupbone in the back, and he dropped on top of the train, but didn't roll off. As the Shine was going down between the cars again, Soupbone shot at him and broke his arm. He got off all right, and went back down the road to find the kid dead—his neck broke.

Old man Muller, the mildest man in the world generally, almost went bughouse when he heard that spiel.
He raved and tore around like a sure enough nut. I've
known him to go backing out of a town with every man
in his mob down on the ground, dead or dying, and not
show half as much feeling afterward. You'd 'a' thought
the kid was his own. He swore he'd do nothing else as
long as he lived until he'd cut Soupbone's heart out.

The Shine had to get out of sight, because Soupbone
would undoubtedly have some wild-eyed story to tell
about being attacked by hoboes and being shot by one.
We had no hope but what the Shine had killed him.

Old man Muller went into town and found out that
was just what had happened, and he was in the hospital
only hurt a little. He also found they'd brought Slim's
body to town, and that most people suspected the real
truth, too. He told them just how it was, especially the
railroad men, and said the Shine had got out of the
country. He also wired Slim's people, and we heard afterwards they sent a special train after the remains.

Muller was told, too, that the train conductor had
notified Pew to let Slim ride, and that the rest of the
train crew had served notice on Pew that if he threw
the boy off he'd settled with them for it. And that was
just what made Soupbone anxious to get the kid. It ended
his railroad career there, as we found out afterwards,
because he disappeared as soon as he got out of the hospital.

Meantime me and Muller and the Shine went ahead
with that job, and it failed. Muller and the nigger got
grabbed, and I had a tough time getting away. Just before we broke camp the night before, however, Muller,
who seemed to have a hunch that something was going
to happen, called me and the Shine to him, and said, his
voice solemn: "I vant you poys to bromise me vun ting,"
he said. "If I don't get der chance myself, bromise me
dot venefer you find Soupbone Bew, you vill kill him
deat."

And we promised, because we didn't think we would ever be called on to make good.

Muller got a long jolt for the job; the Shine got a shorter one and escaped a little bit later on, while I left that part of the country.

A couple of years later, on a bitter cold night, in a certain town that I won't name, there was five of us in the sneezer, held as suspects on a house prowl job that only one of us had anything to do with—I ain't mentioning the name of the one, either. They was me, Kid Mole, the old prize fighter, a hophead named Squirt McCue, that you don't know, Jew Friend, a dip, and that same 'Frisco Shine. We were all in the bullpen with a mixed assortment of drunks and vags. All kinds of prisoners was put in there overnight. This pokey is downstairs under the police station, not a million miles from the Missouri River, so if you think hard you can guess the place. We were walking around kidding the drunks, when a screw shoved in a long, tall guy who acted like he was drunk or nutty, and was hardly able to stand.

I took one flash at his map, and I knew him. It was Pew.

He flopped down in a corner as soon as the screw let go his arm. The Shine rapped to him as quick as I did, and officed Mole and the rest. They all knew of him, especially the Honey Grove business, as well as about the Manchester Slim, for word had gone over the country at the time.

As soon as the screw went upstairs I walked over to the big stiff, laying all huddled up, and poked him with my foot.

"What's the matter with you, you big cheese?" I said. He only mumbled.

"Stand up!" I tells him, but he didn't stir. The Shine and Mole got hold of him on either side and lifted him to his feet. He was as limber as a wet bar towel. Just then we heard the screw coming downstairs and we got away from Pew. The screw brought in a jag—a laughing jag—a guy with his snoot full of booze and who laughed like he'd just found a lot of money. He was a little, thin fellow, two pounds lighter than a straw hat. He laughed high and shrill, more like a scream than a real laugh, and the moment the screw opened the door and tossed him in, something struck me that the laugh was phony. It didn't sound on the level.

There wasn't no glad in it. The little guy laid on the floor and kicked his feet and kept on laughing. Soupbone Pew let out a yell at the sight of him.

"Don't let him touch me!" he bawled, rolling over against the wall. "Don't let him near me!"

"Why, you big stiff, you could eat him alive!" I says.

The jag kept on tee-heeing, not looking at us, or at Pew either for that matter.

"He's nuts," said Jew Friend.

"Shut him off," I told the Shine.

He stepped over and picked the jag up with one hand, held him out at arm's length, and walloped him on the jaw with his other hand. The jag went to sleep with a laugh sticking in his throat. Soupbone still lay against the wall moaning, but he saw that business all right, and it seemed to help him. The Shine tossed the jag into a cell. Right after that the screw came down with another drunk, and I asked him about Pew.

"Who's this boob?" I said. "Is he sick?"

"Him? Oh, he's a good one," said screw. "He only killed his poor wife—beat her to death with his two fists, because she didn't have supper ready on time, or something important. That ain't his blood on him; that's hers. He's pretty weak, now, hey? Well, he wasn't so weak a couple of hours ago, the rat! It's the wickedest murder ever done in this town, and he'll hang sure, if he ain't lynched beforehand!"

He gave Soupbone a kick as he went out, and Soupbone groaned.

Said I: "It's got to be done, gents; swing or no swing, this guy has got to go. Who is it—me?"

"Me!" said the Shine, stepping forward.

"Me!" said the Jew.

"Me!" chimed in Mole.

"All of us!" said the hophead.

"Stand him up!" I ordered.

The lights had been turned down low, and it was dark and shadowy in the jail. The only sound was the soft pad-pad of people passing through the snow on the sidewalks above our heads, the low sizzling of the water spout at the sink, and the snores of the drunks, who were all asleep.

Us five was the only ones awake. The Shine and Mole lifted Soupbone up, and this time he was not so limp. He seemed to know that something was doing. His eyes was wide open and staring at us.

"Pew," I said in a whisper, "do you remember the kid you threw off your rattler three years ago?"

"And shot me in the arm?" asked Shine.

Pew couldn't turn any whiter, but his eyes rolled back into his head.

"Don't!" he whispered. "Don't say that. It made me crazy! I'm crazy now! I was crazy when I killed that little girl tonight. It was all on account of thinking about him. He comes to see me often."

"Well, Pew," I said, "a long time back you were elected to die. I was there when the sentence was passed, and it'd been carried out a long time ago if you hadn't got away. I guess we'll have to kill you tonight."

"Don't, boys!" he whined. "I ain't fit to die! Don't hurt me!"

"Why, you'll swing anyway!" said Friend.

"No! My God, no!" he said. "I was crazy: I'm crazy now, and they don't hang crazy people!"

I was standing square in front of him. His head had raised a little as he talked and his jaw was sticking out. I suddenly made a move with my left hand, as though to slap him, and he showed that his mind was active enough by dodging, so that it brought his jaw out further, and he said: "Don't." Then I pulled my right clear from my knee and took him on the point of the jaw.

The Shine and Mole jumped back. Soupbone didn't fall; he just slid down in a heap, like his body had melted into his shoes.

We all jumped for him at the same time, but an idea popped into my head, and I stopped them. Soupbone was knocked out, but he was coming back fast. You can't kill a guy like that by hitting him. The jail was lighted by a few incandescent lights, and one of them was hung on a wire that reached down from the ceiling over the sink, and had a couple of feet of it coiled up in the middle. Uncoiled, the light would reach clear to the floor. I pointed to it, but the bunch didn't get my idea right away. The switch for the lights was inside the bull-pen, and I turned them off. I had to work fast for fear the screw upstairs would notice the lights was out and come down to see what the trouble was. A big arc outside threw a little glim through the sidewalk grating, so I could see what I was doing.

I uncoiled the wire and sawed it against the edge of the sink, close to the lamp, until it came in two. Then I bared the wire back for a foot. The gang tumbled, and carried Pew over to where the wire would reach him. I unfastened his collar, looped the naked end of the wire around his neck and secured it. By this time he was about come to, but he didn't seem to realize what was going on.

All but me got into their cells and I stepped over and turned the switch button just as Pew was struggling to his feet. The voltage hit him when he was on all fours. He stood straight up, stiff, like a soldier at salute. There was a strange look on his face—a surprised look. Then, as though someone had hit him from behind, his feet left the floor and he swung straight out to the length of the wire and it broke against his weight, just as I snapped off the current. Pew dropped to the floor and curled up like a big singed spider, and a smell like frying bacon filled the room.

I went over and felt of his heart. It was still beating, but very light.

"They ain't enough current," whispered Mole. "We got to do it some other way."

"Hang him wid de wire," said the Shine.

"Aw—nix!" spoke up the Jew. "I tell you that makes me sick—bumping a guy off that way. Hanging and electricity, see? That's combining them too much. Let's use the boot."

"It ain't fair, kind-a, that's a fact," whispered McCue. "It's a little too legal. The boot! Give him the boot!"

The voice of the screw came singing down the stairs: "Is that big guy awake?"

"Yes," I shouted back, "we're all awake; he won't let us sleep."

"Tell him he'd better say his prayers!" yelled the screw. "I just got word a mob is forming to come and get him!"

"Let him alone," I whispered to the gang. Mole was making a noose of the wire, and the Shine had hunted up a bucket to stand Pew on. They drew back and Soupbone lay stretched out on the floor.

I went over and felt of his heart again. I don't remember whether I felt any beat or not. I couldn't have said I did, at the moment, and I couldn't say I didn't. I didn't have time to make sure, because suddenly there run across the floor something that looked to me like a shadow, or a big rat. Then the shrill laugh of that jag rattled through the bullpen. He slid along half stooped, as quick as a streak of light, and before we knew what was doing he had pounced on Soupbone and had fastened his hands tight around the neck of the big stiff. He was laughing that crazy laugh all the time.

"I'll finish him for you!" he squeaked. He fastened his hands around Soupbone's neck. I kicked the jag in the side of the head as hard as I could, but it didn't faze him. The bunch laid hold of him and pulled, but they only dragged Soupbone all over the place. Finally the jag let go and stood up, and we could see he wasn't no more drunk than we was. He let loose that laugh once more, and just as the Shine started the bucket swinging

for his head, he said: "I'm her brother!" Then he went
down kicking.

We went into our cells and crawled into our bunks.
Soupbone lay outside. The Shine pulled the jag into a
corner. I tell you true, I went to sleep right away. I
thought the screw would find out when he brought the
next drunk down, but it so happened that there wasn't
no more drunks and I was woke up by a big noise on the
stairs. The door flew open with a bang, and a gang of
guys came down, wild-eyed and yelling. The screw was
with them and they had tight hold of him.

"Keep in, you men!" he bawled to us.

"That's your meat!" he said to the gang, pointing at
what had been Soupbone. The men pounced on him
like a lot of hounds on to a rabbit, and before you could
bat an eye they had a rope around Soupbone's neck and
was tearing up the stairs again, dragging him along.

They must have thought he was asleep; they never
noticed that he didn't move a muscle himself, and they
took the person of Soupbone Pew, or anyways what had
been him, outside and hung it over a telegraph wire.

We saw it there when we was sprung next morning.
When the screw noticed the blood around the bullpen,
he said: "Holy smoke, they handled him rough!" And
he never knew no different.

If the mob hadn't come—but the mob did come, and
so did the laughing jag. I left him that morning watching
the remains of Soupbone Pew.

"She was my sister," he said to me.

I don't know for certain whether we killed Soupbone,
whether the jag did it, or whether the mob finished him;
but he was dead, and he ought to have died. Sometimes
I wonder a bit about it, but no ghosts come to me, like I
say, so I can't tell.

They's an unmarked grave in the potter's field of this
town I speak of, and once in a while I go there when I'm
passing through and meditate on the sins of Soupbone
Pew. But I sleep well of nights. I done what had to be

done, and I close my eyes and I don't never see Soupbone Pew.

He turned once more to gazing out of the window.

"Well, what is there about condemned men to make
you so nervous?" I demanded.

"I said some condemned men," he replied, still gazing.
"Like this guy next door."

A loud, shrill laugh rang through the corridors.

"He's that same laughing jag," said Chicago Red.

The Main Event *

A big murder trial possesses some of the elements of a
sporting event.

I find the same popular interest in a murder trial that
I find in any city on the eve of a big football game, or
pugilistic encounter, or baseball series. There is the same
conversational speculation on the probable result, only
more of it.

There is even some betting on the aforesaid probable
result.

Before a big horse race, or football game, or baseball
series, the newspaper writers and fans sit around of an
evening and argue the matter with some heat. At a trial,
the newspaper men—and women—do the arguing, but
without the heat. They lack partisanship in the premises.
That is furnished by the murder-trial fans.

Perhaps you did not know there are murder-trial fans.

* Runyon was assigned to practically all the "big" murder trials
of the twenties, thirties and early forties. It was reportage that
usually didn't interfere with continuance of his daily sports column,
and there were asides on murder trials in the sports column at
various times. *The Main Event* is a collection of these asides.

They are mainly persons who have no direct interest in the affair. They are drawn by their curiosity.

Some come from long distances, but do not marvel over this. Persons have been known to travel halfway across the continent to see a basketball game.

I am not one of those who criticize the curiosity of the gals who storm the doors of the court room, as we say in the newspaper stories of a trial. If I did not have a pass that entitled me to a chair at the press table, I would probably try an end run myself.

If I had not seen them, I know I would have been consumed with curiosity to peer at Mrs. Snyder and Judd Gray just to see what manner of mortals could carry out such a crime. It is only a slight variation of the same curiosity that makes me eager to see a new fistic sensation, or a great baseball player.

It strikes me that the courtroom, with a murder trial in issue, develops a competitive spirit, if I may call it such, more tense and bitter than is ever produced on any field of sport. Of course, this is not surprising when you consider that as a rule human life is at stake.

The trial is a sort of game, the players on the one side the attorneys for the defense, and on the other the attorneys for the State. The defendant figures in it mainly as the prize. The instrument of play is the law—it is the ball, so to speak. Or perhaps I might call it the puck, for it is in the manner of hockey more than any other sport that it is jockeyed carefully back and forth by the players.

And the players must be men well schooled in their play, men of long experience and considerable knowledge of what they are doing. They must be crafty men, quick of thought and action, and often they are very expensive men.

There are about as many newspaper men at a big murder trial as ever covered a heavyweight championship fight or a world's series—perhaps four hundred of them, counting the telegraph operators.

They discuss the form displayed by counsel for one

side or the other during the day's session of court, just
as the boxing writers chatter about the form displayed
by the principals in a big match after the day's training.

They discuss the different witnesses as they appear
to them, just as the boys go over the members of a football line and backfield, or over the horses carded to start
in the Kentucky Derby.

And the thrills are just as numerous as in any sporting
event I ever saw, with something new popping up at
every turn, something in the form of what you might call
a new play by the State or the defense. Often it starts
off as involved as a hidden-ball maneuver and it takes
you a little time to figure it out before the play gets in
the clear.

The game or murder trial is played according to very
strict rules, with stern umpires called judges to prevent
any deviation from these rules.

Someone is killed, perhaps in a peculiarly cold-blooded
manner. You might think that the idea would be to get
the guilty into court as speedily as possible to hear the
details of the crime briefly related, and to at once impose
the penalty of the law.

But this is not the way the game of murder trial is
played, especially if it is played under the rules of circumstantial evidence, which are very intricate rules.
Under these rules everything must be done just so. The
game must be played by what strikes the layman, like
myself, as roundabout and unnecessary and tedious
methods.

If the defendant has money enough to engage an im-
posing team of players, or attorneys, the game becomes
more complicated than ever, for high-priced players in
the game of murder trial know all the rules from A to
Izzard. They can see a play by the other side coming up
a long way off and take steps to circumvent it.

And for some reason the feeling on both sides often
becomes very bitter. I sometimes wonder if the players
feel toward each other the bitterness that they not in-

frequently express in court, or do they hobnob all friendly together, like Brown's cows, as baseball players fraternize after a game in which they have attempted to spike each other. I suppose they do.

And yet they are supposed to be engaged in a sort of common cause, which is to determine the guilt or innocence of the defendants. I believe they are presumed to be innocent until they are proven guilty.

A player of the game or murder trial for the State represents the people. His function, as I understand it, is to endeavor to convict any person who has transgressed the law to the end that justice may be done and the majesty of the law upheld. It is inconceivable that he would wish to convict an innocent person.

But it has been my observation that the player or attorney for the State is quick to take advantage of the rules of the game of murder trial that puts his side in front, and equally quick to forestall any moves by the other side. I presume the player for the State is generally firmly convinced beforehand by his study of the evidence that he is playing for the life of a guilty person, hence his enthusiasm in his cause.

Or perhaps I should call it zeal. I doubt that any State's attorney is ever enthusiastic over contributing to the taking of human life. He but does his duty. His remuneration financially is rarely that of the players on the other side, who might naturally be expected to show plenty of zeal on defense.

It is a strange game, this game of murder trial, as played under the rules of circumstantial evidence. I suppose if a defendant is really innocent he has all the worst of it for a time, yet, paradoxically enough, if he is guilty he has all the best of it.

It nearly always is the case in a murder trial that the personality of the victim of the crime remains very shadowy and vague. From what I heard in the Snyder-Gray trial, I never got a right good picture of Albert Snyder except that he was a fellow who liked to putter around with motorboats.

Why Me?

When physical calamity befalls, the toughest thing for the victim to overcome is the feeling of resentment that it should have happened to him.

"Why me?" he keeps asking himself, dazedly. "Of all the millions of people around, why me?"

It becomes like a pulse beat— "Why me? Why me? Why me?"

Sometimes he reviews his whole life step by step to see if he can put his finger on some circumstance in which he may have been at such grievous fault as to merit disaster.

Did he commit some black sin somewhere back down the years? Did he betray the sacred trust of some fellow human being? Is he being punished for some special wrongdoing? "Why me?"

He wakes suddenly at night from a sound sleep to consciousness of his affliction and to the clocklike ticking in his brain— "Why me? Why me? Why me?"

He reflects: "Why not that stinker Smith? Why not that louse Jones? Why not that bum Brown? Why me? Why me? Why me?"

Was he guilty of carelessness or error in judgment? "Why me? Why? Why? Why?"

It is a question that has been asked by afflicted mortals through the ages. It is being asked more than ever just now as the maimed men come back from war broken in body and spirit and completely bewildered, asking: "Why me?"

I do not have the answer, of course. Not for myself nor for anyone else. I, too, am just a poor mug groping in the dark, though sometimes I think of the words of young Elihu reproving Job and his three pals: "Look into the heavens, and see; and behold the clouds which are higher than thou."

The Book of Job may have been an attempt to solve the problem why the righteous suffer and to point out that such suffering is often permitted as a test of faith and a means of grace. They sure put old Job over the hurdles as an illustration.

He was a character who lived in the land of Uz, 'way back in the times recorded in the Old Testament. He had more money than most folks have hay and he was also of great piety. He stood good with the Lord, who took occasion to comment favorably on Job one day to Satan, who had appeared before Him.

"There is no one like Job," remarked the Lord to Satan. "He is a perfect and upright man. He fears God and eschews evil."

"Well, why not?" said Satan. "You have fixed him up so he is sitting pretty in every way. But you just let a spell of bad luck hit him and see what happens. He will curse you to your face."

"You think so?" said the Lord. "All right, I will put all his belongings in your power to do with as you please. Only don't touch Job himself."

Not long afterwards, the Sabeans copped all of Job's oxen and asses and killed his servants and his sheep were burned up and the Chaldeans grabbed his camels and slaughtered more of his servants and a big wind blew down a house and destroyed his sons.

But so far from getting sore at the Lord as Satan had figured would happen after these little incidents, Job rent his mantle and shaved his head and fell down upon the ground and worshipped and said: "Naked I came out of my mother's womb, and naked shall I return thither; the Lord gave, and the Lord hath taken away; blessed be the name of the Lord."

Now had I been Satan I would have given Job up

then and there but lo, and behold, the next time the Lord held a meeting Satan again appeared and when the Lord started boosting Job for holding fast to his integrity, Satan sniffed disdainfully and said: "Skin for skin, yea, all that a man has he will give for his life, but just you touch his bone and his flesh and see what your Mr. Job does."

"All right," the Lord said, "I will put him in your hands, only save his life."

Then Satan smote poor Job with boils from the soles of his feet to the crown of his head. I reckon that was the worst case of boils anyone ever heard of, and Job's wife remarked: "Do you still retain your integrity? Curse God, and die."

"Woman," Job said, "you are a fool. Shall we receive good at the hand of God and not evil?"

But when those pals of Job's, Eliphaz, Bildad and Zophar, came to see him he let out quite a beef to them and in fact cursed the day he was born. In the end, however, after listening to discourses from his pals of a length that must have made him as tired as the boils, Job humbly confessed that God is omnipotent and omnipresent and repented his former utterances and demeanor "in dust and ashes" and the Lord made him more prosperous than ever before.

"Why me?"

"—Therefore have I uttered that I understood not; things too wonderful for me, which I knew not."

A Handy Guy Like Sande

[This, perhaps the best known of all Runyon poems, and possibly the best known of all his writings, preceded his account of the 1930 Kentucky Derby for International News Service—a dispatch that appears in a number of anthologies and textbooks as a classic example of sports reporting.

Unlike most of his verses with sports themes, this was not spontaneous—it was not written wholly on the spur of the moment to precede a sports report or fill part of a column of comment. It was Runyon quoting himself, rewriting a sentiment he had been expressing repeatedly since 1922. None of his other poetic praise of Sande (and of other jockeys before Sande) had caught on as this one did, and the earlier versions of "gimme a handy guy like Sande" were unknown to or forgotten by most Runyon readers.—C.K.]

> Say, have they turned back the pages
>> Back to the past once more?
> Back to the racin' ages
>> An' a Derby out of the yore?
> Say, don't tell me I'm daffy,
>>> Ain't that the same ol' grin?
>>> Why, it's that handy
>>> Guy named Sande,
>>> Bootin' a winner in!

> Say, don't tell me I'm batty!
>> Say, don't tell me I'm blind!
> Look at that seat so natty!
>> Look how he drives from behind!
> Gone is the white of the Ranco,
>>> An' the white band under his chin—
>>> Still he's that handy
>>> Guy named Sande,
>>> Bootin' a winner in!

> Maybe he ain't no chicken,
>> Maybe he's gettin' along,
> But the ol' heart's still a-tickin',
>> An' the ol' bean's goin' strong.

Roll back the years! Yea, roll 'em!
   Say, but I'm young agin',
   Watchin' that handy
   Guy named Sande,
   Bootin' a winner in!

[The "white of Ranco" refers to the racing colors of
Harry F. Sinclair's Rancocas Stable, for which Sande was
contract rider.

On August 12, 1922, from Saratoga, Runyon had
limned:]

Sloan, they tell me, could ride 'em,
   Maher, too, was a bird;
Bullman was a guy to guide 'em—
   Never worse than third.
Them was the old-time jockeys;
   Now when I want to win
Gimme a handy
Guy like Sande
   Ridin' them hosses in.

Fuller he was a pippin,
   Loftus one of the best—
Many a time come rippin'
   Down there ahead of the rest.
Shaw was a bear of a rider,
   There with plenty of dome—
But gimme a dandy
Guy like Sande
   Drivin' them hosses home!

Spencer was sure a wonder,
   And Miller was worth his hire.
Seldom he made a blunder
   As he rode 'em down to the wire.
Them was the old-time jockeys;
   Now when I want to win

Gimme a handy
Guy like Sande
Bootin' them hosses in!

[Two weeks later, on August 27, 1922, the day Sande
rode Edict to victory in the Spinaway Stakes, Runyon's
lead was:]

McAtee knows them horses,
    Ensor's a judge of pace;
Johnson kin ride the courses
    In any old kind o' race.
All them guys are good ones,
    But, say, when I want to win—
Gimme a handy
Guy like Sande
Bootin' a long shot in.

[On September 10, 1922, Sande, riding Kai-Sang,
beat Clarence Kummer and Albert Johnson, both of
them top jockeys then, to win the Lawrence Realization
Stakes at Belmont Park, and Runyon began his story:]

Kummer is quite a jockey,
    Maybe as good as the best.
Johnson is not so rocky
    When you bring him down to the test.
But, say, when they carry my gravy—
Say, when I want to win,
    Gimme a handy
    Guy like Sande
Bootin' them horses in.

[When, in 1924, Sande was hurt badly in a spill at
Saratoga and announced he would not ride again, Runyon brought out a new version, beginning:]

Maybe there'll be another,
    Heady an' game, an' true—

Maybe they'll find his brother
   At drivin' them hosses through.
Maybe—but, say, I doubt it.
   Never his like again—
Never a handy
Guy like Sande
   Bootin' them babies in!

Green an' white at the quarter—
   Say, I can see him now,
Ratin' them just as he orter,
   Workin' them up—an' how!
Green an' white at the home stretch—
   Who do you think'll win?
Who but a handy
Guy like Sande
   Kickin' that baby in!

Maybe we'll have another,
   Maybe in ninety years!
Maybe we'll find his brother
   With his brains above his ears.
Maybe—I'll lay again it—
   A million bucks to a fin—
Never a handy
Guy like Sande
   Bootin' them babies in!

[As Sande lay in the hospital, doctors said he would never ride again. Next Spring he was riding again, and Runyon's INS story from Louisville on May 16 simply began:]

"Riding as if he was hurrying home ahead of the fast on-coming storm that broke soon after the finish, Earle Sande, the master horseman of these times, drove Flying Ebony to victory in the Kentucky Derby this afternoon."

[Sande retired and became a trainer for a while. After a year's absence from the saddle, he resumed riding again. And then, in 1930, Runyon had occasion to write the best-known version of his paean to Sande.

The differences in the versions have been productive of countless café arguments, with one disputant remembering 'Booting them babies in' as the tag line and another swearing it was 'Bootin' a winner in.'

Ironically, in one of his sports columns, Runyon hailed "Pony" McAtee, a contemporary of Sande's, as the greatest jockey.

The Old Horse Player, a Runyon sentiment probably quoted as often as the Sande verses, antedated the earliest of the latter. A California race track once circularized the verses among its patrons—without any noticeable effect on wagering.]

The Old Horse Player

For forty years he's followed the track
And played them hosses to Helenback,
And they ain't a thing he shouldn't know, that bloke.
So I sez to him, "I want advice
On beatin' this dodge at a decent price.
And what have you got to tell me, old soak?"
"Well, son," he sez, "I've bet and won,
And I've bet and lost, and when all is done
I'm sure of one thing—and only one—
    All hawss players must die broke!"
Sez I, "But I see a-many a chump
With plenty o' sugar around this dump"—
Sez I, "What system do they employ, or what is the
        brand they smoke?
You study the form, you study the dope
And you're goin' O.K., or so I hope,

I want you to gimme a line or two on how I can fill my
    poke!"
"Well, son," sez he, "this racket's tough,
And I try to learn as I do my stuff,
And I haven't learned much but I've learned enough—
   All hawss players must die broke!"
Sez he, "Some live to be very old,
Till their hair gits gray and their blood gits cold,
And some of 'em almost fall apart before they up and
    croak."
Sez he, "I've seen 'em, these noble men
Up in the dough, and out again,
In fact, I bin there a-many a time myself—and that's no
    joke!"
   Sez he, "I've seen 'em in limousines
With rocks on their dukes and dough in their jeans,
But they're all alike when they quit their scenes—
   All hawss players must die broke!"

The Funeral of Madame Chase

A big black hearse; 'twas Dougal's hearse,
   Creaked down through Union Street,
And old, old echoes were aroused
   By the horses' heavy feet.
And all our town knew Dougal's hearse
   Bore to some resting place
The last of her who once was known
   As Madame Sarah Chase.

And all the old men of our town
   Were on the street that day.
With senile stealth, it seemed to me,
   They tried to hide away.
They did not meet, and stand, and gas,

As old men love to do,
But seemed to slink, each by himself,
And why nobody knew.

One lone hack; 'twas Pitkin's hack,
With Pitkin on the seat,
Was all that followed Dougal's hearse
As it creaked through Union Street.

One lone hack, and in that hack
Was one lone man, and he
Was Banker George S. Hamerslough,
As all the town could see.

So slim, so gray, so very old,
He sat erect, and stern,
And glanced about from left to right
With eyes that seemed to burn.
And wagging tongues of gossip stopped,
And none that glance could meet,
As slowly passed the hearse and hack
Along through Union Street.

And my old man who hadn't bowed
To Hamerslough for years,
Stood at the curb, and bared his head,
And leaked some senile tears.
"I know him for a skunk," he said,
"And my hate'll never quit—
A liar, cheat, two-thirds a thief—
But, by God, he's no hypocrite!"

One lone hack; 'twas Pitkin's hack;
With Pitkin on the seat,
Was all that followed Dougal's hearse
As it creaked through Union Street.
One lone hack, and in that hack
Was one lone man, and he
Was Banker George S. Hamerslough,
For all the town to see.